Barbara's Bivouac

The Army Cadets

C.R. Cummings

Also By
CHRISTOPHER CUMMINGS

Barbara's Bivouac

The Army Cadets

C.R. Cummings

DoctorZed
Publishing
www.doctorzed.com

Published 2018 by DoctorZed Publishing

DoctorZed Publishing books may be ordered through booksellers or by contacting:

DoctorZed Publishing
10 Vista Ave
Skye, South Australia 5072
www.doctorzed.com

ISBN: 978-0-6485726-8-8 (hc)
ISBN: 978-0-6485726-7-1 (sc)
ISBN: 978-0-6485726-6-4 (ebk)

National Library of Australia Cataloguing-in-Publication entry

    Author: Cummings, C. R., author.

    Title: Barbara's Bivouac/ Christopher Cummings.
    ISBN: 9780648572688 (hardcover)

    Series: Cummings, C. R. The army cadets.

    Target Audience: For young adults.

    Subjects: Adventure stories, Australian.

    Military cadets--Queensland--Fiction.

Cover image © ID 43479258 Ivan Kmit | Dreamstime.com
Cover design © Scott Zarcinas

Printed in Australia, UK & USA

DoctorZed Publishing rev. date: 14/08/2019

Dedication

Special Thanks to
The Officers of Cadets of 130 Army Cadet Unit (Heatley)

This book, while a work of fiction, is dedicated to all the Officers of Cadets and Instructors of Cadets of 130ACU (Heatley) who have attended bivouacs at Millaroo and who have shared in the trials, tribulations and dramas of such activities. You have done a magnificent job in preparing young people for life as good citizens. By being good role models and by showing compassion and sympathy to young people under stress and in need you have helped many. Your wisdom has assisted the OC in delivering what he hopes was justice in particular cases and in ensuring activities were well and safely run.

Thank you.

Thanks also to the Cadet Forces of Clifton College, Bristol, England and, in particular, to Major Ron Cross and Lieutenant Chris Hutchings for a memorable bivouac and for your hospitality and friendship over the years and for your hospitality when my wife Cheryl and I visited your magnificent college.

.

Also a special thanks to
Bill and Elizabeth Tudehope of 'Landers Creek' Station, Millaroo
for the use of their property for cadet exercises over many years.

Chapter 1

SHE'S GOT TO GO!

4:15pm Friday afternoon 28 August.
Heatley Secondary College, Townsville, North Queensland.
130 Army Cadet Unit preparing to go on a weekend bivouac.
Cadets are being dropped off in the rear car park and the Officers of
Cadets and Cadet Under-Officers are meeting in a downstairs classroom
in F Block. The cadets are grouping in platoon areas outside.

Lieutenant(AAC) Caitlin Cavendish, a 28-year-old Officer of Cadets,
glanced out the door at some cadets walking up the pathway from the
car park and her jaw almost dropped open at who she saw.

Shaking her head in disbelief, she cried, "That bloody Chloe! I didn't
think we would ever see her again."

"Nor did I," 2nd Lieutenant Peters agreed.

Cadet Under-Officer Barbara Brassington, an 18-year-old university
student, turned to look and also shook her head. She was about to agree
but then held her tongue. Over the last few years she had been involved
in some dramatic adventures with Chloe, and while she did not approve
of the other girl's morals and attitudes she did have a high opinion of her
ability and strength of character.

Chloe's not a quitter, she thought. *She's tougher than that.*

The other OOCs and CUOs all nodded or shook their heads and most
agreed with Lt Cavendish. The other four Cadet Under-Officers (CUOs)
in the room were all younger than Barbara and were still at school. They
were the commanders of the unit's four 'rifle' platoons. Three were male
and only one, CUO 'Robbo' Roberts, was female. Barbara did not like
two of the male CUOs: Milikin and Bailey, but she was careful to hide
this.

The object of their discussion, 16-year-old Chloe Cummings, a long-
legged blonde with a very prominent bust, was walking along beside
her best friend, Cadet Sergeant Jane Carson. Barbara noted this with
approval.

Well at least Jane has got the guts and loyalty to stick by her friend, even when she is in disgrace, she thought. She really liked Jane, even though she had a reputation almost as bad as Chloe's.

Barbara shifted her gaze back to Chloe, first studying her face for signs of emotion and then, briefly, her body. *Even in that baggy camouflage uniform Chloe is still very curvy,* she thought. Having seen Chloe naked on a dozen occasions, Barbara knew that she had what was considered an almost perfect female form.

As the two girls, lugging their duffle bags of gear, passed out of sight Lt Cavendish turned to the Officer Commanding, Major Wickham.

"Oh sir, that Chloe has got to go! She is a very bad influence and is causing the unit a lot of harm."

Major Wickham, a tubby, middle-aged man who was a teacher at the college in his civilian job, turned back from watching Chloe to meet Lt Cavendish's angry eyes.

"Headquarters has allowed her to stay," he replied.

The sad note in his usually brisk voice and the look in his eyes caused Barbara to again think that Major Wickham really liked Chloe.

He's got a soft spot for her, she surmised.

Barbara liked and respected Major Wickham who had also helped her through a few life crises and she felt sorry for him being pressured to take action he obviously did not agree with.

He likes to give people a chance to change and to improve, to learn from their mistakes, she thought.

Lt Jennifer Peters, another of the lady OOCs, nodded vigorously. "I agree. She has got to go! She gives Cadets a bad name and this unit in particular."

"She is on a warning," Major Wickham replied. "And she has been demoted."

"And not before time!" Lt Peters snapped.

Lt Cavendish nodded. "Do her good! But I still think she should have been chucked out."

Lt Forster, a handsome young male OOC, frowned. "If she is now only a sergeant, I am surprised she has come this weekend. If it was me, I would have been too ashamed."

"She has no shame!" Lt Cavendish snapped. "Flaunting herself and selling her favours like..."

Major Wickham pursed his lips. "That's enough! Her other alleged behaviour is only hearsay and did not happen at Cadets," he said. "The Brigade Commander determined that she should be reduced from warrant officer to sergeant and I have determined that she will not remain in her posting as company sergeant major."

"Who is to be CSM then?" Capt Buchan, the 2ic, queried.

He was the only one in civilian clothes because he was not going on the bivouac and had only come along to help with the admin.

"Sgt Warren," Major Wickham replied.

"Does he know?" Capt Buchan asked.

"Yes, I spoke to him on Wednesday and he agreed," Major Wickham confirmed.

Barbara nodded. She had seen Sgt Warren take over the company as CSM three days earlier. Capt Buchan, who was a teacher at William Ross State High School and commanded the cadet unit's detachment, there had not been present at Heatley that afternoon. Barbara sighed. It had been a very busy few days and had left her feeling tired and worried.

In fact the last few weeks have been very stressful, Barbara told herself.

It had now been four weeks since the incident that had led to Chloe being disciplined and in those weeks she had been required to write a written statement and had twice been interviewed by senior officers from the cadet brigade Headquarters at Lavarack Barracks. She knew that Major Wickham and the other officers had been interviewed as well and that the OC had spent two Tuesday evenings at HQ, that being when the HQ staff, most of whom were Army Reservists or OOCs, 'paraded'.

The incident had occurred on a weekend bivouac at Clemant State Forest, about 40 kilometres north of Townsville. As CSM one of Chloe's duties had been to run the morning Check Parade after the 0600hrs 'reveille' (They did not actually play a bugle tune). To do this she normally got out of bed at about 0530 and woke the platoon sergeants who then had time to get ready. On the Sunday morning Chloe had apparently not woken up when her alarm went and had only woken a few minutes before 0600.

As the whole company now knew (although most had always known it) Chloe usually slept nude, except on 'tactical' exercises. In this case she had judged it was still dark enough to hide this fact and she had just pulled on her boots and hurried a few paces across the Headquarters bivouac, an area of dark bush, to wake the HQ Sgt, Sgt Warren. At the same time she had sent Jane, the Signals Sgt and who had slept in her uniform, to wake the other platoon sergeants. She had then hurried back to her own 'hutchie' to dress while the sergeants got their platoons up and out on the vehicle track that was being used as a 'parade ground'.

But one of the platoon sergeants, Sgt Shane Brady (a male with a grudge) had seen her and complained, alleging that he had been offended (Which Barbara strongly doubted if half the stories she had heard about him were true!). The OC had no option but to investigate and then involve the army HQ. The upshot was that Chloe's behaviour had been officially investigated and obviously proven. As she had been in trouble a dozen times before for nudity and 'lewd and offensive display' she had been demoted from Cadet Warrant Officer Class 2 to Cadet Sergeant. This had been sanctioned by the army Brigade Commander as the OC did not have that legal power. Chloe and her parents had been informed of the results of the official investigation on the Tuesday night at HQ. The demotion had been done then.

At least she was spared any more public humiliation, Barbara mused.

If it had been done at Heatley at the start of the Wednesday afternoon 'Home Training' parade, even in the classroom the unit used as an office and not in front of the whole company, Barbara would not have approved.

That would have been very hurtful.

Chloe had not been at school on the last three days and had not attended the weekly Wednesday afternoon 'Home Training' parade.

Which is why everyone is surprised to see her today, Barbara decided. They obviously felt that after that sort of humiliation she would just leave Cadets. *I think I would,* she mused. *I'd be so embarrassed that I would just want to run away and hide, or curl up in a hollow log!*

The incident had divided the company and that was another concern. And now here was Chloe, wearing sergeant's stripes and obviously intending to come on the bivouac!

Lt Cavendish still wasn't satisfied. "I will be watching the little minx like a hawk. One slip and she will be gone!" she snarled.

Lt Peters nodded vigorously, a sour look on her face, and even CUO Roberts nodded. The males, Barbara noted, all looked poker-faced or glum.

But they are males, she told herself, knowing Chloe was probably an object of fascination and attraction to them.

Major Wickham again reacted testily. "Yes, but by the book! We will make sure justice is done. Now let's get this show on the road. It is getting late and we have packs and webbing to issue and the coach is due in an hour."

Lt Cavendish scowled. "She will cause some drama again this weekend, you watch! Headquarters will be involved again and our good name will be in the mud. You will regret keeping her in," she said.

"We will have to take that risk," Major Wickham replied grumpily. "As I said, it is Headquarters' decision. They decide if a cadet is to be discharged for disciplinary reasons, and only after due process. Now let's get on with things."

The meeting broke up and people moved out to get the admin for the bivouac started. This included the cadets handing in Consent Forms and mobile phones (An Army HQ ruling that cadets not have them at Cadet activities); being issued with packs, webbing, shelters and mosquito nets and then packing their gear.

The cadets and their adult staff were all part time volunteers who usually did one 'Home Training' parade for 3 hours once a week and a weekend once a month so it always took a short time to get organized. 130ACU did not allow the cadets to take their camping gear home (So that they did not lose it when cadets left and did not return it) but it was quick to issue as every item had a large number on it and they just had to file past, collecting their gear and having it ticked off by the 'Q' staff (in this case by Sgt Adrian Dunstan, a tall, thin Year 11 student from Heatley and his Q Corporal Billy Keith).

While this process took an hour or so it was a valuable opportunity for the cadet sergeants and corporals to supervise and manage and provide leadership.

"That's the aim of Cadets, to provide leadership opportunities, not to make it easy for the adult staff to run," Major Wickham had explained to Barbara when she first joined 130, as the cadet unit she came from in Cairns did not do things that way.

Barbara, a very attractive young woman with bright copper coloured hair, was in her first year at University. Her hometown was the city of Cairns, 350 kilometres to the north. She had moved to Townsville to study and was in her First Year at James Cook University. Because she believed Army Cadets to be a very important organization to help young people she still devoted some of her spare time to the AAC. This was her fifth year in the Cadets and her second year as a Cadet Under-Officer.

The first four years of her cadet service had been with the unit at her old High School in Cairns and she had stayed on to help out with the Heatley Cadet Unit in Townsville because the OC of that unit, Major Wickham, had asked her. Finding adult females willing to give up their spare time to supervise teenagers on weekend camps was a constant problem for most cadet units.

Barbara had submitted her application to become an Officer of Cadets, one of the adult staff, but had a few more months to wait until she was old enough.

Once outside the room Barbara turned left and walked ten paces along the concrete 'veranda' under the building, then stopped at the end to watch. The end of the building was also under a classroom and the last room was the unit's Q Store. Beyond that was an area of pavers and then two garden beds full of trees and bushes. On the pavers were laid out rows of packs, webbing, Shelters Individual (Nicknamed 'hutchies' by the cadets) and mosquito nets. The platoons of camouflage clad cadets were filing past to pick up their own gear and then moving past the table at the end of the Q Store to have their name ticked off by the Company Quartermaster Sergeant (The CQMS or CQ).

On the curved path between the garden beds were some bench seats for students to use during the school day. The cadets of HQ Platoon not involved in the issuing of gear were seated on or near these. Among them was Chloe.

Barbara moved a few paces to where she could observe Chloe better. *She is certainly beautiful,* Barbara thought.

Chloe had a face that made her look like an innocent but impish teenager, a face that was usually dimpled into a smile or a mischievous grin but was at that moment looking quite blank as she looked down into her pack. Her hair was long and blonde. Because they were going into the field it was pulled back into a pony tail rather than the 'in barracks' bun.

Oh Chloe! What are we going to do with you? Barbara thought, noting Lt Peters also watching her.

When Barbara had first been told about Chloe three years earlier, she had thought she was the biggest little tart she had ever heard of. Meeting her had reinforced this impression, while mixing grudging respect with dislike. On that occasion Chloe had come running naked along a beach to get help to save Jane from a gang of smugglers at Bamfield Beach.

Chloe was a nudist and made no secret of it. At the drop of a hat, or so it seemed, she would throw off her clothes in the most uninhibited way. On numerous occasions she had gotten into trouble at school and at Cadets for doing this. There were also dozens of stories about Chloe and sex, although of late she seemed to have matured and become choosier. But after a few recent adventures Barbara had come to appreciate Chloe's good qualities and now admired her immensely.

As a consequence of their behaviour both Chloe and Jane had not been promoted at the end of their First Year, as many cadets were. But as Second Year cadets both Chloe and Jane had shone as leaders. Both had won bravery medals for taking command of their platoon on a bivouac at a place called Mingela, thereby saving the lives of two wounded cadets and the leader of an Outlaw Motorcycle Gang. Barbara had not been present, but the incident had been described in detail to her several times.[1]

As a result Chloe and Jane had been selected for promotion and they had done their Junior Leaders Course for Corporal at the same time as Barbara had done her CUO's Course. Remembering that caused her to shudder as vivid and ghastly memories flooded through her.

That was when I was kidnapped by the Pig Hunters who tried to rape me, Barbara thought.

She had escaped and then walked naked through the bush for two nights and a day to get back to the army camp at Bunyip River.

And I was naked the whole time, she told herself, shuddering again at the memory.[2]

She then experienced another wave of scorching memories as she remembered being nude when she had deliberately confronted the two American Secret Agents who came to her home to question her about the missing French satellite the previous October. She had stayed stubbornly naked and had used that as a weapon during the confrontation. And then she smiled as she remembered how she had defiantly walked across the flight deck of an American aircraft carrier totally nude.

---

1   Read *Mischief at Mingela* by C. R. Cummings.

2   Read *Barbara in the Bush* by C. R. Cummings.

I can be as bad as Chloe really, she told herself.[3]

Chloe had next come to fame as a cadet corporal when she had won a naked swordfight with a madman. She had been one of the ten cadets from North Queensland on the team for the prestigious Chief of Army Cadet Team Challenge competition at Moorebank in Sydney. She and another girl had been kidnapped and faced rape and worse but had managed to escape. The man had chased them with a Samurai sword, and it ended with the fight in front of the Chief of Army and numerous senior officers and other cadets. As Chloe had been the innocent victim, she had survived that incident but her notoriety had grown.

And she survived because she does Medieval Martial Arts, Barbara mused, that being one of Chloe's hobbies, along with dancing and being a 'life' model for artists.

The most recent occasion had been only four months earlier during the April school holidays when Chloe and Barbara had gone to the South Pacific nation of Bunga Lunga on a school trip. They had become caught up in an armed uprising against the government and had been taken prisoner by the rebels. Both had ended up nude for several days as they attempted to evade recapture. Both had endured some desperate adventures during which Chloe had rescued the president and Barbara and helped prevent an armed clash between French and Australian troops arriving to restore order. The whole incident had been world news and Chloe's fame, and nude images of her, had been widely broadcast.

The thought of those French soldiers caused Barbara to smile as one of them was the man she loved, Lieutenant Raoul de Berg of the French *Marine Commandos*. Raoul had asked her to marry him and she was now torn with indecision over what her answer should be.

Despite her behaviour Chloe had managed to stay in Cadets and had even risen to the rank of Warrant Officer Class 2 and become the Heatley unit's Company Sergeant Major. In this capacity she had, in Barbara's estimation, done a good job in difficult circumstances. As Barbara had spent a year as the CSM of her own unit she felt qualified to make this assessment.

The thought of the incident which had led to Chloe's downfall made Barbara frown. She did not really approve of Chloe's romping around

---

3   Read *Barbara at her Best* by C. R. Cummings.

naked, although personally she actually found the nude female form very pleasing.

It was the fact that the complaint had appeared to be so obviously an act of sour grapes by a male sergeant who had let it be known on many occasions that he thought he was better than Chloe and that he should have been the CSM that rankled with Barbara.

At that she glanced across the lawn to her right to where the sergeant in question, Shane Brady, 1 Platoon sergeant, was laughing with his mates at some private joke.

At least he didn't get to be CSM in her place, Barbara thought with satisfaction. That position had gone to Sergeant Warren, a Year 12 student in his third year. *And he's doing a good job,* she thought.

And now Chloe is in disgrace. I wonder how she will cope? Barbara wondered, again noting Lt Peters and Lt Cavendish both obviously watching Chloe while muttering to each other.

It was obvious to Barbara that if Chloe made even one little slip in behaviour they would use it to get rid of her.

*****

A few paces from Barbara stood Cadet Corporal Colleen McNamara. Colleen was a beautiful, dark-haired girl with a really nice personality. She was a 17-year-old Year 12 student at Heatley. In Cadets she was the company Medic Cpl and was in her third year as a cadet.

Colleen straightened up from picking up mosquito nets that had not been issued. The nets had been laid out in a long line on the pavers, number up, for cadets to collect. The ones she was picking up were for cadets who had not turned up for the bivouac and she was placing them in plastic carry boxes to put back into the store.

I seem to be the only one in Headquarters doing any work here! she thought, annoyance and resentment beginning to stir.

Colleen was a willing worker and always helpful but just occasionally she resented the way some people seemed to dodge work. Knowing that there were nearly a dozen people in the Headquarters Platoon she looked around to find someone to assist with the chore.

A glance showed that Cpl Keith and the CQ were busy controlling a work party from 3 Platoon that was returning unissued packs to the shelves. Looking behind her Colleen saw Sgt Jane Carson standing talking to Chloe. Colleen did not like Jane, the unit Signal's Sergeant, mainly because she was a friend of Chloe. And she disliked Chloe intensely, embarrassed by her reputation and behaviour.

I wish they'd chucked her out! she thought. But then she felt guilty as normally she was very forgiving and considerate and did not wish harm to anyone.

Her gaze settled on Chloe, knowing that Chloe was now posted as the HQ PL Sgt and therefore responsible for supervising and making them all work. For a second Colleen considered calling out to ask for help but she dismissed the idea, not wanting to even speak to her. She had not liked her as CSM and did not want to have anything to do with her now.

Serves the rude witch right for being demoted, Colleen thought, giving Chloe a resentful, yet mildly jealous glance (as she had to acknowledge Chloe's good looks).

As though the thought had been transferred by mental telepathy Chloe looked up and met Colleen's eye. Chloe then stood up and turned to the other HQ cadets nearby. "Come on you lot! Stop packing your own gear and come and help pack away these hutchies and mozzie nets!"

As Chloe led Jane and the other cadets towards her Colleen blushed at her own thoughts and bent to pick up more mosquito nets. Then Chloe called again. "Come on Valerie, stop talking and come and help."

Colleen glanced up and saw that Valerie Metcalfe, the unit Intelligence NCO (A fine pun that one! someone had unkindly suggested) was standing over near where 4 Platoon were packing their gear. She was talking to Cpl Geoff Unsworth, one of the 4 PL section commanders, and Colleen's boyfriend.

What's Geoff doing talking to her, Colleen thought. *He should be looking after his section.*

A little niggle of worry flitted across Colleen's mind before she bent to pick up more mosquito nets.

Chapter 2

BARBARA

1800hrs Friday 28 AUG
On an army coach on the Bruce Highway 40 kilometres southeast of
Townsville, North Queensland.

Barbara shifted in her seat on the right-hand side of the coach and
looked out of the window as the coach roared along the highway
at 100kph. Out on the right side of the coach rose the huge mass of a
mountain, its lower slopes in darkness and the upper slopes a rusty red as
the last rays of the setting sun lit them up.

To Barbara's eyes the mountain looked very pretty, although rugged.
I'm glad we aren't climbing that this weekend, she thought. Then her gaze
shifted to inside the coach and she studied the rows of cadets in front of
her. *I hope we don't have any problems this weekend,* she thought.

Then her mind dredged up a flood of awful memories. *It was along
this road Erika and I were driven when those prison escapees picked us
up,* she thought.

Barbara understood she was a very attractive young woman with
her copper-coloured hair and green eyes. She had a figure which she
knew men found very attractive: with long legs and prominent breasts.
However, while she had no difficulty in attracting men, she wasn't all that
keen on them. Over the last few years she had been subjected to some
horrible experiences by revolting males, so she was a bit ambivalent
about whether she really liked them.

One of the worst of those experiences had been along this very road
five years earlier, when she was only 14. She had run away from home
with another girl and had hitch-hiked to Townsville. There they had been
taken hostage by two escaped convicts from the nearby Stuart Prison.
The other girl, Erika, had been forced to have sex with one of the men
and the other had been about to rape Barbara while their car was parked
at a service station at Home Hill when a bus full of army cadets had
arrived and saved her.

It had been a terrifying experience and as Barbara thought of it now she experienced a wave of fear and disgust which made her shudder.

The person next to her, Lt Cavendish, turned to her. "Are you cold Barbara?"

"No ma'am. Just remembering something," Barbara replied.

Even though she was legally an adult and was in the process of applying to become an ACS (Army Cadet Staff) herself Barbara could not bring herself to call the officers by their first names. She managed a smile but then broke into a cold sweat as her mind brought up more memories from that incident. That weekend had changed her whole life and was one of the reasons she was now willing to give time and effort to help run the cadets. It had given her a group to belong to who had cared for her.

Some of these kids might need help one day, she thought.

At that she glanced across the aisle and frowned. Seated opposite her was Chloe. Beside Chloe sat her best friend Jane Carson.

Barbara covertly studied Chloe and was relieved to see her smile for the first time that day. Having been in the darkest depths of depression herself as a young teenager, Barbara was very aware of how young people who are down could consider suicide as a serious option.

Seeing Chloe talking apparently happily to Jane Barbara was reminded of the incident the previous month.

Chloe was a good CSM. If only she could control herself she would be a real winner, Barbara thought.

And there, sitting just a bit closer to the front of the coach, was the sergeant who had made the complaint, Shane Brady.

I don't like him, she thought.

She had heard some very nasty stories about him and the friends he associated with, some of whom were still in cadets.

The coach had rounded a curve by then and the whole upper slope of the mountains was now in shadow. On the left was the main railway line. On both sides of the highway was a belt of bush which was becoming darker by the minute and seemingly more threatening as the evening shadows closed in.

For some reason Barbara suddenly shivered again. "I hope nothing goes wrong this weekend," she said to Lt Cavendish.

"So do I. The unit has been having a bad year," Lt Cavendish replied.

"That's true. We seem to have a real collection of bad apples this year," Barbara agreed. Only six weeks earlier they had experienced another incident in a run of problems. The unit had held its annual Command Post Exercise. This was conducted for the CUOs and NCOs at Heatley Secondary College over a weekend and was designed to train the corporals in radio operating and signals procedures.

Three of the NCOs: two male corporals and a female corporal, had told their parents they were going to Cadets for the weekend but then gone to one of their houses to party, those particular parents being away for the weekend. But someone had talked too much and Major Wickham had found out. Parents had been phoned and the police had busted in on the party, which had included sex, drugs and alcohol. The three NCOs had been discharged from cadets.

The fact that all three were friends of Sgt Brady made Barbara uneasy. She had heard that Brady had arranged the bashing of another sergeant who was a rival for his girlfriend, herself a sergeant who had left a few months earlier. There was even a rumour that Brady's girlfriend was now pregnant.

"Some of our sergeants aren't very good," she said to Lt Cavendish.

"No. You are right there. There are a couple of weak links," Lt Cavendish agreed. Then she indicated another female sergeant sitting just forward from them. "Heidi is very good though."

"Yes she is," Barbara agreed.

Heidi Hope was a really nice girl who combined a delightful personality with really good looks. She was 2 Platoon sergeant.

"We've got a weak lot of corporals this year as well," Lt Cavendish added.

"Yes, some are not much good," Barbara agreed. "Or they are too old and won't be around to make sergeants next year." She indicated the seat just ahead of them where two female corporals from HQ sat: Katie Melony and Sandra Saunders. In front of them sat Colleen McNamara. Privately Barbara considered Colleen to be the most beautiful girl in the unit, a notion that bothered her slightly as she still struggled with her own sexuality.

Indicating her she said, "Colleen would have made a good sergeant."

"Yes," agreed Lt Cavendish. "It's a pity she is in Year 12 and will be leaving at the end of the year."

Next to Colleen sat her boyfriend, Corporal Geoff Unsworth, a section commander in Number 4 Platoon, the senior platoon which was made up of '2nd Year' cadets or older '1st Years'. Seeing them together caused Barbara a wry smile.

That's one of the problems of this unit, she thought. *There is too much fraternizing.*

To her it seemed as though at times the whole unit was trying to date each other. Certainly there were plenty of short-lived teen 'crushes'.

In the case of Colleen and Geoff Unsworth Barbara wasn't too worried. It had been a fairly open and steady relationship which was accepted by people and neither was known to misbehave at cadets. The thought of that made Barbara frown again and she bit her lip and unconsciously shook her head with disapproval. For some reason she did not like Geoff Unsworth.

I just don't trust him, she told herself, but knew this had no foundation. But it did cheer her up to see Colleen laugh when Geoff spoke to her. *Colleen is very nice. I like her. I hope she doesn't get hurt.*

Barbara's eyes wandered forward to the seat in front of Colleen. Sitting in the aisle seat was Cpl Naomie Furness, a blonde with freckles who was only in Year 10.

Returning to the previous conversation, Barbara said: "Naomie might be alright."

It was a constant pre-occupation by the staff to look ahead to try to select people who might make good leaders in the years ahead.

Lt Cavendish sighed. "Major Wickham is a bit down about all the trouble we've had. He reckons that it is usual to have good years and bad years which alternate, but this time we seem to have bad eggs at every rank level."

"There are a couple of CUOs who aren't worth feeding, that's for sure," Barbara agreed. She made a sour face and glanced along at where two of the male CUOs sat together: CUO Milikin and CUO Bailey. She did not like either and had heard several complaints from the girls about them both. So far nothing had been serious enough to take action about but she knew that Major Wickham had spoken to both about it.

Poor old Major Wickham! she thought.

It was starting to be brought home to her just how much responsibility and stress the Officers of Cadets took on as part-time volunteers.

Not to mention all the work and admin they do in their own spare time after work.

The cadet unit actually had an 'Establishment' of one hundred and was organized into four platoons and a HQ but recruiting had been poor and the numbers were down so that only about seventy were on the two coaches heading for the bivouac area.

Darkness set in. The coach roared on, crossing St Margaret Creek and then Palm Creek before coming out of the belt of forest into more open country with farms on both sides. The coach then headed east across flat land which was mostly covered with sugar cane farms or mango orchards. The lights of farmhouses swept by from time to time and then Barbara saw the glow of cane fires ahead.

The sight of them made her heart rate shoot up. The night she and Erika had been kidnapped the cane fires had been burning too and the images were etched into her memory. She shook her head as she stared out at one of the fires, a whole field of sugar cane alight. The ruddy glow on the undersides of the smoke clouds and the shooting flames and drifting sparks made it a spectacle to behold, but to her it was also one charged with very strong emotion.

Lt Cavendish pointed to the fire they were passing. "Have you ever seen a cane fire before?"

Barbara nodded, "Yes miss, I mean ma'am. I came along this road a few years ago at night."

To her relief Lt Cavendish did not ask about that but instead went on about cane fires. "They don't burn the sugar cane up your way, do they?" she asked.

"No ma'am. It is only here in the Lower Burdekin that they still do that. Something to do with the soil type and evaporation or something," Barbara replied.

The coach raced on through the darkness, ending up caught in a long line of slow-moving traffic. Barbara became edgy and impatient. She had never been to Millaroo, where the bivouac was to be held, and wanted to get off this highway with its awful memories.

Fifteen minutes later they arrived at the small sugar milling town of Brandon. The busses pulled over to stop at the Roadhouse and that also brought back a flood of memories to Barbara. On the night Barbara was rescued she had managed to fight clear of the man who was trying to rape her in a car, and had run across the concrete driveway of a service station to the cadets. The man had taken her top and bra off so all she had been wearing were her jeans and joggers and the situation had been made worse by the fact that most of the cadets had come from her own school and knew her.

Later she had again escaped being raped by the same men in the bush near Bowen and that time she had been stark naked when some cadets had arrived. At the memory Barbara gave a wry smile.

I'm no better than Chloe really, she thought, *except that she runs around in the nuddy for fun.*

Barbara stepped down out of the coach with the others, then stood and shivered in the cool night air as the memories swamped her. It all seemed like just yesterday!

She looked around at the brightly lit driveway and shop windows and then at the surrounding darkness and felt quite uneasy. To shake off the mood she walked across towards the shop door.

As she did, she saw Major Wickham park his car and get out. He had been on that same weekend exercise but luckily had not actually been present when she was undressed. Major Wickham was driving his own car, which would be one of the safety vehicles for the weekend.

A second safety vehicle was an army Land Rover driven by the unit QM, Capt Hamilton. He was an IT expert in his civilian job and was also an Army Reserve captain. Barbara really liked him and thought he was quite handsome, although she did not really like his moustache and did find his many jokes a bit wearing. The Land Rover was parked over near Major Wickham's car on the other side of the service station and Capt Hamilton got out. With him were the CQMS, Sgt Dunstan and Cpl Keith, the Corporal Storeman.

The Roadhouse had been warned and was ready for the swarm of cadets who surged in. Barbara joined the queue inside and studied the array of foods and drinks available. She felt quite hungry and decided on a hamburger.

As she stood in the queue Barbara looked around. Amongst the first people she noted were Chloe and Jane. They were seated at one of the tables and were enjoying hamburgers and milkshakes. Chloe was still looking very dejected but did smile at something Jane said. Sitting behind them, obviously watching them, were both Lt Cavendish and Lt Peters.

Barbara thought that was a bit like harassment and pursed her lips. But then she shrugged.

Chloe and Jane need to be watched, she reminded herself.

Inside the café Barbara felt safe and warm, surrounded by happy, laughing cadets. Only when she went back outside after buying her hamburger did the horrible memories resurface.

So did the first of the problems. CSM Warren came over to her. "Excuse me ma'am," he said. "Could you just have a look in the female dunny? I've heard a whisper that Micki and Sandy have gone there to have a smoke."

Micki Evans and Sandy Saunders were two female corporals and had been frequently rumoured to be smokers. As smoking was not allowed for persons under 18, nor for cadets, it was a point of discipline the unit worried about. To Major Wickham it was a symbolic thing: if people smoked, they could not be trusted and should not have rank.

Oh blast! Barbara thought.

She did not really want any trouble and just wanted a quiet weekend. But nor could she refuse the CSM's request, so she placed her hamburger on a bench, turned and walked towards the side of the building. As she did, she saw a face peek around and then vanish.

Damn! she thought, *They have someone watching.*

Barbara walked to the corner and around it. As she did she met Cpl Valerie Metcalf coming the other way. Valerie smiled (or was it smirked?) and said hello. Barbara thought Valerie was a real little tart but managed to hide her dislike and returned a friendly hello. Then out of the darkness behind the building walked three girls: Micki Evans, Sandy Saunders and another blonde female corporal, Kathy Horn. They gave Barbara a cheeky and cheerful greeting which made Barbara secretly grit her teeth.

Damn! They were warned. I didn't catch them, she thought.

To hide the fact that she had been trying to catch the smokers, Barbara went to the toilet and found when she got there that she really needed to. She also noted the smell of cigarette smoke but knew it wasn't strong evidence.

Barbara returned to the front of the service station and collected her hamburger. As she ate it she stood talking to CUO Roberts. Nearby Kathy Horn and Micki snickered and cast cheeky glances in her direction.

Bitches! Barbara thought. *I will catch you one day.*

She did not like Kathy, having heard some dreadful stories of her behaviour at parties. The mere thought of what the rumours suggested made Barbara's stomach turn with disgust.

CUO Roberts, 'Robbo' to all, nudged her and indicated CUO Milikin and one of the new female recruits.

"That looks like trouble brewing over there."

Barbara looked and noted that the new girl, a young Year 8 named Rosie something or other, was smiling at CUO Milikin but the smile had a frozen, haunted sort of look.

She isn't enjoying talking to him, Barbara thought. *But she is too good-mannered or new to walk away.*

"Colleen McNamara looks unhappy about something too," Barbara said, glancing over at where Colleen and Katie were talking to one side. Even as she looked, she noted Colleen wipe a tear from her cheek.

"Oh that's because she and Geoff Unsworth just had an argument and now he is over there talking to Valerie. He's been deliberately ignoring Colleen. I think he's going to give her the brush off," Robbo replied.

"What was the argument about?" Barbara asked.

"Unsworth kept making crude suggestions that everyone could overhear. Colleen asked him to stop and he nearly bit her head off; shouted at her not to tell him how to behave."

"She would be well rid of him then," Barbara said. "If he keeps doing things she doesn't like then he doesn't love her."

"That's what we told her," Robbo said.

"Boyfriends can be a bit of a trial," Barbara added. That made her think of her own boyfriend and she experienced a warm surge of pleasure mixed with guilt.

It is Raoul who really makes my pulses race, she thought.

She had met him the previous October when she had taken part in an incredibly dangerous and dramatic adventure at Dotswood in the Townsville Field Training Area.[4]

During the Christmas Holidays, after she had turned 18, Barbara had spent two weeks on holiday with him in French New Caledonia and they had explored their relationship further. He had professed passionate love for her and asked her to marry him, but Barbara had put him off, thinking she was much too young.

---

4   Read *Barbara at her Best* by C.R. Cummings.

I'm not ready for that yet, she thought.

But the memory of him saying sweet nothings to her made her smile.

But then, he is a Frenchman, she thought.

CSM Warren came past. "Back on the bus in five minutes. Hurry up and finish eating."

With that encouragement Barbara bit into her hamburger and quickly wolfed it down. It tasted delicious and she stood and stared along the main street of the little town and felt glad to be alive and happy to be there as part of the unit.

Major Wickham joined them, also eating a hamburger.

Barbara swallowed a mouthful and asked: "Is it much further sir?"

"About forty kilometres. Bit over half an hour," Major Wickham replied.

Robbo asked: "What are we doing this weekend sir?"

Major Wickham turned a face of mock severity on her. "Haven't you read your program?"

Capt Hamilton cut in: "Be the same as last year Robbo."

"It might not be," Major Wickham replied.

"It will be. It will be just the usual old navigation and fieldcraft," Capt Hamilton replied.

Robbo shrugged. "Might be, but I don't care," she said. "Millaroo is my favourite bivouac."

"Mine too," Major Wickham agreed. The unit did five or six weekend bivouacs a year, each in a different place, but only one or two were different from the previous year.

Chloe and Jane both came out of the café and walked past towards the toilet. Barbara thought nothing of it until Lt Peters came out of the café a few minutes later and stopped next to her.

"Barbara, would you just check what Chloe and Jane are doing in the toilet," she asked.

A surge of resentment flushed through Barbara. She sensed she was being used as part of the OOC's vendetta against the pair. It was on the tip of her tongue to say, 'Do your own dirty work!' but she managed to hold it back.

Instead she said, "I don't think they are smokers ma'am."

"Just do what I asked!" Lt Peters snapped irritably back. That raised a few eyebrows and really tested Barbara's self-control. Nodding but too angry to trust herself to speak, she put down her hamburger again and walked towards the toilet.

As she turned the corner at the toilet entrance Barbara almost collided with Jane coming the other way. Behind her was Chloe, standing at a washbasin washing her hands. The two girls had obviously just been to the toilet. Jane just nodded and continued walking while Chloe began drying her hands. She looked up, met Barbara's eyes and smiled. "Hi Barbara, I mean CUO Brassington. How are you?" she said.

"Good thanks," Barbara answered. She really wanted a chance to talk to Chloe alone but that was thwarted by another girl coming out of a toilet cubicle. "Nearly time to get on the bus," she added for something to say."

"Yes ma'am. Come on Katie," Chloe said as she headed for the doorway.

To make it less obvious that she had been sent to check on Chloe and Jane Barbara took herself into the vacated cubicle and pretended to go to the toilet again. But she wasn't happy. To her mind Chloe needed counselling and guidance.

Not victimization! Chloe and Jane are worth saving, she thought. *They both have great positive qualities.*

After waiting a minute Barbara fidgeted with her clothing, flushed the toilet and made her way back out. She re-joined the group of adults. Lt Cavendish was now standing beside Lt Peters, but all Barbara did was shake her head and pick up her now cold hamburger. Over near the coach she could see Chloe and Jane and they were standing under a light and chatting to other cadets.

The adults stood eating and talking while the CSM and sergeants began rounding the cadets up and herding them back to the coaches. Here they were checked on board by Lt Cavendish with the 'Bus Roll'. As the cadets climbed aboard Barbara noted that Geoff Unsworth did not get on with Colleen, but went with Valerie to the smaller bus. Barbara noted a look of distress cross Colleen's face before she climbed aboard.

Poor kid, she thought. It made her really sad to see someone having their heart broken. *And that's what is happening here for sure,* she thought.

While Barbara was still standing considering this Major Wickham finished his hamburger and licked his fingers.

"Oh well, let's get moving," he said.

Chapter 3

MILLAROO

From Brandon onward Major Wickham led the way in his car as the route they took was a real spider web of roads. This was across the flat farmland of the Lower Burdekin district. Even in daylight a driver who did not know the way could be easily confused. In the dark it became a real maze. So the two coaches and Land Rover followed the OC's car.

Barbara found it fairly tiring and boring, just an endless tunnel of headlights between fields of sugar cane, with occasional farmhouses or road intersections. Only a few cane fires and glimpses of the distant lights of the town of Ayr out to her left provided variety.

Now that they were off the main highway there was very little traffic, only two vehicles passing in the opposite direction before they came onto the main road which ran south beside the Burdekin River. This was the Ayr-Dalbeg Road which runs parallel to the river for eighty kilometres, passing through the farming districts of Clare, Millaroo and Dalbeg.

It was all flat country and Barbara found that quite boring and she wished they would hurry up and arrive. The main road was two lane and busier, with vehicles passing the other way every couple of minutes. Farms crowded right to the edge of the road on both sides.

From Clare onwards they had a 2-foot gauge light railway on the left and farms on the right. They began to pass long trains hauling bins full of sugar cane north, or empty wire bins south.

"Those trains take that cane all the way to Giru Mill," Lt Cavendish commented.

"They are long," Barbara replied. She noted that each train had a small brake wagon with yellow flashing lights on it at the rear. The peculiar smell of burnt sugar cane came wafting in through the air conditioning.

"Ah! Oh I love that smell," Chloe cried.

"I don't. It makes me want to throw up," Lt Cavendish replied.

"It's the smell of money," Barbara commented.

"Then I like it even more!" Chloe said, laughing as she did.

Hearing that laugh also cheered Barbara up. *That is the first time I have heard Chloe laugh today,* she told herself. Again she resolved to have a good talk with Chloe when opportunity offered.

The journey seemed never ending to Barbara. Chloe pointed to the left. "The Burdekin River is just beyond those trees there."

Barbara was familiar with the Burdekin from camps near Charters Towers and tried to imagine what the river might be like here, hundreds of kilometres downstream.

"Clare Weir," Lt Cavendish commented as they passed a collection of lights and buildings. "We get our water from there."

"Not far now," Chloe added.

It took another ten minutes. There were more farms, sugar trains and then a few kilometres of dark bush before they passed a large building on the left.

"That is the pump station for pumping water to Townsville," Lt Cavendish informed her.

Barbara nodded. She looked out her window and dimly made out the silhouette of a rugged hill close beside the road on the right. The coach went up over a small rise, then down into a dip with a valley full of dry savannah woodland on the right, then up a long, gentle slope around the left side of a rugged hill.

The coach swept around a curve to the right at the end of the hill. As it did Barbara heard Jane say: "There's the river," but she was not fast enough to catch a glimpse before the coach went into a deep cutting.

"Nearly there," Lt Cavendish said.

Barbara sighed with relief. She was getting cramped and stiff and the bus travel was making her nauseous.

The road curved to the right through the deep cutting, then left at the end of it. It crossed over a creek and went on to run on across flat country. Two more obvious creeks were crossed and several curves negotiated. Open bush seemed to predominate on both sides. After a couple of kilometres the coach slowed as its headlights lit up a long concrete bridge in front and a dirt road junction on the right just before the bridge. Major Wickham's car did a U-turn on the dirt and the coach followed it around. As it did Barbara read a sign pointing along the gravel side road. 'Landers Creek' it proclaimed.

Lt Cavendish pointed that way. "That is where the homestead of the cattle station is. We are camping on their land."

"Where are we going?" Barbara asked, as the coach accelerated back the way it had come.

"That is the only safe place to turn a coach," Lt Cavendish explained. "The bivouac site is just back near the base of that hill."

It was. The coach recrossed the three creeks then slowed and came to a stop. Barbara saw that Major Wickham's car was already stopped there, facing down a gravel side road on the left. The Land Rover was parked in front of it.

The cadets debussed and unloaded their gear. Barbara's was in the back of the Land Rover, so she moved to one side to be out of the way. 130ACU did so many camps that unloading was a drill. As cadets came off the coach they went to the cargo bin and were handed an item of equipment which they carried to the rear until a sergeant told them to drop it. They then circled back to join the end of the line to get another item. The gear all ended up laid out in long rows in the grass beside the road. As each pack or set of webbing had a large number written on it in felt pen it was easy for people to find their gear. For a few minutes there was the usual apparent chaos of sergeants calling and of milling cadets. Then order returned as cadets found their gear and joined their platoons. They ended up sitting on their packs in section lines beside the side road.

Barbara was pleasantly surprised to find that the night was not cold. Being the end of August it had the potential to drop to zero this far inland, but it was barely cold enough to need a jacket. As the coaches roared off back towards Townsville she sighed and breathed deeply. All around her was dark bush but it had a nice feel about it and she relaxed.

Major Wickham stood talking on his mobile phone to the property owner. When he finished, he called to Capt Hamilton to go in, then climbed into his car and followed the Land Rover along the gravel road through a gate. The cadets began marching after the vehicles and Barbara went with them, walking beside Robbo. (Refer to Map 1)

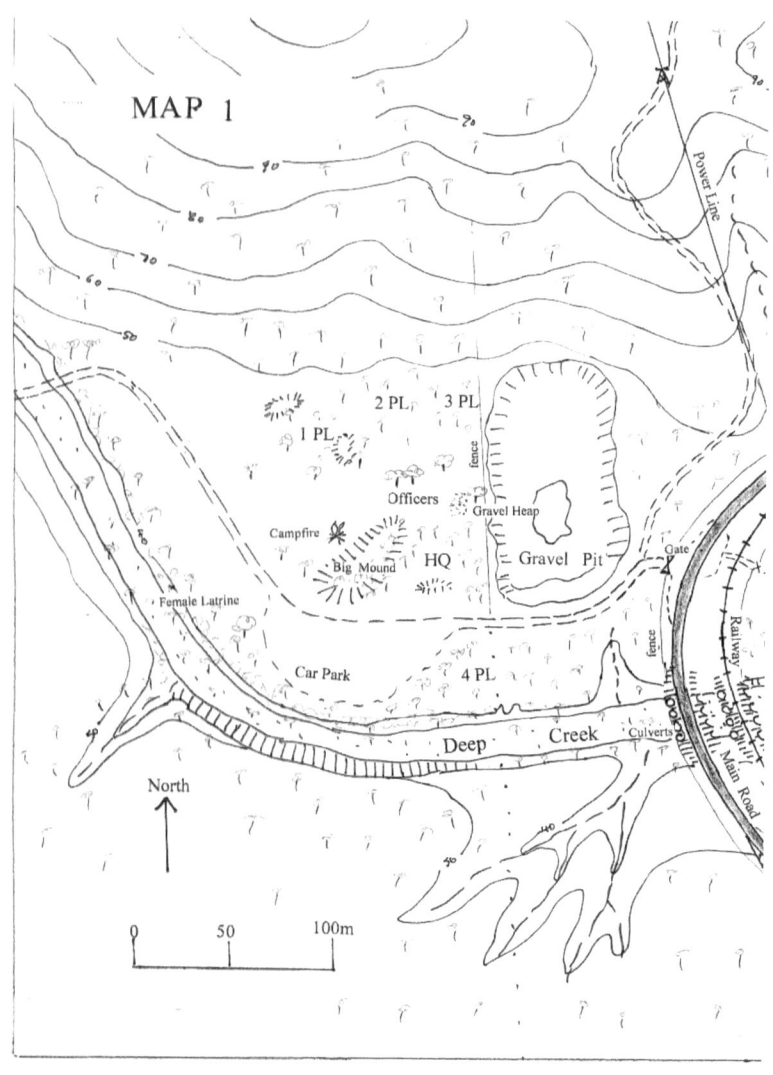

MAP 1

2 PL 3 PL
1 PL
Officers
Gravel Heap
Campfire
Big Mound HQ Gravel Pit Gate
Female Latrine
Car Park 4 PL
Deep Creek Culverts
North
Power Line
fence
fence
Railway
Main Road

0 50 100m

It was only 300 paces from the gate to an old gravel scrape, which was the bivouac area. When told the previous Wednesday that they were to camp in a gravel scrape Barbara had been surprised but now found it quite a reasonable place. As she walked in Barbara noted there was open bush on her left and on the right was a large depression a hundred metres across, extending all the way to the base of the hill. At the bottom of this gravel pit was a small pond, the water just visible in the starlight.

The road went past the gravel pit and through a fence. Beyond this was the old gravel scrape. On the left was a small thicket of stunted trees. The road went past the thicket out into bare, open ground. On the right, opposite the thicket, were some small mounds and more small trees among a stand of large eucalypts. A large mound covered with bushes and long grass stood in the middle of the gravel scrape. Around behind this large mound was more open, bare ground for a hundred metres, then several smaller mounds and then a line of trees along a creek bank.

Between the large mound and the gravel pit was a gently sloping area with trees and short dry grass which extended for a hundred metres up onto the lower slopes of the hill. This was the actual bivouac area. A heap of sorted loose gravel stood near the edge of the gravel pit. The officers had a spot under two small but very leafy trees in the middle of the area and near the pile of gravel. The vehicles were parked on the open ground between the big mound and the line of trees along the creek. Barbara noted that Lt Forster's 4WD was already parked there. He had driven down via a back road through Clare and had the jerry cans of water.

Just beside the road near the big mound the company were seated in section lines sitting on their packs. Major Wickham spoke to them briefly and Capt Hamilton gave a Safety Brief. The platoon commanders were then told to go and set up camp.

All the CUOs and sergeants had been to the area before, so the platoons simply went to their usual areas and began to set up camp. Barbara went to the Land Rover and extracted her pack and webbing. She then dumped them near two small trees just up from where the male OOCs were installing themselves under the largest bushy tree.

The next half hour was taken up with erecting 'hutchies', made by tying the camouflaged plastic sheets called 'Shelters, Individual' between two trees and pegging the corners down. Barbara camped on her own while Lt Peters shared with Lt Cavendish, their hutchie being on the other side of the male OOCs. Barbara opted to have one side of her hutchie almost horizontal, the corners held up by two sticks. That gave a lot more room underneath.

By the time this was done Major Wickham had lit a hurricane lantern and a fire had been kindled in the open area behind the large central mound. There were small groups of cadets in each of the platoon areas out in the darkness, but the campfire quickly became the social focus of the camp. Because of the risk of bushfire only the one fire was allowed and it was on a large patch of bare earth. Barbara carried her pack and webbing down to the fire, arranged her pack to sit on, then settled to brew a cup of coffee on her hexamine stove.

This was one of the activities Barbara most enjoyed on a camp. She was very aware that every time she smelled burning hexamine she was taken back to that very first morning after she had been rescued from the convicts. She had opted to join her section on an infiltration exercise against cadets from Mackay rather than sit around with the adult staff. The immediate result had been to develop an immensely strong emotional bond with her section corporal, Gwen Copeland. It had been Barbara's great affection and admiration for Gwen which had motivated her to continue in Cadets.

The other officers all joined her around the fire. Jokes and stories began and Barbara looked around the circle of happy, smiling faces and felt very much at home. Seated on Barbara's left were Major Wickham, Lt Cavendish and Lt Peters. On her right were Capt Hamilton and Lt Forster. CSM Warren joined them, along with Cpl Andrew Wickham, the OC's son and a dozen of more cadets.

Barbara was mildly surprised to see Sgt Brady sitting opposite her. Somehow, she had expected him to be involved in any mischief that might be going on. Sgt Backer from 4 Platoon joined him.

And it was going on, though not in any serious way. The rumour came by that Micki and Sandy had gone off to have a smoke so the CSM went off, hoping to catch them. Three girls came out of the darkness: Cpl Naomi Furness, Cpl Maree de Beer and Cpl Katie Melony. Barbara overheard them muttering to Robbo that CUO Milikin and CUO Bailey were both being gross.

At that Lt Forster and Lt Peters went off into the night with a torch to ensure the 'little germs' weren't getting out of control. Barbara stirred her coffee and sipped it with real pleasure. As she did, she noted the silhouette of a mountain in the distance. A glance at the stars told her that it must be west of her.

A second look at the stars made her shake her head in admiration. The sky was crystal clear and being so far away from the city lights the stars stood out in millions.

"That is really pretty," she said. It was one of the things she liked best about camping: being closer to nature.

Lt Peters and Lt Forster returned to the fire. Lt Forster sat down but Lt Peters gestured to Lt Cavendish and remained standing. Lt Cavendish nodded and stood up and the two lady OOCs spoke quietly together before turning and walking into the night.

Barbara noted this with disapproval. *Gone to try and catch Chloe and Jane out,* she surmised.

But no sooner had the two OOCs gone away than Chloe and Jane came giggling out of the darkness from the opposite direction. Seeing Chloe giggling lifted Barbara's spirits but also raised her anxiety level.

She's obviously feeling a bit better but if she gets up to any mischief she is doomed, she thought.

Chloe plonked herself down. "4 Platoon are revolting," she commented.

Capt Hamilton looked at her. "Do you mean they are in revolt or they are gross and objectionable?" he queried.

"Gross and objectionable," Chloe said as Jane squeezed in beside her.

Major Wickham frowned then said, "Well you are a sergeant. You should go back and control them."

For just a second Chloe pursed her lips but then she smiled. "We will in a minute sir. The boys just wanted to tell a few jokes."

"They'd better not be breaking the rules," Major Wickham said in a grumpy voice. He moved to stand up but Lt Forster forestalled him.

"I'll go and check sir. Any revolt in the outer provinces will be ruthlessly put down," he said in a joking tone. With that he turned on his torch and walked into the night.

Barbara relaxed and surreptitiously studied Chloe. *She seems more like her old self,* she decided.

For a moment she considered taking Chloe aside for a talk but then decided to wait as Chloe had animatedly joined in the conversation. Twenty minutes of jokes and stories followed which put Barbara in a very happy frame of mind. A few others came and went. Then Chloe told a joke which made Major Wickham frown. The three female corporals went off giggling into the night, to be replaced by four others: CUO Robbo Roberts, CUO Richard Callan, Cpl Colleen McNamara and Cpl Melony.

CUO Callan looked at Sgt Backer and pointed to where 4 Platoon were camped. It was one of the unit's rules that either the sergeant or CUO be always in the platoon area on social nights. Sgt Backer made a face but stood up.

"I'll see you later," he said to Cpl Kathy Horn.

Kathy nodded and went on chatting to the cadets beside her. A few minutes later she stood up and walked into the darkness. That looked a bit suspicious to Barbara and she resolved to walk around and check.

As Barbara thought this Chloe stood up. "I need to go to the toilet," she explained.

"I'll come with you," Jane replied. Chloe hauled Jane to her feet, then dusted her bum. As she did she wiggled and wobbled so much that Barbara could not help noting her curves.

Chloe is really voluptuous, she thought, noting that even the shapeless army camouflage uniform could not hide the fact.

Barbara was not the only one watching. Cpl Bailey, younger brother of the CUO, called out: "Hey Chloe, why don't you give us a dance while you are at it?"

At that Major Wickham scowled. "That will be enough of that sort of talk!" he snapped. "We don't want any more trouble."

Chloe nodded and gave Bailey a sneer before leading Jane off into the darkness. Cpl Bailey shut up immediately and soon afterwards walked off with Sgt Brady. LCpl Lang and Geoff Unsworth sat down and joined in the conversation.

CSM Warren returned, having failed to find Micki or Sandy, both of whom appeared from the other direction a few minutes later. More cadets drifted to the fire: Cpl Ben McPherson, a Year 11 boy, with Sgt Heidi Hope and Katie. Cpl Valerie Metcalf re-joined them. Geoff Unsworth at once stood up and walked around the fire to join her, which caused Barbara to glance sideways at Colleen.

Colleen sat talking to Heidi Hope and appeared at first not to notice or be concerned but then Barbara noted her cast an anxious glance or two in the direction of Geoff and Valerie.

More jokes were told. Cpl Maree de Beer reappeared and sat down next to CUO Callan. That was such an obvious move that Barbara had to smile. Barbara actually thought Maree was an exceptionally pretty girl. She studied her as she stood talking to CUO Callan on the other side of the fire. *Maree is going to develop into a really beautiful woman,* she mused. *I just hope she develops a pleasant personality to go with the looks. If she does she will be a real winner.*

Then, to Colleen's obvious concern, Geoff and Valerie turned and walked off into the night.

Oh dear! Barbara thought. *I hope that isn't what it looks like.*

Barbara noted that Major Wickham had a frown on his face as his eyes followed the backs of Geoff and Valerie. Seeing that decided her. She drained the last of her coffee.

"I'll do a bit of a walk around sir."

"Good. Thanks Barbara," Major Wickham replied.

Barbara packed her cup canteen away and stood up. Robbo also stood up.

"I'll come with you," she said.

"Thanks." Barbara bent and picked up her 'Big Jim' torch and she and Robbo set off into the darkness.

*****

Colleen sat staring into the fire with a churn of sickening emotions swirling inside her. At one level there was embarrassment because she was sure that everybody had noticed what was going on. At another level was almost desperate unhappiness as she realized that Geoff was going to dump her. She found the idea both intensely depressing but also very wounding to her self-esteem.

I must be really boring, she thought miserably.

She knew it wasn't her looks. She was sensible enough to appreciate that, in the conventional sense, she was a pretty girl with all the right curves and looks.

Another thought added to her gloom and anxiety. She had never allowed Geoff to do more than kiss her and do a bit of fondling. When he had tried to go further she had quite firmly stopped him. At 17 she was still a virgin and was determined to stay that way till she was absolutely sure that he, whoever 'he' was, was the right man, that it was true love.

That's probably why he is acting that way, she thought. *Geoff is really randy these days and probably thinks he might get what he wants with some other girl.*

Of late he had really been pestering her to give him more and had been quite abrupt when she had refused. The fact that he was apparently trying to pick up with Valerie tended to reinforce this theory.

Colleen knew the reputations of all the girls in the unit and had mixed feelings about it. Part of her despised the girls who were 'easy' but try as she might she found she could not dislike some of them. Chloe, for example, she had trouble not liking even though she strongly disapproved of her attitudes and behaviour. Kathy and Valerie were another matter. Both annoyed her with their constant deceit and bitchy personalities.

As she sat pretending to listen to the stories about other camps and bivouacs Colleen found she was continually wondering about whether Geoff and Valerie were actually together. Horrible, jealous thoughts of them kissing and worse began to torment her. Along with that her public shame grew as she detected several curious or sympathetic glances.

The idea of going off on her own grew on her. *I'd better go soon,* she thought miserably, *or I will burst into tears.*

The arrival of a noisy group shepherded by Lt Peters and Lt Cavendish provided the opportunity to stand up unnoticed. Amid the confusion Colleen stretched and tried to appear calm and natural, even though her insides were still churning.

As she strolled off into the shadows away from the fire Colleen found she was unable to drive out the horrible thoughts about what Geoff and Valerie might be doing. That gave her a problem. Part of her really wanted to know what was going on, but she also dreaded any sort of scene and public embarrassment. She had no desire to be publicly humiliated by being obviously dumped.

That presented her with a quandary: which way to go?

Initially she had walked back around the central mound towards where HQ was bivouacked but as she reached the first of the 'hutchies' she heard Cadets Williamson and Sauter arguing and bickering. Having no desire to talk to them, much less have them witness her misery, she turned and walked away from them.

That took her over towards the OC's lantern. Just beyond was the heap of gravel. *That will do. I will sit on that,* she thought.

Colleen walked past the lantern and was just about to make her way up onto the pile of loose gravel when the sound of a girl giggling made her stop. The noises came from around the other side of the gravel heap.

Uh oh! Someone there. I'd better go somewhere else, she thought.

She was about turn away when she heard CUO Milikin snarl, "Go on, do it!"

A girl replied but she only muttered the reply so Colleen did not hear what she said. Nor was she able to identify the person.

That doesn't sound right, she thought.

But she hesitated to intervene as she now heard another boy speaking, snickering and making crude suggestions.

But Colleen knew she should do something if a girl was in trouble, so she braced herself for unpleasantness and resumed walking. As she did, she heard Sgt Shane Brady's voice.

"Don't!" he said. "That'll do you blokes."

"Shut up Brady and piss off!" CUO Milikin replied.

By then Colleen had reached the end of the gravel heap and could see around the other side. A tree grew there against the gravel pit fence and its branches grew across to form a sort of natural bower. In the shadows under it she saw a group of people, four she counted.

Sgt Brady was closest and at the sound of her boots crunching on the loose gravel he spun round to face her.

"Who's that? Oh you. What do you want?" he snapped in a voice that was almost a snarl.

"Just... just seeing if... if Kathy is OK," Colleen replied, recognizing the girl as Corporal Kathy Horn. She did not like Kathy at all, disliking intensely the rumours about her character and behaviour.

"I'm fine!" Kathy snapped at her.

Colleen hesitated and then nodded, recognising the other boy as Lance Corporal Jack Lang. There was an awkward silence for a moment and then CUO Milikin said, "We don't want you here McNamara, so clear out!"

Colleen was annoyed and concerned. *This isn't right,* she thought. But what to do?

She decided to tell one of the officers, so she turned and began walking quickly away. As luck would have it the first people she met as she walked back past the lantern were three female sergeants: Heidi Hope, Jane Carson and Sharon Newell. They were strolling towards her from the direction of the fire.

"Hi Colleen! What are you doing?" Sharon asked.

Colleen gestured behind her. "Behind that gravel heap," she said. "There are three boys there with Kathy Horn and I think they are getting up to mischief."

"We'll have a look," Jane replied. She and the other two sergeants began hurrying towards the gravel heap.

As they did Sgt Brady stepped into view from behind the gravel heap and looked in their direction. Immediately he turned and said something to the people behind the heap. Then he walked quickly away towards the road.

The three female sergeants made their way behind the gravel heap and Colleen heard Heidi say, "What are you lot doing?"

She did not hear the replies but there was a babble of talk and Colleen decided that the situation, whatever it was, had been defused. Then she remembered her original reason for leaving the fire and her misery returned. Not wanting anyone to see her cry, she turned away from the fire and walked off into the darkness past another small mound of earth towards the road.

As she passed the small mound the sound of Geoff's voice froze her in her tracks. It came from behind some bushes. Then a girl giggled. A wave of nausea and chill swept over her.

Geoff! And he must be there with Valerie!

Chapter 4

FIRST NIGHT

This was confirmed a second later when Colleen heard Valerie giggle even louder and say, "Stop it Geoff! Not here. Let's go somewhere else. We don't want to get caught."

Colleen felt frozen with despair and shock. Not wishing to be thought a peeping tom she took a step backwards. But she was too late. Around the end of the small mound came Geoff and Valerie, arm in arm.

The guilty pair stopped in surprise as they recognized Colleen. There was moment of embarrassed silence then Geoff destroyed what was left of Colleen's respect for him by trying to lie.

"Oh! Uh hello. We were just looking for you," he said. As he spoke, he and Valerie took their arms from around each other's waists.

"You were not!" Colleen replied, stung by the pathetic nature of the excuse. "I can see what you are doing."

"It... it's not like that," Geoff continued, lowering Colleen's opinion even more. If he was that weak!

She ignored him and faced Valerie in the starlight. "You are welcome to him. If that's the sort of person he is, I don't want him. Good luck!"

Before Valerie could respond Colleen spun on her heel and began to walk away. As she did she almost collided with two people hurrying towards her, their shapes silhouetted by the distant fire. It was Robbo and Barbara. Barbara shone a torch on her and then on Geoff and Valerie.

"Who's that? What's going on here?" Barbara asked.

Colleen could not answer. Her throat choked up with misery and tears blinded her. She heard Geoff mutter, "Nothing," but she did not stay. As she walked off she found Barbara walking beside her.

"You OK Colleen?" Barbara asked.

"Yes... I... I... (sob)... (sob)." Colleen tried to reply.

She found herself turning and being held by Barbara who put her arms around her. Colleen's initial reaction had been to run away but she found Barbara's embrace comforting, so she allowed herself to be held and patted.

"It's alright," Barbara said. "Has Geoff done something?"

"He... he... he's just (sniffle, sob)... just (sob) lied to me so I dumped him," Colleen managed to say.

"Dumped him! What happened?"

"He was there with Valerie Metcalf, but he...(sob) tried to deny (sob) it." Colleen cried. As she tried to speak again, she broke into sobs of misery.

"There, there! Calm down. You are better off without him if he is going to behave like that," Barbara said.

Robbo joined them and Colleen was dimly aware that Geoff and Valerie had walked past in the darkness. Even as they did, Colleen felt a last desperate urge to run over to him, to plead and beg, but two comments doused that desire.

The first was a muttered, "Frigid bitch!" by Geoff. At that she went cold with shock. Valerie's hissed, "Lessos," reversed the process, causing her to seethe with anger at the unkind and unjust accusation.

Geoff has been telling her about me not giving him any sex, she thought bitterly.

For a minute she was too miserable to speak but even in her misery she sensed that the relationship really was over, despite an emotional and irrational wish for it not to be.

This really hurts! she told herself.

Colleen allowed Barbara to hug her for a few more minutes until the tears stopped. As the emotional storm subsided, she became conscious of Barbara's physical proximity and Valerie's jibe about lesbians made her hot and embarrassed.

Gently she eased herself apart. "I'm all right now," she said.

"Is there anything you would like?" Barbara asked.

"A million dollars and a man who doesn't cheat," Colleen replied.

That at least made them laugh and the girls commiserated with each other on males and their many faults. Robbo suggested Colleen wash her face and she agreed. Next to the lantern was a plastic jerry can full of water and she used water from that.

Feeling somewhat refreshed Colleen made an effort to calm herself. *I suppose I could see that coming,* she told herself. Now a host of little clues she had ignored or thought nothing of all fitted together. *No,* she decided, *it's not a stunning surprise.*

But it still hurt.

Feeling very down she considered what to do next.

Barbara suggested going to bed, but Colleen shook her head. "No. I'll go back to the campfire," she replied.

A deep, stubborn streak of pride made her want to try to show Geoff and Valerie that she wasn't hurt at all.

The three girls walked back to the campfire. To Colleen's relief nobody seemed to look at her, so she seated herself and sat quietly. Barbara sat next to her while Robbo went off to supervise.

*****

Barbara made no attempt to talk to Colleen, or to cheer her up. She just sat and stared into the flames.

Poor girl. It always hurts when you end a relationship, she thought.

Barbara considered Colleen to be a very beautiful girl and now, watching the play of the firelight on her face, this impression was reinforced.

After several minutes she said: "Cheer up Colleen, plenty more fish in the sea."

Colleen made a face. "Yes, but mostly toadfish," she said.

Barbara had to laugh at that and made an effort to talk to Colleen. "It reminds me of what my mother said once, that a girl has to kiss a lot of toads before she finds a prince."

That at least made Colleen smile. "Bloody men!" she replied. "They are more trouble than they are worth."

"All they want is sex," Robbo muttered.

"That's probably all they are good for," Barbara agreed.

"Most of them aren't even much good at that, or so I've heard," Colleen replied.

"Cheer up. Prince Charming will come along soon," Barbara said.

At that CUO Callan looked across the fire. "Prince Charming? Did someone call my name?"

That led to good-natured jeers and more jokes. Barbara joined in and allowed Colleen to sit in silence. It was becoming obvious that the story of the bust-up was spreading as she noticed people casting curious glances at Colleen and a lot of whispering and significant looks.

Poor kid! she thought. The public shame would add to the hurt.

The evening went slowly on. From the darkness came constant laughter and talking. Both Chloe and Jane returned to the fire and sat on the other side of the circle. Lt Forster returned and Major Wickham took a turn at walking around supervising. Later Capt Hamilton went for a walk to ensure that there was no mischief. At Barbara's request he particularly checked on Geoff and Valerie.

21:50 came around and CSM Warren went off to get the sergeants to order their cadets to bed. Both Chloe and Jane immediately stood up and ordered their cadets to go. The cadets at the fire were shooed away, leaving only the CUOs and OOCs. As Colleen stood up Barbara laid her hand on her shoulder.

"Cheer up. You'll feel better in the morning," she said.

Colleen gave her a sickly smile which didn't reach her eyes and went off into the darkness. Barbara sighed and shook her head sadly. CUO Callan came and sat beside her.

"Is it true?" he asked.

"What?"

"That Geoff has given Colleen the flick?"

Barbara nodded. "No. She gave him the flick because he was sneaking off with Valerie. She is better off without him."

"Maybe I am the man for her," CUO Callan speculated.

Barbara laughed. "You'd better not let Maree hear that or your days will be numbered."

"No, I suppose not," CUO Callan agreed.

CUO Milikin and CUO Bailey joined them. Later CSM Warren returned to report all cadets in bed.

"As long as they are in the right beds," Capt Hamilton commented.

It had not been unknown for a boy and a girl to get together on a bivouac. Making sure this did not happen was one of the main duties of the CSM and sergeants.

The OOCs and CUOs gossiped for a while before Major Wickham also urged them to bed.

"We have a big day tomorrow and we don't want to be tired out."

"Why sir? What are we doing that is different?" CUO Callan asked.

Major Wickham shrugged. "Oh a bit. You'll see. Now go to bed."

With that enigmatic answer to puzzle over Barbara walked back to her hutchie. She had hung her mosquito net and was glad of it as away from the fire there were mosquitoes. After placing her pack and webbing at her head and unrolling her ground sheet and sleeping bag, she took off her boots and lay down. She was pleasantly tired and drifted into a very contented sleep.

*****

For Colleen is was a long and miserable night, made worse by the fact that Valerie was also in HQ and was sleeping only metres away in the next hutchie. For hours Colleen lay awake, staring out at the stars and thinking. From time to time she slid into a fitful slumber. She was woken from this by someone trampling the dead leaves near her hutchie.

Curious to know who was walking around in the middle of the night she struggled into a sitting position and pulled her mosquito net out of the way, only to have a strong torch beam directed into her eyes, blinding her.

Lt Cavendish's voice came to here. "Who's that? Oh, it's you Cpl McNamara."

"Yes, miss... I mean ma'am. What's the matter?" Colleen queried.

"Nothing. Lie down and go back to sleep," Lt Cavendish replied. The torch beam swung away and Colleen muttered with annoyance and pulled her head back under her mosquito net. She lay back and squirmed into a more comfortable position. As she did she was aware that the torch beam was being shone into the next hutchie.

She is checking on Chloe and Jane, she thought. *Good! They need to be watched. They should both be discharged for being a bad influence.*

Colleen then heard Lt Cavendish grunt with annoyance and then heard her boots crunching on the carpet of dead leaves and dry grass as she walked away.

She was hoping to catch them up to some mischief but hasn't, Colleen surmised.

After the officer had gone Colleen lay back and thought hard about life and human relationships. One of her greatest fears was never meeting her true 'soul mate', the perfect partner who would love and cherish her. She understood that it was going to be difficult because people lived behind a mask, hiding their true selves much of the time.

It is easy to be taken in by appearances, she mused. *Geoff has taught me that.*

Sleep would not come so she lay and fretted. For much of the time she dredged up every one of her perceived faults to try to work out why Geoff had rejected her in favour of Valerie. That made her even more miserable and she tried to tell herself she was being silly, but alone in the night she found it hard to consider things objectively.

I wish I could go home tomorrow morning, she thought.

That led her to consider leaving cadets. She had only joined to be with a friend who wasn't game to join on her own (and who had since left). Much to her own surprise she had found she enjoyed most of it. In particular she enjoyed the feeling of achievement and knew the cadet experiences had done a lot for her self-confidence.

But why Valerie? *Was it the no sex?* she wondered. *If it is, then too bad,* she decided. *I'm not giving in to any Tom, Dick or Harry, just because I feel a bit lonely!*

Very lonely, she added. Geoff had been the first boy she had really dated and at first it had been absolutely wonderful. Now she analysed the relationship, charting its slow decline. Looking back she now saw that the breakdown had probably been inevitable.

But it still hurt, and more tears came. Colleen was careful to stop herself sobbing aloud, experiencing fierce determination not to give Valerie the satisfaction of knowing she was hurting.

As the hot tears trickled down her cheeks she shook her head. *I think I will give boys up for the present and concentrate on my schoolwork.*

In a determined effort to change her mood she shifted her thoughts to her studies and to thinking about her chosen career of being a nurse. She knew her school marks were good enough to make it into university to do the nursing course but decided to make sure by working even harder.

Still thinking about this she slipped into a deep sleep.

*****

Barbara managed to drift off to sleep quite quickly, snug in her sleeping bag. But after an hour or so she found herself awake.

What woke me? she wondered, straining her eyes and ears to listen.

At the top of her mind was fear of snakes but she could not hear any slithering sounds in the surrounding grass. All she could hear was the sighing of a gentle breeze in the trees.

Then she became aware of an odd murmuring, rumbling noise. *What's that?* she wondered.

Puzzled she lay and focused her hearing. The noise grew slowly louder and seemed to make the air vibrate. Then the meaning came to her and she smiled.

A train! she told herself.

It was. The sounds grew louder until they dominated as a cane train, pulled by a labouring diesel engine came slowly from the south. Barbara realized that the sound that had woken her had probably been the distant roar of the train crossing the Landers Creek Bridge. By looking out she was just able to glimpse the locomotive's lights as they came out from behind the gravel heap and before they vanished behind the low rise near the front gate. The night was filled with the squeaking, grinding and rumbling of hundreds of steel wheels as the train rolled past 400 metres away. The smell of burnt sugar and soot came wafting on the breeze and Barbara took several deep breaths to savour it. It was a smell she really liked.

But not as nice as the smell of the sugar mill at work and all that treacle, molasses and brown sugar, she thought, remembering with fondness several visits to sugar mills near Cairns with her family or school.

The train was long and noisy and took several minutes to rumble past, the tail being marked by a flashing yellow light on a yellow brake car. As the sound of the train died away as it went around the big hill Barbara lay back and tried to go back to sleep. But, to her annoyance, she became aware that she really needed to do a pee. Out of laziness and in her state or warm comfort she resisted this for half an hour but finally decided to get up. But where to go? There was no latrine dug yet and she did not feel like walking the hundred metres or more in an area of dark bush she was not familiar with to the area designated for the female latrine.

Behind that gravel heap just there, she decided.

The gravel heap was only 25 paces away and there were bushes and long grass on the other side. So, after sitting up and pulling on her boots (She was sleeping in her uniform as most people in the unit did), she got up and quietly walked around to the other side of the gravel heap. But she found her way blocked by a broken-down barbed wire fence, beyond which the ground dropped steeply into the gravel pit. In the bottom of the pit she could just see the glint of the stars on water, reminding her that the place was dangerous.

In behind the gravel heap was a large, overhanging bush which she did not feel like pushing in to so she just moved onto the relatively flat base of the gravel. Satisfied nobody could see her but a bit ashamed of the poor field hygiene she dug a hole with her boot and then did her pee. As she did, she was conscious of only the murmur of the breeze.

But as she stood up and pulled her trousers up Barbara heard the mutter of voices from over where HQ was bivouacked.

Who is that talking at this time of night? she wondered.

The names Chloe and Jane immediately sprang to mind. Curious to know Barbara began walking quietly back around the gravel heap. As she did, she saw a person walking towards the OOCs area. The person was holding a torch with the beam directed downwards into the grass but the person obviously heard Barbara as the beam was suddenly swung up and directed on her. So bright was the light Barbara was blinded and had to stop and shield her eyes.

Lt Cavendish's voice came to her. "Who's that? Oh, it's you Barbara. What are you doing?"

The beam swung down and Barbara was able to lower her hand. Still blinking from the blinding effect of the torch she stayed where she was as the OOC walked towards her.

"Just going to the toilet ma'am," she admitted.

Lt Cavendish grunted and then shone the torch beam back towards the HQ area, lighting up their hutchies. "I was just checking on Chloe and Jane," she explained.

"Are they there?" Barbara asked anxiously. She had it on the tip of her tongue to ask if Chloe was dressed but decided not to.

But Lt Cavendish answered it for her anyway. "Yes, both sound asleep and both fully dressed," she said in a tone that sounded aggrieved.

She was hoping to catch them out, Barbara thought.

That notion bothered her. She presumed that Lt Cavendish was merely awake because she was the OOC acting as 'Duty Officer' and, as such, she was perfectly within her rights to patrol the area.

Although normally they sit at the lantern, or the campfire if we have one, she told herself.

In fact Lt Cavendish did head towards the campfire after saying good night. As the fire was out of sight behind the large mound and had died down to just embers even before Barbara had gone to bed no sign of it was visible to her. Barbara walked towards her hutchie, slightly troubled that such an obvious vendetta was being waged against Chloe.

Barbara crawled back into her bedding and lay down, her thoughts directed to Chloe and Jane and the lady OOC's. For at least half an hour she lay there, wondering how to help the two girls to succeed in life, before she slipped into a restless sleep.

Several times Barbara stirred during the remainder of the night. At about 0400 she noted that the breeze had died and that a sharp chill had set in. With a few grunts of discomfort she wriggled into a more comfortable position and drifted back to sleep.

The sound of voices roused her at 0600. She looked out of her sleeping bag and saw that the sky was a pale grey. Off to the west the mountain she had noted the night before stood out sharply. Now she saw that it was several kilometres away and had bare ridges rising to a steep pointed summit. This was covered in groups of large pines trees. These looked tiny at that distance, but Barbara suspected they were probably actually very tall.

The first rays of the sun were already lighting up the top of the distant mountain, bathing it with a pinkish glow which changed to honey-red set against a clear blue sky. It looked very pretty.

The cadets were moving past in platoon groups on their way to check parade, so Barbara sat up, pulled on her jacket and then her socks and boots. The other ACS and the CUOs wandered over to talk to Major Wickham while the CSM conducted the morning check parade out on the dirt road on the other side of the large central mound.

Barbara could just see 4 Platoon from where she sat and smiled at the memory of running many similar parades herself. She had enjoyed being the CSM.

Being nearly a hundred kilometres inland the air was almost completely dry and Barbara found her lips were cracking. She put some lip salve on and then had a big drink. After that she strolled over to say hello to Major Wickham and the other ACS and CUOs.

Capt Hamilton was still in bed so Robbo picked up a water bottle and trickled cold water in his ear. That brought him spluttering and muttering to a sitting position. Robbo hastily retreated and hid behind Barbara, who giggled so much Capt Hamilton at first thought it had been her.

Major Wickham laughed then said: "We are going to have a company Orders Group in ten minutes so go to the toilet and get your platoons organized for morning routine. Parade is at 0800. After that I will give an exercise safety brief and ground orientation. You will then give your platoon Orders Groups. Off you go."

Barbara did as she was bid, walking with a sleepy and shivering Lt Cavendish across to the creek line on the far side of the gravel pit to the area which had been designated as the female latrines. None had yet been dug but Barbara knew the CSM would even now be organizing work parties. In the meantime she scraped a hole with her boot and squatted over it.

On her return to HQ she saw that the platoons had returned to their areas and were starting to cook and pack. Barbara was quite hungry but was also curious to know about the exercise they would be taking part in. She rolled up her bedding and strapped it into her pack, then carried it over to where the O Group was to be held. By then the other CUOs and OOCs were starting to assemble.

As she went to sit down on her pack Barbara noted two girls talking to Lt Cavendish over near the gravel heap. Both looked upset but one was in tears.

That is young Rosie. I wonder what is wrong? Oh I hope there hasn't been a problem during the night.

By the grim expression on Major Wickham's face something had obviously happened. He went over and spoke to Lt Cavendish and the two girls, then came back and seated himself in front of the O Group. After shaking his head and clearing his throat he began.

Chapter 5

TROUBLE

It was a full company Orders Group with the four platoon commanders in the front row, then the CSM, HQ Sgt, CQMS, Signals and Medical Sgts and Intelligence Cpl in the back row. The OOCs and Barbara sat at the back or to one side. As the cadets moved to their places and sat down Barbara noted that both Chloe, the HQ Sgt, and Jane, the Sig Sgt, looked fresh and relaxed. *That's good,* she thought, pleased neither had caused any incident during the night.

Major Wickham went through the orders in the exact military sequence. Under 'Ground' he pointed out the Burdekin River, Deep Creek (the dry creek next to them), Snake Gully (a wriggly little creek over near the river), the main road and light railway, Landers Creek and 'Landers Creek' cattle station, a powerline (Refer to Map 2).

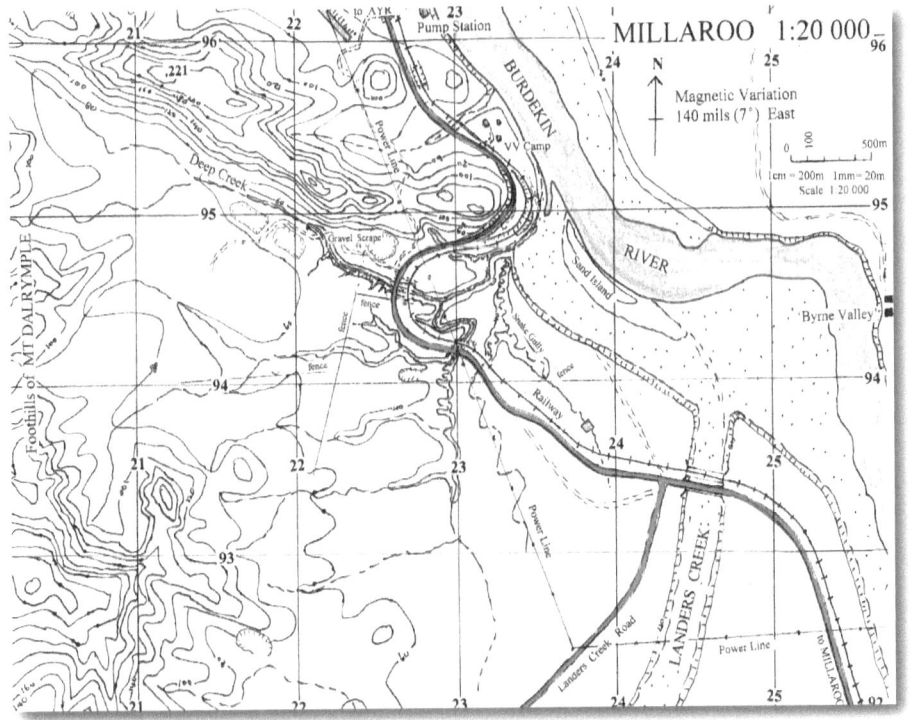

As Major Wickham pointed to the powerline, which came over a saddle on the hill to the north of them, Barbara had to twist around to look at it. As she did so she saw a head poke up over the heap of gravel near them, then duck down again quickly.

That looked like Lance Corporal Lang. He is acting very suspiciously. I wonder what is going on behind that gravel heap? I hope it isn't trouble, Barbara thought.

Bothered by a little niggling concern she shifted her attention back to the orders. Major Wickham pointed to the line of hills to their north. These extended eastwards down from the mountain, whose name Barbara now learned was Mt Dalrymple.

He then indicated on the map the Pump Station on the riverbank north of the hills, and said: "That is the start point for the Opposing Forces in this exercise."

That interested Barbara as all of the unit's platoon commanders were present at the orders. Usually 4 Platoon and HQ provided the 'enemy' (This is what they called them even though the correct term they were supposed to use was 'Opposing Force') for the junior platoons and received separate orders.

I wonder who the enemy are? she thought.

The others wondered that too and CUO Milikin asked: "Who is the enemy sir? Is it 15ACU?"

"Questions at the end CUO Milikin, and cadets are not to use that word," Major Wickham said in mild reproof.

"Probably Mackay or someone," CUO Callan suggested.

"Silence! OK. 'Opposing Force'," Major Wickham went on.

He read slowly from his notebook while the CUOs made notes. Major Wickham described how the opposing force would be operating in groups of five and would be attempting to reach a number of objectives, on which they would attempt to place 'explosives' (plastic cartons with the word 'bomb' on a piece of paper in them). He described the opposing force in the usual terms of being well-trained, fit and aggressive.

"They will be easy to recognize because of their uniforms," he added.

This was normal. The enemy usually wore cloth badges of a particular colour on their webbing or hat. Major Wickham talked about possible enemy tactics. He then covered 'Friendly Forces' and 'Civilians'. After that he went over 'Meteorology' with a gesture at the clear blue sky.

"Fine weather."

Next, he gave their mission, which was to prevent the raiders from reaching their targets. Details of the 'Execution' followed. Barbara learned that each platoon had two 'targets' to guard and that they were also to have one patrol each on the move at all times. Even 4 Platoon had targets to guard. HQ was to deploy an OP with a radio to the big grassy hill which overlooked the area, and another on the low, flat ridge inside the curve of the railway.

When all the details of timings, routes, boundaries, action on contact and so on were covered Major Wickham dealt with 'prisoners'. "Prisoners are to be brought in here under guard by two cadets, or by a section. They are not to be physically manhandled or searched. Four Platoon, you get Lt Barker to drive them here. Intelligence is to then question them here at the CP which HQ is to set up."

That intrigued Barbara even more. *The enemy must be cadets from Mackay, or maybe the local Air Cadets,* she decided.

On her very first cadet exercise the Cairns cadets had travelled all the way down to near Bowen to take part in an exercise against cadets from Mackay and Sarina.

Major Wickham began covering the details of 'Administration and Logistics'. As he did, Barbara saw LCpl Lang walk out from behind the gravel heap over to 4 Platoon, a hundred paces off, and speak to Cadet Sgt Stephen Backer. Backer, a thin, rat-faced boy, got up and followed Lang back to the gravel heap. As the pair went behind it they both cast what Barbara thought looked like guilty glances towards the O Group.

Her suspicion that the boys were up to mischief was reinforced a few minutes later when Backer's head peeked up over the gravel heap. By then Major Wickham was covering 'Command and Signals'.

I will check what is going on as soon as we finish, Barbara decided.

This decision was reinforced when she noted Sgt Shane Brady walk past and also vanish behind the gravel heap. *Definitely up to something,* she thought.

In between copying down the Signals Operating Instructions Barbara again glanced at Cadet Rosie's now tear-streaked face and felt her stomach churn.

She's really upset. Oh well! I suppose we will find out as soon as we finish here, she decided.

Major Wickham obviously thought so too as he looked at Lt Cavendish and nodded and she got up and went to talk to the girls while the OC finished with questions. Barbara then stood up, intending to check behind the gravel heap.

However, Lt Cavendish beckoned to Barbara to come and join her where she stood to one side with Cadet Rosie and her friend.

I'll have a look in a moment, she thought. Then she noted CUO Milikin heading for the gravel heap. *No. He can sort it out. They are mostly from his platoon,* she decided.

"What is it ma'am?" Barbara asked as she reached Lt Cavendish.

Lt Cavendish gestured to Cadet Rosie. "CUO Milikin has been harassing Cadet Rosie, asking her for sex and making crude comments, and now he has given her this."

She held out her hand and on it Barbara saw a condom, still in its packet. She curled her lip in distaste. *Typical,* she thought. *No bloody style at all. What a low-class jerk!*

But she knew the accusation was serious. The AAC Code of Conduct banned any sexual relations at cadets and was particularly strong on forbidding fraternization across the rank levels as an 'abuse of power' situation. She was about to speak when two female sergeants: Jane Carson and Sharon Newell, came hurrying towards them from the direction of the gravel heap.

"Miss! Miss! Quick! Behind the gravel heap," Sharon cried.

"Why? What?" Lt Cavendish asked.

Jane answered: "There are four boys there bothering Kathy Horn."

At that Barbara's stomach turned over with annoyance. *Just what we don't need: more trouble; and real trouble from the sound of it.*

Lt Cavendish frowned. "What are they doing?"

Jane answered wryly. "Arguing, but Kathy doesn't look happy."

As she said this Sgt Brady stepped into view from behind the gravel heap and looked in their direction. Seeing them all looking his way caused a look of alarm to cross his face and he turned and said something to the boys behind the heap.

Lt Cavendish at once hurried over to where Major Wickham was packing his notes in his briefcase. Barbara did not hear what she said but she did see his face. He scowled and set his jaw, then stood up and strode towards the gravel heap.

As he did the four boys and Kathy Horn appeared from behind the heap, walking towards their bivouac area.

"Hold it a moment you lot," Major Wickham called. "What has been going on?"

The cadets stopped and there was an uncomfortable silence and most of the group looked anxious. Major Wickham faced them, his hands on his hips and his face a mask of annoyance.

"Well? What were you people doing behind the gravel heap? Why aren't you with your platoons getting ready for inspection?" he demanded.

CUO Milikin shrugged. "We were only talking sir," he replied.

"About what?" Major Wickham queried.

"Oh... er... er... just about last night," CUO Milikin answered.

"What about last night? What happened?" Major Wickham asked.

"Oh... nothing sir," CUO Milkin replied.

"Nothing eh?" Major Wickham snapped. "So what happened? What's going on? Tell me!"

Major Wickham received no answer to his question, so he said: "Sit there all of you. CUO Milikin, come here. There is another matter I need to discuss with you. Capt Hamilton, you and Lt Forster question this lot to find out what the story is. Question them one at a time. Lt Peters, you and CUO Brassington, watch the others please, and separate them so they can't concoct stories."

Major Wickham and Lt Cavendish led CUO Milikin to one side. It was immediately apparent they were discussing Cadet Rosie as Major Wickham pointed in her direction several times. Barbara realized that the two female sergeants and Cadet Rosie and her friend were all still standing beside her.

"Don't you girls talk about this at all," she ordered. "Wait till the officers have investigated. We don't want a wave of rumours. You two sergeants had better tell Capt Hamilton what you know, then get ready for the exercise. Cadet Rosie, you and your friend stay here."

As she did, Barbara noted the guilty and ashamed looks on the faces of the group from behind the gravel heap and knew it was all going to be very messy.

A CUO, two sergeants, a corporal, and a lance corporal, she noted.

CSM Warren arrived from supervising the digging of new latrines and Barbara called him over.

"What's going on?" he asked.

As discipline was the CSM's job Barbara gave him an outline. "You'd better join Capt Hamilton to find out what has been going on," she advised. She told Cadet Rosie and her friend to wait and walked over with him. He and Lt Forster had begun to question Sgt Backer on his own and the other two boys sat ten paces apart on the gravel heap with Lt Peters supervising them.

As they arrived Capt Hamilton glanced at them. Barbara raised her eyebrows. "What's happened sir?" she asked.

"They say they were only talking and won't say what it was about," Capt Hamilton replied.

Lt Forster nodded. "I heard CUO Milkin say to Cpl Horn, 'and don't you say anything, or else!' and then he saw us and clammed up. I think they are trying to cover something up."

"Something from last night perhaps?" Barbara suggested.

Lt Forster nodded. "Sgt Carson and Sgt Newell said that they were told last night by Cpl McNamara that there was a group up to mischief here behind the gravel heap, but she did not know what."

"Should I ask Colleen, I mean Cpl McNamara?" Barbara suggested.

Capt Hamilton nodded. "Good idea. We aren't getting anything out of this lot except that they were 'only talking!'"

So Barbara walked to the HQ area where Colleen and Sharon were setting up the Company Aid Post (CAP). But Colleen could add very little beyond stating that she thought Kathy Horn was being bullied or threatened in some way and that the boys were trying to coerce or persuade her to do something she did not want to do. Colleen was looking very tired and unhappy, so Barbara did not press the issue. She returned to Capt Hamilton and the others.

By then Major Wickham had spoken to CUO Milikin for nearly ten minutes and now sent him to sit on his own. He was given a clipboard and began writing. By then he looked very miserable. Sgt Brady was now questioned. Major Wickham came over to join Capt Hamilton and CSM Warren. The OC told Sgt Warren to stay.

"It is the CSM's business to know what the sergeants had been up to." he commented.

While this was going Chloe came walking towards them, but Barbara caught her eye and shook her head. Chloe nodded and went back to continue organizing HQ for their routine morning inspection. Jane, as signals sergeant, was busy nearby getting a CP set up and radios ready to issue.

It was apparent to Barbara that a wave of rumour was sweeping the unit. She realized it would have been impossible to stop this anyway, with so many cadets sitting under supervision obviously being questioned. 1 Platoon, in particular, could not help noticing as their CUO, sergeant and one corporal were there.

This is awful, Barbara thought. *It could really harm the unit.*

Lt Peters and Lt Cavendish had both come to stand near Barbara and both looked sour. Lt Peters gestured with her head towards HQ and muttered, "It was that pair I expected to give us trouble last night," she said.

"Chloe and Jane?" Barbara queried, glancing towards HQ. She saw that Jane was now assembling an army radio and Chloe was inspecting Cadets Williamson and Sauter, the only two cadets in HQ. That she was not happy with the standard of their bivouac was very obvious.

"Yes," Lt Peters replied. "I wanted a chance to catch them up to mischief. I gather they were both dressed last night?"

Lt Cavendish answered that. "Yes. Both slept in their uniforms," she answered.

Barbara felt compelled to come to their defence. "Maybe they have learned their lessons," she suggested.

"Leopards don't change their spots!" Lt Peters snapped. "I will get that Chloe yet."

"And Jane Carson," Lt Cavendish answered.

"Oh ma'am, fair go!" Barbara said. "Jane's alright. She hasn't given any trouble for a couple of years."

Lt Cavendish shrugged and grunted. "Maybe so, but as they say: Birds of a feather flock together."

"That's right!" Lt Peters agreed. "As the Bible says: By their friends ye shall know them!"

Barbara was a bit taken aback by the note of venom in Lt Peter's voice and did not know what to say. The notion that what Lt Peter's was doing was not very Christian flitted across her mind but other than deciding to counsel and warn both the girls she could not think of anything to add. She felt relieved when the two OOCs moved away. Their puritanical opinions caused her to wonder if she really wanted to become an OOC in the unit.

There will probably be a clash of attitudes, she worried.

A yellow 4WD came driving in and parked. Barbara recognized it as Lt Ashley Barker's. She really liked Ashley and was glad to see him. In his vehicle were four cadets who had been unable to travel the previous night. As he walked over to join them Lt Barker looked around and raised his eyebrows quizzically. He told the cadets to find their platoons and went over to Major Wickham, who soon told him what had happened.

LCpl Lang was the next one questioned and Barbara saw him hang his head and look ashamed, confirming that something had happened. Barbara glanced at her watch and saw it was now ten to eight.

Parade in ten minutes and One Platoon is not ready, she thought.

CSM Warren also kept looking at his watch but stayed with the OC. Cpl Ridgeway from 1 Platoon came over to Barbara.

"What should we do about parade ma'am?" he asked.

"I will ask the OC. You stay here," she replied. As the OOCs appeared to be busy she again went to the three female sergeants in HQ. "Go around the platoons and get them ready for parade but keep your mouths shut," she instructed.

Chloe, Jane and Sharon all looked serious and nodded. Chloe pointed, "Jane, you go to Three Platoon and Four. I will go to One. Sharon, you go to Two."

The girls split and Barbara then went back over to where Major Wickham and Lt Cavendish had just finished questioning Cpl Horn.

"Excuse me sir, what will we do about parade?" Barbara asked.

Major Wickham looked at his watch and then swore under his breath. As he rarely did anything like this it gave Barbara a clue to how upset he was by the incident. "Go and take parade CSM. I will be there in a few minutes."

"Who will be platoon sergeants for One Platoon and Four Platoon sir?" CSM Warren asked.

Major Wickham glanced at Sgt Brady, who sat nearby writing a statement, then said: "Get Sgt Carson to take One Platoon and Sgt Cummings to take Four. Sgt Newell can take HQ. Stress this is only for this parade. I haven't finished here yet."

Barbara then asked: "Are the CUOs going on parade sir?"

"Yes. Oh, I see," Major Wickham said. "Barbara, would you act as One Platoon commander for the moment please?"

"Yes sir," Barbara replied.

She went off with CSM Warren to get the parade organized. That meant she had to face a barrage of questions from the other CUOs. All she could do was shake her head and say she was not at liberty to say anything. When Jane and Chloe were told to act as platoon sergeants they just nodded and moved off at once.

The cadets were in a very disturbed state, continually glancing over towards where Sgt Backer was now being questioned. Jane Carson marched over to 1 Platoon and called them to form up in two ranks. She then marched them off around to the other side of the big mound to the open area on the road. This had been designated as the parade ground.

Barbara made her way down past the mound to stand facing a very curious 1 Platoon. They kept glancing at her, then turning to look back up through the trees to where the OOCs were talking. The cadets kept whispering to each other. Jane Carson had to call on them a dozen times to stop talking. 4 Platoon was in a similar state, but Chloe was obviously a stronger personality and they soon shut up.

CSM Warren 'right dressed' the company, then told the sergeants to 'call the roll'. While this was going on Barbara resisted the temptation to keep looking to see what was happening. Inside she felt both sick and sad. The incident had spoilt the whole morning and threatened much worse.

Parents could easily take children out of the unit if something serious has happened, she thought.

That made her angry. It wasn't fair that the selfish and disloyal actions of a few could harm so many others, but she knew it could.

Once the parade was ready CSM Warren stood the company at ease, then about turned and stood at ease himself, waiting for the OC. Several times he caught Barbara's eye but she only glanced over his shoulder at where the OOCs were standing in a huddle and then shook her head.

Five minutes dragged by. The cadets became restless and began to whisper. It was hot and Barbara found her mouth dry.

I'd better let the OC know the parade is ready, she thought.

She turned and marched back up to where the OOCs stood. "Excuse me sir. The parade is ready," she interrupted.

Major Wickham nodded. "Thanks Barbara. We won't keep the troops waiting. We will finish this after parade," he said.

As he and Barbara marched down towards the company she asked, "Do we know what happened yet sir?"

Major Wickham shook his head. "Not really. It looks like the four boys were trying to pressure Kathy Horn into some sort of sex, but they won't say and nor will she. Whether they did anything or not, I don't know. And it also looks like they have threatened her to keep her mouth shut. It is all very upsetting," he said.

By then they were near the cadets so stopped talking and made their way to the front of the waiting parade. Barbara halted in line with 1 Platoon, while the CSM called the company to attention and handed over to Major Wickham. He then called the officers to 'take post'.

Barbara came to attention and marched forward to meet Jane Carson. Being in the field they followed Australian Army custom and did not salute. Jane gave her a wry smile.

"They are all here ma'am, except the ones in trouble."

"Fall in then Sgt Carson," Barbara replied.

Jane stepped around her and marched to the rear of the platoon. As she glanced to her left to keep track of Jane's movements Barbara found herself looking into the intensely curious eyes of a dozen cadets and was glad when she was able to right turn to face the front. She had spent the whole of the previous year as a platoon commander in her own unit in Cairns, so all this was routine to her, but she felt very uncomfortable standing in front of someone else's platoon.

Major Wickham then spoke briefly. "You were to be given your ground orientation and safety brief, then your orders for the day's exercise but as you are no doubt aware there has been a serious disciplinary incident. I won't beat about the bush. It is very bad news for the unit. Therefore you will go back to your platoon areas and wait till we have finished. Headquarters, issue the compasses, radios and bandages to commanders. CSM, organize the work parties to complete the latrines."

"Sir!"

"Officers... Fall out! CSM!" Major Wickham called.

Barbara came to attention and marched forward off the parade. Major Wickham handed back to the CSM and then went back to where the OOCs and troublemakers waited. Barbara sat in the shade nearby with the other CUOs and discussed the orders for the exercise, just in case she had to command 1 Platoon during the day.

From a distance Barbara saw Major Wickham call over the troublemakers. She could not hear what he said but it was obvious from their faces and body language that they were very unhappy.

CUO Milikin then said something which caused Major Wickham to explode with rage. He bellowed: "Don't you 'but' me! You are seventeen and I don't have any choice but to phone Cadet Rosie's parents and pass the matter to the army. I can't demote a CUO. Only the army can do that, but if a full investigation finds against you I will recommend that you be discharged from cadets. I will now have to phone the Cadet HQ in Townsville and this story will be in Canberra within the hour. Now, I am suspending you from your duties and ordering you not to attend any cadet activity until this matter is decided. Go and get your gear and hand back any radios or compasses."

Milikin hung his head and Barbara saw his lip tremble. Then he looked up and Barbara heard him say, "Yes sir. But Sgt Brady is innocent sir. He was there trying to stop them, but the others wouldn't do what he said."

At that Barbara's opinion of Milikin, never high, went up a notch. She saw that the other troublemakers appeared to be supporting this statement.

Then CUO Milikin said something about Cpl Horn which made Major Wickham's temper flare again.

"Oh yes she did! I know that she, and all the girls in the unit, have been told on several occasions that they do not have to obey orders they believe are wrong. She was told that on her Recruit Course and on her Corporals Course as well. I know, because I was the instructor. So no more of that!"

"We threatened her sir," CUO Milikin said.

Major Wickham shook his head in dismay. "You could get a prison sentence for saying that. Cpl Horn, do you wish to make a formal complaint?"

Kathy blushed bright red and hung her head. "No sir."

To her annoyance Barbara missed the next bit but she exchanged glances with Robbo, who shook her head and looked upset.

"This is terrible," she whispered. "It could cause us awful trouble."

Barbara agreed, then strained her ears to hear what Major Wickham was saying. He looked at his watch, bit his lip and shook his head. Then he said: "I don't want to make decisions in haste, but nor do I want this to drag on. We have a bivouac to run and other cadets coming to... er... er... take part. There is a field exercise to get underway. But we will investigate the matter fully to ensure justice is both done and seen to be done, and that means by the Policy Manual. I will speak to Brigade HQ in Townsville and see what they say. Meanwhile you will all write a full statement giving your version of this incident. That means the full deal; your rank, name and unit details, date, time and place, and in English people can read. CSM, get clip boards and paper from the Intelligence Box."

"CUO Milikin, you will also write a statement concerning what you said to Cadet Rosie. Now you sit over there with Capt Hamilton and write out those full statements. Sgt Backer, you go with Lt Forster and sit over near the gravel pit there."

Backer hung his head and turned to do as he was told. As he did Major Wickham added: "I am extremely disappointed. It was your job as a sergeant to maintain discipline. You have let the unit down badly. I trusted you and it looks like you have betrayed that trust. I'd say your third stripe is gone. Now off you go and write your explanation."

Major Wickham then turned to Kathy, Brady and Lang. They were told to sit on their own and he asked Lt Peters and Lt Barker to supervise them. Obviously very unhappy, but also looking surly and defiant to Barbara, they moved to obey.

Major Wickham stood for a moment watching them, shaking his head and obviously deeply hurt. Then he shook his head again and took a deep breath.

Turning to Barbara, he said: "We have to go ahead with this exercise as cadets from... from another unit are providing the Opposing Force and are already on their way. But I cannot trust CUO Milikin and do not want to make any hasty decisions without getting all the facts. So we have to decide whether to disband One Platoon or keep it going, and that means a temporary platoon commander until CUO Milikin's fate is decided."

"Keep it going sir," Barbara replied at once. "If you scatter them among the other platoons, they will mostly have a hard time and leave and there are some good kids in that platoon."

Major Wickham nodded. "I think you are right. Are you willing to take on the job of platoon commander for the weekend?"

Barbara had already thought about this. It meant a lot of responsibility and effort, but she nodded. "Yes sir."

"Thanks. Now, get the OOCs to get issued with their radios and compasses please. And CSM, make sure all CUOs and section commanders have been issued."

It was a relief to move away to get routine admin things done. This occupied the next half hour. In 130ACU when in the field every section commander was always issued with a CB Radio, Silva prismatic compass, a packet of two compression bandages (in case of snake or spider bites) and one triangular bandage, and two broom handles. The broom handles were to make an improvised stretcher using webbing to carry an injured cadet across short areas of rough terrain to where a vehicle could pick them up. The platoon commanders and HQ NCOs also got radios and compasses and all the ACS.

By the time that was done the troublemakers had written their statements and handed them in and now sat on the gravel heap in a sullen row. Major Wickham looped his radio onto a buttonhole in his shirt and looked at them.

"Capt Hamilton, get all the OOCs please. CSM, get the troublemakers lined up," he said.

While this was being done Major Wickham turned to Lt Barker. "Sorry Ashley but I must ask you to drive CUO Milkin and possibly some of the others back to Townsville. I am going to send Lt Peters with you. I do not want an adult staff member on their own with cadets in this situation."

Lt Barker nodded. "That's fine sir. We'll be back as soon as I can."

When the troublemakers were lined up there were a few moments of anxious silence while Major Wickham glared at them.

"You have let the unit down. You have let down your platoons. Instead of supervising them after breakfast you take yourselves off and skulk behind a gravel heap while you threaten a girl to keep her mouth shut. Why? What has happened that she needs to stay silent? We don't know yet, but we will find out."

Major Wickham glared at each in turn. Then he told them he did not trust them to be in command of younger cadets and that if he learned they had really broken the Code of Conduct they would probably lose a stripe if they were not discharged. He also warned them that, in that case, parents would be informed and that the police might be investigating. At that Kathy Horn broke down in near hysterical sobbing.

Barbara was not impressed. *What did she do?* she wondered.

Major Wickham went on: "CUO Milikin, you are to be taken home at once and are suspended. Does anyone else want to go home?"

To Barbara's surprise both Sgt Backer and LCpl Lang put up their hands but not Kathy Horn or Sgt Brady.

Major Wickham, his face now a mask of severity, nodded and said, "Alright. We will complete this at the next Home Training parade. Cpl Horn, you move to HQ. Sgt Brady, you stay. You others are all relieved of your commands until this is sorted out. You people who want to go home go and get your gear and take it to Lt Barker's vehicle. Move!"

The troublemakers moved.

It was then Sgt Brady's turn. Barbara was particularly interested in his fate if she really was to take over 1 Platoon.

Unless he decides to disband it, she thought. The platoon was now down to one corporal and 13 cadets.

Barbara did not hear what Major Wickham said but she saw Sgt Brady struggle to keep his composure. He then came over to her and halted at attention in front of her.

"Ma'am, I am to remain as platoon sergeant of One Platoon. Major Wickham would like to see you now."

"Thank you, Sgt Brady. Get them ready for a platoon O Group," Barbara replied. She would actually have preferred to have Jane Carson as her sergeant but admitted that Jane was rumoured to be nearly as bad as Chloe in her behaviour.

She went over to the OOCs. Major Wickham was giving instructions to Lt Cavendish to supervise HQ during the exercise. When he had done that he turned to Barbara. "You OK with Sgt Brady as your platoon sergeant Barbara?" he asked.

"Yes sir," Barbara replied.

"Thanks. Oh well, now for the hard bits, phoning the Cadet Brigade Commander and parents."

Seeing his face Barbara's heart went out to him.

What a lot of trouble those cadets are causing! The officers are only volunteers and they give so much of their spare time to make cadets happen. How unfair!

With her emotions in turmoil she watched as Major Wickham took out his mobile phone and walked away towards the vehicles.

I hope this all doesn't escalate out of control, she thought.

Chapter 6

1 PLATOON

B arbara did not really want to be a platoon commander again but she knew it was important to the unit.

We need to lift things back up after this disaster, she thought. It was really annoying to her that a Cadet Under-Officer, one of the senior leaders of the unit, had been disciplined for doing the wrong thing. Simmering with resentment she called Sgt Brady over and asked to see his roll.

"Who have we got and how is the platoon organized?" she asked.

Sgt Brady showed her his Platoon Roll. "We have three sections ma'am; one of six, and two of five, but they will both be only four now. We had three corporals at the start of the year but if Kathy Horn and Lance Corporal Lang are going then we have only one, Nick Ridgeway. His is the section of six."

"So we need at least another section commander. Is there a lance corporal we can put in the job?" Barbara asked.

Sgt Brady shook his head. "No. Lang was our only lance corporal."

"Are any of the cadets good enough to be promoted to lance corporal?"

Sgt Brady frowned and shook his head. "Aw, not really. The cadets are all new First Year recruits." Then he hesitated and shrugged. "Aw, maybe Wright. He's been in all year and come to everything and he's pretty bright."

Barbara thought hard. One option was to split the platoon into three groups, commanded by herself, Sgt Brady and Cpl Ridgeway.

That might be OK for this exercise today, she thought. Then she shook her head. *No. Start as you mean to go on. It will be better for their teamwork and morale to keep the existing structure. We need two more NCOs.*

She turned to Sgt Brady. "Have them seated ready for orders. I will just have a quick word with Major Wickham."

She turned and walked back across to where Major Wickham was talking to Lt Peters and Lt Barker in front of Lt Barker's 4WD. At the rear of the vehicle a sulky looking trio of cadets: CUO Milikin, Sgt Backer and LCpl Lang, were loading their gear in.

As she approached Barbara noted that Lt Barker was showing Major Wickham a newspaper. She overheard Lt Barker say: "I don't think any of the cadets I picked up this morning have seen it."

"I hope not," Major Wickham said. "It would spoil the surprise."

At that Major Wickham realized Barbara was standing beside him. Her eyes went to the large pictures on the front of the paper and the headline. It read:

BRITISH ARMY CADETS ARRIVE FOR EXERCISE.

Major Wickham quickly folded the paper. "Oh, sorry Barbara. I didn't realize you were there."

"My apologies sir. I didn't mean to snoop," Barbara replied.

So that's it! she thought. *The enemy are these British Army cadets.*

She smiled at the thought. It was typical. Major Wickham was always trying to organize interesting training and surprises.

Major Wickham smiled. "You saw the headline I suppose?"

Barbara nodded. "Yes sir. I won't say anything."

"Good. I am hoping it will add a lot of interest to the weekend. It took quite a bit of organizing," Major Wickham said.

"Who are they sir?" Barbara asked.

"Twenty cadets and two staff from an exclusive private school: Clifton College. Clifton is one of the best schools in England. They only flew in yesterday and are arriving at eleven. I have to go and give them their orders and safety briefing then," Major Wickham replied.

"That will be good sir," Barbara replied. "Do we get to meet them?"

"Yes, after the exercise today," Major Wickham answered. "Now, what is it you want?"

"Two section commanders sir, one for Two Section and one for Three," Barbara replied. She outlined the problem, then added: "I think it is better to set the platoon up again properly immediately if you are not going to disband it."

"Yes, quite right. Now, is there anyone in the platoon we could promote to lance corporal?"

Barbara at once mentioned Cadet Wright. She could picture him, a serious, dark-haired cadet with glasses. Major Wickham looked thoughtful and then nodded. "Yes. It will cause a bit of jealousy, but he is a good lad, very bright. OK, we need one more. Who can we move? CSM! Bring the company roll," Major Wickham called.

CSM Warren collected the roll book and came over. Major Wickham flicked from page to page, scanning the names of NCOs. After a few minutes he said: "It will have to be a lance corporal as an acting section commander. We are running out of qualified corporals."

"Then that will have to do sir. Who is it to be?" Barbara said.

"The best available seems to be Frank Ray. He is in Four Platoon and is a Year Eleven. He is a Second Year so should have the knowledge. Let's go and talk to CUO Callan. He won't like losing him."

Lt Barker said: "We'll get going then sir. I'll try to be back by mid-afternoon."

"Yes Ashley. Sorry about this," Major Wickham said.

Lt Barker shrugged and turned to the troublemakers. "OK you lot, in you get."

As Major Wickham and Barbara walked over to where 4 Platoon were bivouacked Lt Barker and Lt Peters drove off out to the highway. Barbara glanced at the vehicle as it passed and saw that Milikin looked very angry, while LCpl Lang was in tears.

Bloody disloyal troublemakers, she thought. But then she did feel a small bit of sympathy. *They have some very unpleasant interviews with parents coming up. But then, they did bring it on themselves.*

While Major Wickham and Barbara talked to CUO Callan Lt Forster also drove off out to the main road. Barbara knew he was pre-positioning water jerry cans at safety check points.

CUO Callan was reluctant to lose anyone, with only 15 in his platoon, but agreed it was for the best. LCpl Ray was called over and was delighted at the opportunity.

"Get your gear then, and go with CUO Brassington," Major Wickham said.

While LCpl Ray collected his pack and hutchie Barbara stood and talked to CUO Callan and Chloe. Chloe seemed happy enough to be platoon sergeant for 4 Platoon. Barbara and LCpl Ray then walked back to the 1 Platoon area. The cadets sat in the shade of a gum tree. They looked quite down.

I've got a morale problem here, Barbara thought.

Instinctively she sensed that her leadership was going to be really put to the test.

"Put you gear there Cpl Ray, and then sit in front of Three Section," she said.

The cadets watched, their faces a mixture of resentment and curiosity. Barbara stood in front of them and looked them in the eyes. "Cpl Ray is to take over Three Section and Cadet Wright, the OC is going to promote you to lance corporal and you are to command Two Section," she said.

That caused even more looks of resentment. To ease this Barbara asked for one volunteer to move from 1 Section to go into 2 Section. To her relief one agreed and moved over. As Wright was already in 2 Section he was left in command.

That gives me three sections of five, Barbara thought. *That should be workable. Four is our minimum number in the bush for safety. Now, to get things moving.*

She took out her map and notebook and told the NCOs to do likewise. When they had settled, she began: "These are the orders for today's exercise, and I reckon it is going to be a really good one."

At that she noted a gleam of interest in some eyes and she smiled to herself. *Yes, with British Army cadets it should be good. They will be a real surprise!*

She then went slowly and carefully through the orders, explaining so that even the newest recruit understood what was going to happen. This took her over half an hour, and it was 0940 by the time she finished.

While she was giving the orders Barbara noted Major Wickham speaking to the other OOCs and when she finished the CSM came over and said: "The major is going to see the landowner. The sections are to revise patrolling until it is time to move and the platoon commanders are to do a reconnaissance. He wants you to join them."

Barbara at once organized the three section commanders to revise their silent field signals and patrolling and told Sgt Brady to supervise this. As the exercise did not begin until 1230hrs they had plenty of time to get ready.

She made her way across to where Major Wickham was speaking to the other platoon commanders and OOCs. "Capt Hamilton will lead you. CUO Brassington, you go with them. You are to do a walk down to the Burdekin and make sure the tracks are passable," he explained. "Lt Cavendish, you mind the fort please." As he did he glanced at where Cpl Horn sat near the CP but made no reference to her.

Barbara also glanced at her and puckered her lips in distaste. *They are just a bad memory we need to erase,* she thought. She knew the cadets were now well aware of what had happened. *The lesson won't be lost on them.*

Major Wickham went on: "I am heading off for a while to check the area. You lot be back by eleven thirty so you can eat an early lunch and get into position by twelve thirty."

The other CUOs had done two or three bivouacs in the area so knew it well but Barbara was glad of the chance to have a look around. The area looked simple enough on the map, but she was experienced enough to know that maps can be deceptive.

Capt Hamilton led off towards the road, followed by the CSM. The platoon commanders followed, Barbara behind the CSM. Capt Hamilton crossed the gravel road and led them across the flat ground past 4 Platoon's bivouac. After a hundred paces through flat, dry savannah he led them down into the dry bed of Deep Creek. Barbara now discovered this was not deep at all, being only a typical dry stream with a bed about 25 metres wide of stones or sand. The creek bed and banks were lined with Paperbarks.

Turning left Capt Hamilton led them in the direction Barbara deduced was downstream. As the group made their way across the loose stones and sand Capt Hamilton suddenly stopped and held up his hand.

"Watch out! Snake!"

Barbara looked past him and saw a large brown snake sliding along just up on the other bank. She grimaced and stood watching as it slithered off out of sight in the grass.

"Repulsive bloody thing!" she said.

"I thought snakes hibernated in winter," CUO Bailey commented.

"Probably this unseasonably hot weather has fooled them into thinking winter is over," CUO Callan replied.

Barbara could only agree with the 'unseasonably hot' bit as she was perspiring and wiped sweat from her face as they continued on. The comment sprang to her lips that the British cadets would cack themselves at the sight of a snake, but she managed to remember and hold her tongue.

They climbed under a barbed wire fence and then went under the main road through a large culvert, one of four which carried the road across the stream bed. Beyond was another stretch of creek bed with trees in it, then an even steeper and higher embankment. This carried the light railway and there were another four culverts. These were so large the cadets could walk through them upright. The culverts were like gloomy tunnels, being nearly fifty paces long.

"These tunnels are what you are guarding Barbara," Capt Hamilton said.

Barbara knew that and made no reply but set her mind to work trying to work out the best way to do so with her three small sections.

Downstream of the culverts the creek ran on in a bed with steep, vertical sides about two or three metres high. Barbara noted that the sides and bed included a lot of conglomerate rock. Up on the left was an open, grassy flat with a scattering of ironbarks. Up to her right was a tangle of small gullies and a long, low ridge covered with acacias and low bushes.

That will take a bit of watching, she mused, eyeing all the possible hiding places and cover on the ridge.

Two hundred metres further along the ridge ended abruptly in a steep little bluff. A similar creek came in from the right and there was a pool of mucky, slimy, green water at the point where the two creeks met. At this point the power line swooped overhead and an old vehicle track came down from the open ground on the left. The track went up the other bank under the power line but had been reduced to washed-out cattle pads by lack of use.

The group turned right and walked up the cattle pads and along under the power line for a hundred metres. The second creek ran in a deeper bed beside them, then looped around to bar their path. Here its bed was choked with rubber vine and bushes. The power line went on across the creek to a pylon a hundred metres away on the other side of the embankments which carried the railway and main road.

"The culverts up this creek are your problem Two Platoon," Capt Hamilton said, pointing. "And that power pylon and the culverts near it are your responsibility Three Platoon."

They turned and went left up a gentle rise through open bush. The ground underfoot was almost bare of grass, being mostly red earth with a scattering of leaf litter and a few sparse tufts of dry grass. The place was a dry, semi-desert environment but Barbara decided she liked it. Overlooking everything from half a kilometre to her left was the big hill. She could just see the cuttings which carried the road and railway around its eastern end.

As the group walked along the flat ridge several vehicles went past along the road. On top of the gentle rise Capt Hamilton led them left along the flat top of another low ridge. Barbara noted that on her left, beyond a belt of rubber vines and thorn trees, was Deep Creek.

My patrols need to move along down there, she decided.

This decision was reinforced when Capt Hamilton pointed to a large log lying on top of the flat ridge. Several bushes hid both ends of the log. "HQ is to have their second OP here," he said to CSM Warren.

CSM Warren nodded. "I will be in the one up on the hill there, sir," he replied, pointing to the big hill.

"Make sure you aren't right on the crest in case the enemy go up there to get a good look around," Capt Hamilton cautioned.

"We won't be sir," CSM Warren answered. "We will be just down this side, and we have our 'Yowie' suits." Yowie suits were made of camouflage netting and scrim and Barbara knew they were extra-ordinarily effective in this sort of country.

As the group walked along the low, flat ridge towards where the big hill came down to meet the Burdekin River Barbara noted that all the country on her right between her and the river was one huge tangle of rubber vines and undergrowth with tall, white-trunked gum trees growing out of it.

"That looks a bit thick," she commented.

"A bit! It's very bloody thick," CUO Callan said. "If you can get through that you are pretty bloody good."

"Are there any tracks?" Barbara asked.

"There were," Capt Hamilton replied. "We cut them a few years ago for an exercise against the Air Cadets from Ayr but they are probably overgrown by now. That is Snake Gully down to our right. The Burdekin is on the other side of that jungle."

Barbara was tempted to ask why it was called Snake Gully but resisted the urge. *They will let me know soon enough.*

They did. Ahead of them loomed a wall of rubber vine that seemed to go on for hundreds of metres, only ending at a line of trees which marked where Deep Creek squeezed through against the base of the hill. Rather than plunge into the tangle the group turned right and followed a faint trail down a small spur into Snake Gully. Capt Hamilton now led the way, machete in hand.

After sliding down a steep, dusty slope for ten metres Barbara found herself in a steep-sided and very overgrown gully. The bed of the gully was dry, about a metre deep and varying between one or two wide. A thick matt of head-high guinea grass grew on both sides, overhanging the narrow washout so that they had to push through it.

Fear of snakes made Barbara hesitate but Capt Hamilton hacked his way along with a machete and CSM Warren followed, laying some of the grass flat with swipes from a stick. In the gully it was airless and very hot. On either hand a massive thicket of thorn trees, rubber vines and spikey bushes walled them in.

After fifty metres the gully ran in under overhanging trees. Barbara thought this much better as the long grass gave way to bare dry mud and a few bushes. She was now able to see up the banks and into the gloomy tangle which hemmed them in. A peculiar feeling of claustrophobia crept over her.

This is a queer place, she thought.

It was unlike anywhere else she had ever been. The closest she could think of was Dingo Creek at Macrossan, also on the Burdekin but hundreds of kilometres upstream.

The gully wound along through the tangle. It was like being in a gloomy tunnel. Barbara decided that the nickname 'Snake Gully' came from this.

It certainly snakes around, she thought.

The gully went left, then right, then left again, all in under tall trees which met overhead. From time to time they had to climb under or over logs which had fallen across the gully. The smaller ones were removed to make movement easier.

"We don't want people tripping over them tonight," Capt Hamilton said.

"We come along here in the dark?" Barbara asked, looking around at the thickets. It was bad enough in the daylight.

The others laughed. CUO Callan answered: "Of course we do, and with no lights."

"Are there pigs?" Barbara asked. She had a real fear of wild pigs and it looked to her to be just the sort of place to meet them.

Capt Hamilton shook his head. "Never seen one... Oh shit! Snake!" he called, jumping back.

Barbara looked and saw a thin, yellow-bellied black about half a metre long go sliding into a hole in the bank.

"Only a little one," CUO Bailey commented.

CUO Callan chuckled. "Where there are little ones there are big ones don't forget," he commented.

"Thanks! I needed that," Barbara said sarcastically. She walked past the place where the snake had vanished, casting anxious glances at the hole as she did. She decided she did not particularly like Snake Gully.

The gully wound on for another hundred metres, left, then right, then left, then right again. At no time did she see any side-tracks which they could have followed and only once, where a small dry gully came in from the side, did she think she might be able to get out of it.

At length the gully curved to the right in under a huge spreading tree. This formed a really gloomy glade with a steep bank covered with rubber vine on the left and a matt of exposed tree roots leading up to the huge tree. Soon after that the gully curved right, then left and, to Barbara's relief, she saw bright sunlight ahead through the tunnel of vegetation.

They emerged onto flat, clean sand which extended for hundreds of metres: the bed of the Burdekin River. As they came out onto the open riverbed they stopped and looked around. Twenty-five paces to her left Barbara saw that Deep Creek also reached the river bed there, but in a deep, slimy pool which nestled against a steep slope, the end of the hill. The remains of an old bridge abutment rose from the pool. The pool ended just past the rotting stumps and did not extend all the way to the water in the river which was still several hundred metres away.

Upstream, to Barbara's right, the bank of the river was a wall of steep earth cliffs ten metres high. These were topped by the thick tangle of rubber vines and bushes and extended off in a huge sweeping curve to the left as far as she could see.

In front of her the bare, open sand formed a huge dry flood overflow channel three hundred metres wide. Several clumps of bushes grew in it and the far side was a dry, sandy island topped with trees and bushes. Through a hundred-metre-wide gap the flood channel curved away from the steep grassy slope of the hill to where sunlight glittered on water. That was the main channel of the river.

It was, to Barbara's eyes, a pleasant enough spot. Capt Hamilton led the way out to the middle of the dry flood channel, then left around the end of the Deep Creek pool and up the steep grassy slope. This gave Barbara a good view back up the river. She noted the tree covered 'island' was over a kilometre long and several hundred metres wide.

She also noted that the Burdekin came around in a wide, sweeping curve, with a long, deep pool several kilometres long. As she studied the pool the warning from Major Wickham's safety brief came to mind: 'Estuarine crocodiles inhabit this river!' She shuddered at the thought. The distant water looked brown and sluggish and she was glad her platoon were not to go anywhere near it.

The group climbed under a fence onto the light railway at the end of a steep-sided cutting. Capt Hamilton pointed up. "There is a tourist lookout up there, and the main road goes around the end of the hill. We will have a safety vehicle parked there most of the time."

They turned left and set off walking along the light railway. For a hundred metres it ran through a very deep, steep-sided cutting below the Lookout. By this time Barbara was sweating profusely and she kept taking sips from her water bottles.

If it is as hot as this we need to watch the cadets for heat exhaustion, she thought.

They followed the railway back to near the camp. For much of the way the railway ran on a high embankment with the overgrown bed of Deep Creek beside it. After the creek trended away they were able to see right across the bare flat inside the curve of the railway.

It was easy walking and they arrived at the turnoff to the Gravel Scrape ten minutes later. They were just in time as the sound of a train came to them. From the shade across the road at the turnoff they watched it go clanking past: a chunky little yellow diesel locomotive and hundreds of the square wire mesh bins on their tiny little wheels.

Capt Hamilton jerked his thumb towards the bivouac area. "OK, let's get back and have lunch, then get this exercise underway."

The group walked along the dusty gravel road back to the Gravel Scrape. Barbara checked her watch. It was just on 11:30.

Chapter 7

THE 'OPPOSING FORCE'

Major Wickham was a kindly man in his fifties. Many years before he had been a soldier and had experienced the hard and bitter test of war. Now he was a teacher and also served as an Officer of Cadets. In this capacity he had commanded the cadet unit for many years, finding it the most rewarding thing he had ever done, save raising his own family.

This morning he was feeling sore at heart and even wondered if he was not getting too old for the job. He felt tired and sad. The disciplinary incident had upset him more than he cared to show.

"We seem to be lurching from one disaster to another," he muttered as he drove his car around the base of the hill heading northwards. To his mind the unit seemed to be crumbling as numbers fell and leaders were found wanting.

That is six corporals I have sacked this year, and the first time I have ever had to relieve a CUO of his command, he thought unhappily.

It was usual to have at least one sergeant give trouble each year. The 3rd Years seemed to grow too cocky and even arrogant in that rank, but it was the corporals which really worried him. They were the leaders of the future and he needed at least sixteen to get the seven or eight good sergeants and CSM needed for the next year.

We are down to fourteen corporals, he counted in his head, *and some of them are either too old and will be leaving, or are doubtful.*

Still worrying about how to rebuild the unit he drove down across the small valley on the north side of the hill, then up over a low rise with a small conical hill on the right and large conical hill on the left. On the other side of the rise the road went down to run along a straight for several kilometres. Half a kilometre past the rise was a gravel road on the left. Opposite, beyond the light railway which paralleled the road, were the large buildings of the pump station. These stood on the riverbank.

Major Wickham pulled over and parked his car at the junction of the gravel road, then sat there thinking hard. Outside it was hot and the glare made him pucker his eyes against it. The grass was brown and dry, and a heat haze shimmered off the bitumen.

"These Pommies are going to find the heat a bit trying," he said to himself.

Heat exhaustion and how to prevent it in the visitors, occupied his thoughts for the next ten minutes. While he waited, he read the newspaper article Lt Barker had given him.

There were two photos, both in colour. One showed the British cadets as a group and had the caption: 'British Army cadets arrive for exercises with Australian Army cadets'. The second photo was of only four of the cadets, three males and a female. 'Jolly pleased to be here,' says Cadet Warrant Officer Class 2 the Honourable George Summerfield, eldest son of Lord Bramley.

"Bloody hell!" Major Wickham groaned. "The bloody British upper class in all its glory!"

He studied the photo and concluded that the future Lord Bramley looked quite a normal looking 'chap' (the word sprang to his mind). Fair curly hair and a cheerful grin in a nuggety face.

The female cadet then held his attention. She was, he noted with surprise, a Warrant Officer Class 1. This was a very rare rank in the Australian Army Cadets. The only ones he knew were the Cadet Regimental Sergeant Majors of each of the 8 cadet regions. The name of the British WO1 was Adelaide de Vere Lisle and to Major Wickham she looked very plain.

She might find Chloe a bit of a shock, Major Wickham chuckled. Then he frowned as he remembered that Chloe was in disgrace and no longer his CSM.

The next person in the picture was a very good-looking youth, fair, blue-eyed. Colour Sergeant the Honourable Frederick William Masters, son of the current Commander of the British Army in Europe, General Sir William Masters.

"Well, he shouldn't have any trouble passing his selection board if he decides to go into the army," Major Wickham murmured. "A bloody general's son, and an 'Honourable' at that. What a collection!"

The fourth cadet in the photo was a solid, 'Rugby' type with black curly hair and a confident smile. His name was also reassuringly normal: Cpl Alec Nobbs.

No silver spoon there I suspect, Major Wickham thought.

It had been several months since the British cadets had first made contact. They were planning a tour of Australia and wanted to meet Australian cadets during it. Major Wickham had proposed the exercise and their OC had enthusiastically embraced the idea, even though it would be the first thing they did after arriving.

The cadets all came from Clifton College, an exclusive and very expensive private school in Bristol. The school had its own cadet unit and specialized in preparing young people for entry into the armed forces. From his briefcase Major Wickham extracted the list of names and studied them. His first impression remained, and was even reinforced: very British, very upper class.

He read down the list again, noting Sgt the Honourable Charles Fosdyck Havelock, another lord to be. There were several names with historical connections: Haig, Allenby, Gough-Gore, which made Major Wickham wonder if they were related to the famous people.

I must find a tactful way to ask, he decided.

There were a number of ordinary sounding names such as Derbyshire, Topping, Crossly and Gosford, but he knew that could be very misleading as to their actual social and economic status.

They must all have a few bob to go to that school, he mused.

He had met the British cadets the previous day at the airport. Friday had been their first day in Australia and they were all tired and jet-lagged. Despite that they had been very keen and friendly. Their OC, Major Grogan, was a veteran of similar vintage to Major Wickham and they had got on well.

The British cadets had been billeted at Lavarack Barracks and had spent the remainder of the day resting. There had been no opportunity for them to see the sights of Townsville.

I hope they weren't on the TV news last night, Major Wickham worried.

It had been a big effort to keep their involvement in the exercise secret and he did not want it spoilt at the last minute.

Just after 11:00 an army coach appeared from the direction of Townsville. Major Wickham climbed out of his car and waved it down. The coach swung round to stop on the gravel side road. The faces of the British cadets grinned out at Major Wickham.

Major Grogan, clad in his British Army 'Woodland Green' camouflage uniform, climbed out and at once wiped his face.

"Whew! Bit hot," he commented.

"Sorry about that, but this is North Queensland," Major Wickham replied. "If your people can unload their gear and place it here we will make sure it is collected by my 2ic. Then they can sit themselves in the shade of that tree for their briefing."

He pointed to the only tree nearby, a lone gum tree, which cast its meagre shade on the side of the gravel road.

A tall, thin British lieutenant climbed off the bus. For a moment Major Wickham struggled to remember his name. Then it came to him: Jeffries, John Jeffries. They shook hands and Lt Jeffries also wiped perspiration from his face and commented on the heat.

So did nearly all of the twenty cadets who stepped down off the coach. As they did the impression of the previous day was reinforced: that the British cadets were all bigger and older then the average Australian cadet. From his notes Major Wickham knew they were all 16 or 17.

The British cadets were formed into a line by the female RSM and then set to work to unload the gear from the bus. When she spoke Major Wickham had to suppress a smile. Her voice was so obviously English 'upper class' that she sounded like a caricature. From time spent in Britain and at British universities Major Wickham was familiar with the type but still found it odd to listen to, here on the other side of the world in the Australian bush.

As they worked, Major Wickham studied their uniforms with interest. Their 'Woodland Green' camouflage was the most noticeable thing, the dark green and dark brown pattern being such a contrast to the pale green, light brown and khaki of the 'Austcam' disruptive pattern uniform he wore. The badges of rank, while similar in pattern were larger and more obvious than the tiny black badges worn by Australians.

Our cadets are going to love seeing this, he thought happily.

Lt Jeffries looked around in wonder and wiped his face again. "Well, I haven't the faintest idea where I am. We seem to have travelled forever to get here," he said.

Major Wickham smiled. "About one hundred and fifty kilometres,"

"That would be from one side of a small European country to another," Lt Jeffries commented.

Major Wickham nodded. "You have travelled across a district called the Lower Burdekin. It is about the size of Belgium."

"As big as Belgium!" Lt Jeffries commented.

"Australia's a big place," Major Wickham reminded him. "Great Britain will fit about six times into Queensland from memory."

"Bloody hell. And it is hot!" Lt Jeffries replied, but he grinned and was obviously happy to be there.

A Land Rover arrived from the south and Capt Hamilton got out. He did a radio check on the company safety net, then came over to join them and was introduced. By the time that was done the British cadets were moving to the shade of the tree.

Major Wickham collected his briefcase, map board and a bundle of maps from his car, then walked over with the other officers to stand in front of the British cadets. The female RSM called them to sit at attention and saluted her own OC. He returned the salute and told them to sit easy, then handed over to Major Wickham.

He introduced Capt Hamilton, then said: "I hope you all slept well."

There was a chorus of laughs and cheerful curses about the heat, the humidity, the insects and the birds. "Jolly laughing jackasses woke us up at cock crow!" exclaimed one cadet.

The others laughed and one rumpled his head. "You are the jackass old boy!" he said.

At the 'old boy', Major Wickham met Capt Hamilton's eye and had to bite his lip.

When the laughter subsided Major Wickham handed out the maps. He then held up his map board, on one side of which was a 1:250 000 scale map of the Townsville region. He then orientated the British cadets to where Townsville and the Coral Sea were. The Burdekin River was pointed out and the roads they had followed. He made the same comment to them as their OOCs had made about the size and distance. To emphasize this he placed a plastic overlay on top of the map with southern England on the same scale.

This brought forth exclamations and shaking heads and a few muttered comments about quality being more important. One of these was by the female RSM who said: "It isn't how big it is that matters."

"You'd know then would you Adelaide?" asked a lad with a mischievous grin.

The female RSM scowled. "Keep your filthy thoughts to yourself Hinchley, and address me as RSM."

With memories of his own unit's morning incident Major Wickham blushed. He glanced at Major Grogan but he seemed content to let the RSM deal with the situation, so he went on with the briefing.

The map board was turned over to show the enlargement of the local area and the cadets were referred to the map photocopy they had been handed. Major Wickham then gave a full set of Verbal Orders for the exercise. Some of the British cadets seemed surprised by this while others took careful notes.

The mission of the British cadets was to infiltrate the area and place 'demolitions' (plastic containers with 'bomb' written on them in felt pen) on selected targets. They were also to make detailed sketch maps. To achieve this they were divided into five patrols of four. Three patrols were given the task of infiltrating from the north. The other two patrols were to be taken by Capt Hamilton to the southern edge of the exercise area and were to move in from there.

Patrol 1, led by the female RSM and moving in from the south, had the mission of reaching the culverts over Deep Creek. Patrol 2, also coming from the south, and led by WO2 Summerfield, was to 'destroy' selected pylons on the electricity transmission line from Landers Creek to the Hill. Patrol 3, led by the General's son, Colour Sgt Masters, was to attack the road and rail bridges over Landers Creek. Patrol 4 (The Honourable Charles) was to come in from the north and raid the culverts defended by 3 Pl and 4 Pl. Patrol 5, led by Sgt Cecil Gough-Gore, was to locate and hit the defenders HQ.

The giving of the orders, in all the details of routes, timings, boundaries, action on contact and so on, took nearly an hour. This was partly because the safety briefing had to be so detailed. At the mention of snakes all the British cadets looked nervously at the grass they were sitting in. The warning about staying away from the river because it had crocodiles in it added to their dismay.

Major Wickham described in detail how big and how fast crocodiles were and how they dragged their prey into the water and so on. But what he was really worried about and laboured was the heat and how to avoid, or treat, heat exhaustion and heat stroke.

Each of the raiding parties was issued with a radio so, in the event of an accident or illness, they could report. The radios were hand-held VHF radios with 16 channels and were on loan from the NQ Cadet Brigade HQ. They worked on a different set of frequencies from the 80 channel UHF CB hand-held radios that the unit was using so neither side could listen in to the other. Major Wickham had a VHF and now issued a UHF CB to Major Grogan and another to Lt Jefferies. The British cadets were told that if the radio did not work, they were to make their way to the nearest 'friendly' patrol, or out to the road. The location of the safety vehicles and safety check points was then given to them.

To reinforce the message on heat Major Wickham had them all then drink a complete water bottle, then refill it from jerry cans in Capt Hamilton's vehicle. By then it was lunch time and the British cadets settled in the sparse shade of the single eucalypt to eat the cut lunch provided for them.

While the cadets ate in the shade the officers stood and talked beside the vehicles. By then Major Wickham was feeling better. The British cadets had arrived and been briefed. They seemed keen and their arrival was still a secret from his own people. There was only the looming ordeal of continuing the investigation after lunch to try to find out what the troublemakers had actually done. Very briefly he hinted at the nature of the problem to Major Grogan and Lt Jeffries, but only because it would impact on the exercise.

As they ate their lunch Capt Hamilton commented: "Only one girl and she is the highest rank?"

Major Grogan grinned and looked over towards where she sat with a group of friends. "The Lady Adelaide? Yes, she can really dish it out. She is a very capable operator."

"Lady Adelaide eh?" Capt Hamilton said, raising an eyebrow.

"Definitely top drawer that one." Lt Jeffries added. "She looks very pretty and ladylike, but she is as tough as old boots underneath; the original steel fist in a velvet glove."

"We've got a couple like her," Major Wickham said, thinking of Barbara and Chloe.

"Many girls in your unit?" Major Grogan asked.

"About thirty," Major Wickham replied.

At that moment the radio in Capt Hamilton's vehicle crackled. He went and answered it, then came back. "The friendlies are moving out now," he said.

Major Wickham looked along the highway to the south to where The Hill rose beyond the conical hills.

There will be an OP up there soon. We had better get this lot moving or under cover.

"Time to start moving," he said.

Major Grogan nodded. "Right RSM, get them up. Make sure there is no litter and get their packs here to load into the vehicle trailer."

"And have them all have another big drink and refill their water bottles," Major Wickham added.

Ten minutes later the British cadets began moving. Two patrols squeezed into the back of the Land Rover and the other three started walking nervously off into the long grass. The exercise had begun

Chapter 8

HOT WORK

After doing radio checks, Barbara led her platoon out to the junction of the main road and the vehicle track to the Gravel Scrape. At this point Cpl Ridgeway led his section off along a rough vehicle road which went off through the bush on the left towards the Big Hill. That track then led up under the power line to the saddle on the crest. Guarding the power pylon there was the task of that section.

At the gate beside the main road Barbara stopped and pointed out the lay of the land to the remainder. She then lined them up beside the main road in extended line, and when she was sure there were no vehicles coming, she signalled and they all walked across at the same time.

On the other side she turned right. After trampling her way down through long grass and weeds for 50 metres she reached the dry bed of Deep Creek between the culverts under the main road and those through the railway embankment. The platoon followed.

Here Barbara deployed them with 2 Section sent to the right to guard the main road culverts and 3 Section sent left to guard the culverts under the railway. To put them in position she led four members of 2 Section through the culverts under the main road. Walking through the long, dark culvert set the young cadets acting silly and they called out and tried to frighten each other.

Having placed two of the cadets up on top of the bank and two down in the creek bed Barbara made her way back to the others and led them east through the railway culverts. 3 Section were then shown their positions when not on patrol. Two cadets, one from each section, were sited there facing downstream.

"When the whole section is here, have a cadet watching the long grass between the railway and the main road," Barbara explained. Once she was sure they all knew where to be and what to do 3 Section were all grouped at the downstream end of the culverts.

Barbara had decided that she must take risks and that a patrol would add 'depth' and better security so after checking that LCpl Ray knew where he was on the map and which way to go Barbara sent his section off as the first patrol. LCpl Ray led three of his cadets off down the creek. One stayed as guard with the cadet from 2 Section. Sgt Brady and Barbara also remained at the downstream mouth of the tunnel.

Sgt Brady sat down, screwed the long antenna onto the army radio that was on the Company Command Net, then did another radio check. To Barbara's relief the radio worked well and they got good clear coms with HQ, which was back at the Gravel Scrape.

Barbara had a small hand-held UHF CB radio, as did each of the section commanders. These had been tested before moving from the bivouac area, but she now tested them again and was dismayed to find that she could barely hear LCpl Ray, even though he was only a few hundred metres down the creek. Cpl Ridgeway came through clearer and Barbara presumed it was because he was now up on the Big Hill.

"I wish we had been given the better radios," Sgt Brady grumbled.

The unit also owned ten larger CB Radios, but these had been given to the other platoons as they were to operate further from HQ. Nine army radios provided the Company Command Net: one at the CP, one with each platoon, two with the HQ OPs, and two with safety vehicles.

"We have a pretty good radio set-up all the same," Barbara said. "Better than my old unit could normally round up."

"Yeah, the OC is trying to buy enough small radios so we can have a platoon net for every platoon as well as the company net," Sgt Brady replied.

Barbara sat in the cool shade of the culvert and talked radios and other exercises with Sgt Brady. As they talked Barbara covertly studied him.

If this platoon is to be pulled out of the muck then he is an important person, she thought.

She knew Brady had been in quite a bit of trouble earlier in the year, had even been suspended on suspicion of having organized the bashing of another sergeant who had since left the unit. The case had gone to court but there it was proved that, in fact, Brady had been the victim. He had been lured into a trap in a car park at night and had been saved by his friends. It was they who had bashed the other sergeant.

"It's none of my business," Barbara said, aware that she was treading on delicate turf, "but do you ever see Candy Dickson anymore?"

Earlier in the year Brady and Candy had been going together and Brady had been very obviously smitten by her. Now he just shrugged and made a face before shaking his head.

"Nah, not really. She left school and works in town."

"Sorry, I don't mean to probe, but if we are to save this platoon you and I have to work together and I need to know a bit about you," Barbara explained. She had noted the look of pain which had filled Brady's eyes and decided that he was still in love with Candy. The rumour was that she had dumped him for the other sergeant; that the fight had been over her.

At that moment the Coy Net radio crackled into life. CSM Warren's voice sounded: "All stations, this is Hotel One. We can see movement beside the main road to the north of the hills, near the pump station. Four figures in dark coloured uniforms moving south between the railway and the river, over."

The CP acknowledged the message, so Sgt Brady waited till they had signed off, then also confirmed they had heard it. Barbara picked up the small radio and called both corporals. This time she got LCpl Ray easily but had difficulty getting through to Cpl Ridgeway. After passing on the message she took out a map photocopy and a red pen and marked the sighting with the military symbol for a recon patrol, plus a red arrow showing direction of movement, and the time.

As she did this Barbara experienced a surge of excitement. *Now things should start to hot up. I hope the cadets find having the British cadets as enemy interesting,* she thought. She knew she was curious about them. *I can hardly wait to see them. It will be so novel to have an enemy who are from a real foreign army, with different uniforms and badges and so on,* she thought.

That got her remembering her previous experience with British forces. That had been during the annual camp the previous year. In that case they had been Royal Marine Commandos from the famous Special Boat Squadron, and she had been very impressed. She had even developed a crush on one of them, Lt Mark Guy.

I wonder where he is now? she thought. *He is so handsome, and so nice.*

That set her mind thinking about the other Special Forces officer who had been involved: Lt Raoul de Berg of the French Marine Commandos. Despite being only in his mid-twenties, he was a decorated veteran of half a dozen wars and conflicts around the world and a very brave man. Having been with him in a real battle Barbara knew he was the sort of man you could depend on unto death. A powerful image of him in all his rugged toughness made her heart beat faster.

He is such a charmer, she thought.

At that she smiled and felt a warm glow. To have two such men both obviously interested in her was a real boost to the ego.

Another radio call came over the Coy Net. This was from 4 Platoon who were patrolling near the bridges over Landers Creek, 4 kilometres to the south. They had seen an enemy party of four who had gone into the close country near the junction of the Burdekin and Landers Creek.

Barbara marked this information on her map and then called both the section commanders. Neither had anything to report but were obviously cheered up to be told there actually were enemy.

"It's bloody hot," LCpl Ray reported. "We are on our way back up the creek now, over."

Barbara checked her watch and saw that it was already 1330. An hour had gone by with no action and she knew the cadets would be starting to get bored. That stirred her to get up and walk through the culverts to check on the four cadets watching upstream.

Two were lying down and one of these was asleep. The other two were awake and Barbara climbed up and tried to talk to them. She found this heavy going as they returned monosyllabic grunts and did a lot of shrugging to her questions.

I don't think they like me much, she decided. As she made her way back through the culverts, she pondered this and revised her estimate. *No, they are probably just unsure and upset after losing their CUO and corporal.*

On her return she was greeted by Sgt Brady with a report that four enemy were standing in the open at Cornford Lookout refilling their water bottles. This report did not come from the safety vehicle there, which was neutral, but from CSM Warren's OP up on the Big Hill.

"I wonder if that is the same group they saw earlier?" she pondered aloud, marking the sighting on her map.

As she finished doing this LCpl Ray and his patrol arrived back. They were all red in the face and perspiring from the heat. Barbara organized Sgt Brady to place them as the guards at the upstream end of the culverts, leaving the smallest cadet, Cadet Simpkins, as radio operator with her. LCpl Ray and the other three replaced 2 Section who were then sent off as a patrol led by LCpl Wright. Their patrol route was the same: down Deep Creek to the Burdekin, then back up again.

"You will have real trouble getting down the last part of Deep Creek," LCpl Ray commented. "It is easy going till you reach the place where the creek turns right at the base of the hill, but from there on it has water in it, long, deep pools of horrible slimy looking muck. We tried to go along both banks but they are too steep and overgrown. We had to go up along an overgrown track just below the railway."

"Thanks. Do I need to cut my way?" LCpl Wright asked.

"No. We cleared a path," LCpl Ray replied, indicating the secateurs on his belt.

"Thanks," LCpl Wright replied.

"Be back by fourteen thirty Cpl Wright," Barbara said.

Wright nodded and led his patrol off down the creek, sending one cadet up onto the top of the bank to extend the search more effectively.

That was a sensible move, Barbara thought. *Wright seems capable enough.*

More time dragged by. Down in the creek bed the heat increased, although Barbara found sitting in the shade in the culvert was cool enough as a breeze was funnelled through it. More sightings came in; again from 4 Platoon. They reported they were chasing four enemy along the power line in a northerly direction.

This group eluded the pursuit in a creek line near the culvert guarded by 3 Platoon who were warned by radio and assured HQ they were alert.

But the next sight of the opposing forces was by Cpl Ridgeway up on the Big Hill. His excited voice broke into Barbara's thoughts saying that he was chasing two enemy. Soon afterwards he called again to say there were actually four enemy and that his section was pursuing them.

"Keep someone guarding the power pylon," Barbara cautioned, remembering an exercise years before when she had been able to sneak in and place a 'bomb' on the target because all the guards ran off to chase two of her own team.

That was the exercise near Innisfail where Chloe and Jane went missing, she remembered.

Barbara informed the other Call Signs on the Coy Net of the action and then waited anxiously, wondering if Ridgeway was coping. He had seemed to her to be a level-headed and competent corporal.

So he proved to be. A few minutes later he called again. "One One, this is One One Alpha. We have captured one enemy and the others have run off, over."

"Good. Keep him there and I will come up with a cadet to collect him and take him to HQ, over," Barbara replied.

"Roger One One. He is a pommy, over," Cpl Ridgeway replied.

"Say again One One Alpha, over," Barbara asked. She knew what he had said but wanted the others to hear it. Cpl Ridgeway replied, confirming that his prisoner was a British Army cadet. "Says his name is Cpl Barry Cranwell, and that is all he will tell us, except that he thinks it is er... very hot. He looks it. He is beetroot red and I think he is suffering from the early stages of heat exhaustion, over."

"Roger One One Alpha. Give him a drink and sit him in the shade. I will be up in a few minutes, out."

With that Barbara sent Cadet Simpkins to get Cadet Polsen from the upstream end of the culverts. While he did this, she used the Coy Net to inform HQ and the other platoons. It gave her real satisfaction to report the presence of the British cadets and that 1 Platoon had captured a prisoner.

When Cadet Polsen arrived Barbara took the CB radio, checked that Sgt Brady knew what was going on, then headed off back up to the main road. She had a niggling concern about leaving the culverts with the platoon sergeant in command but reasoned she was actually making it safer by patrolling. She was also fired by curiosity to see what the British cadet looked like. Her curiosity and anxiety set her walking quickly. Polsen trotted along behind her without complaining. She had picked him because he seemed to be the biggest and fittest cadet.

They walked across to gate and went through it to the road junction, then along the side-track that led to the power lines. Within a couple of minutes they were puffing up the steep gravel track towards the power pylon on the summit. It wasn't far, only 400 metres and a climb of about 60 metres but it was enough to bring her to a puffing standstill near the crest.

After recovering her breath she plodded on up, stopping to look back over the flat country behind her as she did. From there she could clearly see the gravel pit area and also the bare ground inside the curve of the railway. There was no sign of any movement. She called LCpl Wright and he confirmed he was now at the Burdekin and starting his patrol back up the creek.

A minute later Barbara and Cadet Polsen reached the crest of the saddle. There, seated under the shade of a straggly gum tree, was the British cadet. Cpl Ridgeway stood nearby with another of his cadets. The British cadet was very red in the face and looked thoroughly disgusted with himself.

As Barbara approached, he looked her up and down with evident surprise, followed by approval. That annoyed her.

Bloody males! That's all they can think about! she thought crossly.

She stood and studied his foreign camouflage and different badges with interest. Cpl Ridgeway said: "His mates came back to see if he was alright. They accepted that he was captured and went off back over the crest there." He pointed northwards.

"How did you catch him?" Barbara asked.

"He ran too slowly and tripped on a rock," Cpl Ridgeway replied.

"I were lookin' out fer bluidy snakes I were," the British cadet grumbled.

That caused a gust of unfeeling laughter from the Australians. Barbara gestured: "Come on. Get up and come with us."

As he stood up and swung on his webbing the British cadet said: "Have yer got any water? I'm ferk... er.. very hot."

"Down at HQ," Barbara said. "There's plenty there." She pointed to where the gravel pit could just be seen through the trees.

She and Polsen led the British cadet down the slope and across through a fence to HQ. By the time they arrived she was sweating heavily herself and was glad to arrive. She noted that Lt Forster was in the Command Post with the HQ signallers led by Jane. They all came out to look. Lt Cavendish stood near the gravel heap and was also watching them walk in.

The British cadet was seated in the shade and questioned. Barbara would have loved to stay and listen, but she knew that trouble could strike her platoon at any moment so she and Polsen quickly refilled their water bottles and set off back along the road to the gate.

Five minutes later they were back at the culverts. LCpl Wright had just arrived back with his patrol. The defenders were then re-arranged so that 3 Section could do another patrol. This included the two cadets who had not yet done a patrol. LCpl Ray was happy to lead a second patrol and Barbara nodded with approval as he explained to the cadets what he wanted them to do. He then led them off down the creek.

Barbara sat down and questioned LCpl Wright about his patrol.

"Very hot," he said. "And Ray was right. It was hard going along the part of the creek right beside the hill, that last few hundred metres before the river."

"Why is that?" Barbara asked. It had looked reasonably open to her when she had walked back along the railway.

"Really steep bank ma'am, and that bloody great tangle of rubber vines hems it in on the right and the creek is full of water in long deep pools."

"Too deep to wade?" Barbara asked.

LCpl Wright made a face. "I wouldn't care to try. They looked deep and were full of green slime. I reckon it is the sort of place a croc would live."

Barbara nodded and asked: "What about the bank beside the railway?"

"There is an old road but parts of it are washed away and it is really overgrown with spiky weeds and lantana ma'am. We had to..." LCpl Wright paused and looked anxiously around. "Strewth! What's that noise?"

Barbara realized she was aware of it too, a peculiar rumbling vibration which made the air quiver. Then the sound of a labouring diesel engine came to her. "A train," she said.

The sugar train came from the south. They could hear it for a couple of minutes before it arrived. Both walked out to look up as it went grinding past along the top of the steep gravel embankment. Barbara saw the driver, but he did not see them as he was leaning out staring along the track ahead.

She was seized by the childish urge to be in the tunnel under the train, so she walked back into the culvert and along it. To her surprise she found her heart beating faster from what she knew was entirely irrational fear of the culvert collapsing. Inside the culvert the sound became a deep vibration which made the air quiver and caused dust to rise from the floor.

Sand trickled down from a crack in the corrugated steel pipe, causing her to glance anxiously at the roof.

Sgt Brady had followed her in. He gave a forced looking grin and said: "I hope it doesn't collapse."

"It won't. It's been here for years and is obviously built for the job," Barbara replied. Even so she knew she was a little bit scared and she did glance anxiously at the roof a couple more times. "The train is certainly long enough," she added.

That gave her an excuse to walk back out to watch. She found it quite fascinating to watch the hundreds of wire bins full of short lengths of freshly cut sugar cane go clicking and rattling past on their tiny steel wheels. The end of the train was some sort of bright yellow wagon with flashing lights. The pungent sweet smell of burnt sugar cane filled the air.

As the sound of the train died away Barbara realized someone was trying to call them on the radio. She picked it up. It was Sgt Dunstan's OP on the low ridge between Deep Creek and Snake Gully.

"We can see an enemy patrol in the rubber vines beside Deep Creek," Sgt Dunstan replied.

"I will send you some help," Barbara replied. She used the walkie talkie to call LCpl Ray. He reported that he was just passing under the power lines.

That is right near there, Barbara thought.

She gave him instructions to search carefully eastwards along on the south bank.

This was rewarded a few minutes later by a call from Sgt Dunstan that LCpl Ray's patrol had flushed the raiders out. He reported that the four British cadets had run up the open slope past the OP and were pretend 'fired on'. They had then swerved away and run over into the creek beyond into the area 2 Platoon was guarding.

Barbara called LCpl Ray and told him not to chase the enemy past the OP. When he replied he sounded quite pleased.

Good! she thought. *A few successful actions will lift their morale and platoon pride.*

LCpl Ray's patrol returned to Deep Creek and resumed their search down it. 2 Platoon came on the radio to report having ambushed the four British cadets, capturing two. Two escaped and vanished in the top end of the same creek towards 3 Platoon. Barbara knew that the exercise orders would have forbidden two cadets to be running around on their own but could only shrug. That was a problem for Major Wickham.

Cpl Ridgeway called next. He was in touch with another enemy patrol which was on the hill between him and the OP. At the same time the Coy Net radio called: a girl's voice.

"There are at least four enemy just near us heading for the power lines, over," she said.

"Who was that?" Barbara asked Sgt Brady, who had taken the call.

"Colleen McNamara, up at the OP on the hill," Sgt Brady replied.

"They must be a second group of raiders," Barbara said. "We had better reinforce Cpl Ridgeway, and warn him."

She called Cpl Ridgeway and did this. Once again Barbara told him not to leave the power pylon unguarded. She then selected Cadet Norris, a big strapping lad, and told him to come with her. That left Sgt Brady again in charge at the culverts.

As quickly as they could Barbara and Norris walked out to the road and set off up the hill. To Barbara's annoyance she lost radio contact with Cpl Ridgeway and could only wonder what was happening.

Chapter 9

GETTING EVEN

Barbara walked as fast as she could without running. Cadet Norris trotted along at her heels. By the time they reached the bottom of the hill both were puffing and sweating freely. As they plodded up the steep track under the power lines Barbara kept scanning the hillside for any sign of movement.

It was only when they were near the top that she regained radio contact with Cpl Ridgeway. "One One Aplha, what is going on?" Barbara asked.

"One One, this is One One Alpha. We are chasing four enemy along the top of the hill heading east, over," Cpl Ridgeway replied, his panting breath sounding clearly over the radio.

"Don't follow them too far, over," Barbara said.

"Roger that, puff... puff... we... oh bugger!"

"What's happened, over?" Barbara asked anxiously. She pushed herself to keep on climbing the slope but had to slow down to allow Norris to keep up. He was falling behind and looked very red in the face.

"Cadet Rowland has hurt herself, over," Cpl Ridgeway replied.

"Where are you?" Barbara asked.

"Right near the highest point of the hill, over," Cpl Ridgeway replied.

"What is wrong with her, over?" Barbara asked.

"She's tripped in the grass. I'm not sure how bad it is, over," Cpl Ridgeway answered.

"Is it serious?" Barbara asked.

"No, don't think so. Sprained ankle I think, over," Cpl Ridgeway answered.

"Wait there and carry out First Aid. I am almost up at the crest," Barbara replied.

"Roger, over."

"What are the enemy doing, over?"

"They have run away down the hill towards the river. I can't see them anymore, over," Cpl Ridgeway said.

Barbara slowed again to allow Norris to catch up, then gritted her teeth and plodded up to the power pylon on the crest. A cadet stood there, looking anxious. Barbara struggled to remember his name and failed.

"What's going on Ma'am?" the cadet asked.

"Cpl Ridgeway has chased some enemy off towards the river. You stay here and keep guard. We will be back soon," Barbara said. She turned off the track and began walking along the crest of the hill.

This was fairly wide and studded with clumps of rock and a scattering of trees. Worse, it was clothed in waist high grass which hid hundreds of rocks of all sizes. Barbara disliked walking in the long grass intensely as she feared stepping on a snake, but she had done such exercises dozens of times and just walked quickly along, more annoyed by the prickly spear grass seeds which stuck in her clothing.

It was a gentle uphill for a hundred metres to an outcrop of rocks on what appeared to be the crest and by then Barbara was already heartily sick of stumbling on the hidden rocks. The crest turned out to be a false one and she saw that the true top of the hill was another hundred metres on, across a shallow, flat dip.

She had to stop to allow Cadet Norris to catch up again. He was even slower walking through the long grass than he had been coming up the hill. While waiting for him Barbara looked around and was quite struck by the view.

Away on her right was the area of bush where the exercise was going on but in the distance beyond that was the bright green of sugar cane fields. These stretched away for many kilometres southwards until lost in the shimmering heat haze near a line of distant mountains. Somewhere in that direction she knew was the gorge through which the Burdekin made its way to the coastal plain.

In front of her she could see the lines of trees marking the river and part of its sandy bed. On the other bank was open savannah woodland and grassland which again extended to distant mountains. In this case the mountains did not form a continuous range but instead were a chain of isolated but rugged outcrops.

The closest of these was only a few kilometres away on her left front, just across the river. Barbara studied the range for a minute, then looked out to her left. Somewhere in that direction was the sea but it was 70 kilometres away and not visible. All she could see was a vast plain covered with bush or cane fields, the winding ribbon of the river trending away northwards. Distant blue mountains to her left rear indicated the Mt Elliott range near Townsville.

"It's certainly a great view," she said as Cadet Norris puffed up to join her.

He grunted and glanced around but was clearly unimpressed. Barbara did not wait but hurried on along the crest line to the next clump of rocks. Here she came upon Cpl Ridgeway and four other cadets. One of them was CSM Warren, still wearing his 'yowie' suit and talking on the radio about some enemy group he could see out on the plain below.

Kneeling down over Cadet Rowland with Cpl Ridgeway was Cpl Colleen McNamara and the sight of her caused Barbara to heave a sigh of relief. Colleen was a medic and she clearly had the situation in hand. The other person was Cadet Bundy from Cpl Ridgeway's section.

Colleen looked up and flashed Barbara a smile. Barbara knelt beside her and looked at Cadet Rowland's leg. Cadet Rowland was a really tiny girl who looked as though a good wind would blow her away. Now she sat on a rock, her grimy, tear-streaked face looking thoroughly miserable.

"How is she?" Barbara asked Colleen.

Cadet Rowland cut in first. "It hurts! And I feel sick. I hate this and I want to go home."

Barbara gave her a hard stare and turned again to Colleen who smiled and said: "She is alright. The ankle is twisted but I don't think it is serious. There is no real swelling. I think her main problem is actually heat. She hasn't drunk enough and is on the edge of getting heat exhaustion."

Barbara flicked an accusing glance at Cpl Ridgeway then turned back to Colleen. "We will take her down the hill then."

"Which way?" Colleen asked.

CSM Warren had finished his radio message by then and chipped in: "There is the safety vehicle down at the Lookout. It would be the closest."

"That will do," Barbara agreed.

"You might flush out those raiders on the way," CSM Warren added.

"Or get captured by them," Barbara replied dryly.

"I will come with you," Colleen said. "I need to refill my water bottles." She turned to CSM Warren. "Can I go CSM?"

CSM Warren thought for a moment, then said: "Take Cpl Foggarty with you. I don't want you walking back to us through the bush on your own."

Barbara looked around, then told Cpl Ridgeway to go back to the power line with Cadet Bundy. "We will look after Cadet Rowland. You keep up the good work Cpl Ridgeway. You are doing a very good job," she added.

Cpl Ridgeway nodded and flushed with pleasure at her praise, then set off back towards the power line, followed by his cadet. Barbara turned to CSM Warren. "Where is your OP?"

CSM Warren pointed. "Just down past those rocks. We heard the yelling and joined in. Gave the Poms a real shock when we just stood up out of the grass in our yowie suits. Nearly caught them too, but then Cadet Rowland here hurt herself, so we stopped."

Barbara laughed as she conjured up the images. By then Cpl Foggarty, a HQ NCO, had joined them with a bundle of empty water bottles. Colleen helped an unwilling Cadet Rowland to her feet.

"It hurts!" she whimpered.

Colleen made an unsympathetic face. "It probably does but we aren't going to bust our guts trying to carry you down this hill on a stretcher just for a sprained ankle. Just take it slow and start walking," she said.

Her tone of voice clearly indicated she wasn't convinced that the sprain was all that real or all that serious.

Cadet Rowland muttered and grumbled but set off, supported on one side by Colleen and on the other by Barbara. Cpl Foggarty and Cadet Norris were sent ahead to scout, just in case the British cadets were hiding somewhere in the long grass and rocks on the hillside.

The group angled to the right but found themselves on top of a steep cutting which was quite impassable. Faced by that they had to angle around the hill to the left. It was slow going as they waited for Cadet Rowland to limp and lower herself down from rock to rock. That gave Barbara plenty of time to look around.

Below her was the main road and the Lookout. A Land Rover was parked there but no-one was visible. Beyond it was a steep drop to the light railway and the deep cutting. The hillside then dropped away to Deep Creek.

LCpl Wright was right, the weeds along that creek line look pretty thick, Barbara mused.

She was able to study the extensive tangle of rubber vines which extended off across Snake Gully and along the riverbank and decided it was not a place she would want to be.

The steep slope of the cutting continued on so that they had to keep working their way around to the left. The hill seemed larger on this side and Barbara fretted that she had made a wrong decision.

The enemy might strike while I am away, and here I am on the far end of the hill!

Their route now led down to the very eastern end of the hill. The Lookout and Deep Creek area went out of sight and instead they had a view out over the river. Barbara noted once again the wide, deep main stream. She estimated this to be several hundred metres wide, with a large pool four or five kilometres long. From up on the hill the layout more nearly resembled the map; the river coming around in a sweeping curve, with the tree and scrub covered sandy 'island' on their side of the water, then the wide sandy flood channel which was edged abruptly by the line of sandy cliffs.

The glint of sunlight on distant rooftops caused Barbara to pause and take out her map. The buildings were several kilometres away and on the far side of the river at the point where the river began its curve. The map informed her that these were the homestead buildings of the 'Byrne Valley' cattle station.

After a drink and waiting a dozen times for a grumbling Cadet Rowland the group at length reached the main road just at the point where the cutting ended. In front of them, directly across the main road, the light railway curved into view again. Up to their right a hundred metres away was the turn-off of the gravel road to the Lookout.

After waiting for a car which sped past at high speed, they crossed the main road and walked up the verge to the Lookout Track. As they puffed up this in the still, hot air Barbara noted with mild dismay that the Land Rover was no longer there. Instead a white utility stood parked in the middle of the Lookout. CORNFORD LOOKOUT read a welded steel sign on the outside edge.

Two young men dressed in jeans and work shirts stood beside the utility. They were looking out at the riverbed. One was talking on a mobile phone and the other was using a pair of binoculars. They did not hear the cadets coming until they were quite close and the one with the mobile phone started with surprise and tapped his companion on the arm.

The young man with the binoculars lowered them and looked around, his eyes widening in surprise.

Gosh! He's handsome, Barbara thought, noting a rugged, ruddy face with bright blue eyes and wavy black hair.

"Sorry," she said. "We didn't mean to sneak up and give you a fright."

The young man with the mobile phone, a big, solid older version of the one with the binoculars, grunted and shrugged. The smaller, better looking one smiled and shook his head.

"You didn't," he said.

As he spoke his eyes swept over Barbara and then over the others. "Who are you people?" he asked.

"Army cadets doing an exercise," Barbara replied. "We are chasing some British army cadets. You haven't seen any people in a dark green sort of camouflage uniform, have you?"

The young man met her eyes and smiled, then pointed along the dry bed of the river. "Would that be some of them?"

Barbara's eyes followed his finger and she saw four tiny figures plodding away from her across the bare white sand just below the steep line of soil cliffs. The figures were at least a kilometre away and were moving slowly in single file.

"That looks like some. May I borrow your binoculars?" Barbara asked.

"Sure," the young man replied. He handed Barbara the binoculars and she quickly focused them. Into the blurred circles leapt brown and dark green mottled clothes.

"That is them," Barbara said. She handed the binoculars back.

Colleen stepped up beside her. "Can I have a look please?"

"Sure," the young man agreed, handing the binoculars to her. As he did Barbara noted his eyes widen with interest as he realized just how pretty Colleen was.

Colleen focused the binoculars and stared, then said: "They can't be the ones we chased. They couldn't have gotten that far that quickly."

"No, you are right," Barbara agreed. She turned to the young man. "You didn't see any of them come down the hill there just now did you?"

The young man shook his head. "No, sorry. We just got here."

"Just testing our mobile phone," the older one added. "I want to see just where we can get reception."

Barbara nodded. She had often seen Major Wickham or Lt Barker doing just that. She said: "Was there a Land Rover here when you arrived?"

"Didn't see one," the young man replied, but his eyes were on Colleen, who smiled and blushed.

Barbara gestured to Cadet Rowland, who now sat in sulky silence on the grass. "She's twisted her ankle and is hot. The Land Rover is our safety vehicle."

"Can we help?" the young man asked.

"Oh we'll be right thanks. It isn't an emergency," Barbara replied. "The Land Rover will be back in a minute."

Cpl Foggarty interrupted to say, "Those Pommy cadets are climbing up into those rubber vines."

Barbara turned and watched as the distant British cadets clambered up the steep slope one at a time, to vanish from view. She unclipped her CB radio and called up LCpl Ray. He reported he was nearly back at the culverts.

Barbara asked him to use the radio there to pass on the location of the British raiders as soon as he got there and said she would be back in ten minutes.

While she was doing this the Land Rover arrived back. Capt Hamilton was driving. He parked the vehicle and got out.

"Everything alright Barbara?" he asked, eyeing the two young men suspiciously.

Barbara pointed to Cadet Rowland. "Cadet Rowland is sick from the heat, and says she has sprained her ankle. Could you take her back to camp sir?"

"Just been there," Capt Hamilton replied. "Took another British cadet in, sick from the heat, Charles Bletchley, poor chap!" As he said this his voice changed to an imitation English accent and they all smiled, even the two young men.

"Get in Cadet Rowland," Barbara said, gesturing to the Land Rover. She turned to Capt Hamilton. "Can you give us a lift back to the turn-off near camp please sir?"

"What, all of you?"

"No, only Cadet Norris and myself. Colleen and Cpl Foggarty are going back up the hill," Barbara replied.

"We need water sir," Colleen added.

"Yes, here's a jerry can," Capt Hamilton replied. He heaved out a plastic water jerry and they all set to work to fill their water bottles.

As they did Barbara became aware that the two young men were staring at them. She glanced up and met the eyes of the big, solid one. He was looking at her with the male look she hated: a sort of undressing-her-with-his-eyes leer. She curled her lip and looked away, noting as she did that the handsome younger one was studying Colleen with open admiration.

As Colleen completed filling her water bottles, she moved behind the Land Rover. She gestured with her head towards the young man. "Isn't he handsome," she whispered.

"He's OK," Barbara agreed.

"I reckon he's a real hunk," Colleen added.

"He likes you," Barbara said, noting the coy flush mottle Colleen's neck and cheeks. Her black eyes danced with pleasure.

"Pity he lives way out here in the sticks," she said. "Do you think they are brothers?"

"They look like it," Barbara agreed.

The two young men had struck up a conversation with Capt Hamilton and Barbara heard the older one ask if there really were British cadets in the area. When told they were he said: "Strewth! They are a long way from home. They must find it a bit bloody hot here."

The younger man came over to where Barbara and Colleen stood. *He is only about seventeen or eighteen,* Barbara decided, noting his clear skin and good teeth.

The young man waved his hand. "Hi! I'm Michael. Sorry if we were rude. I didn't know there were girls in the army cadets."

"Well there are," Barbara answered, but she noted his eyes were on Colleen, who met his and blushed.

"Where do you come from?" Michael asked.

"Townsville," Colleen replied.

"So do I! How come I have never seen you around?" Michael asked.

"Probably went to a different school," Colleen replied. "Which school did you go to?"

"Columba Catholic College, the boarding school in Charters Towers," Michael replied.

"I go to St Pats," Colleen replied.

For a second Barbara wondered if Michael was going to ask straight out if Colleen was a Catholic. She noted Colleen smile and her eyes sparkle.

Bloody hell! He's a fast worker this bugger, she thought.

Then she experienced what she knew was a spasm of jealousy as young Michael obviously had eyes only for Colleen.

Capt Hamilton saved them. "OK Cpl McNamara, you and Cpl Foggarty get going back up that hill. The exercise has only an hour to run. Get in Barbara, and you Norris."

"See you then," Colleen said to Michael.

For a moment Barbara thought Michael was going to ask Colleen for her phone number or address but he just gave a wry smile and nodded. Colleen and Cpl Foggarty set off down the gravel track back to the main road. Barbara and Norris climbed into the Land Rover and Capt Hamilton got in and started up. As he turned the vehicle Barbara saw the two brothers get into the ute.

It followed them down onto the main road and along it. As they turned left along the bitumen Barbara saw Michael give Colleen a wave as she climbed up the bank into the long grass.

What a bloody smoothie! she thought, but she smiled. *Lucky Colleen! She needs a bit of a lift.*

The two vehicles drove down through the cutting and around the curve. At the turn-off to the gravel scrape the Land Rover slowed and pulled in. As it did the ute went past and Michael gave her a wave as well. She gave one in return and watched the vehicle vanish around the bend towards Landers Creek.

Barbara climbed out and extracted her webbing. So did Cadet Norris. Capt Hamilton leaned out.

"Open the gate for us Cadet Norris," he called.

Cadet Norris walked the twenty paces to the wire gate and tried to open it. He fumbled so much that Barbara lost patience and went to help him. It was a typical wire gate, held back by a straining latch but, like many city kids, Norris had obviously never seen one.

"Like this," Barbara said, showing him how to undo it.

Norris blushed and grunted his thanks. He began dragging it aside.

"Keep the wires taut," Barbara cautioned, "otherwise they get tangled."

Norris did as he was told. He had just finished opening the gate when sudden yells from the region of the Gravel Scrape sounded.

"An attack! They are attacking the HQ!" Barbara cried. She gestured to get down. "Cadet Rowland, get out and join us."

Very unwillingly Cadet Rowland did this. She then crouched in the grass beside the road. Barbara listened. The sounds of people shouting 'bang' seemed to be coming from the far side of the gravel pit. She could just make out where the CP hutchie was under its camouflage net. There was movement there but the people she could see were in Australian army DPCU. She had a glimpse of Lt Barker dashing down past the infamous gravel heap towards the CP.

"We will go to help sir," Barbara called to Capt Hamilton. He nodded assent so Barbara gestured to Norris and Rowland and began running along the gravel road towards the HQ.

She had only gone a hundred paces, to where the track curved slightly right beside the gravel pit, before she spotted movement among the trees off to her left. A glimpse of dark green and brown camouflage uniform alerted her, and she scuttled sideways to her right and dived for cover. As she opened her mouth to warn Norris and Rowland there were loud shouts of 'Bang! Bang! Gotcha!' from the bushes twenty metres to her left.

Oh damn! Ambushed! Barbara swore angrily to herself.

It was such an obvious tactic, to set a trap for the relief column, that she mentally berated herself for rushing in like a fool, even as she rolled off the road and down the bank into the overgrown depression of the gravel pit.

To her relief Norris and Rowland both joined her and began pretending to shoot back, or at least Norris did. Barbara yelled at Rowland to do likewise. Barbara then bobbed up to look around, noting that there were probably only two or three of the British cadets in contact with them, although there were obviously more attacking the HQ. As she did, she was almost paralysed by terrible flashbacks to the real fighting she had been involved in the previous year at Dotswood. Horrific images of stuttering automatic weapons, blood and dead men filled her mind. Then she blinked and shook her head to chase the mental demons away.

This is only an exercise, she told herself. Then she thought, *Oh heck! What should I do now?*

Barbara looked anxiously around as she tried to calm her anxiety and save her own and the unit's reputation. She glanced left and noted that Capt Hamilton was still at the gate, watching with interest and obviously not going to join in.

As she crouched under cover there was a lull in the shouting. Then a voice called out from the bushes across the track, in a very English upper-class accent: "Britannia One, Colonials Nil!"

Ooh! You cheeky, arrogant bugger! Barbara thought. The tone of patronizing superiority got right up her nose. *I'll show you, you stuck up bloody Pom!*

But she had to laugh, as the call was so apt.

Chapter 10

THE HONOURABLE FREDDY

Barbara wiped perspiration from her face and blinked to clear her eyes, then cautiously raised her head again, this time behind a small bush. After a rapid sizing up of the situation she ducked and grabbed her CB Radio.

"One One Charlie, where are you? Over."

Almost at once LCpl Ray answered, although the signal strength was weak and the voice distorted. "At the railway, Sunray, over."

"Get your patrol to Company HQ fast," Barbara said. "Tell Sgt Brady that the Company Headquarters is under attack. He is to guard the culverts with three cadets. You bring the others, got that? Over."

"Roge... (crackle...crackle), ove..."

"Come up the creek to the fence across it. Go past that and turn right, then line up on top of the bank and advance towards the dirt road leading in from the main highway. We are pinned down by two or three enemy near the gate. We will be on your right front, over."

"Roger, over," LCpl Ray replied.

"Move fast! Out," Barbara ordered.

She found she was shaking with excitement and wondered if she had made the right decision. She knew Sgt Brady would have been a better choice to lead the counterattack but was still worried that the raiders might strike at the culverts and she wanted a strong leader there in that case.

When Ray gets here I can take command, she reasoned.

There were more shouts and sounds of mock battle from the Gravel Scrape area, which gave Barbara the information that Coy HQ was still holding off the raiders. The loudest of the voices was Lt Barker's, from which she deduced he was back from taking the troublemakers back to Townsville. The thought of them caused her a sour twist of the lips.

She glanced at her watch. 1605. Time seemed to drag. The thought occurred to her that the raiders across the track might pull out before Ray's patrol arrived.

She squirmed around and called to Norris and Rowland, pointing as she did. "Get up and pretend to shoot back. Be ready to attack."

Norris at once obeyed and began yelling 'Bang! Bang!' as loud and fast as he could. Rowland made a half-hearted attempt to lift her head but then just hunched down and looked pained. Barbara shook her head in annoyance and joined in the action herself.

As she raised her head, she detected movement thirty metres away. "Bang! Got you!" she shouted.

A figure in the dark green camouflage dived for cover and rolled behind a log in the short brown grass. He began to 'shoot' back, calling to his companion to pull back as he did.

They are trying to get away, Barbara thought. *Oh! Where is Ray?*

She raised her radio. "Hurry up Cpl Ray. They are pulling out!" she snapped, forgetting to use correct radio voice procedure in her excitement.

There was no answer from LCpl Ray so she did not know if he heard her. She again raised the radio to her mouth, then stopped. Coming into view through the spindly trees on her left front and behind the two British cadets were moving figures in Austcams.

Voices began to shout. At the same moment LCpl Ray yelled charge one of the British cadets spotted them. He shouted:

"Run for it Jeremy old boy, the jolly colonials have got around behind us."

It sounded so quaint and 'put on' that Barbara had to laugh, even as she 'opened fire' again. Then she stood up and shouted: "Cpl Ray, keep going. Here we are."

She saw two figures in green cams start running but the one who was doing the ordering had left it too late and almost collided with LCpl Ray, who shouted at him to surrender.

The British cadet made a run for it but a small anthill, hidden in the grass, was his undoing. He went down in a sprawling heap and LCpl Ray and another cadet were standing over him before he could rise. By then Barbara was up and running, yelling to Norris and Rowland to follow.

Fifty paces in twenty seconds had Barbara standing over the British cadet as well. His companion was still withdrawing through the bushes towards the Gravel Scrape, firing as he went, and being hotly engaged by two of Ray's cadets.

"Surrender!" Barbara shouted, looking down at the British cadet as he went to rise. Dust and grass coated his face and beads of sweat trickled down through a coating of grime.

He looked up at Barbara, then grinned. "To you, willingly," he said.

"Don't get fresh!" Barbara snapped. "Now get up, and don't try any funny business." As he rose, Barbara turned to LCpl Ray. "Wheel your section left and keep attacking across to the far side of the Gravel Pit between the road and Deep Creek. Co-ordinate with HQ so you don't run into them. Cadet Norris, guard the prisoner."

LCpl Ray shouted to his two cadets and changed direction. They began running towards the Gravel Scrape, obviously enjoying themselves immensely. Barbara turned back to her prisoner and got a little shock. He had wiped his face and now smiled at her, grey eyes twinkling in a ruggedly handsome face.

The British cadet was about her own age she decided. As she went to speak, he got in first. "Cadet Colour Sergeant The Honourable Frederick William Masters at your service ma'am."

Barbara was taken aback by the formal introduction and 'upper class' speech. It sounded so 'put on' to her she had to smile. "Cadet Under-Officer Brassington," she replied.

The Honourable Frederick raised a quizzical eyebrow and indicated the cloth rank slide on her uniform. "Is that what that indicates, that you are a cadet officer?"

"A CUO, a Cadet Under-Officer. That is the highest rank a cadet can reach in Australia," Barbara corrected. As she did a trickle of blood ran out of The Honourable Frederick's nose and down his face. "Oh! You are hurt!"

The Honourable Frederick used the back of his hand to wipe the blood away. He glanced at it and said off-handedly: "Yes, came a bit of a cropper then on that beastly rock. Nothing serious though."

Before she could stop herself, and knowing as she did that she was being silly, she said: "I would have thought it would have been bluer than that."

The Honourable Frederick burst out laughing and grinned. "Jolly good that one! Sorry sweetie, but my family are not real 'blue bloods'. Daddy got his peerage for being a jolly good general. If you want a proper 'blue blood' then you had better meet Charles Handley. His family go back to the Norman Conquest at least."

"Sorry. I didn't mean to be rude," Barbara replied. "Pardon my ignorance, but who is your father?"

"General Sir William Masters. At the moment he is the General Officer Commanding British Forces in Europe," The Honourable Frederick replied.

Barbara realized she knew very little about the English aristocracy, and even less about the British Army and its command structure. As more blood trickled out she said: "You'd better come over to HQ and we will get a medic to look at that."

"Oh, I will be alright sweetie," The Honourable Frederick replied.

"Don't call me sweetie!" Barbara snapped. She didn't care what his title was at that moment. He was now just another patronizing male and that always made her blood boil.

"Sorry!" The Honourable Frederick replied, but he smiled and winked at Norris, who had to hide a grin.

As they walked through the short stretch of open bush beside the Gravel Pit, they met LCpl Ray and his two cadets. They had captured the other British cadet. The Honourable Frederick called out to him: "You should do more exercise Jeremy old chap."

Jeremy laughed. "You should talk Freddy. I ran into a bloody great open area and got cut off. Those other rotters withdrew and left us to face the beastly colonials on our own."

Barbara noted that Jeremy wore corporal's chevrons. "Who are you?" she asked.

Jeremy was a big lad, with bright hazel eyes and freckles. He looked her up and down with evident approval. "Cpl Jeremy Parkhurst, and that is all I am going to tell you. Who are you gorgeous?"

That nettled Barbara. "I'm a cadet under-officer, so show some respect!" she snapped. "Now go that way."

To her annoyance Jeremy smirked and winked at The Honourable Freddy, who laughed again. Barbara marched her prisoners over to the overgrown Gravel Scrape to the area near the central mound where Lt Barker and Lt Peters waited. Nearby, lying in a line under cover, were the HQ cadets with Jane very obviously in command and enjoying herself. She stood up and came to join them.

Lt Barker looked the prisoners over then said: "Thanks Barbara. You arrived just in time. Who have we here?"

"Barbara eh?" Jeremy said, giving Barbara a cheeky look.

She pretended not to notice this, but Jane Carson did and she giggled, attracting the attention of both British cadets. As Jane was a very attractive girl, they gave her an appraising stare, which she returned.

Oh dear! Barbara thought. *I hope Jane and Chloe aren't going to get up to their old tricks.* In their younger days both Jane and Chloe had been notorious for nudity and sex. Despite this Barbara had come to like them. *If they muck up the OC will chuck them out, which would be a pity,* she thought. Jane had been well behaved recently and both she and Chloe seemed to be maturing.

Lt Barker called out and Sgt Newell, the medic Sgt, and her assistant, Cpl Katie Melony, both came down from among the bushes on the central mound. The Honorable Frederick's nose had begun to bleed again, and Barbara felt a spurt of satisfaction when she noted he was very pale under the grime.

The medics took him and sat him in the shade of the tree beside the CP tent, then proceeded to fuss over him. That caused Barbara to experience another spurt of annoyance and emotion, which it took her a moment to recognize as jealousy.

Oh nonsense! He is just a cheeky boy, Barbara told herself.

Lt Barker turned to Barbara. "You had better get your people back to guarding those culverts Barbara, just in case there are more of these blokes around."

"Chaps sir, not blokes," Barbara replied.

At that The Honourable Frederick laughed again. He looked up and met her eyes, his own twinkling: "You should call her cadet under-officer sir. She doesn't like being called Barbara or sweetie," he said.

"Not by rude strangers!" Barbara snapped. She spun on her heel and strode away, annoyed that she had risen to the jibe, and at the fact she was blushing.

"You are rude Freddy old boy," Jeremy added. "I wouldn't speak to a lady like that, particularly one as beautiful as her."

Barbara blushed even more at that and was simultaneously pleased and peeved. She pretended not to hear.

"Come on Cpl Ray, bring your people."

As she walked back along the track, she passed Cadet Rowland, who was still sitting under a tree looking miserable.

"Oh for heaven's sake Cadet Rowland! HQ is just there. Go to the medics," she snapped.

Barbara waited till Cadet Rowland had stood up and begun limping towards HQ then walked on with her cadets to the gate where she found Major Wickham talking to Capt Hamilton. She gave Major Wickham a brief account of the action. He praised her platoon's effort, then looked at his watch.

"Go back to the culverts but you can call your people in after another ten minutes. Four Platoon are already on the way back. Have all your people in by seventeen hundred."

"Yes sir," Barbara replied. She walked on, feeling quite pleased with the way the afternoon had worked out.

The platoon has had some success and that should help them pull themselves up after this morning's disaster, she thought.

Two minutes later she re-joined Sgt Brady at the railway culvert. As she did, he warned her and pointed down the creek. Two figures in green cams had appeared. A second glance revealed them to be adult officers. They were making no attempt to use concealment, so Barbara stood and waited for them.

As they got closer, she saw the leader was a tubby, grey-haired major. The man behind him was a tall, thin lieutenant. They made their way up to Barbara and Sgt Brady. The major stopped a few paces away and wiped his face.

"I'm Major Grogan, OC of the British cadets. Don't you people salute officers?"

He said it mildly, but it was still a rebuke to Barbara's military etiquette. She made a move to salute, then restrained herself.

"The Australian Army doesn't salute in the field sir. Sorry, no disrespect intended. I'm Cadet Under-Officer Barbara Brassington, commander of One Platoon, and this is Sgt Brady, my platoon sergeant."

"Oh I see. Well, thanks for clearing up that little misunderstanding," Major Grogan said. "How do you do? This is Lt John Jeffries."

The lieutenant stuck out his hand for Barbara to shake. *He looks a nice sort of chap,* she thought, then smiled at the choice of the word chap.

Major Grogan asked: "Can you show us the way to your HQ please?"

"Certainly sir. We are all going there in a minute. Sgt Brady, call in Cpl Ridgeway's section. Tell them to go straight back to camp."

Sgt Brady did this then informed Coy HQ they were moving in. He knelt to unscrew the ten-foot rod antenna while Barbara explained the rank of Cadet Under-Officer, the British not having any equivalent.

By the time the radio was packed ready to carry the OP party from near Snake Gully had appeared down the creek. There were three of them led by the CQMS, Sgt Dunstan. Cpl Keith followed then Cpl Forest, the Sig Cpl. He was carrying an army radio. All three wore yowie suits and looked very business-like.

Major Grogan looked at them in surprise. "By Jove! That is jolly good camouflage. Where did you chaps spring from?"

"You walked right past us back up on that low open ridge sir," Sgt Dunstan replied. He introduced himself and there were more handshakes. The whole party then set off back towards the camp, Barbara and her platoon bringing up the rear.

As they emerged on the main road, they met 4 Platoon marching back in single file. Four British cadets followed them.

"Did you capture them?" Barbara asked CUO Callan as they met.

CUO Callan shook his head. "Met them just back at the last creek. They were on their way here. We chased off a different lot several times though."

"How do you know it was the same group?" Barbara asked.

"They were led by a big female cadet," CUO Callan answered.

"And you didn't catch her! That's not like you," Barbara chided. She knew CUO Callan considered himself to be God's gift to women.

Like most stupid males! she thought.

By then 2 Platoon and 3 Platoon had also appeared, marching back around the bend. Barbara led her platoon on as part of the line. At the gate they were met by Capt Hamilton who told them to keep going.

Back at the Gravel Scrape CSM Warren met them and ordered the platoon sergeants to seat their platoons in section groups. This meant each section sat in a line behind its section commander, the platoons side by side. This was normal procedure for the end of every exercise. It enabled a careful check to be made to ensure no-one was missing. At the same time it got them in a compact group so the OC or whoever could debrief or give instructions.

Barbara joined the officers over to one side. Major Wickham went to introduce her to the two British officers, but they all smiled and assured him they had already met. As they talked, she looked around and noted a dozen British cadets seated nearby. By a process which seemed like magic her eyes met those of the Honourable Freddy. He grinned and winked, causing her to experience a simultaneous rush of pleasure and annoyance.

Blushing and trying not to, Barbara turned her back on them and began to discuss the exercise with CUO Roberts. Robbo looked hot and tired and not too happy. Her platoon had only briefly encountered two British patrols all afternoon and her cadets were bored.

From the conversation Barbara gathered that one of the British patrols was still missing, the one led by the girl. Barbara noted Cpl Ridgeway's section come in through the bush and gave him a smile of approval. She was pleased with how 1 Platoon had performed and realized she already had a proprietorial feeling of identification.

Lt Forster came in from the Landers Creek direction with a sick cadet from 4 Platoon. His vehicle was parked with the others and the sick cadet limped over to join his section.

CSM Warren came over and reported to Major Wickham that all the Australian cadets were present. Major Wickham looked at his watch.

"1715. It will be dark in an hour. We'd better get this organized then go looking for the missing patrol."

Having said this he asked Major Grogan to bring his cadets over to stand in a group at the side. The British cadets and their officers were then introduced. After the introductions Major Wickham said: "I hope they gave you all a good surprise and a good run for your money."

This raised a chorus of ribald comments and jibes about who had won and who had lost. Barbara noted several of the British cadets looking at Chloe, who stood near them and she had to smile.

I had better have a word to Chloe, she decided.

Major Wickham went on: "We are going to do a night exercise later. It will be our seniors plus the British cadets against the juniors."

"Oh sir!" CUO Callan interjected. "That won't be fair. We can beat the juniors on our own anytime."

This caused another chorus of laughter and jeers. Major Wickham held up his hand for silence. "Orders for that will be at eighteen thirty and the exercise will start at twenty hundred. Between now and then you are to eat and get ready."

Major Wickham handed back to the CSM and turned to discuss finding the 'lost patrol' with Major Grogan and the other officers. It was clear to Barbara that neither OC was worried as they had radio contact with them and were assured they were safe and making their way in. The CSM instructed the platoon sergeants to take their people back to their platoon areas to eat. There was a general scatter as lines of cadets filed off in all directions.

Chloe came striding over and stood with her hands on her hips facing the British cadets. "I am Sgt Cummings. You people are to camp next to Four Platoon. Get your gear and I will show you where."

Barbara looked at Chloe and shook her head. As usual the usually shapeless camouflage uniform did little to hide Chloe's ample curves and she appeared to be standing in such a way as to emphasize her shape.

One of the British cadets leered at her. "Camp next to you eh?" he said with evident approval.

"Dream on!" Chloe replied, but she smiled and her eyes twinkled mischievously.

She turned and led them over to where their packs lay in a line near the CP tent. With nothing better to do Barbara strolled over to watch the British cadets as they picked up their packs.

As she did, she saw one of them point to Chloe and say: "What about her then Freddy?"

The Honourable Freddy grinned with approval and was about to reply when he caught sight of Barbara. Instead he smiled at her and picked up his pack. Then he turned to Barbara.

"Where is your platoon bivvied up Cadet Under-Officer Barbara ma'am?"

"Not near you," Barbara replied. She tried to give him a look of disapproval but found herself smiling instead.

"Too bad," The Honourable Freddy replied. "I was hoping you might be able to advise me on how to survive in the jolly old Australian bush, what with all these drop bears and hoop snakes and whatever."

Barbara had to laugh. It was obvious that the Aussies had been practicing on the credulity of the newcomers. It was equally apparent they were not in the least deceived. "You had better follow Chloe and have your tea before it gets dark," she said.

"Who's Chloe?" asked a tall, handsome British colour sergeant.

"Sgt Cummings," Barbara replied, indicating Chloe as she walked away.

The colour sergeant stared after her and stroked his chin with evident appreciation. "By Jove yes!"

That nettled Barbara. "And you behave yourselves. We don't approve of that sort of behaviour in this unit."

The colour sergeant turned to smile at her and said: "So we heard. Is that the famous gravel heap?"

The question was very innocently put but caused Barbara to flame with embarrassment and annoyance.

Bloody hell! she thought. *Some big mouth in our unit has already aired our dirty linen in public!*

At that The Honourable Freddy came over. "That was a bit below the belt Charles."

The colour sergeant named Charles nodded. "Sorry. You are right. I apologize. Quite uncalled for. Please accept my apology."

It was so sincerely said that Barbara nodded. As she did The Honourable Freddy said to her: "This is the chap I said you should meet. Charles, meet Cadet Under-Officer Barbara Brassington. Barbara, ma'am, meet The Honourable Charles Handley, the future Lord Matchlock."

As she looked into the hazel eyes of The Honourable Charles Barbara felt quite flustered. Two thoughts swamped her consciousness: that The Honourable Freddy had remembered her whole name; and that she was meeting a true-blue Pommy aristocrat.

And a very handsome one at that!

Chapter 11

SPARKS

For a minute Barbara watched Chloe flirting with the British cadets, then, noting both Lt Peters and Lt Cavendish watching, decided she must warn Chloe.

With that in mind she marched towards Chloe, who luckily glanced around and saw her. In answer to a quizzical look from Chloe Barbara beckoned her over.

"Yes ma'am?" Chloe asked.

"Chloe, for God's sake don't give the officers any reason to discipline you," Barbara said. She gave a faint indication with her head in the direction of the two lady OOCs as she did.

Chloe glanced in that direction then looked squarely at Barbara. "Thanks Barbara, I mean CUO Brassington. I know that pair of... er... officers, are watching me like hawks. They are just itching for me to make a slip so they can complain and get me tossed out."

"So don't give them any reason please. I want you to survive and succeed," Barbara answered.

The hard look on Chloe's face softened back to its usual deceptive 'Little Miss Innocent' look and she smiled. "You are a really good person, Barbara. Thank you. Now don't worry. Jane and I just intend to do a bit of flirting. It's not every day a girl gets a chance like this. Some of these boys are real true-blue English upper class."

Barbara gave a wry smile. "If you get attached to one of them you could end up living in a foreign country and your kids wouldn't be Australian."

"Isn't that what you are thinking of doing?" Chloe replied.

"What do you mean?" Barbara answered, her mind filling with images of Raoul and France.

"Hasn't that hunky French commando asked you to marry him?" Chloe riposted.

Barbara was instantly swamped with a mix of emotions. "Yes, he has," she replied.

If it had been any other person but Chloe, who had done so much for her and who had saved her life, she was sure she would have told them to mind their own business.

"Well?"

"I... I haven't made my mind up yet. And what I just talked about is one of the main negatives. I want my kids to grow up in Australia," Barbara replied.

"Me too," Chloe said, but she looked wistful. "If I ever have any," she added.

"Oh you will!" Barbara cried. "You have no trouble attracting male attention."

"Yes," Chloe replied, her lips twisting into a wry smile. "But mostly the wrong sort."

"Oh Chloe, Mr Right will come along, your knight in shining armour."

Chloe shook her head vigorously and looked quite downcast. "No Barbara. It's easy for you. You are normal. But I'm not."

"You are! You are a beautiful young woman," Barbara protested.

Chloe again shook her head. "I know, but I'm also something of a freak. Ever since I was little, I have been aware that I am an object of erotic fascination to males of all ages, but they mostly just want to do things to me."

Barbara was appalled at the sadness and anxiety in Chloe's tone. "You will be alright," she said in an attempt to comfort her.

"Maybe, but most men are afraid of me. I don't know what I will do," Chloe said.

"Well, you take care anyway. And thanks for everything," Barbara said.

Chloe smiled at her, but the smile did not reach the eyes. "Thanks Barbara. You are just the most caring person. I hope life goes really well for you."

Barbara was so touched by Chloe's genuine comment that she had to nod and turn away quickly before her face betrayed her. Quickly she walked back towards 1 Platoon area, acutely conscious that both female OOCs were watching. As she went past she managed a smile for both and then a nod at Jane and the HQ cadets as she walked back past the CP Tent to HQ.

Lt Cavendish came with her and they found Sgt Newell and Colleen talking to CUO Roberts and some of the HQ girls.

Barbara gestured behind her. "We had better watch those British cadets Miss," she said. "They are very fresh."

A little frown of concern crossed Lt Cavendish's face. "Anyone in particular?"

"All of them I'd say," Barbara replied, although the faces of The Honourable Freddy and The Honourable Charles both flitted across her mind.

Colleen McNamara chipped in: "Some of them look real dreamy to me. I hope we do get a chance to meet them."

At that all the girls giggled. Barbara had to smile and then said: "We had better watch you carefully then. That is twice in one day you have been making eyes at strange men."

Colleen went crimson, helped by the glow of the setting sun. "Oh I did not!"

"Oh yes you did!" Barbara replied with a laugh.

"What's this?" Lt Cavendish asked.

"There were two young blokes at the Lookout," Barbara replied. "Colleen pretended she wasn't interested but she certainly gave them the once over."

Colleen blushed even more, but she laughed. "Well? The young one was a real dreamy hunk. You thought so too Barbara."

It was Barbara's turn to blush and the others laughed at her evident discomfiture. "Well, yes. He was nice. But you should pay attention to what your mother taught you about strange men Colleen."

She said this with mock seriousness and caused another ripple of laughter. At that moment Major Wickham came over.

"Lt Cavendish, let's go. If we don't find this lost patrol soon it will be dark."

"Have we got coms with them sir?" Lt Cavendish queried.

Major Wickham nodded. "Yes. They sounded like they were in all that rubber vine and stuff along Snake Gully. They were told to just go southwest until they reach the main road and then to wait. They have just reported they are now out in open country and can hear cars on the main road," he explained.

Lt Cavendish walked off with Major Wickham and they drove off in his car to join Lt Barker in a road search for the missing British patrol. Barbara watched them go.

I hope they find them quickly. The night exercise will be cancelled otherwise. She found she was quite looking forward to the night exercise.

By then the sun had gone behind Mt Dalrymple so Barbara walked back to the 1 Platoon bivouac area.

If I don't eat quickly it will be dark, she thought.

On arrival at the platoon area she was pleased to note that the cadets seemed to be happy. They were busy telling jokes and recounting how they had chased the British cadets. Barbara seated herself on her pack and extracted her stove and tins of food.

Spaghetti and Meatballs, she decided, *then tinned peaches and condensed milk.*

130ACU had a simple ration plan for bivouacs. Every cadet just went to the shop beforehand and bought five or six cans or packets of food they liked. Every cadet was issued with a small stove and a packet of hexamine.

Barbara settled to heating the food. As she did, she drank from her water bottle repeatedly, aware that she had become quite dehydrated during the day.

I hope it isn't as hot tomorrow, she thought, noting that some of the cadets looked a bit tired and down.

She ate as quickly as she could, conscious that Major Wickham would want to give orders for the night exercise as soon as he returned. It was as well that she did as she was just repacking her mess tins and stove when two vehicles drove in from the main road.

By then twilight was setting in and the vehicles had their headlights on. Barbara quickly fastened her webbing and stood up. To Sgt Brady she said, "I will be at HQ. Have the platoon ready to go and with full water bottles." She then quickly walked over where the vehicles had pulled up.

From the movement in front of headlights, voices calling and the general stir, it was obvious that the 'lost patrol' had been found. Barbara arrived just as Chloe led them over to where their packs lay in the grass near the CP tent.

The leader of the 'lost patrol' was a big, strapping blonde girl. She directed her cadets to collect their packs. As she did, she caught sight of Barbara and looked at her in the glow of the vehicle headlights.

"Hello," Barbara said. "I'm Barbara. I'm a cadet under-officer."

The girl straightened up. "I'm Adelaide and I'm a cadet WO1. I'm sorry to be rude but should I salute you?"

Barbara shook her head. "Technically yes, but the Australian Army doesn't salute in the bush. It is a custom dating back to World War Two when the Japanese snipers made a practice of shooting the people who got saluted."

"That's sensible. I only asked because I am the RSM and need to be able to advise our people," Adelaide replied. She had a very upper class accent that made Barbara want to smile when she heard it.

At that moment Colleen and Sgt Newell joined them. Sgt Newell asked: "Does anyone need any doctoring?"

Several admitted they had blisters from walking.

Barbara asked: "Did you have to walk far?"

"Bloody miles!" Adelaide replied. "We tried to sneak up on those beastly bridges three times and got seen and chased away each time. The last time we ended up bushed in all this terrible springy vine."

"That will be rubber vine. It can be awful," Barbara said. "How did you get out?"

"We hacked our way west on a compass course till we came to the road, then started walking north along it," Adelaide replied.

"That was sensible. Did you walk all the way back?" Barbara asked.

"Not quite," Adelaide replied. "Two very nice young men in a small white truck gave us a lift, then we saw the army Land Rover and asked them to let us out."

"Oh, that'll be Michael and his brother," Colleen said. "Where did they go?"

"Drove on north along the highway," Adelaide said. "Who's Michael?"

"Oh, just a man we met today," Colleen replied.

Colleen was kneeling in front of one of the male British cadets examining his blistered foot while she talked. She used a torch to provide light to study the young man's foot. By way of conversation she said to him: "What do you think of Australia?"

The male British cadet gave a wry smile. "Not sure yet, but if all the girls are as pretty as you then it must be alright."

Colleen blushed but smiled. "Don't get fresh or I will put antiseptic on this that stings."

The male British cadet returned her smile. "Sorry, no offence meant, but you are very pretty. What's your name?"

"Colleen, Colleen McNamara," Colleen replied.

At that the smile was wiped from the young man's face. Barbara was watching the by-play with mild amusement and was astonished at the abruptness of the transition. The British cadet stared hard at Colleen for a moment, then said: "Are you Irish?"

Colleen had bent her head to apply ointment to the blister so did not notice the change in the young man's expression. She nodded and replied: "Yes, well, no, not really. I was born in Australia, but mum and dad both come from Ireland."

"Catholic?" the British cadet asked in an odd tone which caused a sharp twinge of alarm to Barbara.

"Yes," Colleen replied, looking up and smiling.

As she did the young man wrenched his foot out of her grasp and out of her reach. He stood up, clutching his boot and sock and stared down at her.

"In that case I will do my own doctoring thank you," he snapped.

Before Colleen could even ask what was wrong the young man swung around and limped away, leaving a silent and astonished group behind. Barbara saw a look of bewildered hurt spread across Colleen's face.

"But... but what did I do?" she asked anxiously.

Another male British cadet, seated next to her while Sgt Newell attended to his blisters, answered that one. "You didn't do anything. You are Irish and Cecil hates the Irish."

Once again, a look of hurt confusion crossed Colleen's face. "Hates the Irish! But... but why?"

"They killed his father, in Ulster. It was years ago but he won't let go of it," the British cadet replied.

"I... I... I don't understand. Who did? Why?" Colleen asked.

Adelaide shook her head in disbelief. "You are certainly insulated from things here in Australia. Didn't you ever listen to the news about what used to go on in Northern Ireland?"

Colleen bit her lip and shook her head. "No, not really. I know there was some sort of trouble. Why did the Irish kill his father?"

This time all the British cadets present shook their heads in disbelief.

Even Barbara made the gesture. Once again Adelaide answered: "Cecil's father was a lieutenant in the British Army, on peacekeeping duties in Ulster. An IRA gunman named Shaemus O'Malley shot him at a roadblock."

"What... where... What does IRA mean?" Colleen asked. She looked flustered and Barbara felt sorry for her.

"Irish Republican Army," several people answered. Adelaide added: "They are a secret terrorist army who want Ulster to be part of Ireland, not part of the UK."

"Where's Ulster?" Colleen asked.

Again people looked astonished. "It is the six counties of Northern Ireland," Adelaide replied.

Colleen nodded and ended the conversation by bending to study another cadet's foot.

Barbara, however, was intrigued. "Did they catch this man, the murderer?"

Adelaide shook his head. "No. He escaped. I hope they get him one day."

"How come you know so much about it?" Barbara asked.

"Because Shaemus O'Malley also shot our OC, Major Grogan. That is why he is here. Major Grogan was so badly injured he was medically unfit and was not allowed to continue serving in the army. He told us about it."

"He actually knew the enemy's name?" queried Barbara.

Adelaide nodded. "Major Grogan used to be in Intelligence. He identified this O'Malley character as he tried to escape through a roadblock after a bomb attack."

"Freddy's dad was the CO of the battalion that Cecil's dad was in," added another British cadet, "Isn't that right Freddy?"

"That's right," Freddy replied.

Barbara had not noticed him join them but now their eyes met and he smiled at her. Barbara frowned. She knew that a battalion CO was only a Lieutenant Colonel.

She said: "Isn't your dad a general?"

Freddy nodded. "That's right. This all happened years ago; sixteen or seventeen or so at least."

Colleen looked up. "Has this trouble in Ireland gone on that long?"

At that all the British cadets burst out laughing. Another look of hurt bewilderment crossed Colleen's face. Freddy saw this and said: "Sorry, we didn't mean to laugh at you. The Irish 'troubles' have gone on for hundreds of years."

"But why? What's it all about?" Colleen asked.

"Nationalism and Religion ostensibly; Catholics versus Protestants," Freddy replied, "But really I think it's just bigotry and nationalism run mad."

"And they kill people?" Colleen asked.

"That's right. They used to. By midnight murders, sniping, bombs in shops, and all that," Freddy replied. "Pretty ugly business really. Luckily there has been relative peace the last dozen years or so."

Colleen wrinkled her nose. "It all sounds stupid and ignorant to me. Why did they do it?"

At that moment CSM Warren called out: "Hurry up you lot. CUOs, over to the OC for an Orders Group."

"What about us?" Adelaide asked.

"No. Your OC is giving you your orders," CSM Warren replied. He came over and introduced himself.

Barbara hurried back up to where Major Wickham waited. He was seated on a box and had a hurricane lantern placed on the ground in front of him and was reproving Lt Barker for making flippant comments about the CSM going to check behind the gravel heap during company orders. That made Barbara glance that way and she puckered her lips in sour disapproval of what might have gone on.

*****

That left Colleen with the British cadets for a few more minutes before they were also called back to their platoon area. She was glad when they went as she was feeling resentful and hurt. In all her life she had never really experienced any racism directed at her Irish origin, or at least none worse than 'Irish' jokes. She also felt quite inadequate at not knowing things that everyone else seemed to take for granted.

Thankful it was dark Colleen went over to her gear and sat on her pack to have her tea. It had been a long day for her and one filled with conflicting emotions. When she had woken up she had been quite happy, until she saw Geoff Unsworth in the distance and remembered the rejection of the previous night.

Hurt and annoyance had seethed in her for a while after that, before being swamped by scandalized disgust over the rumoured incident behind the gravel heap the night before. She wasn't sure what had happened, but the rumours certainly hinted at some sort of sexual activity.

Disgusting animals! she had thought.

To her physical love was a special thing, to be done in private with the one you loved; although she had never actually done it and only had a rough idea of what it might be like. To act the way those people were rumoured to have acted left her feeling something precious had been abused and debased. She was also deeply concerned that they were possibly committing mortal sin, one that Father Flannigan had often warned them against.

Disgust had given way to concern as she thought about what she had witnessed. *It can't have been... been too serious,* she told herself. *After all they were all dressed when I saw them and they were only trying to pressure Kathy into doing something then, and the sergeants went there straight after I told them.*

Still feeling disturbed by the possibilities Colleen had offered sincere prayers for their forgiveness and in the hope that they would see the error of their ways and change.

Confused and depressed she had gone off on the exercise, puzzling over whether there was something wrong with her, rather than with them.

Geoff dumped me after all, she thought unhappily.

She had been thankful to busy herself with the observation, map marking and radio work of the exercise as it took her mind off such things, at least until she had helped Barbara get Cadet Rowland down to the Safety Vehicle at the Lookout. There she had noticed the two brothers and had been quite amazed at her own reactions. The moment she had met the younger brother's eyes she had found it hard to breathe and had felt as though she had been charged with electric current. When she went to the Land Rover with Barbara, she found her heart beating rapidly and was astonished to find that she wanted to keep glancing at him.

"Michael!" she had whispered to herself. "His name is Michael."

As she sat in the darkness opening a can of food, she whispered the name again and shook her head in amazement at her own reaction.

I'm being silly, she told herself. *I'll probably never see him again anyway.*

Telling herself that all boys were stupid brutes who only wanted one thing she settled to cooking her food.

Twenty minutes later she joined the other members of HQ for orders. CSM Warren seated them in a group and had them use torches so they could study their maps and take notes. Colleen was tired but still keen to go on the night exercise. She always found them exciting and knew they helped to build up her self-confidence.

CSM Warren explained that it would be a two-sided exercise with HQ and the three 'First Year' platoons on one side and 4 Platoon and the British on the other. HQ and the First Years were the defenders.

CSM Warren pointed to the map. "The whole exercise is to be in the river bed between the end of the hill and the mouth of Landers Creek. We are to be on this long, sandy island with the trees and bushes on it and are to set up HQ and be one of the targets. The other platoons are to be the defenders, working in section patrols."

It took CSM Warren nearly half an hour to explain the orders. By then it was 1930 and the OC was urging them to move. There was a last-minute check of who was staying behind (Lt Cavendish plus three sick); and of radios. Some cadets had failed to refill their water bottles, and this caused more delay which got the CUOs and NCOs urging them to hurry up and to get their act together.

Colleen rolled up her pullover and strapped it to the back of her webbing, then picked up the First Aid Kit and stretcher and moved over to where HQ was lining up in single file in the darkness. A few minutes later Major Wickham joined them and after the CSM and platoon sergeants had done another count of their cadets, led them off into the night.

Chapter 12

NIGHT EXERCISE

At the gate near the main road the company halted while two safety vehicles drove out. Each turned and went in a different direction. The company filed through the gate, being counted by CSM Warren as they did. He then closed the gate and walked to the front of the line which was now halted at the side of the bitumen. The CSM reported the number to Major Wickham, who repeated it.

Standing behind Major Wickham was Cpl Forest, who carried an army radio. CSM Warren stayed out of line, waiting to count the company again. Barbara was the next person after Cpl Forest and her cadets were in single file behind her. They stood quietly talking, for a couple of minutes, until radio messages from both safety vehicles reported they were in position.

Major Wickham then led the company across the road. On the other side they turned right and walked into the grass between the road and light railway. Barbara knew the way quite well after the day's exercise but still had a few twinges of concern about possible snakes.

She was in a good mood and was interested to note her own emotional reactions to having command of a platoon thrust back on her. To her own surprise she found she cared about 1 Platoon and that she wanted it to do well.

I wish we had a few more troops, she thought.

Fourteen wasn't many for the task they had been allocated; the first line of defence against the raiders. The thought of Cadet Rowland staying back at HQ because she was 'sick' annoyed her.

Silly little thing! What did she think she would do when she joined the army cadets?

The line made its way slowly down the creek bank and into the culvert under the railway. As they were doing this without any lights as an exercise in night movement it was almost pitch black in the tunnel. The sound of their boots echoed and the sillier cadets began to make noises and cry out.

Barbara made no attempt to shut them up as she knew it would be a waste of energy in the circumstances. It was obviously a scary experience for the younger ones.

I wouldn't be too keen at going through this on my own without a torch either, she thought wryly.

After traversing the tunnel Major Wickham led the line along the creek bed for 50 metres until they could climb safely out of it. He led the way up onto the creek bank on the left. The company then walked slowly along through the knee-high grass until they reached the creek junction at the powerlines. Here they crossed over to the other side of the creek and went slowly up the cattle pad under the powerlines, then left up onto the crest of the wide, flat ridge which led along between Deep Creek and Snake Gully. Every hundred paces Major Wickham halted to allow the tail end of the line to catch up.

It was easy walking and the stars gave enough light for Barbara to clearly see obstacles such as logs and sticks. It was when they turned right and made their way down the small spur towards Snake Gully that she felt her heart rate really speed up. She had known they were going that way but had tried to thrust out of her mind what it might be like. Now, to her own annoyance, she found she was not looking forward to the experience.

I'm not scared, she told herself, but she had to admit her breathing had sped up along with her heart rate.

She found she was perspiring but put this down to the high temperature. The mass of rubber vines and tall trees now loomed as a real challenge, far more daunting than they had been in daylight. Barbara was glad that Major Wickham was leading. He passed the word back to go very slowly and they made their way, slipping and sliding, down the steep little slope into the gully.

That was bad enough. The tall grass blocked out much of the starlight and seemed filled with menace. The rustling sound of people brushing against it added to Barbara's concern. The grass on both sides of the gully was so close she could touch it. Into her imagination flitted images of an aroused snake striking at her as she walked past. She tried to push this thought out of her mind, telling herself that the company was making so much noise that any snake would have long since fled.

But it might have woken up and not be able to get out of its hole in time, she considered, then wished she hadn't.

After 50 paces of winding along the gully they came to a log and had to crouch to crawl under it. That was much worse as Barbara could imagine spiders as well as snakes lurking there.

Another hundred slow, shuffling paces further on things got even worse as they reached the end of the grassy area and entered the section of gully which wound its way through the thicket of trees and rubber vine. Now it became so dark that she could barely make out the person in front of her and quite literally could not see her hand in front of her face. She knew that because she tried it.

Major Wickham stopped and waited for the tail of the column to catch up, then passed back the instruction for people to hold onto the webbing of the person in front of them. Barbara groped and took hold of CSM Warren's web straps and felt Cpl Ridgeway grab hold of her own webbing. The company then began to grope and stumble its way along the bed of the gully.

Every few paces Major Wickham called a quiet warning as he encountered an obstacle. These were usually tree roots, exposed by flood rains eroding the bottom of the gully. At one of these Barbara climbed carefully over it and said: "Root."

Behind her a boy's voice muttered: "That's what I need!"

Barbara wasn't sure which one of them it was, but it annoyed her and she had to suppress the urge to snap a rebuke into the darkness. Instead she concentrated on moving carefully along.

Snake Gully in the dark took them nearly half an hour to go 500 metres. The last part, in under the big spreading tree, was the worst. Hundreds of tree roots formed a tangle to snare their feet and two large logs half-blocked the gully. They had to clamber over one and crawl under the second. Worse still a large bird swished close overhead, emitting a loud 'hoot' as it did.

"Shit! What was that?" Cpl Ridgeway cried in alarm.

CSM Warren answered. "An owl, I think. I saw two here earlier in the day."

Barbara wiped perspiration from her face and steadied her breathing. "I hope it wasn't a bat," she muttered. She disliked bats with an irrational passion.

"Vampire," Cpl Ridgeway commented.

"Shut up!" Barbara snapped.

"All of you be quiet," Major Wickham called. "Here is the end of the gully."

Thankfully Barbara noted a circle of lightness in the black. She sighed with relief as they stumbled out of the end of the gully and onto the open sand of the riverbed. Major Wickham led them 50 metres out to where a small drop on the edge of a washed-out area of sand gave them a slope to sit on.

CSM Warren ordered 1 Platoon to sit in section lines. Barbara stood and supervised this till Sgt Brady joined her. He reported all present and Barbara then moved to one side to wait. It took nearly five minutes for the remainder of the company to grope and stumble their way out of the black tunnel of Snake Gully. During that time Major Wickham struck a match and lit the hurricane lantern he had carried.

The lantern provided a cheerful and comforting circle of light which helped settle the cadets down after their experience in the dark gully. Major Wickham allowed the cadets five minutes to drink and cool down. While they waited Lt Barker joined them. Barbara knew he had parked one of the safety vehicles up at the Lookout.

He must have walked down, she decided.

Major Wickham next gave the cadets a safety brief, stressing once again that there was to be no physical contact or throwing things. "And stay together in your groups and stay away from the river. There are saltwater crocodiles in it. I don't want anyone eaten by a croc."

He paused to let that sink in, then held up the lantern. "If you get separated or lost then just walk to the light. We will put the lantern up there on the old highway below the Lookout. That is the RV at the end of the exercise."

He handed the lantern to Lt Barker, who set off towards the base of the nearby hill. Major Wickham then ordered them to stand: "Let's move. We need to get into position fairly quickly."

He led the way out across the sand of the riverbed. Barbara got her platoon in line and followed. She quickly discovered that walking on the soft sand was hard going. She also found that her eyes played tricks on her. There were no shadows, so she was quite unable to detect the sudden drops or rises where flood waters had scoured away the sand. Only when she saw Major Wickham suddenly slide downwards, followed by CSM Warren and Cpl Forster, did she realize what was going on. She slid down several metres, calling a warning to those behind her as she did.

The flood channel was a hundred paces wide and ended in a sharp up-slope of a couple of metres. On top of this was a scattering of bushes and flood bent trees. Major Wickham stopped and waited till the line had caught up. By then Barbara found she was panting and perspiring.

"This is the area where your platoon is to deploy CUO Brassington," Major Wickham said.

"Thanks sir," Barbara replied. She told her people to wait while Major Wickham led the remainder of the company on past them. As soon as they were gone Barbara looked around to get her bearings.

The first thing she noted was the dark bulk of the hill a few hundred metres back behind them. She turned to face it. A bright pin-point of moving light indicated where Lt Barker was climbing up with the lantern. Off to her left, back where they had come from, the line of sand cliffs and rubber vine jungle formed a dark mass. Off to her right front were open sand and the faint glint of stars on water. A shallow backwater of the river ran in there halfway to the base of the hill. On her right the steep drop continued on up to a line of trees which she knew were on the sand island.

The sand formed a real dune at the river end. Barbara had noted this in daylight and estimated it to be 5 metres high or more. All the way along her side of the flood channel it formed a steep slope which was difficult to run up.

After a drink she called her NCOs in and pointed right and left. "This is our line to defend. The enemy will come from the north, from the direction of the hill. OK, off you go. Sgt Brady, you take your group back over to the far side of the dry riverbed, right next to the sand cliffs below the rubber vine. Cpl Ridgeway, your group is to be on this small rise with the bushes on it. I will be next just up on the edge of the sand island and LCpl Ray, your group will be over near the river."

"Thanks!" muttered LCpl Ray sarcastically. The others laughed at this and Barbara ignored it, except to say: "Keep your group up on the high part of the sand island and away from the water."

"What do we do if we see a croc?" LCpl Ray asked.

"Shine your torches on it and run," Barbara said, "Now stop fussing and get going. The raiders must already be on their way."

With that she led her own group over to the trees and bushes on the landward edge of the sand island. A grumbling LCpl Ray led his patrol of three on along the edge of the steep slope. As soon as she was in position Barbara called up Sgt Brady and Cpl Ridgeway on the radio. Both answered almost at once.

"And keep your people quiet. I can hear them from here, out," Barbara added.

She could too. The cadets were excited and enjoying themselves and the sound of their voices carried clearly on the still night air. So did other sounds. The most noticeable was the noise of vehicles up on the main road half a kilometre away. The glow of their headlights showed plainly as they rounded the end of the hill through the cutting near the Lookout.

As the sound of a car receded Barbara noted another sound. This caused her to look up. She saw the lights of a jet airliner high overhead. It moved fast across the sky, its navigation lights sliding across the stars towards Townsville.

We must be right under the flight path from Brisbane to Townsville, she decided, remembering seeing several other aircraft during the day.

Then another sound came to her. This caused her to look in all directions until she was sure it was coming from behind her, from the south. She looked that way and noted a glow which could only be headlights, but a long way off. The sound was an odd vibrating noise which changed to a rumble and then to hundreds of tiny clicks.

For a few minutes Barbara puzzled over this. Then she shook her head. *It must be a cane train,* she decided.

She was right, but it took nearly ten minutes to reach the area and by then Barbara's attention was taken up by movement over near the edge of the water. Although she strained her eyes she could not tell if it was a group of raiders or not.

A rumbling roar indicated that the cane train was crossing the Landers Creek Bridge. Barbara kept glancing over her shoulder to monitor its progress, the glow of its headlight just visible among the distant trees. She spent the rest of the time scanning the open sand to her front. The cane train went away from the river as it followed the curve towards the Gravel Scrape, then came towards them through the deep cutting.

As it did the glow of its headlight lit up the far bank of the river and the reflection illuminated the bed of the river. Movement to her right front attracted Barbara's eye. Yes! That was a person. Whoever it was, they had made the mistake of moving, crawling into a dip.

"Over there," Barbara said to the two cadets with her. She unclipped the radio and warned LCpl Ray.

The cane train locomotive went around the bend out of the cutting below the Lookout and on northwards. For what seemed like ages the hundreds of small wire carriages clicked and rattled along behind it until at least a yellow brake van with orange flashing lights suddenly rolled into view briefly, before vanishing.

As the sound of the train died away Barbara heard shouts over to her right towards the river. *LCpl Ray's patrol is in contact,* she thought. She looked that way and tried to call him on the radio. No luck. *He isn't listening,* she told herself.

The shouting grew louder and torch beams flashed out from the edge of the trees where Barbara had seen LCpl Ray lead his people to. In their glow she saw at least five running figures out on the sand flat towards the backwater.

"There they are," she said, pointing so that her two cadets could see them. As Barbara watched several more dark figures scuttled forward across the sand. They were about a hundred metres away. They did not run straight and kept dropping down to crawl or to hide behind small sand hummocks. Barbara tried to count them and was seized by a strong feeling that she had made a mistake.

There seem to be an awful lot. I hope the whole enemy group isn't trying to punch through at one point.

With that thought in mind she decided to go there. "Stay here you two. I am going to help LCpl Ray," she said. With that she set off running across the sand.

She had run only about twenty paces before she slowed. *I'm not being very smart here,* she thought. *I can't do much on my own.*

At that she turned and ran back. "Norris, Croucher! Come with me, quick!"

The two cadets stood up and ran over to her. As they did Barbara turned and resumed running, spurred on by a fresh outbreak of yelling and pretend firing.

Running on the sand was hard going and the three quickly slowed to a rapid plod. Barbara found she was happily excited and knew she was really enjoying herself. She pushed herself to hurry, ignoring her rapid heart rate and panting.

"Hurry up you two, run! Keep up!" she urged as the two cadets began to fall behind.

She reached the upslope and line of flood twisted trees along the edge of the sand island, scrambled up and cast around for the easiest way through the tangle. By then the sound of yelling had died down so she paused in among the trees and bushes to try her radio again while waiting for the two cadets catch up.

This time LCpl Ray answered. "There were five of them," he reported. "They have withdrawn back towards the hill."

The moment she heard this, Barbara was assailed by doubts and suspicions. "Who were they?" she asked. "Were they the Poms, or Four Platoon?"

"Poms, over," replied LCpl Ray.

By then the two cadets had caught up. They stood puffing and perspiring while Barbara bit her lip and tried to decide. With a shake of her head she made up her mind. She pointed back to the west.

"We will go back," she said.

"Aw bloody hell! We just ran here," complained Croucher.

"Tough. That lot have withdrawn, and I think they might have been a feint," Barbara replied.

"A what?"

"A feint, a decoy to draw us away. Come on!" Barbara set off walking fast back the way they had come.

She had only gone ten steps when Cpl Ridgeway called. "One One this is One Three, there is a group of enemy crossing our front towards One Two, over."

"Roger. Stay there, over," Barbara replied.

As she went to call Sgt Brady, he called her. "One One, this is One Two, we are about to be attacked."

No sooner had he said this than shouts and whistle blasts shattered the night over at the riverbank. Barbara began running, sliding down the slope out of the trees and pounding across the lumpy hummocks of the clear flood channel towards the tree-studded rise she had been on earlier.

Even as she reached this and scrambled back up onto the higher ground, she saw shadows moving ahead of her. Enemy! Her heart leapt and she raced forward. In the starlight she saw three figures rise up and start running but she experienced a sharp sense of exultation. They had left their run too late.

"Got you!" she shouted. "Surrender! Bang! Bang!"

The three figures kept running for a few more paces, then dropped flat and pretended to fire back. Barbara dived into a sandy hollow and yelled with the sheer pleasure of the game. As she came up and resumed pretending to shoot, she was joined by Norris and Croucher, both of whom joined in enthusiastically.

As Barbara again called on the three enemy to surrender, she glanced around, aware that her group were not in very good cover. Ten metres to her right front was a clump of bushes and what appeared to be a good dip in the sand.

"This way," she called to her cadets.

She sprang up and dashed across to the bush. As she reached it her heart seemed to stop in fright as a large, dark figure rose up from behind it.

Chapter 13

SURPRISED AND ANNOYED

Before Barbara could call out or stop herself an arm reached out from under the bush and grabbed her leg. She cried out in fright and tried to break free but fell headlong on the sand, right at the feet of the person who quickly stood up.

Hands grabbed her and a very 'English' voice called: "Got you, by Jove!"

"Let me go!" Barbara tried to yell, but sand had gotten into her mouth and she spluttered and spat angrily. "Let me go! Help, Norris!"

The voice in her ear chuckled and said: "Good heavens Freddy old chap, it's Barbie Doll."

At that Barbara's already ruffled dignity exploded into anger. If there was one thing that was a red rag to her it was being likened to a Barbie Doll.

That bloody freak of a bimbo! she thought. *How dare they!*

Anger fuelled her struggles and she broke free. As she rolled over in the soft sand, she felt hands clutch at her, one even brushing her bosom. It was The Honourable Charles, she realized. "Keep your hands off me! Let me go!" she shouted.

By then she was on her knees with Freddy close beside her and Charles a pace in front.

Where are those cadets of mine? she wondered, her annoyance sparking more anger.

As Charles reached out to grab at her again, she struck his hand away and shouted angrily: "Keep your hands off me! You touch me again and I'll have you charged with assault!"

At that Charles held up both his hands. "Here, I say! Steady on! No offence meant Barbie. I was only trying to take you prisoner," he said. He sounded genuinely shocked and concerned.

"Don't you listen to exercise orders?" Barbara snapped. "No physical contact they said. So don't start grabbing hold of anyone. I don't care what you do in England, but they are the rules here."

"Sorry Barbie. I..." Charles began.

At that Barbara exploded: "And stop calling me Barbie! I'm not a bloody plastic toy! I'm a person. And you call me Cadet Under-Officer Brassington or ma'am."

"Oooh, yes ma'am!" Charles replied, but he had a chuckle in his voice which infuriated Barbara even more.

"And you can both put your hands up. You are my prisoners!" she yelled.

Freddy stepped forward. "Oh I don't think so. You've only got two with you and there are five of us. I think you are our prisoner."

Barbara felt a surge of embarrassment. Captured! She did not want to look foolish. *That is twice in one day Freddy has ambushed me,* she thought with annoyance.

At that moment she heard the thud of running boots and the gasp of laboured breathing. To her relief Cpl Ridgeway's voice came to her from 50 paces away: "CUO Brassington, where are you?"

"Over here Cpl Ridgeway. Bring your section. I've got five prisoners," she shouted back. She could not resist giving Freddy a grin.

Freddy grinned back. "Touche!" he cried with a laugh. "That makes it a bit awkward. Let's call it a draw."

Before Barbara could agree Freddy turned and started running off south up the sandy riverbed. "Come on chaps, let's get out of here before the cavalry arrive," he ordered.

The other British cadets dashed into the night after him. Barbara yelled at them to stop and Norris and Croucher started pretending to shoot from a hollow ten metres off. Cpl Ridgeway shouted again and his group of three came pounding through the bushes.

By the time they arrived the five British cadets had vanished among the trees and bushes upstream. Barbara pointed and said, "They went that way," but Cpl Ridgeway and his two cadets were too puffed from their run on the soft sand to follow. They stood with heaving chests, gasping for breath while Barbara recounted what had happened.

She then asked, "What happened over the other way?"

Cpl Ridgeway gestured. "Sgt Brady's patrol got driven off by about ten of them."

"British or 4 Platoon?" Barbara asked.

"Poms," Cpl Ridgeway replied.

Barbara snatched up her radio and called Sgt Brady. He answered at her second call. She asked, "Did they catch you? Over."

"No Sunray, over," Sgt Brady replied.

"Good. Remain in position, out," Barbara replied.

She then called Norris over and used the CB to call up HQ. She sent them a full report and also warned 2 Platoon that at least two groups of British raiders were heading for their area. Major Wickham answered and told her to keep her platoon where they were. Barbara passed this on to her patrols, then took out her water bottle for a drink. A check of her watch showed it was only 20:50.

An hour to go, she mused.

She sent Cpl Ridgeway's patrol back to their position, then posted Norris and Croucher to watch both directions. Feeling suddenly tired she then sat down.

*****

Colleen was also feeling tired and annoyed. At that moment she was a thousand metres Southeast of Barbara at the eastern tip of the sandy island, part of the HQ group who were the third objective for the raiders. She was tired because of the long day, followed by the long walk on the soft sand to get into position. Her annoyance was the result of an argument and being teased about boys, Geoff in particular, by Valerie Metcalf.

To compound her annoyance Cpl Keith, the Q Corporal, had made a suggestive remark to her, hinting he would like to get her alone in the dark.

"Keep your disgusting ideas to yourself!" Colleen hissed between clenched teeth. To avoid further trouble she walked over to where Jane Carson and Sharon Newell were seated.

Jane raised a quizzical eyebrow. "What was that about?" she asked as Colleen sat down.

"Just Keith being gross," Colleen replied. "Boys! They are just crude animals."

"Yes, they can be," Jane agreed.

"Too right," Sgt Newell added, but she sounded a bit wistful.

Colleen knew Sgt Newell was a standing joke among the boys

because she was so fat. That annoyed her too because she knew Sharon had a very kind heart and obviously wanted to have romance in her life.

"Why is life so cruel and unfair?" Colleen muttered, but she did not elaborate. Instead she stared off into the darkness.

HQ was arranged in a 50-metre circle among the fringe of the trees. In the centre sat Major Wickham, CSM Warren and Cpl Forest. They had two radios there and were continually calling someone. Colleen knew this was deliberate. They were simulating an enemy HQ so that the raiders could locate them and have an objective to raid. The HQ area was almost at the southern tip of the 'island', among the last few trees and bushes.

From where she sat Colleen could see fairly clearly in all directions. Behind her the trees thickened up to a black mass within 50 paces. Off to her left the sand dropped away, then rose in a series of small parallel dunes studded with clumps of black rocks. Somewhere in that direction was the water but she knew it was at least a hundred metres away and she could neither see, nor hear it.

In front of her the sand and gravel stretched away into the night. A few hummocks, rocks and bushes were studded around but they offered little cover. In the distance she could see a black line which she knew was the tree-lined far bank of the river as it curved around from the south. A bright light and several smaller lights showed clearly on top of the bank. The lights, she knew from their briefing, were at the homestead of a cattle station named 'Byrne Valley'. The homestead was on the other side of the river.

To her right the sand undulated to the edge of the island twenty metres away, then dropped abruptly for three metres to flat, smooth sand which extended for hundreds of metres to the left bank of the river. This was much closer, the actual shapes of some of the trees lining it being quite distinguishable against the background of stars. Other members of HQ faced that way.

A cool breeze had begun to blow along the river, directly into Colleen's eyes. It was just cold enough to make her shiver slightly as her perspiration chilled and she felt her eyes water in an attempt to stay moist.

"I wish they'd hurry up," she muttered. They had all heard the hullabaloo downstream when 1 Platoon had been attacked.

"Which way are they coming?" Jane asked.

"Not sure," Sharon replied.

At that moment there was a burst of shouting and pretend shooting a few hundred metres north of them.

"That will be the pretend mortar positions being hit," Jane said. 2 Platoon had that job and Colleen had heard them from time to time calling out 'Boom!' to represent mortars firing.

The 'battle' raged for a few minutes before dying down to occasional shouts and laughter and a lot of 'We won!', 'No you didn't' yelling.

Colleen heard Major Wickham calling 2 Platoon on the radio and strained to listen. He asked whether the attackers were Brits or 4 Platoon. Even as she heard him say: "Brits," she saw movement to her front.

For a moment she wasn't sure. She rubbed her eyes and tried to look out of the side of her eyes as she had been taught to do at night. *Yes, definitely movement.*

"Here they come. There are people moving out there," she said, pointing east along the riverbed.

The others turned to look and Sgt Newell called a warning to Major Wickham. He and CSM Warren quickly came over. By then Colleen could see the moving figures quite clearly and was surprised at how close they were; only about 50 paces away.

How did they get that close out on that open sand without being seen? she wondered.

"Ten of them, no more than that," Jane counted.

"They must have come down Landers Creek to get at us from that direction," Sgt Newell added.

Colleen stared hard at the line of advancing figures. Even now they were hard to see against the black background of trees. Just as she crouched ready, wondering what would happen next, Cpl Melony called a challenge. In response one of the approaching figures shouted, "Bang!"

At once the advancing line broke into a run and began screaming and blowing whistles.

4 Platoon, Colleen knew instantly on hearing the voices. She began yelling excitedly, pretending to have a machine gun.

The attackers raced up to her and then past, still yelling and screaming. Colleen found she was very tense. She did not want to have anything to do with 4 Platoon. However it seemed to her to be inevitable that she heard Geoff's voice yelling to his section, and that he should run directly towards her.

Geoff Unsworth ran the last few paces and Colleen thought he was going to knock her flat with his rush. She sprang up to get out of his way.

He managed to stop in time and shouted, "Got you, you're dead."

"No you didn't. I got you first," Colleen managed to say.

Geoff recognized her and sneered. "Oh you! Get out of my way," he snarled. He ran on past her, leaving Colleen feeling her emotions boiling: hurt and rejection and anger, all mixed together.

As ordered, she stayed where she was and lay down again. She was glad that it was dark as she felt tears well out. 4 Platoon swept through the position and then halted on command from CUO Callan. They then dropped flat, facing in all directions.

"Re-org!" CUO Callan called.

Colleen saw three of the attackers get up. One was Chloe. As platoon sergeant her job was to check that no-one was hurt or missing. The other two went over to where Major Wickham and CSM Warren sat watching. Chloe made her way quickly along the line of raiders and then walked around the defenders.

"Anyone hurt?" she asked.

As she reached Colleen Chloe stopped and grinned. Colleen forced herself to smile back. She did not approve of Chloe at all, being appalled at her nudity and low morals, but she tried not to show this.

It's not my place to judge, she often told herself as she tried hard to live up to Christ's injunction to forgive.

Chloe stopped and took out her water bottle. "No customers for you Colleen," she said.

"Good," Colleen replied.

Chloe took a swig, then spluttered and pointed off to the north. "CUO Callan! Counter-attack coming on the right flank!"

It was 3 Platoon. As rehearsed, they had waited under cover a hundred metres away until the re-org was under way. Now they advanced swiftly in extended line. For the next few minutes there was hectic activity. 4 Platoon quickly redeployed to face left, before starting to withdraw rapidly.

Even so the two forces intermingled and there was a lot of furious yelling and excited running about before 4 Platoon broke off the action and ran down onto the flat and off into the night. During this some of the HQ group came back to life and joined in and this added to the confusion.

Colleen found herself in a yelling match with two members of 3 Platoon who had gone to cover near her and were pretending to shoot at her and Sgt Newell. She recognized them by their voices and screamed to make them understand. It was LCpl Derran McArtney and Cadet Hinchley. She could tell McArtney by his stammer, which always got worse when he was excited.

"McArtney! Stop shooting at us! We are friendly," she yelled.

After several attempts she at last made herself understood and McArtney and his friend stood up and charged past them towards where several other members of 3 Platoon were following 4 Platoon, ignoring the yells of CUO Bailey to stop.

It took a few minutes for the noise to die down. CUO Bailey called his troops back in while CSM Warren got HQ to their feet. "Make sure you have everything," he added.

Colleen checked she had her First Aid Kit and picked up the stretcher. She got Katie to help carry this. Major Wickham shone a torch around to ensure there was nothing left lying on the sand.

"I don't want to have to walk all the way back to here just for a lost hat or water bottle," he commented.

At that moment there was another loud outburst of battle in the direction of 2 Platoon's 'mortar' position. Major Wickham grabbed the radio handset from Cpl Forest.

"It is 4 Platoon. We will go to help. 3 Platoon commander, take your platoon back to the northern end of the island as quickly as you can and reinforce 1 Platoon's line to try to catch them escaping. Quick!"

CUO Bailey called on his platoon to follow him and ran down onto the sandy flat. Major Wickham turned to where HQ now stood in a ragged line. "Have we got everyone CSM?"

CSM Warren did a quick count. "Yes sir."

"Let's go. We don't want to miss all the fun," Major Wickham said. He led them at a fast walk into the trees and bushes.

Colleen had expected to find this difficult to move through but soon found there were numerous gaps and trails between the bushes and trees and HQ moved at a brisk walk. As they moved Major Wickham gave instructions to the platoon commanders by radio.

Long before they reached the scene of action the enemy had withdrawn. Major Wickham warned 1 Platoon to be ready to catch the raiders on their way back and led the line on. Five minutes later they arrived panting and perspiring at the 2 Platoon position.

Just as they reached them distant shouting down river indicated that some of the raiders were fighting their way past 1 Platoon's line. Colleen heard Major Wickham answer the radio and say, "Brits. OK, 1 Platoon, watch out for 4 Platoon, they are heading your way too. So is Three to reinforce you. We are on our way."

Major Wickham passed the handset back to Cpl Forest and turned to CUO Roberts. "Have you got all your people?"

CUO Roberts called to Sgt Hope who instantly assured her all were present and ready to go. Colleen asked if 2 Platoon could take turns at carrying the stretcher and this was agreed to, being normal practice on field exercises. Major Wickham then led them on again, heading back for the start point.

Long before they arrived they heard the screams and shouts of 4 Platoon battling their way past 1 Platoon. This was confirmed by radio. Major Wickham then slowed his pace, for which Colleen was very thankful as she was now sweating and tiring fast. Her shoulder was starting to ache from carrying the First Aid kit and she just wanted to get back to camp to lie down.

For her the walk began to assume the feeling of a bad dream. The soft sand made walking hard and she sweated so much her shirt chafed and the perspiration dribbled into her eyes, stinging them and making her blink. She found it a relief to come out of the bushes at the Northwest side of the island but was then disheartened by being able to see how far they still had to walk.

Out on the flat sand she could clearly see the black outline of the hill. Halfway up it was the tiny pin-prick of light she knew was the lantern. It seemed a long way away and never seemed to get any closer as they trudged along.

There was a pause when they reached the line where 1 Platoon and 3 Platoon were waiting. Major Wickham told them to follow and led the way on. Colleen just had time for a drink before transferring the First Aid kit to her other shoulder as they resumed the march.

The last two hundred metres seemed to be the worst. They tramped down across soft, damp sand and then stumbled and slogged up the rough animal pads to the Old Highway where the lantern was hanging from a tree. Here they were ordered to sit in sections so they could be counted. Colleen collected the stretcher off 2 Platoon and moved to the rear of HQ where she thankfully slumped down.

She shoved the stretcher against Katie Melony. "Your turn to carry this thing now," she insisted.

Katie began to grumble but was silenced by Sgt Newell. "Be quiet while I count you," she ordered.

Colleen sat back and mopped the sweat off her forehead, glad to be seated. The company soon seated itself and the sergeants called for silence.

CSM Warren then called, "1 Platoon, Sgt Brady, are all your cadets here?"

"Yes CSM."

"2 Platoon, Sgt Hope?"

"Yes CSM."

"3 Platoon?"

There was muttering and CSM Warren called again. "3 Platoon, Sgt Milikin, are all your cadets there?"

Again there was a pause, then Milikin replied nervously, "Er... no CSM. We seem to be missing one."

Chapter 14

THE LIGHT

The moment Major Wickham heard Sgt Milikin say that a cadet missing from 3 Platoon he felt his stomach tighten up.

Oh no! he thought.

The possibility of a cadet getting hurt or lost was always a major worry for him when he planned and conducted exercises. While the CSM and sergeants did a second count he turned and looked around.

How the devil could anyone get lost here? he wondered.

The steep hill he was standing on blocked off the northern end of the exercise area; the line of steep sand cliffs and tangle of rubber vine walled the area in from the west, and the river was on the other side.

The river! Oh my God! Not the river, Major Wickham thought.

The river had always been a worry but before each exercise he had always checked personally for any signs of crocodiles and then made a point of warning the cadets several times to stay away from it. There were, he knew, warning signs put up by Parks and Wildlife warning that 'Estuarine Crocodiles inhabit this waterway'. The image of a cadet, lost and in panic, going too close to the edge of the water and being dragged in by one of the monster reptiles rose to add to his feeling of apprehension.

CSM Warren reported. "Lance Corporal McArtney is definitely missing sir."

"Thank you CSM. Right, everyone quiet," Major Wickham called.

It took a second order to still the excited babble which had broken out. When all was silent Major Wickham filled his lungs and bellowed in his best 'parade ground' voice.

"Lance Corporal McArtney! Corporal McArtney!"

The yell carried out across the riverbed and echoed faintly from the distant banks. They all strained their ears and Major Wickham cursed the faint breeze which made a noise around his ears. Nothing. He shouted again. He was sure that his voice was carrying all the way to the far end of the island as he had shouted that far on previous exercises when radios had failed.

There was no reply, other than some startled bird noises down in the tangle. Major Wickham felt his stomach churn again and he turned to CUO Bailey. "When did you last see him for certain?"

Bailey hesitated. "Not sure sir. He was with us when we counter attacked 4 Platoon at the far end of the island. I am sure of that."

"Is that right Sgt Milikin?" Major Wickham asked. He was both worried and annoyed.

"Yes sir."

Major Wickham turned back to CUO Bailey. "After that you led your platoon in this direction, didn't you?"

"Yes sir, along the open bed of the river," CUO Bailey agreed.

"Did you have any action or contacts?"

"No sir. We were too late."

"Did you stop and do a head count at any time?" Major Wickham asked. It was a unit rule to do this after every action and exercise.

CUO Bailey hesitated and shuffled from one foot to the other. "No sir," he admitted.

Anger welled up in Major Wickham, but he forced himself to keep a grip on his emotions.

I can deal with leaders later, he told himself.

So he again turned and bellowed into the night. He was aware that the other staff members were grouped nearby, all as aware and anxious as himself. There was no answer to his shout. He scanned the dark riverbed. The only lights visible were the distant lights of 'Byrne Valley' homestead, nearly three kilometres away and on the far side of the river.

A radio crackled and Cpl Forster handed the handset to him. "Lt Barker sir."

Lt Barker was up at the Lookout with the safety vehicle. He wanted to know what was going on. Major Wickham told him, then added, "You'd better wait there Ash, with your mobile phone ready in case we need the ambulance. I'll turn mine on and call you to check we have coms."

He did this, the distinctive sound of the phone ringing also sounding loudly in the night. Having checked that his mobile phone was working Major Wickham called the adult staff, CUOs and CSM to one side of the company.

"We will have to search. For the time being we will keep everyone else here in case we need to be even more thorough. CSM, you and the

First-Year sergeants are to stay here. Do a radio check so that we are sure you have coms with us and with the safety vehicle."

"Yes sir."

Major Wickham went on, "We will do a sweep of the riverbed upstream as far as the end of the island. I will go along the edge of the water. 4 Platoon and HQ are to form an extended line on my right, 4 Platoon on the left and the other CUOs and HQ on the right. I want the CUOs and their corporals to extend the line across to the west bank. Captain Hamilton, you go on the right-hand end please. And I want another two, plus the First Aid kit and stretcher, to be with the medics in the middle of the line."

CUO Bailey asked, "Do we use torches sir?"

"Of course we do! This isn't an exercise! Cpl McArtney may be lying injured under a bush or in a hollow. We walk slowly, stay in line and search every possible place."

"How long for sir?" CUO Roberts asked.

"Until we find him! All night if necessary, now let's get organized and get moving," Major Wickham replied.

It took ten minutes to arrange for all radios and other equipment to be checked and for the people detailed to move into a line. There was some grumbling from the First-Year cadets that they would have to remain waiting.

"Why can't we just go back to the bivouac and sleep?" Cadet Norris whined.

Barbara at once snapped a reply. "Because we might need all of you to help with a more thorough search later," she said.

Major Wickham checked his watch. 2115. *The time I'd planned for us to be starting back for the bivouac,* he thought. *Oh well! The social activities will just have to wait.*

He wondered if the British cadets had managed to safely get back, then shrugged and led the line of thirty people back down the rough cattle pads to the flat sandy riverbed.

Once there he turned left and headed directly towards the water. The others began spreading out behind him to form an extended line. This would be 500 metres long at least and that meant only one person every ten or fifteen metres. That was a very worrying thought to Major Wickham.

If they don't search every place thoroughly we could easily miss him, he thought.

As he drew closer to the black water Major Wickham shone his torch across its surface, checking to see if any pairs of red eyes glowed back. Relieved that none showed he walked on, aware that the sand underfoot was becoming wetter and slushier as he went. Twenty paces from where the sand shelved gently into the water he stopped.

"OK CUO Callan, line your people back out to the right," he said.

CUO Callan did this. The person next to Major Wickham was his signaller, Cpl Forest. Next came Chloe, 4 Platoon's sergeant. After that the cadets became just dimly seen black shapes lined up across the bare expanse.

Torches flickered and there was a good deal of calling out and angry orders before the line was formed. As he waited Major Wickham again studied the river to his left. In the beam of his torch the water looked almost still and had an evil, forbidding look to it. The stars were reflected off it and only an occasional piece of drifting stick hinted at a gentle current.

The radio crackled. It was Capt Hamilton reporting that he was in position at the right of the line, near the mouth of Snake Gully.

Major Wickham listened and then pressed his 'press to talk' button. "All Call Signs, this is Sunray, advance," he called on his radio.

They began walking slowly forward. Torches began sweeping their beams back and forth in front of the line. Some cadets began calling out but Major Wickham ordered this stopped.

"Only myself, Capt Hamilton and CUO Callan are to call out. If everyone yells out, we may not hear Cpl McArtney," he explained.

Within a hundred paces the easy bit ended. They reached the northern end of the sand island. Major Wickham had been watching it with foreboding, but he now steeled himself to do what was necessary. While everyone else climbed up the steep sand slope onto the higher level he went left through the trees and bushes right beside the water. Cpl Forest wanted to follow but Major Wickham sternly ordered him up on top of the bank.

"Walk along up there and keep visual touch with me," Major Wickham said.

Walking beside the river in the dark quickly became the stuff of nightmares. The bank was steep and plunged almost straight down in many places. The beam of Major Wickham's torch revealed the water to be both deep and to have an eerie green tinge to it. He anxiously swept his torch beam across the surface.

"Bloody hell!" he muttered, "A croc could just come sliding up and pull me in."

He began to sweat with fear and fervently hoped he would get enough warning to spring clear. Despite this he doggedly kept on along the edge of the water, searching the mud for boot prints or signs of a struggle.

It was difficult going as many of the trees grew out at an angle over the water, so he was forced to continually clamber over their trunks and across masses of flood debris. That got him worrying about snakes as well as he knew such places were a favourite habitat for the reptiles.

Worst of all was the fact that his vision was both blinded and focused by the beam of his torch. *If a croc comes up beside me or behind me, I won't see him,* he thought.

That worry caused him to swing the torch beam back and over the water every few steps and that slowed him even more. From time to time he spoke to Cpl Forest whose torch he could see flickering through the trees and bushes five metres above him.

Cpl Forest called him messages from time to time and reported that the line was getting further ahead on the right than on the left.

"Can't be helped," Major Wickham replied. "We have to search this area thoroughly."

He grimly struggled on, his sense of dread growing with every minute. From time to time he stopped and yelled LCpl McArtney's name. The sound carried flatly across the water and he hoped McArtney was alive and conscious and could hear it.

With luck he has only hurt his ankle or leg or something, he reasoned.

Once he thought he heard a reply but then decided it was the echo of Capt Hamilton calling out as well.

If we don't find him soon I will have to get the whole unit down and busy searching, he thought.

Even more unhappily he knew he would then have to start telephoning army HQ, police and parents to inform them.

Blast and damn! I don't want us to be on the six O'clock Sunday news, he thought angrily.

After forty minutes of sweaty, muddy trudging and clambering Major Wickham realized with relief that he had reached the part of the river where the water trended left, away from the trees along the edge of the island. That made searching easier for him but also raised a serious difficulty in keeping the search line intact.

He called Capt Hamilton on the radio. "Where are you 'Playtime'?" he asked, using the army nickname for 'transport', Capt Hamilton being an officer in the part-time, active army reserve in a transport unit as well as being a cadet officer.

Capt Hamilton called back to report he was nearly at the mouth of Landers Creek. They agreed on a short halt while the line was checked and re-aligned, so it could swing left around the curve of the river. While this was organized by the CUOs and OOCs Major Wickham had a big drink and wiped sweat from his face and eyes. It was getting late and he was becoming a very worried man.

Twenty past ten, he muttered. According to the program the exercise should all be over and they should all be back safely in the bivouac area.

At that moment there was a radio message from CUO Callan. "We have found a hat sir, over."

"I'll be right up. Wait where you are, over," Major Wickham replied. He turned and strode quickly along the line, Cpl Forest trotting along behind like the good signaller he was.

It took five minutes of sweaty slogging through sand, waist high bushes and grass to reach CUO Callan. He was standing with Jane Carson and Valerie Metcalf. They held up a camouflage cloth hat.

"Any name in it?"

"No sir. It was just here, lying on the sand," Jane replied.

Major Wickham took the hat and looked at it in the light of his torch. It looked fairly new and he tried to remember what LCpl McArtney's hat looked like.

Older and more faded I thought.

Another idea came to him and he had Cpl Forest call the CSM and ask if any of the cadets had lost a hat.

After a couple of minutes the answer came back. "Yes sir. Cadet Sherry has lost her hat sir," Cpl Forest replied.

"Sherry. She is in 2 Platoon. This is the area they had their fake mortar position in isn't it?"

"Somewhere around here sir," CUO Callan agreed.

"We will have to keep on searching. Wait till I get back to the edge of the river," Major Wickham replied.

Major Wickham and Cpl Forest set off again back along the line of tired and sweating cadets towards the riverbank. As they came out of the bushes Major Wickham became aware of some sort of commotion ahead of him. A group of cadets were standing on the bank shining their torches out onto the water.

Major Wickham looked and his heart skipped a beat. In the beam of the torches, about twenty metres out from the bank, was what looked very much like a body.

"Is that... is that?" Cpl Forest asked.

"It might be," Major Wickham replied grimly. He felt sick in the stomach. The thing was flattish and looked exactly like the back of a person's head and body.

Three torches were now focused on it. "It doesn't seem to be moving," Cpl Forest offered.

"Stuck on a snag or rock?" Cpl de Beer suggested. Both of these things were visible nearby in the water.

"I will have to check," Major Wickham said. The idea of swimming in that black water made his stomach contract with fear. He sat down on a rock and reached down to unlace his boots.

"Chloe's already doing that sir," Cpl de Beer replied.

"She's what!"

"Chloe's looking now," Cpl de Beer replied, swinging her torch to the right. Major Wickham felt his heart lurch with alarm as he saw Chloe's head and shoulders in the water. She was swimming out to the object.

"Chloe! Come back here! Get out of that water at once!" he shouted.

Chloe shook her head and kept swimming. She was now only a couple of metres from the thing. Major Wickham called out again, his heart pounding with anxiety. At any moment he expected to see a flurry of water and Chloe vanish.

She reached the thing and stood up. In the beams of the torches it was obvious she was almost nude. All she wore was a very brief bikini. She turned and shook her head.

"Only a rock sir."

"Get back here at once!" Major Wickham cried. The tension caused him to break into a cold sweat.

Chloe slid off the water-smoothed rock and struck out for the shore using a powerful breaststroke.

"Shine your torches out to each side and behind her, not on her," Major Wickham ordered.

The three cadets present did so. Major Wickham did likewise, the beam of his 'Big Jim' torch reaching right across to the far bank. At any second he expected to see the glowing red orbs of evil but apart from a few ripples there was nothing.

Chloe came scampering out of the water, her near nakedness plain in the reflection of the torches. That confirmed that all she wore was the tiniest bikini.

"Look away you boys," Major Wickham ordered.

He turned away himself, but not before he got a good eyeful of Chloe's barely concealed charms. But it was enough to make his heart hammer, both with admiration and fear. The thought of Cadet HQ hearing about more misbehaviour by Chloe after the recent investigation which had resulted in her demotion from cadet warrant officer was enough to make him feel ill.

Chloe stopped beside him. "It was only a rock sir," she said.

Anxiety exploded in anger. Major Wickham turned on her angrily. "What the devil do you think you are up to! Weren't the exercise orders to stay out of the water? Why did you do such a stupid thing? And get dressed!"

He glanced at Chloe and even in the torchlight could see she was incredibly attractive. Hastily he looked away again, then snapped at the boys who had all turned to goggle.

"Turn those torches off and look away you boys!"

Chloe stooped to pick up her trousers and shook sand off them. She stood behind Major Wickham and dusted sand off her feet. As she dressed, she said, "It had to be done sir. Someone had to go out and investigate."

"That was my responsibility. You cadets are in my care. I am the one who has to take the risks," Major Wickham replied angrily. His chest was heaving with emotion. A wave of cold shock passed over him as he thought of the dreadful risk Chloe had just run.

Chloe again dusted her feet dry before pulling her trousers on. "I am a better swimmer than you sir. Besides, I have swum in worse places for crocodiles than that. Crocs and I are old friends," she said.

"Don't remind me!" Major Wickham replied, remembering with a chill of sweat that dreadful exercise three years earlier when she and Jane had been kidnapped by smugglers during an exercise near Innisfail. There were also the fantastic stories of how Chloe (naked again!) had rescued the President of Bunga Lunga during the April school holidays. Major Wickham had seen some of the TV News footage and could only shake his head in bemused wonder.

At that moment Major Wickham's mobile phone rang. The sound was so loud and so unexpected that he jumped nervously. He snatched the phone from his belt.

"Major Wickham."

"Lt Barker here sir. I have got Mr Tudehope from 'Landers Creek' station here with me at the Lookout. He has just had a phone call from the people at 'Byrne Valley' homestead across the river to say that one of our cadets is calling out to them across the water. It is Lance Corporal McArtney."

"Thanks Ash," Major Wickham replied. "I will get a group along there at once. Keep me posted if there are any developments. I will call you back."

As he ended the call Major Wickham let out a huge sigh of relief. McArtney was safe! He turned to Cpl Forest. "Call Capt Hamilton."

"Is that LCpl McArtney sir? Is he safe?" Chloe asked. She was standing beside him, her upper body plain to see in the starlight. The other cadets there had all turned to watch and Chloe seemed, as usual, quite unfazed by this.

Secretly Major Wickham really liked Chloe and she certainly had an effect on him. This effect he tried to mask by being angry and gruff. "Yes. Now get dressed Chloe!" he snapped.

"Yes sir, if I have to."

"Chloe!"

"Oh sir! It's much cooler and nicer like this," she said, but she bent to pick up her shirt. Before the interested gaze of the three boys she continued dressing. The sight so aroused and exasperated Major Wickham that he turned his back and swore under his breath.

He snapped, "Stop looking you boys! It might be cooler for you

Chloe, but it isn't for the boys. They are getting all hot and bothered; and I don't want another investigation by Cadet HQ thank you, or any more wild stories leaking to the media."

At that moment Capt Hamilton answered the radio. Major Wickham passed him the news. Capt Hamilton replied, "I am closest. I can see the homestead lights clearly from where I am. I will take a radio and the CUOs and go and get him."

"Roger. Take the medics too. I'll round the others up and start back," Major Wickham replied. Beside him Chloe shrugged on her shirt and began to button it up. He shook his head and sighed with exasperation.

Arrangements were quickly made. All the search party, except Capt Hamilton, the CUOs and two medics, were ordered to concentrate at the southern end of the island. Major Wickham had to wait while Chloe pulled on socks and boots and then her webbing. As she stood up and swung her webbing on he gave one last shot.

"And don't you take any more silly risks Chloe!"

"No sir. Only if the situation warrants it sir," she replied.

Major Wickham steamed and was about to snap at her again when he shook his head.

No point, he thought, *and besides, that is a sensible answer.* So he held his tongue and waited.

When Chloe was dressed the group walked along the line of 4 Platoon and HQ collecting them into a single group. By 2245 they were all grouped near the southern end of the island. By then Capt Hamilton and his group were well on their way. Major Wickham started the others walking back northwards along the open sand beside the island.

They went slowly as all were tired by then. Even so they perspired and found it solid slogging. Major Wickham looked ahead and saw the gleam of the lantern on the black shape of the hill. It still seemed to be a long way off and he ruefully decided he was getting too old for such activities.

As the group walked along the riverbed the CP at the bivouac site radioed to report that the British cadets were all safely back. They had just arrived.

"Get a campfire going. We will be half an hour yet," Major Wickham replied.

Ten minutes later, just as the long line of trudging cadets was nearing the northern end of the island, Capt Hamilton called on his radio. "We have reached Lance Corporal McArtney. He is OK. We are on our way back, over."

"Do you need any extra help, over," Major Wickham asked.

"No, over."

"Then I will start the others moving back and just leave Ash and the safety vehicle at the Lookout, over."

"Roger, over."

Curiosity made Major Wickham then ask, "Why did McArtney walk all that way? Over."

There was a pause then Capt Hamilton replied, "He says he got separated from the others, so he just did what he was told to do in the orders and walked towards the light, over."

Major Wickham looked up at where the lantern glowed on the hillside ahead and silently swore, then shook his head in disbelief. "Bloody hell!" he muttered. "He just walked towards the light! Pity it was the wrong light."

He again shook his head and wondered how such a simple instruction could cause such confusion.

Chapter 15

CAMPFIRE

Colleen shook her head in disbelief and stood with trembling legs while leaning on the stretcher she had been carrying. She had been part of the group that had walked along the riverbank to find LCpl McArtney and now stood beside the water opposite the lights of 'Byrne Valley' homestead.

Capt Hamilton shouted across the water, "Thank you. We've got him."

Answering shouts acknowledged this and Colleen saw the flicker of torch lights from the top of the steep bank about a hundred metres away. At this point the water flowed along the base of the far bank and in the torchlight the channel appeared to be littered with numerous rocky outcrops.

Capt Hamilton called on the radio to inform Major Wickham and Lt Barker. While he did CUO Callan spoke to LCpl McArtney.

"You walked to this light! Why didn't you go the other way to the lantern?"

"I c… couldn't see it. I g… got d... dis... disoriented," LCpl McArtney replied. He sounded upset and his stutter was worse than usual.

CUO Callan pointed upstream. "But you can see the bloody hill from here! You must have been able to see it."

"I... I c... couldn't. All I c... could s... see was the r... ri... riv... river."

Capt Hamilton swung round. "That'll do CUO Callan. I think he's been punished enough. Come on you lot, let's get back." He turned and led the way back across the sand.

Colleen went to hoist the stretcher onto her shoulder when Barbara said to her, "Here, give me one end. I'll help you."

Thankfully Colleen did so. She felt a warm glow of gratitude. *Barbara is nice,* she thought. *She remembers and she cares about people.*

HQ and LCpl McArtney started walking behind Capt Hamilton. The other CUOs followed them.

As they trudged back along the riverbed, skirting numerous rocky outcrops, the cadets behind Barbara resumed the discussion with LCpl McArtney on how he got lost. He was unable to explain, and it was obvious to Colleen that the kid was embarrassed.

He probably just got separated from the others and then panicked in the dark, she thought.

CUO Callan was the most annoyed. "Bloody hell! You walked two bloody kilometres in the wrong direction on this bloody sand McArtney."

LCpl McArtney made no reply, but CUO Bailey added, "Yeah, and now we have to walk another three all the way back."

That was a daunting idea to Colleen and she wondered if she could make it. *That makes it about six or seven kilometres on the sand tonight,* she calculated.

She felt very tired and was getting chafed in several places, worst of all on her shoulders. She was also perspiring, and the sweat rubbed under her armpits and down her back.

After twenty minutes they halted for a few minutes and to Colleen's relief Barbara insisted that the two male CUOs take over carrying the stretcher. By then Colleen had emptied all her water bottles and was feeling dry in the mouth and her eyes were so tired she had trouble focusing in the starlight.

They resumed the walk, slowly rounding the inshore curve of the island. A tiny pin-prick of yellow light came into view.

CUO Callan pointed to it. "There is the bloody lantern McArtney. That is the light you were supposed to walk towards."

"I... I... did... didn't s... see it," McArtney mumbled unhappily.

The sight of the light both cheered and depressed Colleen. It looked to be a long way off and she was now yearning for an end to what had become, for her, a physical ordeal. However she made no complaint and kept trudging gamely on, thrusting the sore muscles and tiny aches to the back of her mind.

CUO Callan began to grumble and again loudly speculated at how anyone could get lost in the riverbed. Barbara replied to him, "Give it a break Rick. The poor guy has learned his lesson."

That comment sent Colleen's opinion of Barbara even higher. Thankfully CUO Callan made no further comments.

It took them nearly twenty minutes to reach the lantern. By then it was 2320hrs and the temperature had at last begun to drop slightly. Major Wickham was waiting at the lantern. He gave them a couple of minutes to rest then called up to Lt Barker at the Lookout to let him know they were alright.

After that it was a ten-minute slog back along the railway. They rolled under the barbed wire fence and tramped along between the rails on the gravel ballast. To Colleen it was all a bit of an ordeal as she was now feeling dry and slightly dizzy. As they walked through the big cutting, she wished she could just sit down and rest but pushed herself.

Get it over with, she told herself.

She found walking along the railway in the starlight a peculiar experience. For several hundred metres it was on a bench cut with a steep drop on the left down into the dark tangle of jungle along Deep Creek. This looked very sinister in the dark. After that it ran on an embankment and Colleen felt quite dizzy and knew she was having trouble with her perception of depth as the creek below looked a long way down.

At 2340hrs they reached the turn-off to the Gravel Scrape. Colleen sighed with relief and forced herself to keep walking. Lt Barker was waiting at the gate with his vehicle. The vehicle headlights lit up the bush ahead and he gave them cheerful greetings. Once through the gate he stayed to shut it then drove slowly along behind the plodding line.

"Well, we missed the bloody social night at the campfire anyway," muttered CUO Bailey.

"So what?" CUO Callan asked. "There was only one girl with the Pommies, and she looks a bit too tough even for me."

"You might prefer the boys," Sgt Dunstan suggested.

"That's enough of that sort of talk," Major Wickham snapped from the head of the line.

By then they had arrived at the Gravel Scrape. CUO Callan asked, "What do we do now sir?"

"You can stay up for a cup of hot drink and a chat if you like and then into bed," Major Wickham replied.

Even as he said this there was a muffled burst of cheers and laughter from the other side of the large mound. Colleen looked up and saw the glow of a fire on the treetops.

"Sounds like someone is still awake and having a party," CUO Bailey commented.

"Yes. Let's go and see," Major Wickham replied.

Colleen made her way to the CAP hutchie and placed the stretcher and First Aid Kit there, then went to her own hutchie. Her first thought was to just crawl into bed, but another outburst of laughter and clapping changed her mind.

I'll have a hot drink and relax first.

She refilled her water bottles from a jerry can, then walked around the big mound, carrying her webbing. On the other side she found about fifty cadets, all seated around a large campfire. Lt Cavendish and the two British officers were there, as were all of the British cadets. To Colleen's eyes the darker green and brown of the British camouflage uniforms was very noticeable.

They were cheering Chloe, who was standing out front and doing a wriggle and dance of some sort while telling a joke.

Bloody Chloe! What a show-off! Colleen thought.

Major Wickham walked over to the fire and looked at his watch. CSM Warren rose to meet him. "Sorry sir. We thought it would be nice to entertain our guests. I hope you don't mind. I wanted to keep people ready in case you needed them."

Major Wickham nodded. "Yes CSM. That is alright. I had planned to have a campfire until midnight anyway. We will stay up a bit longer."

Colleen knew they should all now be going to bed but was suddenly glad they were going to stay up a bit longer. She felt the need for some cheering up and she usually loved the campfire sessions on bivouacs. For a minute she stood at the back and looked around for somewhere to sit herself down.

As she looked around her eyes met those of the British cadet who had snubbed her earlier for being Irish. He gave a smile and Colleen felt a rush of confused emotions before looking away. She noted Sharon Newell, Jane and Katie and went over to sit behind them. They asked her what had happened and she told them while having a big drink of water. They then related the latest story about Chloe's goings-on.

"She stripped off and swam out to check if it was a body or not," Sharon said in a scandalized tone.

"She had a bikini on," Jane said.

"Only a tiny little one that hardly hides anything," Katie said.

Colleen looked at Chloe and her lips pressed firmly together in disapproval. She could not imagine herself wearing only a tiny bikini and she certainly did not like the way Chloe was behaving.

She is just teasing those boys and flaunting herself, she thought.

She then unpacked her hexamine stove and mess gear and began to heat some water for a cup of Milo.

Capt Hamilton had the circle around the fire moved out to make more room and he and Major Wickham sat down. Lt Barker parked his vehicle and walked over to join then. Barbara and the other CUOs also joined the group.

"What's going on?" Major Wickham asked.

There were hoots of laughter and Major Grogan replied, "Your people have been telling us jokes and my boys have been trying to persuade this girl to do a strip tease."

He indicated Chloe, who was still standing in the middle of the circle. She was still fully dressed but her eyes were dancing with mischief.

Major Wickham snorted. "That won't take much doing," he replied shortly, "but she'd better not. Not if she wants to stay in cadets."

"We heard she's already taken her clothes off tonight sir," Sgt Milikin yelled.

In the firelight he looked positively hostile and Colleen remembered that it was his brother who had been suspended and sent home.

He probably wants revenge, she thought.

"Yes," Major Wickham replied.

He shook his head. Chloe appeared to blush, but Colleen suspected it was just the effect of the firelight. She again heard the story of what had happened down in the riverbed and had felt a sour taste of dislike for Chloe and her loose morals.

She just gives us a bad name, she thought.

Major Wickham firmly told them to change the subject and to tell some jokes instead. To start them off he told the 'Dad and Dave' joke about Dad being suspicious of what young Dave and Mabel might be getting up to and sending Jackie to keep watch on them.

This was followed by several 'Travelling salesman' jokes and a couple of riddles. These led to 'Irish' jokes. The British cadets seemed to know dozens of these. Colleen had heard most of them before and had never really taken them personally before. Even now she laughed at most, but she was also aware that they were irritating her.

It was the same British cadet, Cecil, who finally got her annoyed. He stood out in front of his friends and told several more Irish jokes. Most were just silly 'one-liners' like the Irish submarine with deckchairs, or the Irish sea scouts drowning while trying to put up their tent. Then he said, "You all heard about the Irish terrorist who burnt his mouth badly? He was told to go and blow up a bus and used the exhaust pipe."

The image was funny, but Colleen began to get really annoyed at her ethnic origin being continually put down. When the laughter had died down Cecil went on, "Mick and Paddy were driving through Belfast and Mick says to Paddy; 'Bejeezes Paddy, I don't like drivin' around wit' dat bomb you are holdin' in yer lap. Wot if it blows up?'; and Paddy replies, 'Dats alright boyo, I got another one in the back.'."

As Cecil finished the joke his eyes again met Colleen's. She glared back and then spoke up loudly enough to over-ride the voices of others.

She said, "You know why Irish jokes are so simple don't you?"

There was a hush and Cecil looked at her and gave a quizzical smile and shook his head. "No darling, why?"

"So the English can understand them!" Colleen snapped.

Cecil flushed but managed to laugh while the crowd cheered and jeered. Freddy clapped Cecil on the back and cried loudly: "Got you that time old boy!"

Feeling pleased at having scored a point yet unhappy at hurting someone Colleen looked away and went on with making her Milo. There was a short lull while people tried to work out exactly what had just happened. Luckily for Colleen the situation was interrupted by Micki and Sandy. They came walking in out of the darkness.

"What was that all about?" Micki asked.

CUO Callan called to them: "Where have you two been? Smoking?"

Both looked guilty. "No. We just went to the toilet," Micki replied. Sandy glared at CUO Callan.

Major Wickham looked up from stirring a cup of coffee and gave them a hard look but said nothing. Micki and Sandy moved back into the semi-darkness at the back of the group.

Chloe came and crouched near Colleen. "Come and help Jane and me do a skit," she said.

"Which one?" Colleen asked.

"What about the trained elephant? We will catch some of these snooty Poms with it," Chloe said.

Colleen looked up. "Good idea. I know the one to pick. I will be the back end of the elephant."

"Good girl. Get a blanket," Chloe said.

Colleen and Jane hurried into the darkness to get a blanket and a cup of water. Chloe came and arranged the blanket over them. They spent a few minutes rehearsing their lines then Chloe led them slowly forward.

As she shuffled along, Colleen whispered, "Get that Cecil bloke."

"OK," Chloe agreed.

She led them through a gap in the crowd, then walked forward and held her arms up for silence. This aroused a chorus of yells and whistles.

"Take it off!" yelled a boy.

"Come on Chloe, show us what you've got," said a British voice.

"That's enough of that!" Major Wickham growled warningly.

Finally Chloe got silence. She went on with her patter. All the Australian cadets had seen the skit before and tensed in gleeful anticipation.

Chloe said, "Here we have Bessie, the famous trained elephant. She is so clever she can do many tricks. For example Bessie can count to three. Watch this. Bessie, count to three."

Under the blanket Colleen stamped her feet twice and Jane once. The crowd laughed and clapped. Chloe next got them to count to four. Colleen nearly got it wrong.

Chloe then said, "Bessie has marvellous muscle control. She can stand on an egg and not crack it. She also has great dexterity. Now, we need a volunteer from the audience to demonstrate this."

There were more shouts and laughter. Colleen wished she could see but could only follow the sound of the voices and laughter. At last one of the British cadets was pushed forward by his laughing friends. Colleen waited then walked forward when Chloe led them across.

Chloe said, "Bessie will now demonstrate her great skill by stepping across this person without once hurting him. Come on Bessie."

Colleen shuffled forward, gripping the cup and blanket and straining to see down behind Jane. She glimpsed the British cadet and to her annoyance saw it wasn't Cecil. It was Freddy and he was lying on his back and laughing, clearly expecting some trick. Jane stepped carefully across him and Colleen did likewise. Chloe then grabbed them and turned them around.

"Just to demonstrate that wasn't a fluke Bessie will now go back again," she said.

This time, as Colleen stepped over Freddy, she tipped the cup and the water poured down onto him. The crowd roared with delight and Freddy laughed and rolled aside. Colleen flung the blanket off and laughed as well.

As soon as they had walked to the side of the group, Colleen hissed at Chloe, "He wasn't the one I wanted."

"Which one do you want? I'll get him next time."

"I don't want him. He's annoyed me and I want to pay him back," Colleen said.

"Then let's do 'The Fire Engine'," Chloe suggested.

This was agreed to. Sharon and Katie were roped in to make up the crew of the fire engine and they made their way off into the darkness to rehearse while more jokes were told.

This time Chloe acted the speaker again. Colleen could only shake her head as Chloe strutted around in the limelight, pouting, wriggling and flaunting herself.

"This skit is called 'The Fire Engine'," Chloe explained. The group then acted it. Chloe pretended to use the telephone. "Hello, is that the fire department? Come quick, there's a fire at 3 Wombat Drive."

Katie made siren noises and the girls scurried out to sit as though in a fire engine. Colleen managed to keep another cup of water hidden from the British cadets during this. The four girls then pretended to drive quickly, making sound effects and moving in unison to portray turning sharp corners at speed or stopping and starting suddenly.

Sharon cried, "Brakes! Here we are. Where is the fire?"

As the four girls ran over to Chloe she pointed to Cecil. "Here!"

Colleen raced over and dashed the cup of water into Cecil's face. She did it harder than she meant to and for a moment feared she had made a serious mistake as anger flashed in Cecil's eyes. For a moment he glared at her, their eyes locked. Then Charles and Freddy clapped him on the back.

"Just what you needed old boy," Charles cried.

"What's that, a bath?" CUO Callan cried.

The Australians roared with laughter.

"No, cooling down after looking at all these beautiful girls," Freddy said.

Chloe pouted and put her nose up but Colleen could tell she was really enjoying their attention. She turned and walked back to where she had left her drink and webbing. As she reached there, she found Geoff Unsworth beside her.

"That was good Colleen," he said.

"Thanks," Colleen replied coldly. She had no desire to speak to him.

He wasn't put off. "Colleen, I'm sorry for what I said. Can... can we go somewhere and talk?"

Colleen sat down and put her head down. "There's nothing to say," she replied.

"But I want to make it up to you," Geoff whispered.

"And I don't. It is over. Please leave me alone," Colleen replied.

For a second she thought Geoff was going to drag her to her feet. The arrival of Katie and Sharon stopped this. Instead Geoff bent over near her. "Bitch!" he hissed.

Then he was gone. Colleen felt her stomach turn over with distress and distaste. Sharon and Katie sat down and looked at her.

"You OK?" Katie asked.

Colleen nodded, but did not trust herself to speak. She sipped her drink and looked at the happy group around the fire. She then became aware that two of the British cadets were walking around towards her. One of them was Cecil.

Oh dear! I hope he isn't going to be unpleasant, she thought.

Cecil stopped and knelt down. He looked her in the eyes and Colleen was relieved to see he didn't look angry.

"Yes?" she asked.

"I just came over to say I am sorry for what I said to you earlier in the evening," Cecil said.

"Thanks," Colleen replied. She wanted to look away.

Cecil smiled. "You are really beautiful," he added.

"And you are really fresh!" Colleen replied.

She was embarrassed and acutely conscious that all the cadets near them had heard Cecil. She flushed, but with pleasure as much as annoyance.

"I mean it," Cecil said. "I am really sorry, and I'd like to make it up to you. Can we talk?"

Two males in ten minutes! Colleen thought, *and I don't like either of them!*

She shook her head. "Sorry. I'm tired and I am going to bed in a minute."

"Tomorrow then?"

Colleen shook her head. "No, I don't think so."

Cecil nodded and managed to smile. "Thanks anyway."

He and his friend turned and made their way back to the other side of the fire. Sharon bent over and whispered, "You didn't have to be that hard Colleen. He seems nice."

"You can have him then," Colleen replied.

"Oh, I wish!" Sharon said. She looked eagerly across the fire at the laughing faces and Colleen felt a twinge of guilt.

Poor Sharon! She really wants a boyfriend.

Colleen looked and noted that Chloe had now seated herself between The Honourable Charles and The Honourable Freddy, both of whom were obviously trying to win on. That made her smile.

Good luck to them, she thought. She had no doubt that Chloe would relish such a situation.

Katie nudged her as she finished her drink. "Come to the dunny with me Colleen."

"OK," Colleen replied. She rinsed her cup and packed it, then took out her torch and stood up. She and Katie moved around the rear of the group just as Major Wickham stood up.

"Zero One hundred," he said. "Time you all went to bed."

Colleen and Katie hurried on into the darkness across the open Gravel Scrape towards Deep Creek. They used their torches to be safe, neither wanting to step on a snake in the dark. As they reached the creek bank and made their way carefully down a foot trail between the clumps of rubber vine, Katie commented, "That Pommy likes you Colleen. You should go out with him."

"Why?"

"Because he's good looking and he must be rich," Katie replied.

"No thanks. That doesn't mean he is a nice person," Colleen replied.

Chapter 16

MICHAEL

Cecil was not the only one who thought that Colleen was beautiful. Lying in the darkness under a bush beside Deep Creek was 18-year-old Michael O'Malley and he had been admiring her for the last half hour, her face drawn close by the binoculars he was holding. Beside him lay his older brother Dylan.

The two brothers had been watching the cadets all day, trying to keep out of sight and trying not to attract too much attention to themselves. The hardest part had been during the night and it had been with relief that they had noted the return of the last of the cadets from their exercise.

As the two girls had walked towards them at the end of the campfire the two brothers had hidden their faces in their black balaclavas and flattened themselves into the sparse grass. For a second Michael had been sure they would be discovered and he tensed himself to run. At the last minute the girls had detoured to the other side of the bush the brothers were hiding under and had gone down the slope behind them.

As the sound of the girls voices receded behind them Michael had swivelled his head to watch the flicker of their torches.

"That was close," he whispered. "I thought we were going to be sprung then."

"Wonder where they are going?" Dylan said.

"To the toilet probably," Michael replied.

"Might be going to have a smoke like that other pair of tarts," Dylan suggested.

Michael shook his head. "No, I don't think so."

"We could follow them and check," Dylan was suggested.

Michael was shocked and offended. "We will not!" he hissed. He had been struck by Colleen's beauty that morning and had again admired her spirit when she had taken part in the campfire acts. And he was disgusted with his brother's lewd suggestion. Even so, as he thought of her, he had to stifle a yawn.

"Time we went," he suggested.

"Yeah. Looks like that mob are off to bed," Dylan agreed.

"Then let's go," Michael said. He eased himself to a crouch and looked behind to where he could just hear the murmur of the two girls talking in the darkness.

Dylan stood up beside him, his eyes glinting in the glow of the distant fire. Outlined as they were by the black balaclava, they appeared positively evil to Michael.

Dylan said, "I wish we knew why dad wanted us to watch this mob. We might have been able to get what he wanted while they are asleep."

Michael shrugged. He did not know what their father wanted. "They might have guards," he suggested.

"Maybe," Dylan replied. He turned and led the way slowly down the bank into the bed of the dry creek. There was just enough starlight for them to see and they made their way slowly and as silently as they could on the dry leaves and loose stones down towards the main road.

It had been a long day for both of them and Michael was now very tired and not a little mystified. He had been routed out of bed at 0745 that Saturday morning by Dylan.

"It's dad," he had explained. "He wants us to go and find a bunch of army cadets."

"Army cadets!" Michael had echoed incredulously. He knew such people existed but had never in his life actually met one, nor even, to his knowledge, seen one. "What do we have to find army cadets for?"

"Dad wants us to report on them. Liam will tell us more in a minute. He's on the phone to Uncle Shaemus. Now get up ya lazy bugger and get dressed."

Grumbling about the unfairness of getting up early on his day off Michael had risen, dressed and carried out a hasty toilet, then settled at the kitchen table to eat. Soon afterwards their eldest brother Liam, a big, solid young man of 21, had come into the room.

"This is the story. Dad wants us to go and find a bunch of army cadets who are having some sort of training exercise at a place called Millaroo. He particularly wants to know if there are any British cadets with them."

"British cadets!" Michael had echoed, even more mystified.

Liam thrust a newspaper under his nose. Across the front page was the headline: BRITISH ARMY CADETS ARRIVE FOR EXERCISE. Several photos with captions were underneath.

Dylan sniffed. "They must be bloody hard up for news today!" he had muttered as he buttered more toast.

Michael knew that his father had once been involved in some sort of trouble with the British Army in Northern Ireland, but it had been many years ago, around the time when he was born. Because of it the family had migrated to Australia when Michael was a baby, but he had never heard the details. With such a family background however the boys had been subjected to an anti-British tirade from their earliest years, so that all of them had no doubts that the British were evil enemies to Ireland's freedom.

Curiosity made Michael ask, "Why does dad want to know where these British cadets are?"

"He didn't say," Liam replied, "but Uncle Shaemus is coming to see us. Now, I've got to go out and get a few things. You pair get going in the ute. Take your mobile phones and keep in touch with me."

"Where the hell are we going?" Dylan had asked with a scowl. Michael knew Dylan wanted to go and see his girlfriend.

"Place called Millaroo, so Uncle Shaemus says," Liam replied.

"Where the hell is that?" Dylan asked.

"Somewhere south of Ayr. Find it on a road map. Now get going," Liam snapped.

"But I haven't got a road map," Dylan replied.

"Then use your GPS Navigator!"

"I haven't got one of them either," Dylan answered.

Michael stood up, "We will use the app in our phones."

Dylan scowled at him but nodded. "What if our phones go flat?"

"Use a car charger," Michael replied.

Dylan scowled again. "I haven't got one of them either."

"Then bloody well buy one!" Liam retorted. "And take your camping gear and some grub. You might be quite a while."

"Oh pigs! I'm taking Jess out tonight," Dylan replied.

Liam shook his head. "Not if dad wants a job done. Now get going," he replied.

The brothers all worked on a construction site managed by their Uncle Shaemus and had the weekend off. Michael finished his breakfast then went to collect his swag. Since leaving school he and his brothers had worked at several isolated places and were equipped to live rough.

As he was rolling a spare shirt into his blanket roll Michael was surprised to have Dylan toss a black woollen balaclava onto his bedroll.

"What the hell is this?" he asked.

"Just a little precaution. It can get cold at night there," Dylan said.

As they went out to the ute Michael noted that Dylan bought their binoculars with him. He also noted with some disquiet that Dylan checked the two guns that were kept in the ute behind the seat.

"What's going on Dyl?" he asked.

"Dunno. Might see some pigs. There'll be roos for sure," Dylan replied.

Michael knew Dylan and Liam were keen hunters, but he was personally disgusted by it. He said no more and climbed into the ute.

"How do we know where to go?" he asked Liam, who came out to see them off.

"Dunno. Uncle Shaemus told me to go to the Millaroo place. Now get going, and keep reporting what you find out, but don't let on you are interested in them. Say you are just out for a drive or something."

This all had such an air of mystery that Michael felt vaguely uneasy. He then shrugged and settled back as Dylan started the ute up and drove it out of the driveway of their Townsville flat. He then relaxed. A day driving in the country would make a nice break he decided.

It was 1:30pm before the two brothers reached Clare. They had taken several wrong turns and stopped to ask the way twice. At Clare, which was a tiny town with only about three streets each way, they stopped and asked again where Millaroo was. They also tested the mobile phones.

From there they had driven south along the main road, the Ayr-Dalbeg Road, to the Pump Station at Steepy Banks. Here they parked the ute and went looking for someone to give them information. However the place was locked up and deserted. From the top of the high riverbank Michael got a good view out along the wide, deep reach of the river.

"What river is this?" he asked.

"The bloody Burdekin ya nong!" Dylan replied.

"Looks bigger here than near the 'Towers'," Michael replied.

"Course it is. It's got some big rivers join it between here and there," Dylan explained. "You should'a paid more attention in school."

Michael scowled. He hadn't really enjoyed school, although he had achieved quite reasonable marks. "Where to now?"

"Drive on a bit further," Dylan said.

The brothers walked back to the ute and drove slowly south along the road. Within a few minutes Michael had tapped Dylan's arm and pointed.

"There, up on that ridge ahead of us. Are they army cadets?"

Dylan pulled the ute over to the side and stopped. Michael used the binoculars. Into the focused lenses sprang the images of four figures in dark camouflage uniforms. "Yep, army cadets, or maybe soldiers," he said.

Dylan had taken the binoculars and carefully studied the distant figures, which were descending the rugged hillside towards the road. "They look like army," he agreed.

"Let's go and ask them," Michael said.

Having no better plan Dylan agreed. They drove forward but, to Michael's annoyance and astonishment, lost sight of the figures as they neared the end of the ridge. "Can't see them now. Where the bloody hell did they go?"

Dylan kept driving slowly around the end of the ridge. Just as the road curved right into a deep cutting they saw a gravel side-track on the left which led up to a small lookout. "Go up there," Michael had suggested.

They did that. A sign informed them it was CORNFORD LOOKOUT. The ute was parked and they climbed out. Michael then realized that the Lookout was on a small area of flat land between two very deep cuttings. On one side it dropped down to a railway and on the other the main road. He took the binoculars and scanned the hillside above them, then the riverbed below them. As soon as he did this he noted a group of four figures in camouflage uniforms walking along the dry sandy riverbed. He pointed them out to Dylan who grunted and took out his mobile phone and called Liam. The phone had worked but the signal had been weak.

While they were doing this Michael had been surprised to find a group of people in camouflage uniforms walking up the gravel track from the main road. They were only 20 paces away when he first noticed them and he was astonished they could have gotten so close without him seeing them.

That they were army cadets was instantly obvious from their youth. What was an even bigger surprise was that three of them were girls. One of them was a tall red-head who looked very self-assured and attractive. It was when Michael's eyes shifted to the dark-haired girl following that he was really shocked. She was so beautiful he felt something akin to an electric charge pulse through him and, for a minute, he could only gape in open admiration.

The girl with the red hair spoke first. "Sorry," she said. "We didn't mean to sneak up and give you a fright."

Michael managed a smile and shook his head. "You didn't," he said.

As he spoke his eyes had swept over the red-head and then over the others. "Who are you?" he had asked.

"Army cadets doing an exercise," the red-head had replied. "We are chasing some British army cadets. You haven't seen any people in a dark green sort of camouflage uniform, have you?"

Michael met her eyes and smiled, then pointed along the dry bed of the river. "Would that be some of them?"

The red-head looked and nodded, then said, "That looks like some. May I borrow your binoculars?"

"Sure," Michael replied. He handed the red-head the binoculars and she quickly focused them.

"That is them," she said. She handed the binoculars back.

The second girl, the beautiful one with the black hair and bright blue eyes, stepped up beside her. "Can I have a look please?"

"Sure," Michael agreed, handing the binoculars to her. As he did he found he could hardly tear his eyes from her.

She is bloody pretty! he thought. He felt his pulse quicken with interest. *She looks about my age. I wonder how old she is?* He guessed at sixteen or seventeen and hoped he was right.

The dark-haired girl focused the binoculars and stared, then said: "They can't be the ones we chased. They couldn't have gotten that far that quickly."

"No, you're right," the red-head agreed. She turned to Michael. "You didn't see any of them come down the hill there just now did you?"

Michael shook his head. "No, sorry. We just got here."

"Just testing our mobile phone," Dylan added. "I want to see just where we can get reception."

The red-head nodded and asked: "Was there a Land Rover here when you arrived?"

"Didn't see one," Michael replied. He glanced at the pretty, dark-haired one and noted her smile and blush.

The red-head gestured to the third girl, a tiny, skinny little thing with a look of misery on her face, who now sat in sulky silence on the grass.

"She's twisted her ankle and is hot. The Land Rover is our safety vehicle."

"Can we help?" Michael asked.

Quite irrationally he wanted to find a reason to prolong the meeting so that he could get to know the pretty, dark-haired one. He ignored Dylan's frown.

"Oh we'll be right thanks. It isn't an emergency," the red-head replied. "The Land Rover will be back in a minute."

A male cadet pointed along the riverbed. "Those Pommy cadets are climbing up into those rubber vines," he called.

They all turned and watched as the distant British cadets clambered up the steep slope one at a time, to vanish from view. The red-head unclipped a walkie-talkie radio from the webbing she wore and called up another group of cadets. She asked them to use the radio there to pass on the location of the British raiders and said she would be back in ten minutes. That got Michael wondering just how many cadets there were and where they were.

While she was doing this the Land Rover arrived back. An adult officer, a man with a moustache, was driving. He parked the vehicle and got out.

"Everything alright Barbara?" he had asked the red-head.

Barbara had pointed to the small girl. "Cadet Rowland is sick from the heat, and says she has sprained her ankle. Could you take her back to camp sir?"

"Just been there," the officer replied. "Took another British cadet in, sick from the heat, Charles Bletchley, poor chap!" As he said this his voice changed to an imitation English accent and they all smiled, even Dylan.

"Get in the Land Rover Cadet Rowland," Barbara had said, gesturing to the vehicle. She turned to the officer. "Can you give us a lift back to the turn-off near camp please sir?"

"What, all of you?"

"No, only Cadet Norris and myself. Colleen and Cpl Foggarty are going back up the hill," Barbara replied, gesturing towards the black-haired girl.

Is her name Colleen? Michael thought. Once again he studied her with irrational interest.

The black haired one, Colleen, said, "We need water sir."

"Yes, here's a jerry can," the officer replied. He heaved out a plastic water jerry and they all set to work filling their water bottles.

While this was going on Michael had stood studying the black-haired girl with open admiration.

She is the prettiest thing!' he thought.

After the black-haired girl completed filling her water bottles, she moved behind the Land Rover. Michael badly wanted to talk to her but was drawn into a conversation with the officer.

Dylan asked if there really were British cadets in the area. When told they were, he said: "Strewth! They are a long way from home. They must find it a bit bloody hot here."

While they talked Michael took the opportunity to walk over to where Barbara and the black-haired girl stood. He was now gripped by an intense desire to speak to her, in the vague hope that he might get to know her. With an effort he mastered his nervousness and tried to appear calm and cool.

After swallowing to moisten his suddenly dry throat, he said, "Hi! I'm Michael. Sorry if we were rude. I didn't know there were girls in the army cadets."

"Well there are," Barbara answered.

Michael nodded, but his eyes were drawn to the black-haired girl, as though by an invisible force. She met his gaze and blushed. "What's your name?" he managed to ask, although his mouth felt dry with anxiety.

"Colleen," the black-haired girl had replied.

Colleen, Michael mentally whispered.

"What a lovely name," he said. "It's Irish isn't it?"

"Yes," Colleen replied. "My family come from Ireland."

"So do mine," Michael replied. For a moment he could only stand and stare in awe at Colleen as hope and wonder filled him. Desperate not to lose the link with her he asked, "Where do you live?"

"Townsville," Colleen replied.

"So do I! How come I have never seen you around?" Michael asked.

"Probably went to a different school," Colleen replied. "Which school did you go to?"

"Columba Catholic College, the boarding school in Charters Towers," Michael replied.

"I go to St Pats," Colleen replied.

For a second Michael was sorely tempted to ask straight out if Colleen was a Catholic. From the name and the school she went to he thought it likely. Unable to think of what to say he smiled at her and noted her return smile and a sparkle in her eyes. He was so struck by her beauty that he could not think of anything sensible to say to continue the conversation. But he was also aware that Dylan was frowning at him.

The male officer saved them. "OK Cpl McNamara, you and Cpl Foggarty get going back up that hill. The exercise has only an hour to run. Get in Barbara, and you Norris."

"See you then," Colleen said to Michael.

For a moment Michael felt an intense desire to ask Colleen for her phone number or address but he was then overcome by shyness.

She will think I am silly, or too forward, he thought.

He was also constrained by the presence of the others. Instead he gave a wry smile and nodded. To his regret Colleen and the male cadet set off down the gravel track back to the main road. Barbara and the other cadets climbed into the Land Rover and the officer climbed in and started up.

As he did, Dylan pointed and said, "Come on, get in the ute. Let's go."

Reluctantly Michael did so, his eyes following Colleen all the way down the track and across the road. He wistfully watched her cross the road and begin climbing the hill through the dry bush. "Jesus she's pretty!" he had said.

Dylan snorted. "Just a bloody kid! You'll end up in bloody jail if you start messing with school kids. Now stop mooning about sheilas and get your mind on the job. Liam wants us to find out how many cadets there are, where they are camped and what they are doing."

"Oh, is that all!" Michael replied sarcastically, taking a last look up at where Colleen had vanished up the hill.

Chapter 17

WHY?

As the army Land Rover drove back down to the main road the two brothers followed it in their ute. Michael cast a last wistful look up the hill, hoping to get another glimpse of Colleen. Then he focused his attention on what the cadets were doing.

After only half a kilometre the Land Rover slowed and turned right off the main road onto a gravel side-track. Dylan glanced at it and gave a wave in reply to one from the red-head. Then he kept driving on along the main road.

"That must be where they are camped," he suggested.

Michael looked but could only see the back of the Land Rover and bush. No tents or people were visible.

Only about 50 metres past the turn-off was a creek. The main road crossed this on a large embankment. As they reached it Dylan slowed the ute and pulled over.

"What are you doing?" Michael asked.

"Going to have a better look," Dylan replied. He stopped the ute and they both climbed out. Michael wiped perspiration out of his eyes and squinted against the glare as he peered into the bush. As he looked, he puzzled over what exactly they were looking for. He had such a hazy idea of how army cadets were organized and what they did that he really felt quite ignorant. The closest experience he could relate to was a couple of Scout camps a few years earlier.

"Do cadets go around in small groups or are there lots of them?" he asked Dylan.

"Army cadets? Don't they go around in big bunches and have rows of tents all lined up and things like that?" Dylan suggested.

Michael did not know. He turned and bent into the ute to get the binoculars. As he straightened up again, he realized with a shock that there was an army cadet sitting in the grass beside the road only ten paces further along.

"Bloody hell! Sorry, I didn't see you," he said.

The cadet, a boy in his early teens, grinned with embarrassment. Michael then saw that a second boy sat behind a bush a couple of paces beyond the first. Michael tried to act casual.

"What are you kids doing?" he asked.

"We are on an exercise," the cadet replied. "Our platoon has to protect these tunnels against raiders."

"Tunnels?" Michael asked, mystified.

The cadet pointed to the nearby railway embankment and Michael understood. "Oh you mean the culverts."

"Yeah, that's right."

"How many of you are there?" Michael asked.

"Only two of us here, but there are two more across the road and another two on the other side of the railway," the cadet replied. Then he looked suspicious and asked, "You aren't a spy for the enemy, are you?"

At that Michael felt a surge of guilt, but this was smothered by laughter.

"Spy! Fair go! We are just looking for a couple of stray cattle."

Dylan had joined Michael by then. He said to the cadet, "Who is the enemy?"

"Bunch of Pommy cadets I think," the cadet replied.

"Pommies? Are you sure?" Dylan said.

"So the platoon commander said," the cadet replied.

"Have you seen any?" Dylan asked.

The cadet shook his head. At that Michael said, "We might have. We saw some cadets in a darker green sort of camouflage uniform back at the lookout there."

The cadet looked very interested and he and his companion exchanged glances.

"Which way did they go?" he asked.

"Along the riverbed, upstream," Michael replied, pointing south.

Dylan asked, "How many cadets are here?"

"Oh, about seventy I think," the cadet replied.

"Are you staying here all weekend?"

The cadet shook his head. "No. We are only doing the exercise till this afternoon. Then we go back to camp."

"Are you camped over there?" Dylan asked, pointing up the creek.

"Yeah, in the old gravel scrape," the cadet replied.

"Thanks. Well, if you see two young steers with a BQ brand on them let us know eh?" Dylan said.

"Sure. Are they wild?"

Dylan shook his head. "No, not really. Well, see you around," he replied. He moved to the ute and got in. Michael did likewise. They started up and drove on south along the road.

"That was useful," Michael said.

"Yeah, but I wanted to look at their camp," Dylan replied.

"We can always drive in and look," Michael suggested.

"Nah. Liam said don't attract any attention," Dylan replied.

That puzzled Michael as he still wondered what their father's interest in the army cadets was. He said, "We could walk in through the bush."

"Yeah, but we'd need to be careful. They seem to have little groups all over the place. Look, there's another bunch."

As he said this Dylan pointed to the right. Michael saw three cadets with a radio standing near the base of a steel power pylon.

So as to look like normal locals Dylan kept driving. This took them south across fairly open and flat country. On the way they spotted another group of cadets walking through the bush on their right and then found a vehicle and three more cadets at the turn-off to 'Landers Creek' station. More cadets stood guarding the road and rail bridges over Landers Creek.

To avoid any complications Dylan kept on driving across the bridge and on southwards.

"How far are we going?" Michael asked.

"Better go on for a bit," Dylan replied.

They drove for five more minutes, passing through a range of small hills in dry bush, before coming back out into sugar cane country. After driving for a few more kilometres Dylan slowed the ute and stopped. He got out and checked the mobile phone, then called Liam and passed on the information they had collected.

When he finished the call he said, "Liam says to have a look at their camp but not to be seen."

"That sounds easier said than done," Michael replied. He was getting hot and tired and wanted to go home.

"Have to park the car and walk," Dylan agreed.

"Wish we had a map," Michael added.

"Well we haven't, so too bad," Dylan replied.

He started the ute and turned it round, then headed back northwards along the main road.

"Where we going?" Michael asked.

"Might try that side road, the one that leads to that cattle station," Dylan replied.

They drove across the Landers Creek bridge and turned left at the turn-off. One of the cadets there raised a hand in greeting and Michael waved casually back.

The road was gravel and well maintained. It went up a slight rise through open bush. An old, overgrown road curved off to the right but there was no gate giving access to it. The gravel road curved gently and they were soon out of sight of the cadets at the junction. After about a kilometre they came to where the power line crossed the road. Dylan braked and pulled the ute off to the right-hand side.

"This might do us," he commented, turning the ute onto the dirt track below the powerlines. He then drove about a hundred metres northwards along the two wheel ruts in the long grass. Coming to a padlocked gate in a fence he stopped. He then switched off the engine.

Dylan pointed and said, "They are camped just near that line of hills. We can follow this power line most of the way," he said.

"We might meet some cadets," Michael suggested. He wasn't keen on such a long walk in the heat.

"So what? They won't know we aren't the local landowners," Dylan replied.

He clapped an old felt hat on his head and reached in behind the seat, extracting a rifle with a telescopic sight.

"What do you want that for?" Michael asked, reluctantly getting out.

"Never know. We might run into a pig, or a snake. Anyway, we can say we are looking for roos or something. Besides, I can use the scope. You bring those binoculars," Dylan replied.

Michael did as he was told and followed his older brother along the track. Ahead of them he could see for a long way along the power line clearing. In the distance he saw that the powerlines went up over line of hills that ended at the Lookout. He was unsure how far it was but guessed at several kilometres.

Too bloody far anyway! he thought, unhappy at the idea of walking for hours in the heat.

And that is what it took, and because they were not properly prepared and had no water they both became very hot and thirsty. It took them about half an hour to reach a point where they could see the group of cadets guarding the power pylon beside the main road. On seeing them Dylan turned left and walked west into the bush, crossing a dry creek and then walking up a gentle slope through open savannah woodland and waist high spear grass.

Michael hated walking in the long grass, for fear of snakes, but knew his brother would pour scorn on any mention of being afraid so he trudged on in silence. He was thankful he wore his jeans and riding boots.

At least we won't get lost, he thought, noting that the line of hills was very much closer and made a very clear navigational feature.

After skirting a big, overgrown gravel pit the brothers stopped. Satisfied they were out of sight of the cadets at the road Dylan turned right and led the way north again. Another twenty minutes of tramping through savannah woodland, crossing a fair sized, but dry creek, and crawling under a new barbed wire fence had them at the bank of a third, larger, dry creek. On the far side was the bare red earth of a gravel scrape and beyond that rose the hill. They had not seen any cadets until now.

"There they are," Dylan said, moving to a crouch behind a tree.

He raised the rifle and sighted through the scope. Michael also took cover, feeling slightly foolish about it. He raised the binoculars and looked.

Just visible among the trees and bushes on the other side of the gravel scrape were several army cadets. A few small camouflaged tents showed among the bushes. He could only see two people standing beside a bush, but when he focused the binoculars he saw the bush was actually a camouflage net over a small tent fly. Two more cadets sat under it, talking on radios.

"Not many of them," Michael observed.

"No. Hello! Look at this!" Dylan hissed.

He pointed down to his right. Michael had to move to see what he was talking about and was surprised to see a line of cadets creeping towards them in the dry creek bed. These cadets wore dark green camouflage uniforms.

Six, he counted.

"Who are they? Are they British?" he asked.

Dylan had swung the rifle to study them more carefully. "Yep. No doubt about it."

Michael looked. The British cadets were obviously unaware of their presence and had their attention also focused on the camp in the gravel scrape. Into the lenses of the binoculars sprang red faces, flushed by the heat and burned by the sun.

Poms alright, he decided, *and feeling the heat.*

Dylan kept the telescopic sight fixed on the leading British cadet. Michael noted the barrel swing slowly as Dylan kept his aim. Dylan gave a grunt and placed his finger on the trigger.

Grinning he muttered: "I could drop that Pommy bastard easy."

"Jesus Dylan! You be careful. Please take your finger off the trigger. We don't want anyone hurt," Michael cried softly.

He was feeling unhappy enough about the whole operation without Dylan making those sorts of comments.

As the brothers watched them the British cadets split into two groups. Two cadets went creeping up the bank along the line of an old fence while the others crept on along the creek below where Dylan and Michael crouched watching. They then climbed out of the creek and moved forward across the flat through some bushes.

In the centre of the gravel scrape a voice shouted a warning and then cried, "Bang!" The British cadets began pretend firing back. Michael stared with interest at the mock battle which then broke out. The defenders in the camp quickly took cover behind trees and mounds and pretended to fire back.

More shouts and bangs broke out across the creek to the right along the entrance road. Michael could just make out figures flitting from cover to cover. This went on for a few more minutes before more figures appeared in the creek bed near the main road. These wore Australian Army camouflage, which Michael noted really blended in with the local vegetation.

This new group went up the bank in the same direction as the two British cadets, who were then seen to run and get captured. Dylan followed the action with the scope. "There's that red-headed sheila we met at the Lookout," he said.

Michael focused the binoculars and agreed. He scanned the distant faces hoping to spot Colleen but could not see her.

There were more voices to their right rear. Dylan stared that way, then stood up and gestured to move back away from the creek.

"Time we were gone I reckon. We have seen enough."

Michael agreed. He had no desire to be caught and have to make embarrassing explanations. The two brothers backed off into a thicket of mulga scrub as a patrol of cadets came hurrying past fifty metres away.

Once clear of the immediate area Dylan led the way back to the ute at a fast walk. By then Michael was feeling very dry and was longing for a drink. He was also bothered by blisters and by chafing which was beginning between his thighs. He wasn't used to walking.

It was after 1700 when they reached the ute. Both had a drink from the water they carried for topping up the radiator. The water was warm and tasted slightly oily, but Michael was still glad of it. He sat and wiped his face while Dylan made another call on the mobile phone.

"Liam wants us to keep a close watch on them tonight. He says he wants to know every last little thing about them, particularly where they camp and if they have any guards or not," Dylan said.

"Why? What's going on?" Michael asked. He had a headache now and was feeling peevish and slightly worried.

"Dunno, but he says he and dad will be joining us sometime early tomorrow. He will let us know when."

"Dad! Coming here! Why?" Michael cried. He was amazed. Their father and mother lived in Mount Isa, a thousand kilometres to the west.

Dylan shrugged. "No idea. Maybe he wants to do something to hit back at those bloody Pommies?"

That idea sent a shiver of apprehension through Michael. He vaguely knew that their father had been a member of the IRA many years before, and that he had been forced to flee Ulster to avoid arrest, but he did not know any details.

"It wouldn't be anything serious would it?" he asked anxiously.

Dylan shrugged again. "Doubt it. He might just want to embarrass them. There's no love lost between him and the British Army, that's for sure."

At that the old ditty flitted through Michael's mind. It had been often sung at home when he was small and now he hummed it.

'Some people say the Devil's dead,
Others say it's blarney,
Others say he's rose again,
And joined the British Army!'

Dylan heard him and grinned. "Might be good to teach the bastards a lesson," he said. "They've got no place being in Australia now either."

"So what's the plan?" Michael asked, his excitement rising at the thought of possible action, and of striking a blow for Ireland against her ancient foe.

"We park the ute and sneak in to watch everything they do," Dylan replied.

Michael was aghast. "Fair go! What about a feed and a bath? I've had enough of this bush bashing for one day." He did not say it, but the idea of creeping around the bush in the dark terrified him.

"Crap little brother!" Dylan snarled. "If dad says we watch, we watch! If he wants information to put the bloody Brits in their place, then we will give it to him."

Michael still did not give up. He had a splitting headache and felt sticky and dirty. "What about driving back to that town, Clare, to get a hamburger or something first?"

"No. We've got grub with us. We will cook for ourselves."

"What about water?" Michael persisted.

"Shut up you soft little shit and get in," Dylan said. He climbed in and started the vehicle's engine. Reluctantly Michael got in. Dylan backed the ute out onto the gravel road and turned it towards the main road. They set off in that direction.

As they drove Michael asked, "Is mum coming too?"

Dylan shook his head. "Don't think so."

Michael had not seen his father for nearly a year and felt mixed emotions. He loved his dad but found him a forbidding figure. It had been no real hardship to spend those years at boarding school away from him.

They reached the road junction after a minute's drive. The cadets were gone from there and from guarding the bridge. Dylan swung the ute left and headed north along the main road. By now the afternoon shadows were reaching out across the plain from the mountain away to the west and the fierceness had gone out of the air.

They had only driven a few hundred metres when Dylan let out a hiss and pointed. Michael looked and saw a group of four cadets walking along the side of the road, marching in the same direction.

"Brits!" Dylan said as they got closer.

To Michael's surprise Dylan slowed down and came to a stop beside the marching group. Michael noted the red faces, sweat soaked uniforms and tired expressions. He was even more surprised to see that the leader of the group was a big, strapping blonde girl.

"G'day," Dylan called in his broadest Australian accent (easy as both brothers naturally spoke that way from a childhood in Australia). "What'ya doin'?"

"Just heading back to our camp for the night," the blonde answered. Her voice was so obviously English, and upper class at that, that Michael had to suppress a smile.

"You aren't Aussies," Dylan commented.

"No, English," the girl replied.

"Strewth! You're a long way from home. Yer must find it a bit hot eh?" Dylan suggested.

The girl gave a rueful smile. "We do. We've only been here two days."

"Would ya like a lift?" Dylan offered, giving a friendly grin.

"Yes thank you. We are a bit late," the girl replied.

"Mike, get out and shift some of that junk in the back," Dylan ordered.

Michael did as he was told. While he was rearranging the swags and oil drums in the back, he was annoyed to hear Dylan invite the girl to sit in the front with him. He found himself climbing into the back with three male British cadets.

As they settled themselves one put out his hand. "Cecil Gough-Gore. Thanks very much. We've had a long day."

Feeling quite guilty Michael took the proffered hand and shook it. "Mike," he said. "Where you from?"

As the ute started up, he listened to Cecil describing his school and home in England. The youth's accent was so 'English' that Michael found it both amusing and irritating.

They had only driven about a kilometre when the ute abruptly braked. Michael swivelled his head to look and saw Dylan's arm out the window, waving at a Land Rover coming the other way. The Rover stopped beside them and Michael noted that the officer with the moustache was the driver.

"Been looking for this lot," the officer explained, indicating the British cadets. "Thanks for giving them a lift."

"No problem," Dylan replied.

"Thanks awfully," Cecil said as he climbed out with the others.

"Think nothing of it," Dylan replied. "See you again."

Michael climbed back into the cab. "What now?"

Dylan engaged the gears and started the ute moving while the Land Rover did a three-point turn behind them. "Like I said, we find somewhere to eat, then watch this mob."

They drove on past the turn-off to the gravel scrape and on around the hill beyond the Lookout. Finding nowhere else they went all the way back to the turn-off to the pump station at 'Steepy Banks'. Here they found an old vehicle track that led back to an overgrown campground on top of the riverbank near the end of the hill.

"This will do," Dylan said.

It was dusk by then. The place was overgrown with waist-high grass but Dylan declared it perfect as they were close to the main road and railway but completely hidden from both. They quickly cleared an area and lit a fire. Their dinner was nothing much, just heated baked beans from tins and some bread, washed down with strong, black tea.

By the time they were finished it was dark. Dylan then organized them for the night. He dug out a torch and knife, plus the two balaclavas.

"Put this on," he ordered, handing the balaclava to Michael.

Michael did so but felt very uncomfortable and foolish. It was also very hot, so he soon rolled the woollen garment up above his ears. The two brothers then made their way through twenty metres of long grass and through a barbed wire fence to the railway line. Dylan opted to follow this, so they turned left and set off walking around the base of the hill.

"We'll look a bit odd walking along the main road," Dylan explained, gesturing towards where the headlights of a passing car lit up the hillside.

At the big cutting below the Lookout they got the shock of almost walking into a line of dark figures coming the other way. Dylan stopped abruptly and hissed.

"What's that noise?"

Michael stopped and listened. The odd crunching noise came clearly to him. Then he heard the chink of stone on metal and realized what the noise was: boots crunching on the gravel ballast. A voice confirmed the sound was being made by people.

"Someone coming," he whispered, his heart rate shooting up with excitement.

"Hide, quick!" Dylan said.

In the nick of time the two brothers scrambled into the long grass on the side of the embankment. Michael crouched, sweating and with beating heart as about twenty cadets went past, the sound of their boots trudging on the gravel ballast sounding very loud.

After the group had passed the two brothers crawled back up onto the railway. Michael dusted himself down and wished he had a water bottle as his tongue was sticking to the top of his mouth from thirst.

"Bloody Poms," Michael commented. He had heard some of them talking.

"I wonder where they are going?" Dylan said.

"Down to the river from the sound of it," Michael replied.

"Yeah. Sssh! Listen," Dylan said.

They stood still and strained their ears. From down in the riverbed came the faint sound of voices.

"They must be doing some sort of exercise down there," Michael suggested.

"We'd better check," Dylan replied.

"That was only a few of them," Michael reminded.

"I know, but we will look bloody silly if we walk all the way to that gravel scrape and find the cadets are all here. Come on," Dylan replied.

The brothers made their way back through the cutting. Sounds indicated that the British cadets had gone out onto the grassy hillside below on their right, so the brothers crawled under the fence and followed a trail of crushed grass. They were just in time to see an adult officer hang a hurricane lantern on a tree branch nearby. By then it was obvious that the cadets were in fact taking part in some sort of exercise down in the dry riverbed.

For the next three hours the brothers sat in the long grass watching and listening, trying to follow what was going on. After a while the pattern became clear, but Dylan vetoed going down to find out.

"They will come back this way to get back to their camp," he said.

"What if they stay out all night?" Michael grumbled.

He was now feeling stiff and sore and just wanted to lie down and sleep. In fact he had almost drifted off by the time cadets began collecting in a group near the lantern only 50 paces away. These were British cadets and Michael clearly heard their officer counting them. The British cadets then walked past them to the end of the cutting and set off along the railway back towards the gravel scrape.

"Do we follow them?" Michael asked.

"Not yet. Wait for the rest of them to go back," Dylan said. So they lay in the grass and waited as more cadets, Australians this time, began gathering at the lantern. On one occasion a cadet came over and had a leak near them. The two brothers lay flat in the grass, their balaclavas over their faces. Then Michael got a real lift. Into the light of the lantern came a girl he recognized as Colleen. He focused the binoculars to check and felt his heart skip. It was her!

But then the two brothers had to sit and wait while the search for the missing cadet went on. What was going on was obvious from the calling out and lines of torches out on the riverbed. That made Michael even grumpier as he really was worn out by then.

When the main group of cadets tramped past on their way back along the railway line the two brothers waited, then followed them all the way to the gate. Here they sat behind bushes and waited till the last group arrived. When they did, Michael was glad they had waited because he clearly saw Colleen in the headlights of the Land Rover.

It was the desire to see more of her that made him willing to agree to Dylan's suggestion to creep around to the other side of the camp along the dry creek to see what was going on beyond the big mound in the middle of the gravel scrape. Thus it was that he was able to watch Colleen at the campfire.

She really is lovely, he thought as he and Dylan reached the main road again at about 1:30am.

Then it was a twenty-minute trudge back along the railway to their camp. By the time they arrived Michael was so dehydrated and tired that he was happy to gulp the last of the oily water, and was even happier to roll in his blankets without caring too much about snakes.

Chapter 18

A NEW DAY

When Barbara had reached the bivouac that night after LCpl McArtney had been found she felt quite worn out. Despite this she made an effort and moved to the campfire to unwind emotionally and to enjoy a hot drink. A cup of Milo and the antics of the cadets cheered her up enormously so that she felt much happier when she at last stood up to go to bed.

She said goodnight to Colleen and Katie as they went off into the darkness to go to the toilet. Feeling very mixed emotions she had made her way to the 1 Platoon area and located her hutchie. It had taken her another five minutes to tie up her mosquito net. Sighing with relief she unrolled her bedding and sat down. Removing her boots from her tired and swollen feet was real bliss and after massaging them she lay back and stretched.

For a few minutes she lay with her eyes closed, expecting sleep to embrace her. To her mild annoyance she found her mind was still too active to allow her to relax. The day had been something of an emotional roller coaster for her and she now re-lived much of it. What gave her the most satisfaction was how well 1 Platoon seemed to have coped and pulled together as a team. To her own mild surprise she found she really cared about the platoon and its future.

Unable to sleep she sat up and had a drink. That prompted a need to go to the toilet again, so she pulled on her boots, picked up her torch and made her way across the gravel scrape towards the dry creek bed where the latrine was located. As she did, she noted that several people still sat around the campfire, which had now subsided to a small pile of glowing embers.

Having relieved herself Barbara climbed back up the bank to the open area. On the way back to her bed she detoured over to the fire, expecting to find a couple of the adult staff still talking. Instead she found it was Chloe and Jane, plus three of the British cadets: Cecil, the Honourable Charles, and Freddy.

Bloody Chloe! she thought. *Trust her!*

As she drew closer Barbara noted that Chloe had several of the buttons of her shirt undone, allowing a considerable amount of cleavage to show. Seated beside her the Honourable Charles was gazing at Chloe with a look that Barbara could only interpret as hopeful admiration.

As Barbara reached them, they looked up.

Chloe smiled. "Hi CUO Brassington! Care to join us?"

Barbara shook her head. "You should all be in bed. You have to get up in about four hours don't forget. You will be very tired tomorrow."

Chloe pouted but nodded. For a moment Barbara thought she was going to argue but instead she agreed. "Yes, you are right. Bedtime you lot. Come on, help me up."

Both the Honourable Charles and Freddy sprang to their feet and offered their hands to Chloe. They did it so fast Barbara had to smile. Cecil helped Jane to her feet. As they did Major Wickham and Lt Barker appeared from behind the mound.

"What are you people doing up?" Major Wickham asked. "It's after two O'clock. Go to bed!"

"Just making sure the campfire died down sir," Chloe replied. "We don't want a bushfire."

Major Wickham gave her a wry smile. "No."

As they all began to move off Barbara beckoned to Chloe. Chloe left the two British cadets and came over to her. "Yes ma'am?"

"Don't you do anything silly Chloe," Barbara cautioned.

Chloe shook her head. "Don't worry. I won't. I want to be a CUO before I get to be Lady Matchlock."

Barbara had to laugh at that. "That sounds very mercenary," she replied.

Chloe grinned. "Maybe, but you must admit that the Honourable Charles has got a few good points."

"Oh yes?"

"Well, he's rich, he's good looking, and he's an English lord," Chloe replied. She gave a mischievous grin.

"I know. But please behave Chloe," Barbara said.

"I will. We were just getting to know each other," Chloe replied. "Besides, I promised Major Wickham I wouldn't cause any problems."

"Thanks. Take care," Barbara said.

Chloe smiled and Barbara felt a surge of genuine liking for her. They said goodnight and went their separate ways. Barbara was quite sure that Chloe would keep her word, so she went back to her own bed with a clear mind.

This time when she lay down, she fell asleep almost instantly. It was a deep, refreshing sleep and she woke feeling quite alert when CSM Warren called on the sergeants to get the cadets out on check parade at 0600.

Barbara pulled on her boots and followed the platoon as it marched down past HQ. She stopped there to say good morning to Major Wickham and the other OOCs and CUOs. CUO Callan was retelling the story of the search.

"I just walked to the light," he said, mimicking LCpl McArtney. "The bloody light! Three bloody kilometres there on that sand, and then another three back! I feel wrecked."

CUO Roberts smiled. "Aren't you tough enough to command 4 Platoon?" she teased.

CUO Callan snorted. Major Wickham stood up. "I hope we don't have any problems today. I don't want another day like yesterday."

"We couldn't have anything worse than that," Lt Cavendish said.

"Has anyone looked behind the gravel heap?" CUO Bailey quipped.

"That will be enough of that!" Major Wickham snapped. He looked tired and irritable and Barbara felt sorry for him. "I want a nice easy day today," he added.

"That bloody Chloe," CUO Callan said, "she did her usual trick this morning."

"What was that?" Barbara asked, although she suspected the answer.

"She slept with almost nothing on and when she got up she sat up and pulled on her shirt so that some of the Pommy cadets all got a good eyeful," CUO Callan replied.

"Was she naked?" Lt Cavendish queried.

CUO Callan shook his head. "Nah, she had a bikini on, but not a very big one."

"She should be chucked out," Lt Peters added, her face a mask of bad temper.

Lt Cavendish scowled. "I hope she wasn't up to any of her other tricks," she said.

Barbara wanted to defend Chloe but had no proof so held her tongue. The conversation was diverted by CSM Warren coming over after dismissing the parade.

"Any missing CSM?" Major Wickham asked.

"No sir. Two sick, but all here," CSM Warren replied. He sat to mark the company roll.

Major Wickham nodded, then said, "OK CUOs, go and get your platoons ready. Inspections at 0730. Have them packed up by zero seven forty-five. CSM, Company parade at zero eight hundred."

"Yes sir."

The CUOs dispersed to their platoon areas. As Barbara passed HQ, she met Colleen, who had just returned from parade. Colleen looked pale and drawn.

"You OK Colleen?" Barbara asked, remembering her bust-up with Cpl Unsworth.

Colleen nodded and managed a weak smile. "Yes thanks. Just a bit tired. It was a late night."

"Yes it was. That blasted light!" Barbara agreed.

They both laughed and made wry smiles. Barbara walked on back to the 1 Platoon area. She arrived just as the cadets returned from the check parade. The cadets were fallen out and told to get on with their morning routine and Sgt Brady at once reported to her that all the cadets were present, but that Cadet Rowland said she was sick.

"Where is she?" Barbara asked.

"In her hutchie," Sgt Brady replied.

Barbara walked over and knelt down to speak to the sick cadet. Cadet Rowland sniffled miserably and said she felt too sick to get up, but Barbara thought she was just feeling sorry for herself, although she didn't say so.

Instead she said, "When we go out for this morning's exercise you had better go over to the CP and be with them."

Cadet Rowland raised a teary face and said, "I want to go home."

"Well you can't. So just stay at the CP," Barbara replied.

"Why not? They took some people home yesterday morning," Cadet Rowland replied.

Her sulky look and selfishness annoyed Barbara. "That was different. They were being chucked out for misbehaviour. Besides, you can't expect two of the adult staff to drive for three hours just because you feel a bit down. You will be on the bus to go home at lunch time."

Cadet Rowland still looked sulky, but Barbara gave up wasting her breath trying to convince her and went over to her own gear. She rolled up her mosquito net, groundsheet and sleeping bag and then led the platoon out to the bare ground of the Gravel Scrape to cook breakfast.

As she sat cooking and eating her breakfast Barbara carefully studied the cadets in the platoon. Most seemed to be cheerful enough and she decided they had accepted the changes from the previous day. She thought Sgt Brady looked a bit moody but was pleased to note that Cpl Ridgeway was talking happily to his cadets and LCpl Ray was telling jokes and laughing.

We might be able to save this platoon, she mused.

That it would take an on-going effort she was well aware, but she steeled herself to make the commitment.

As quickly as she could Barbara washed up, packed away her stove and mess gear then cleaned her teeth and then tidied her hair. She then hurried away to the girls latrine. As she reached the creek bank two female cadets came into view from behind the bushes in the creek bed: Sandy and Micki.

What have those two been up to? Barbara thought. *Smoking I suppose.*

But she had to concede they might have just been going to the toilet as she was. Both girls smiled and said cheery good mornings. Barbara felt like scowling and questioning them but knew she had no proof so answered in like fashion.

A minute later she was alone among the bushes and sniffing. No doubt about it, the tang of tobacco smoke hung in the still morning air.

The sneaky bitches were smoking! she thought angrily, knowing she would be unable to make a case of it.

She quickly went about her business and hurried back to her platoon, passing Katie and Valerie on the way back. By 0730 she was packed and ready to inspect the platoon. The cadets were not all ready, so Barbara called Sgt Brady aside.

After a meaningful glance at her watch Barbara said, "They should be ready by now Sgt Brady. Get them moving. You inspect them and then come and get me from HQ. Don't be more than ten minutes."

Sgt Brady pursed his lips and looked unhappy, but he just nodded and replied, "Yes ma'am," then went to yell at the cadets to hurry up. Barbara walked over to where the adult staff were talking near the gravel heap.

The conversation was about the problems of the previous day, and who might be promoted the following year to keep the unit functioning well. Major Wickham asked Barbara how she thought 1 Platoon was going and she gave a positive report.

Major Wickham nodded and added, "I am going to have to ask you to stay on as the platoon commander for the rest of the year. If you can't I will disband the platoon."

Barbara nodded. "I will do it sir. I don't mind. It will be a challenge."

"Good. Thank you for that... what? What the bloody hell is going on over there?"

They all turned to face towards the area where 4 Platoon and the British cadets were bivouacked and from which was coming shouts, laughter and ribald yells.

CSM Warren hurried in that direction but the yelling had subsided and only laughter could be heard by the time he reached them. He returned a few minutes later.

"Well?" Major Wickham asked.

"Chloe sir," CSM Warren replied, as though that explained everything.

For a moment Barbara assumed the worst and so, obviously, did everyone else.

"What is she up to this time?" Major Wickham asked in a resigned tone of voice.

"Just teaching one of the Poms a lesson in manners sir," CSM Warren replied. "One of them teased her and made a couple of crude suggestions, asking her if she liked wrestling. So she challenged him to a wrestle to prove she was better than him. She dropped him in a second and was holding his face in the dirt when I arrived."

Major Wickham rolled his eyes. "Wrestle!" he muttered.

Barbara had to smile. She knew that no red-blooded boy could resist such a challenge. She said, "I suppose she didn't warn him beforehand that she is a specialist at Martial Arts?"

They all laughed and CSM Warren shook his head.

"Serves the silly bugger right then," Lt Barker offered.

"Are there liable to be any repercussions?" Major Wickham asked.

"No sir. Don't think so."

Major Wickham pursed his lips. "CSM, go and remind Sgt Cummings that the AAC is a 'no touching' organization."

"Yes sir."

"Who was the Pom?" Barbara asked.

"Some guy named Topping," CSM Warren replied.

Lt Barker at once quipped in a mock English accent, "Oh I say, that's jolly topping what?"

They laughed again, all except Lt Cavendish and Lt Peters, both of whom scowled. But the group had to restrain themselves when Major Grogan and Lt Jeffries came walking over. At that moment Sgt Brady came to report to Barbara so she left the group and moved to inspect her platoon.

By the time she had done this it was time for company parade. During the parade, Major Wickham thanked them for good behaviour during the night and then explained the outline of the morning's activities. This was to be a series of fieldcraft and observation exercises set up along the creeks.

For the exercise various objects would be placed along the creeks and gullies, such as trip wires and pretend land mines, plus other items of gear. These would be laid out to tell a story. Each cadet would then move along the route on their own, trying to detect the perils while noting every object and working out what might have happened. Barbara had done several similar exercises and knew the cadets really liked them.

Radios were tested and the CP organized. Lt Barker and Lt Peters were left in charge at the camp, while Capt Hamilton and Sgt Dunstan drove off to refill the water jerries in Clare. Barbara noted that the CP was staffed by Micki and Sandy, and that Cpl Horn and Cadet Rowland were lying in the shade near them.

When the radios had been tested Major Wickham led the company out along the gravel road to the main road. As before CSM Warren and Cpl Forest followed him, then 1 Platoon. It was 0825 by then and already it was so hot they were perspiring even before they began walking.

Once at the main road they crossed it. Major Wickham then led the company down between the road and the railway and left through the culverts under the railway. Barbara assumed they would go along Snake

Gully as they had the night before, but instead he then led them down Deep Creek for a hundred metres until he could easily climb the bank and then led the long line of cadets across a wide paddock dotted with a few trees. Again he halted every hundred paces or so to allow the tail of the line to close up.

From out there Barbara could clearly see the Big Hill, the main road and the railway and felt pleased with her efforts the previous day. As she drank from a water bottle during a short halt, she studied the route she had taken up the Big Hill and was amused to hear the cadets talking and boasting about the exercise. Obviously they had enjoyed it and thought they had done well.

They made their way under the Power Lines and on along a cattle pad through a patch of quite dense scrub to where Deep Creek curved sharply right at the base of the steep slope up to the railway. After following the bed of the creek for a hundred paces they climbed out on the left and made their way up and along the old, overgrown road on the side of the slope below the railway.

They walked quickly along this towards the river. Barbara found it easier walking in the daylight except for the heat. Sweat trickled down her forehead and she had to repeatedly wipe her face.

Ten minutes later they came out on the hillside above the river on the old highway. Above them to the left was the steep slope up to the railway and Lookout. Below on the right was the sandy bed of the river. As they came out into the open where the whole sweep of the riverbed was visible Barbara heard people muttering about the 'bloody light' and how far they had walked the previous night. She looked out and noted the morning sun glinting on the corrugated iron roofs of 'Byrne Valley' homestead and shook her head in disbelief.

How could he have walked so far without realizing it was the wrong way? she wondered.

Others obviously thought the same thing as it was the main topic of conversation as they made their way down the cattle pads to the dry sand of the riverbed. There was some teasing of LCpl McArtney till Major Wickham called on them to stop it.

The company was seated in section lines just near the mouth of Snake Gully. The British cadets were last to arrive and were seated on the left-hand end. Once they had been allowed ten minutes to drink and cool down Major Wickham began his briefing. He explained that the aim of the training exercises was to hone their scouting skills and to improve their observation.

Five activities, each of half an hour, were to be conducted. 4 Platoon, HQ and the British cadets would first do the moving individual and section observation courses and then do fieldcraft training back at the bivouac area. The three '1st Year' platoons were to work in the bed of the river revising creeping and crawling, playing 'Mr Wolf' and doing a Static Individual Observation exercise. They would then move along Snake Gully and Deep Creek doing the individual and section moving observation courses. All would end up back at the bivouac. The platoons were rostered to rotate so that each had a different time to go along Snake Gully.

Major Wickham explained the scenario for the Snake Gully exercise. "This exercise assumes there is an Opposing Force. It is a situation where you are on your own and the only way you can navigate is by following the route we lay down. There are no actual enemy, but you will meet Directing Staff along the way. You must observe and note all objects and try to work out the story. Try not to step on any pretend land mines or touch any tripwires. Just follow the direction from the DS and keep moving at a slow walk."

Having explained the program Major Wickham set off with Lt Forster, CSM Warren, two HQ NCOs with radios: Sgt Jane Carson and Cpl Forest, and Colleen McNamara with a First Aid Kit. Barbara noted that Unsworth gave Colleen a hostile sneer as she walked past. Colleen looked quickly away and bit her lip. It was 0900 by then and Major Wickham instructed Lt Cavendish to start sending the first members of 4 Platoon in five minutes, at intervals of two minutes, starting with the CUO and ending with the platoon sergeant. HQ and the British cadets were to go last.

Chloe moved to stand out the front of her platoon and looked at her watch. She nodded to CUO Callan who moved off alone, pursued by ribald comments and suggestions that someone who knew what they were doing should go first. Two minutes later Chloe sent Cpl de Beer. As more of 4 Platoon moved off Barbara noted Chloe give the Honourable Charles a wink and a little wave, which he cheerfully returned, only to be nudged and teased by Freddy and Cecil.

Bloody Chloe! she thought. *What a flirt.*

Barbara moved with Sgt Brady to put 1 Platoon through a 'Mr Wolf' exercise. For this she selected the area where she had been the night before. This gave her an area of about a hundred metres square studded with small bushes and a few trees and pitted with hundreds of small dips and depressions in the sand.

And the sand is nice and soft so the cadets won't hurt themselves when they go to ground, she thought.

The game was simple. One of the DS was Mr Wolf and stood on a high point at the edge of the 'island' and the cadets started from 100 metres away. Mr Wolf stood with their back to the cadets and the other DS, in this case Sgt Brady, shouted 'Go!' and then counted down ten. On 'Go' the cadets ran forward but by ten they all had to be hiding. Mr Wolf immediately turned around and directed the DS to any cadets who could be seen. These were sent back to start again. The process was then repeated until all cadets had reached Mr Wolf. Because it was a bit of a challenge and a bit of fun the cadets mostly really enjoyed it.

At the same time CUO Roberts and Sgt Hope set up and started the Static Individual Observation at the base of the steep slope around closer to the river where the best track came down. 2 Platoon's cadets and corporals sat in the shade near there and were called one at a time to try to spot 25 items within 25 paces in two minutes. After they had had their turn the cadets were sent to sit near the mouth of Snake Gully. 3 Platoon stayed nearby on the flat sand and worked in section groups revising 'Ghost Walks;' and 'Leopard Crawls'.

When the half hour was nearly up Barbara swapped with Sgt Brady and moved with her cadets to the start point of her activity. By then most of 2 Platoon's corporals and cadets had completed their observation exercise and were seated near the British cadets.

So far everything seemed to be going well and Barbara felt relaxed. She noted that the last two cadets of 4 Platoon were now waiting to go along Snake Gully. She also noted that Chloe was devoting more time to flirting with the British cadets.

Bloody Chloe! Lady Matchlock indeed!

Then the radio crackled, and she tensed.

Uh oh! Some problem, she thought.

Chapter 19

NEW ARRIVALS

The sound of the mobile phone ringing penetrated Michael's sleep fuddled mind. He groaned and tried to block the sound out by rolling over and pulling his blanket over his ears. In this he was unsuccessful as Dylan's voice broke into his dreams. He had answered the phone.

"Hello dad... No dad... Yes dad. Fifteen minutes?... Yes dad... Bugger!" Dylan groaned and then prodded Michael. "Get up slug. Dad and the others will be here in fifteen minutes. We have to meet them out on the highway."

"Ah bugger!" Michael muttered.

He felt very tired and his eyes seemed to be gummed together. There were also stiff and sore muscles which instantly became apparent when he moved to sit up.

"What time is it?" he asked, squinting out and noting it was already daylight.

"Six fifteen," Dylan replied. He stood up and stretched, then jabbed Michael with his toe. "Come on little brother, get up."

Mumbling with resentment Michael did so. Dylan tugged on his boots and then walked over to the riverbank and urinated. By the time he had finished Michael had sat up and found his own boots. He pulled them on and stood up, groaning at the stiffness in his muscles as he did.

Dylan strode to the ute and opened the door. "Come on little brother, get moving."

"Yeah. Just a minute," Michael grumbled. He needed a pee as well and stood to do this while Dylan started the ute up and turned it around. Michael quickly finished and climbed in. Dylan glanced at his watch and let in the clutch.

Two minutes later the brothers were at the turn-off to the pump station. Dylan parked the ute and they got out. Michael stretched again and gingerly tested the places where he had been chafed.

"A few more hours sleep would have been nice," he muttered.

"You're a lazy little slug," Dylan commented unsympathetically.

Michael muttered but did not reply. He was hungry and very thirsty as well and was in no mood for being teased. Still mystified as to why they were there at all Michael swore and grumbled. About the only good thing in the whole situation that he could think of was the girl: Colleen.

She is real pretty. I wonder if I can get to meet her in Townsville?

While he was speculating about this Dylan stepped out onto the road and began waving. "Here they come."

Michael saw a car pulling up; Liam's old brown 'Ford'. There were four people in it. Three he recognised instantly: his father, Liam and Uncle Shaemus. The fourth man Michael had never seen before and he did not like the look of him at first sight. The man was middle-aged and was a big, burly looking brute with dark hair and a hard face. The four climbed out.

Michael followed Dylan over to shake his father's hand. As he did, he studied the old man's face. Patrick O'Malley was a solid, red-faced man with grey hair. He gripped their hands and gave them a gruff greeting. As always Michael felt inferior and anxious in the presence of his father. "G'day dad, how's mum?" he asked.

"Fine. How are you?" Patrick replied, studying him with alert blue eyes.

"Good," Michael replied.

He nodded to Uncle Shaemus, a middle-aged but ruddy-faced and cheerful looking version of his older brother. Uncle Shaemus grinned and joked about him and Dylan being 'bushies'. As Michael saw him every day at work the greeting was perfunctory. Uncle Shaemus then indicated the big, burly man.

"This is Kevin."

Kevin just glanced at Michael and grunted in acknowledgment to the introduction. This caused Michael to instantly dislike the man, but he hid this and stood quietly while his father and Uncle Shaemus questioned Dylan about what they had seen. After a few minutes of this Michael became irritated. He was tired and grumpy and felt dirty and hungry.

He interrupted to say, "Can we go and have something to eat? I'm bloody hungry."

Liam rounded on him at once. "You shut your trap little brother. We eat when dad says so."

Michael pursed his lips and tried to hide his resentment, particularly when the burly man, Kevin, gave him a look of contempt. He was saved by his father. "Food ain't a bad idea. I ain't had anything since yesterday and I'm starving."

"Oh all right!" Liam snapped irritably. "Take us to your camp then."

They climbed back into the vehicles and drove to the old campsite. On arrival there Dylan said to Michael, "Go and get some firewood and get a fire going."

Michael resented being ordered about but did as he was told. While he did this the others sat in a group and talked. Having kindled a fire Michael found himself in the role of cook. As he fried eggs and heated tinned meat in a skillet Michael tried to listen in to the conversation but missed most of it. His mind was mostly taken up with trying to find a way to feed six people from the limited stock of food they had.

As he worked Dylan called across, "A cup'o tea would be nice."

That was a problem. They had a billy but a quick search of the ute revealed no water. By this time Michael was acutely conscious of his thirst, as well as being annoyed.

"No water," he replied. "Did you bring any with you?"

Liam answered. "No, don't think so."

"Then we have to get some. We will need it if we are going to be here a while," Michael replied.

"What about the river?" Dylan suggested.

Liam shook his head. "Nah! Might make us sick. We need proper council water."

Michael was not amused. "There isn't any here," he said.

"So get some little brother, and be bloody quick about it," Liam replied.

"Have to go to a farm," Michael answered.

"So bloody get going! And make it fast," Liam snapped.

Michael stood up. "Someone better watch this food. Give us the car keys Dylan."

Dylan fished out the keys to the ute and Michael climbed in, started it up and drove back out to the main road. By then he was feeling quite irritated and was glad to get away from his brothers for a while. At the main road he hesitated, then turned right and drove northwards. He remembered passing farms in that direction. The first farm turned out to be a bit further than he remembered but by the time he reached it he had changed his mind. Instead he drove back all the way to the small township of Clare.

This took a bit of finding as it was off the main road and the road signs were small. He turned left and drove along beside some sugar trains in a siding for a kilometre and came to another road junction. A glance to his right showed building beside a wide bitumen road so he turned that way. The buildings were all on the left, with a field of sugar cane on the right.

Then Michael noted that one of the buildings was a police station and his heart rate shot up. He did not know if what his father and uncle planned was illegal, but he had a nasty suspicion it might be. To his relief the police station and house next to it appeared to be deserted and closed up. But he still felt uneasy as he drove past.

He had no trouble finding a tap against the wall of a toilet block beside the hall in the side street and quickly filled the plastic juice containers. He also took the opportunity to drink his fill and to wash his face and hair. Feeling much better he set off back to re-join the others.

It was 0740 by the time he arrived back, to find that most of the food had been eaten. He was immediately told to put the billy on for tea and that annoyed him even more.

"Do it your bloody self," he retorted to Dylan.

"Just do what you are told little brother," Dylan threatened.

For a moment Michael bristled with rebellion, then noted his father watching and frowning so he knelt to arrange the fire. As soon as the billy was hung over the flames on a tripod of sticks, he picked up the skillet to heat up the left-over bacon and eggs. These had congealed in the pan and the sight of the greasy mess made Michael's stomach turn.

Uncle Shaemus came over to light a cigarette from the fire. "How are you boy'o?"

"Good thanks Uncle Shaemus," Michael replied. "What's going on?"

"We aim to teach the bloody British a lesson, that's what," Uncle Shaemus replied.

A surge of anxiety swept through Michael. "You aren't going to cause any trouble, are you?"

Uncle Shaemus laughed and slapped him on the back. "No sonny. We just got a few little scores to settle. It'll be a good laugh."

Michael wasn't entirely convinced by this answer. To his mind the whole thing was extraordinary. *For dad to drive a thousand kilometres it must be important,* he thought, but he kept this to himself.

"What are we going to do?" he asked.

"Have a look at them first," Uncle Shaemus replied.

Liam looked at his watch. "Ten past eight. We'd better move."

"Cup'o tea first boy'o," their father replied.

Five more minutes passed before the drinks were poured. They then stood and talked about family gossip while they drank. The hot, sweet drink did a lot to restore Michael's good temper, even though he had to roll up and pack the camping gear. At 0835 they climbed into the vehicles and set off. They drove out to the main road, turned left and went around the hill through the cutting. Dylan led the way, driving past the turn-off to the gravel scrape and across the dry creek beyond. He went on for another couple of hundred metres before parking the ute at the side of the road near a power pylon. The Ford parked behind them.

As they climbed out Michael was concerned to see that Liam had a rifle. He recognised it as his hunting rifle. It had, he knew, a x10 magnification telescopic sight. To Michael's further consternation his father extracted a shotgun from the boot of the car, then Kevin appeared, shrugging on an old army green jacket with four pockets on the front. Kevin then bent into the car and reappeared with an ugly, black sub-machine gun.

"Jesus dad, what do we need the guns for?" Michael asked.

"Because this is the British Army we are fighting," his father replied.

"Fair go dad, they are only cadets, just teenage kids. They don't have any guns," Michael replied. He now had a bad feeling about the situation but could not think of a way to control it.

Dylan snapped at him, "Stop snivelling ya little coward. There's a gun for you in the ute too."

Michael saw that Dylan had taken out the rifle he had been carrying the previous day. Uncle Shaemus took an automatic pistol from the glove box of the car and checked it. That action Michael found really worrying. When the others all took out balaclavas and rolled them on to the top of their heads, he thought he was having a bad dream.

Dylan thrust a rifle into Michael's hands. "And put your balaclava on too little brother. We don't want anyone recognising us."

"What's going on? What are you going to do?" Michael asked anxiously.

"Going to have a look, now stop blabbing," his father replied.

"Stay with the car and keep your mouth shut if you want," Uncle Shaemus added.

Michael noted that he was no longer smiling and had a grim set about his mouth.

Liam turned to him. "That's right. You are either for Ireland or against her."

"But this is Australia," Michael protested, but he said it feebly and despised himself for it. "You aren't going to shoot anyone are you?"

"No we aren't," his father snapped.

"Or plant a bomb?" Michael was ashamed of the use of terrorist bombs by the Irish freedom fighters and had frequently said so. To him they were dark stains on the good name of the Irish, stains that would harm their reputation for hundreds of years, long after freedom had been won. He wanted no part of any such thing.

Liam jeered and curled his lip in a sneer. "Gawd you're a soft little bloody sook. You can't win a war by being weak."

"No, but you have to be in the right!" Michael retorted.

"Stop arguing!" their father snapped. "I didn't come all this way to debate. I want that bastard Grogan to pay for my Bridie. Now lead on Dylan."

Dylan did as he was told. He rolled his balaclava down over his face and walked into the bush. The others did likewise. Michael felt sick with anxiety but also pulled the balaclava over his face and followed. The whole thing had turned into some sort of unreal nightmare. He found the sight of the line of armed and hooded men to be quite sinister and felt a chill of fear. He wished he could think of some way to take control but could only tamely follow along.

As he walked through the bush behind the others Michael's mind turned over what his father had just said. Bridie had been his little sister, or would have been if she hadn't been shot by the British Army. It was an old family tale. It had all happened before Michael was born. Michael's mother had been driving along in the country outside Belfast with the newborn baby Bridie in the car and had been ambushed by a group of British Army soldiers at a roadblock. There had been shooting and the baby had been hit and killed. Later Uncle Shaemus had shot the officer in charge of the platoon at the roadblock, which was why the brothers had fled the country with their families.

With every step Michael became more and more anxious. He wished he was not there, and he urgently wanted to stop any trouble. Self-loathing surged in him for giving in so easily. He hefted the sporting rifle to a more comfortable position and shook his head. He was a good shot but actually hated guns.

What can I do? he wondered.

The group crossed several small gullies before arriving on top of the bank of the dry creek near the place where he and Dylan had observed the cadet's camp the previous afternoon. As they approached the top of the bank they slowed down and began to creep from tree to tree, further heightening Michael's sense of dread.

"Looks deserted," Liam commented as they crouched behind bushes and looked across the creek into the gravel scrape area.

"Don't tell me the bastards are gone!" hissed Uncle Shaemus angrily. Michael could see his eyes flashing through the eyeholes in the black balaclava.

Dylan pointed. "No, they are still here. They've got a signal tent or something over there. Look, you can see two people sitting under it."

They all studied this. One of the cadets was lying down and the other sat with their back to them.

"So where are the others?" their father demanded.

"This is where they were camped last night," Dylan said. "Maybe there are some around behind that big mound?"

"You sure this is the right place?" Kevin asked.

"Definitely. We hid here yesterday and watched a bunch of Pommy cadets creep past just down there in the creek. I could have dropped the lot, no trouble at all," Dylan replied.

"You should have. The bastards!" Kevin snarled. He spat and glared across the clearing.

"Let's go down that way along the creek and look around behind that big mound," Dylan suggested.

For lack of a better idea they agreed to this. Liam and Dylan led, followed by Uncle Shaemus, Kevin, Patrick, and with Michael very reluctantly trailing along. Liam led the way down a small washout so that they arrived in the dry creek bed unseen by the cadets across in the gravel scrape. The dry creek bed was a mass of football sized rocks and was choked with clumps of rubber vine and bushes. The group had to wend its way through these. Michael found the sight of the line of armed, hooded men creeping along the creek bed chilling.

Dylan paused and pointed up the bank. "This is where we watched from last night."

Liam was about to go up the bank when a sound made them all turn. From behind a bush only a few paces away emerged a girl in cadet uniform. Her mouth opened in surprise and she cried, "Micki!"

A second girl in Australian camouflage stood up from behind the bush; a well built girl with straw blonde hair and hazel eyes. Her eyes goggled in disbelief and fright. By then the others were pointing their guns at them.

"Don't move, and don't call out," hissed Liam.

Michael saw that one of the girls was trying to hide a cigarette in her hand. Even as he watched she dropped it. The first girl, tall and red-faced and with quite a nice body, stared at them wide-eyed.

"Who are you?" she gasped.

"We ask the questions," Liam answered. "Who are you and what are you doing here?"

"Army cadets. We were just going to the toilet," the straw-blonde replied.

Dylan snorted. "Snuck away for a smoke more like!"

Michael saw the girl flush with guilt and flick a smouldering cigarette aside. "Who are you? What do you want? Are you British cadets?" she asked.

Liam answered. "No, but you are our prisoners, and don't do anything silly like trying to run or yelling out, these guns are real," he replied.

Both girls were obviously scared but unsure. The straw-blonde grabbed her friend's arm. "Come on Sandy, let's go back."

"No you don't! Grab them boys!" Uncle Shaemus suddenly barked.

The straw-blonde, Micki, let out a cry and tried to run but Liam pounced and grabbed her, his hand going around her neck and over her mouth. Kevin also moved, so fast that Michael barely had time to register the movement. He struck the one named Sandy hard on the side of the head. She collapsed on the sand. Micki's eyes goggled with fear as she struggled but Uncle Shaemus stepped up to her and thrust his pistol in her face

"Sorry girlie, but this is for real. Stop struggling and shut up or you'll get hurt."

Micki stopped her struggles but looked terrified. Uncle Shaemus looked around, swore, then said, "OK gag them both, then let's go back somewhere where we can question them."

"We should just let them go and get out of here," Michael cried. He was really scared now. This was breaking the law: assault and kidnapping and so on.

"Shut up boyo!" his father snapped at him.

By then Dylan had shoved a handkerchief in Micki's mouth. Kevin did the same to the one lying groaning on the sand, Sandy. By now Michael could see that the girl was really scared, terror showing plainly in her eyes.

Kevin hauled Sandy to her feet and gripped her arm roughly. He then led the way back along the creek. Micki was forced to walk with them, and the group retraced their steps along the creek and up onto the south bank. As they went over the top, they looked carefully across at the gravel scrape in case the cadets there could see them. Five minutes later they were crouched in one of the small dry gullies a hundred metres back.

The girls were then separated and seated. Micki had her gag removed and Uncle Shaemus stood threateningly in front of her. To Michael his harsh manner was an unpleasant revelation. He had only ever seen Shaemus as the jovial uncle, full of jokes and good cheer. Now a much harder man emerged.

"What are your names?" he demanded.

"Micki and Sandy," Micki replied, "Who are you?"

Uncle Shaemus did not answer. Instead he asked, "Where are the rest of the cadets?"

"You aren't going to hurt us are you?" pleaded Micki.

"Not if you answer our questions," Uncle Shaemus replied. "Now, where are the rest of the cadets?"

"They all went down to the river," Micki said. She was sweating and trembling now, on the edge of tears.

"Which river?"

"The Burdekin," Micki said. "Please let us go. We won't say anything."

"Are the British cadets with them?" Uncle Shaemus asked.

"Yes."

"All of them?"

"Yes."

"Is there a major named Grogan with the British cadets?" Uncle Shaemus asked.

"I don't know! I didn't meet their officers. Please don't hurt us," Micki cried.

Tears had now started to course down her cheeks. All this made Michael feel sick inside. He intensely disliked brutality to women.

They are scared we are going to rape them, then murder them, he thought.

Uncle Shaemus then asked about some of the British cadets by name. Micki could only shake her head and cry.

"I don't know any of them. I didn't meet them," she said.

"What are they doing now?" Uncle Shaemus asked.

"They are going to do an individual scouting exercise up the creek," Micki replied.

"What does that mean? Which creek?"

"This creek. They will be sent one at a time up the creek and there will be things along the way that they have to spot," Micki explained.

"Do they have guns?" Uncle Shaemus asked.

Micki shook her head. "No."

"How many adults are there and where are they?"

"Six with our unit and two British officers," Micki replied. "They all went with the cadets except Lt Barker and Lt Peters. They are in the camp here."

"Who else is in the camp?"

"Only two other girls and one is sick," Micki replied.

"Where are the other adults?"

"Captain Hamilton is driving the Land Rover. He went to the Lookout near the river. I think the others are walking with the cadets," Micki said.

During this Michael had been listening intently. He was sweating, as much with anxiety as from the heat. It was so hot he fervently wished he could take the woollen balaclava off.

Kevin now spoke. "So what are we waiting for? Let's go and get them."

Uncle Shaemus nodded. "Yes. But let's be sensible. We need a map to plan this." He turned to Dylan. "Did you make a map?"

"No."

"Bloody useless idiot!" Uncle Shaemus snapped.

Micki spoke up, "I've got a map."

It was only a photocopy, but it was detailed and clear. The men grouped to study it and Michael's father pointed and said, "Some of us should go down the creek and a few go 'round to the river to get behind them. That way we should catch them easily."

"Yes," Uncle Shaemus agreed. "And we need someone to meet Murty and Rory. They are due soon."

"We need to capture the officer with the safety vehicle at the Lookout too," Liam added.

"Right," Uncle Shaemus agreed. "OK, this is the plan. I will go with Dylan to the Lookout and we will capture the officer there. Then we will go down to the riverbank. You others go down the creek to meet the cadets as they come the other way."

"What about these girls?" Liam asked.

"Leave 'em here," Uncle Shaemus said.

"They might escape," Liam disagreed,

"Then leave Michael to guard them," Dylan suggested.

"Nah! The little softie might let them go," Liam said.

Kevin now spoke. "We gotta keep 'em under guard. You stay with the car Liam and guard 'em. Dylan can go with Shaemus and I'll go with Pat and young Michael here. That way you can also stop anyone crossing the road and keep tabs on the entrance to their camp."

"Good idea," Uncle Shaemus agreed. "Let's get going."

Michael badly wanted to back out but found himself moving. The two frightened girls were hauled to their feet and set walking. "Please don't hurt us," Micki pleaded.

"We won't, as long as you co-operate," Kevin snarled.

It took ten minutes to reach the vehicles. The two girls were seated behind a bush just off the road. Dylan and Uncle Shaemus climbed into the ute and drove off back towards the Lookout. Kevin checked his sub-machine gun and said, "OK Michael me boyo, lead us down this creek."

Michael bit his lip and desperately wished he could back out but knew it was some sort of test of loyalty he was being set. With his father watching he could not back out. Reluctantly he led the way along the side of the road to where it crossed the creek. As he looked for the best way down through the weeds and long grass, he glanced around to check that no-one was watching. As he did, he noted a column of dense white and grey smoke billowing into the clear blue sky from further up the creek.

"What's that smoke?" he asked, pointing.

They all stared. It was obviously a fire. Kevin suddenly hissed and gestured. "Get down! People!"

They crouched into the weeds and long grass beside the road. Michael saw four people in camouflage uniforms run across the road towards the gravel scrape. One was a tubby, middle-aged man and another carried a radio.

"Heading for their camp," Michael said.

"To investigate the fire probably," his father suggested.

"They will find two girls are missing and might start searching," Kevin said. "We had better stop them. Come on!"

He stood up and hurried along the road after the group, which had now vanished into the bush towards the camp.

Chapter 20

SMOKE?

Major Wickham walked slowly along the bed of Snake Gully and stopped. With him were Lt Forster, CSM Warren, Colleen McNamara, and two cadet signallers: Sgt Jane Carson and Cpl Forest. They waited at a sharp bend in the gully while Lt Forster and CSM Warren 'buried' an empty food can and lightly covered it with leaves. It was to represent a land mine and was deliberately left just visible.

They moved on and another was placed on the other side of a small log just where a person would normally put their boot down when stepping over the log. A length of green nylon hutchie cord was tied across next to represent a 'trip wire'. A camouflage shirt was next placed beside the gully and then a 'bloodstained' bandage.

It was just after 0920 and Major Wickham and his group had worked their way up Snake Gully laying out the Individual Moving Observation Course—25 items, not counting the land mines and trip wires.

They had reached the point where the rough foot track led up out of the gully onto the low flat ridge. Major Wickham stopped and said, "OK CUO Callan, you wait here and direct them all to go up to the top of the bank. Cpl McNamara will be up there and she will direct them down the other side into Deep Creek where Cpl Forest will send them west up the creek and back to camp."

"Yes sir."

Major Wickham nodded with satisfaction. "Good. Now, let's go and lay out the moving section observation course. And we'd better hurry, the first one must be nearly up to us by now. You hold them for five minutes to let us get ahead," he said.

He led the party up the steep little track to the open ridge between Snake Gully and Deep Creek. As he came out of the rubber vines onto the flat, open ridge top his eyes were instantly drawn to a column of smoke billowing into the sky from the direction of the camp.

"Holy mackerel! I don't like the look of that," he said. "That looks like it is pretty close to the camp."

"Yes it does," Lt Forster agreed.

Major Wickham turned and reached out for the radio handset of the radio being carried by Cpl Forest. "Hotel, this is Sunray, over."

There was no response. Major Wickham tried again. Even as he watched he could see the smoke increasing in volume. It was now towering into the clear blue sky and was obviously quite a sizeable fire.

"God, I hope that isn't a bushfire out of control," he muttered.

The last thing he wanted was to burn out the pastures of the cattle property. He knew it would cost the station owners a fortune in either shifting their cattle to agistment, or on trucking in hay. That would make the cadets very unwelcome in the future.

Once again he tried calling the CP, 'Hotel' being the call sign he allocated to HQ. There was no response. He turned and said: "Sgt Carson, stay here and hold the cadets here. Remain as the safety link and get the cadets ready to move as a group if we call for it. We will hurry back to camp to see what is going on. Relay for us if you have to. Is that clear?"

"Yes sir," Jane replied.

She swung off the radio she was carrying and leaned it against a log right on the crest of the ridge.

Major Wickham beckoned to the others. "Cpl McNamara, come with us and bring your First Aid kit," he ordered.

He then set off at a fast walk along the track to Deep Creek. As he walked, he kept trying to contact the CP. All the while the smoke cloud grew larger and he became more worried.

"Try to get the safety vehicle at the Lookout," he instructed Cpl Forest as they hurried through the belt of rubber vines and bushes along the bank of the creek. Cpl Forest did so but received no response.

"What the bloody hell is going on?" Major Wickham muttered. "Try again."

"Hello Safety Vehicle, this is Nine, over," Cpl Forest called.

There was no answer. By now the group were moving at a fast walk and Major Wickham was sweating and biting his lip with anxiety.

"Try to get the check point at the river," he said.

Cpl Forest called Call Sign 'Bravo' and immediately got an answer. It was Lt Cavendish. "Loud and clear, over," she answered.

"See if you can contact the Safety Vehicle or the CP, over," Major Wickham instructed.

Lt Cavendish began calling. Major Wickham strode on, wanting to run but knowing he was not fit enough. As it was, he was panting from the exertion. He led the way down into the junction of Deep Creek and the other creek at the point where the power line crossed, then hurried up the far bank. Once there he headed across the grassy flat along a rough vehicle track which led to a gate opposite the gravel scrape gate.

The group was halfway across the paddock by the time Lt Cavendish called back to say that she could not raise either the safety vehicle or the CP. She did add that she knew the safety vehicle was at the Lookout because Sgt Dunstan had come down to join them after the vehicle had returned from refilling the water jerries.

"Thanks. Stop the exercise while we investigate a fire near camp, over," Major Wickham replied.

"Roger, over," Lt Cavendish answered.

By this time the smoke cloud was a massive column which was drifting towards Mt Dalrymple. Worse still, to Major Wickham's worried mind, the closer they got to the gravel scrape, the more obvious it was that the fire was in that area.

Major Wickham, now puffing with exertion and feeling distinctly anxious, reached the gate. As quickly as he could he opened the gate and made his way through. As soon as the others were through, he said, "Close the gate Duncan." The last thing he wanted was to cause the landowner more trouble by allowing cattle to escape onto the main road.

Major Wickham at once resumed walking at a near trot, crossing over the railway and across the main road to the gravel road leading to the gravel scrape.

As he hurried along the dirt road Major Wickham called the CP again. To his intense relief a voice answered, a girl's voice he did not recognise. "Who is that?" he asked.

"Cpl Horn sir," came the reply.

"Is Lt Barker there?"

Major Wickham was at the bend in the access track where he could see over the gravel pit area by this and could just see the vehicles parked in the bivouac area on the other side of the gravel scrape. He could also see that the smoke was billowing up from directly beyond them and that the smoke was rising from a fairly small area beyond the gravel scrape, apparently on the bank of Deep Creek.

Cpl Horn answered nervously, "He is asleep sir."

"Wake him up!" Major Wickham snapped.

By then the others had joined him. Lt Forster had closed the wire gate behind them. As Major Wickham looked anxiously at the huge column of thick smoke Lt Barker answered. "Hotel here, over."

Major Wickham wasted no time on the army call signs or system. "Ashley, what's that smoke?"

"Smoke? What smoke? Holy shit!" crackled Ashley's voice over the radio.

Major Wickham had a glimpse of a running figure heading down through the trees towards the smoke: Lt Barker running flat out.

He broke into a run himself. "Come on!"

The group raced along the dirt road past the gravel pit. As they reached the more open area between the CP and where 4 Platoon and the British cadets were bivouacked Major Wickham saw that the fire really was on the bank of the creek directly ahead, a hundred paces away across the bare open ground and just past where the vehicles were parked. By then Lt Barker was flailing at it manfully with a green sapling. A sleepy-eyed Lt Peters, Cpl Horn and Cadet Rowland stood nearby, all in an anxious dither.

As the group arrived Ashley cast them a thankful, but guilty look. "It is only on this bank so far," he called. "If we can cut it off it won't spread across the creek."

Major Wickham paused to take stock of the situation and saw at once that Ashley was right. The fire was unlikely to spread across the dry creek bed except by jumping from one clump of rubber vine or bush to the next but could easily and quickly spread along the bank towards the hills as dry grass extended much of the way. Or it could spread the other way to where 4 Platoon and the British cadets had been bivouacked.

"We must stop it spreading to the hill," he cried.

That would be a disaster! Already Major Wickham could picture the Tudehopes standing on the veranda of their homestead at 'Landers Creek' saying, 'I wonder what that smoke is? I hope those bloody cadets haven't started a bushfire!' With that in mind and the image of the flames racing up the grassy hills, pushed by the breeze, Major Wickham shrugged off his webbing and cast around for a small tree to use as a beater.

"Caitlin, help here please. Corporal Horn, you and Cadet Rowland, go back to the CP and sit by the radio," he ordered. "You other cadets do the same." The last thing he wanted was a cadet burnt. That would be even worse than a bushfire.

CSM Warren, Cpl Forest and Cpl McNamara all protested. "But sir, we can help," Cpl Forest said, as he took the radio Major Wickham thrust at him.

"I know you can, but only the adults are going to do any firefighting, now get out of the way. Put that radio over there in the open and keep listening to it."

Reluctantly the cadets backed off. Major Wickham dashed to a tree growing on the bank near the fire and wrenched a branch from it, then snapped off the end with its green leaves. He moved forward and studied the fire to decide where to best attack it. Both Lt Forster and Lt Peters also grabbed branches and joined him.

The fire wasn't very big at all, but it was burning dry grass and rubber vine and a dead tree had caught alight. The flames were fairly small, but the fire was pumping out an astonishing amount of smoke. Having considered the problem Major Wickham directed Ashley to go down into the creek bed while he and Lt Peters moved to the downwind end to attack the flames spreading along the top of the bank.

As Major Wickham began beating at the flames CSM Warren called to him from nearby, "Will we get some water sir?"

"Yes, bring a bucket and some jerry cans, and keep listening to that radio!"

To his relief the cadets all moved away, and Major Wickham noted Cpl Forest direct Cpl Horn to sit beside the radio. Cpl McNamara hurried to the vehicles to get a bucket. For the next few minutes Major Wickham, Lt Peters and Lt Barker worked like demons to beat out the fire. It became rapidly apparent they were winning.

"We've caught it in time," Major Wickham cried. He paused to wipe sweat from his face as CSM Warren and Cpl Forest returned carrying two jerry cans each. "Duncan, pour the water into the bucket and cast it on that bush," Major Wickham ordered.

Lt Forster did as he was told but his first attempt was not very successful. "Swing the bucket so that the water comes out in a spray rather than in a big heap," Major Wickham suggested. Lt Forster did this and the water had an immediate effect. The four officers redoubled their efforts and within another couple of minutes most of the flames were out. Most importantly the fire was no longer spreading along the bank and across the creek. As there was no danger of it crossing the bare earth to where the bivouac area was Major Wickham began to relax. Now the firefighting became just a grimy chore, with attacks on specific spot fires. Several dead sticks and small logs had caught fire and were smouldering inside, and the officers set to work to break these open or douse them.

Major Wickham grabbed the end of one of these burning sticks and dragged it up the bank and out onto the bare earth. As he did, he glanced around. Cpl Forest was about to hurry away and Cpl Horn was answering the radio. She called to Cpl Forest, who took the handset and answered, then turned to Major Wickham. "It is Lt Cavendish sir. She says they have stopped the exercise and want to know if you want any cadets back here to help with the firefighting?"

"Tell her no. We will have this out in a minute, and they can restart the exercise then," Major Wickham replied. He glanced at the sky and noted thankfully that the smoke cloud was noticeably smaller and already becoming ragged.

Hopefully the landowner won't spot it, he thought.

Then another worrying thought came to him. He glanced at Cpl Horn who still stood beside the radio and then at Cadet Rowland who had moved back to sit in the CP.

"Ashley, how many cadets were left at camp?"

Lt Barker paused in his efforts to stamp out smouldering leaves on the steep bank. His face creased in concentration, then a look of doubt crossed it. "There were four girls. Cpl Evans and Cpl Saunders were here too."

Major Wickham swore under his breath and then snapped angrily, "Bloody Micki and Sandy! I'll bet that pair of troublemakers have been down here smoking."

"Sounds likely," Lt Barker agreed. "Now where the Devil are they?"

The officers looked anxiously around. For a fleeting instant Major Wickham feared the two girls might have been burnt by the fire but a glance showed him that was unlikely. The charred area was only about 50 paces long and 10 paces wide on the steep bank of the creek.

"They have probably made themselves scarce and are preparing their alibi now," Lt Barker suggested.

Major Wickham turned to Cpl Horn. "Have you seen Micki and Sandy? When did you last see them?"

Cpl Horn looked afraid and shook her head. "I don't know where they are sir. They were at the CP but they went off somewhere."

"When?"

"About half an hour ago," Cpl Horn replied.

By this time Lt Forster, Lt Peters, Cpl Forest and Cpl McNamara had joined them and continued splashing water on the few smouldering embers. Horrible fears flashed across Major Wickham's mind.

Two girls missing! Oh no, not again!

"Where the hell can they be?" he asked irritably.

"Here they come. Holy mackerel! Who are they?" Lt Barker cried, looking into the creek bed behind him.

Major Wickham looked and saw the line of armed men in green jackets and black balaclavas and his stomach turned over. He knew instantly they spelled real trouble.

Then Major Wickham's eyes noted the two missing girls and his heart rate shot up with intense anxiety. Micki and Sandy were both gagged and were roped together. Seeing that moved Major Wickham's concern to a whole new level.

"Who the devil are you? What do you want? Let those girls go!" he cried, fear adding an edge of anger to his voice.

In response the first man pointed a rifle at him and shook his head. "Sorry mister, but we give the orders. Now don't try anything stupid because this gun is loaded."

Major Wickham shook his head in disbelief as he swept his eyes over the group, taking in the glaring, hate-filled eyes of the big man facing him.

"What do you want?" he managed to ask.

The second man, a much older fellow by his build and voice, answered. "You don't need to know. Now major, where are the British cadets?"

"Why do you want to know?" Major Wickham replied, casting desperately around for some way to discover what was going on.

He noted that the others had been pushed into a group by a big, burly fellow with a sub-machine gun. Cadet Rowland was called over and she reluctantly did so. She looked scared and was on the edge of tears.

I hope Ashley and Duncan don't try any heroics, Major Wickham worried, certain in his own mind that the men meant business.

The older man gestured with his gun. "Just answer the question major and no-body will get hurt. Where are the British cadets?"

Irish, Major Wickham thought, noting the man's accent. He said, "IRA are you?"

"None of your business, now answer me before someone gets hurt bad," the man snarled.

At that one of the hooded men, a tall young man standing at the back guarding Micki and Sandy, called out, "Dad, you promised no-one would get hurt."

The older man answered shortly, "And they won't if they are sensible, now keep your mouth shut boyo."

At that Colleen McNamara stepped forward. "Michael? Is that you?"

The tall young man nodded, and Major Wickham noted with astonishment the way the two stared at each other.

How the devil do they know each other? he wondered.

"No names, ya idiots," snapped the big burly man with the sub machine gun.

At that moment the tension was interrupted by the ringing of a mobile phone hooked to one of the men's belts. He answered it and had a short conversation, then spoke to the older man.

"It's Dylan, dad. He says that reinforcements have arrived."

"Give me that," the older man snapped. He took the phone and spoke rapidly, then listened. After nodding a few times he said, "You've captured the officer at the Lookout? Good.... Now, keep Murty there and send Rory here. We will meet him."

As he ended the conversation the older man handed the phone back to the other younger man and said, "We have a friend arriving. Run out to the road and show him the way in."

"Yes dad," the young man replied. He ran off along the gravel road toward the main road.

The older man now turned back to Major Wickham, who stood in a state of growing dismay. "Now Major, can you call all these cadets in on that radio?"

Major Wickham nodded, his lips pressed hard together with bitterness.

"Then do so."

It was an order and Major Wickham could see no way to disobey it. With a heavy heart he walked over towards the radio. As he bent to pick up the handset the radio suddenly crackled into life.

"Nine, this is Bravo, emergency, over."

It was Lt Cavendish and she sounded frantic. Major Wickham picked up the handset. As he did the big, burly man prodded him with the muzzle of the SMG.

"No tricks major, or else these girls get hurt."

Major Wickham nodded and answered the radio. The tone of voice told him things were about to get much worse. Lt Cavendish at once answered, "Oh Major! Quick! There are men in black hoods shooting at us. They have shot one of the cadets and the two British officers. We need the medics fast!"

Shot! Major Wickham was stunned. It was too unlikely and unreal to be easily taken in. He stared grimly at the older man and thought he noted an anxious flicker cross his eyes. But it was the young man named Michael who acted first. He swore and turned on his father.

"Dad! You said no-one would get hurt."

"Quiet boy!" the older man snapped.

Michael shook his head. "I will not be quiet! This isn't right! We shouldn't be doing this. If someone has been hurt then we must call the ambulance."

"No!" snarled the big, burly man. "Shut up kiddo and let us get on with things."

"I will not! If they need medical help then we must give it," Michael replied angrily.

"Don't be weak boy, this is war!" shouted the older man.

"Crap! It is not! It is just bloody murder!" Michael yelled. He turned to Colleen. "Have you got a First Aid kit here?"

Colleen nodded. "I'm a medic."

"Good. Grab your First Aid kit and let's get going," Michael said.

"And a stretcher," Colleen added. She turned to go.

"Don't!" warned the older man.

"Try and stop me!" Michael retorted. "I won't have murder on my conscience for some stupid old idea."

By then Colleen had turned and she began walking towards the CP.

The big, burly man snarled at her and Michael, "Stay where you are, or I'll shoot."

"Like hell you will Kevin," warned the older man. For a minute the two men glared at each other, their eyes glittering with anger in the black hoods. The older man then said, "Go on Michael, go and see what the hell is going on, but be careful boy."

"Yes dad. Come on Colleen," Michael replied.

He and Colleen hurried across the bare gravel scrape. For an instant Major Wickham feared that the man named Kevin would shoot but he then just shrugged.

"Bloody stupid," he commented. Then he gestured with his SMG, "What do we do with this lot then?"

"Tie them up," the older man answered, "Then go and find out what is happening."

Chapter 21

RECOGNITION

Barbara had just walked over to where to Major Grogan, Lt Jeffries and Lt Cavendish stood in the shade near the mouth of Snake Gully. Nearby most of 2 Platoon sat in the shade, as did the British cadets and the remaining couple from 4 Platoon. 3 Platoon was also nearby in groups in the shade on the sand of the riverbed. At the end of Snake Gully stood Chloe, her watch in one hand and a broom stick in the other. Chloe was timing the cadets of 4 Platoon, sending one along Snake Gully every two minutes. In between she talked to the British cadets. For an amused few moments, Barbara watched as Chloe twirled the stick she held, then wiggled her hips, to the obvious interest of the boys.

Bloody Chloe! Barbara thought with wry amusement. *She never misses an opportunity!*

Barbara studied the British cadets and had to smile at the sight of the Honourable Charles and Freddy both devoting all their attention to Chloe. That Chloe was aware of this and playing on it was plain to Barbara.

She is very attractive, she conceded.

Indeed Chloe seemed to exude a powerful sexuality and desirability that set her apart from any other female Barbara had ever known. Having watched Chloe on other activities Barbara had no doubt that she was one of the strongest characters she had ever met.

She will go far, if she doesn't get into too much trouble over her nudist behaviour, Barbara mused.

Barbara turned back to answer a query from Lt Jeffries about how much army support the Australian cadets received on their annual camp. She was busy describing this when the radio message about the fire came in. Cpl Valerie Metcalfe answered the call. She was seated on the sand with the army radio and at once turned a questioning face to Lt Cavendish.

"A fire?" Lt Cavendish asked anxiously. "Does the OC want us to go back to camp?"

Valerie asked this question over the radio and then shook her head. "He says to stop the exercise and to hold the cadets ready in case, Ma'am."

Lt Cavendish called across to Chloe, "Sgt Cummings, don't send any more cadets."

Chloe looked at her in surprise, still twirling the stick. "Why not ma'am? There are only two to go from 4 Platoon."

"There is a fire back at the camp. The OC is going to investigate," Lt Cavendish explained.

During this conversation Barbara had been scanning the sky off to the west but she was too close in under the trees beside the river and could not see any smoke. To get a better view she walked further out onto the open riverbed. From there she saw the column of smoke rising into the clear blue sky. CUO Bailey joined her and they discussed the fire for a few minutes, wondering if it was serious or not.

"You had better get your platoon here in case we have to move," Barbara told him.

CUO Bailey nodded and went to collect the sections of 3 Platoon and Barbara radioed to her corporals and told them to stop their exercise and to move to her.

As she finished this call CUO Roberts came on the radio from her Observation stand. "What about us One One? Over," she queried.

"Better move all of your platoon here as well, over," Barbara replied.

As she walked back to join the others, movement up on the steep bank attracted Barbara's attention. It was Sgt Dunstan and his offsider, Cpl Keith. They came sliding down the grassy slope, dragging two jerry cans each with them. They slid to the bottom just near the end of the pool.

Lt Cavendish noted their arrival and asked, "Is the safety vehicle up at the Lookout?"

"Yes ma'am," Sgt Dunstan replied. Then he pointed as he spoke to Cpl Keith, "Put these jerry cans in the shade over there at the mouth of the gully Keithy."

Cpl Keith grumbled but obeyed. It was then that Major Wickham called asking if they could contact the CP or safety vehicle. Valerie tried calling both but had no luck and Lt Cavendish then tried, before reporting the failure to Major Wickham. During this Barbara stood, feeling vaguely uneasy but not sure why. "I hope the fire isn't serious," she said.

"We wouldn't be in danger here would we?" asked Lt Jeffries.

"Oh no! We wouldn't be in danger up there at the gravel scrape either," Barbara replied.

"I thought bushfires were really bad news?" Major Grogan commented.

"They are in southern Australia, in areas where they have eucalyptus forests," Barbara explained. "But all we normally get in this part of the world are grass fires and they don't burn nearly as fast or as fiercely."

"You could still get burnt though," Lt Cavendish said.

"Only if the grass was very long and there was strong wind," Barbara countered. She had watched such a fire destroy a farm near Mareeba once but all the other fires she had seen had been much less threatening. "It is rare for the tree canopies to catch fire here," she added. "That is what is so dangerous in the real bushfires down south."

"How does that happen?" Lt Jeffries asked.

"Well, I'm no expert, but I believe the gumtrees weep eucalyptus oil into the air when temperatures get very hot," Barbara said. "The oil evaporates or something to form an explosive vapour. Then, when a fire begins somewhere, it can leap through the air, burning this vapour."

"That's right," Lt Cavendish agreed. "I spent a couple of years in Sydney and saw a bush fire in the Blue Mountains and that is what happened. The flames just leapt from tree top to tree top. It was really frightening."

"So why doesn't that happen here?" Major Grogan asked. "The trees around the camp are eucalypts aren't they?"

"Most of them," Barbara agreed. "The trees are further apart mostly, and it just doesn't get as hot here as it does down south."

"But this is the tropics!" said Lt Jeffries.

"Yes, but they get a long dry summer down south. Besides this is winter now," Barbara said.

"Winter?" Lt Jeffries mopped his forehead and they all grinned.

They continued discussing bushfires while trying to follow the progress of events on the radio. They heard the OC call Lt Barker asking about the smoke and were amused by Lt Barker's response.

"Poor Ashley," Lt Cavendish said, "The OC won't let him forget this one."

"He was probably asleep," CUO Bailey suggested.

"He was on duty as the Duty Officer after me, between zero two hundred and four," Lt Cavendish replied in his defence.

"They are fighting the fire now," Valerie added.

More minutes went by. All of the cadets were grouped in platoon lots sitting in the shade at the mouth of Snake Gully. They were seated in section lines for a roll check with 4 Pl and the British cadets nearest Snake Gully, then 3 PL, 2 Pl and 1 PL.

The air became hotter as the sun rose higher. Barbara found she was perspiring just standing talking. The cadets began to fidget restlessly.

"Stop throwing sand!" Barbara snapped. Several of her cadets had begun to annoy each other out of boredom. "We don't want someone with sand in their eyes," she muttered.

At that moment CUO Roberts said, "Hello, who is this?"

Barbara looked in the direction CUO Roberts was facing and felt an instant thrill of fear. Two men wearing black balaclavas and green jackets were sliding down the steep grassy slope near the end of the old ruined bridge. Barbara knew that some of the cadets had balaclavas and that they sometimes wore them on night exercises but a glance showed her that these people were not cadets. The leading person was a solidly built, middle-aged man. Behind him was a taller, slimmer man carrying a sporting rifle with a telescopic sight.

"Are these men part of the exercise?" Lt Jeffries asked as the men reached the bed of the river and began striding across the sand towards them.

"No, I don't think so," Barbara replied.

She was puzzled and also felt distinctly uneasy. There was something about the way the first man was walking that told her this was serious. The fact that both had their faces covered by balaclavas added to her feeling of concern.

The men skirted the end of the deep pool and strode over to them, stopping a few paces away. Before any of the cadet staff could speak the first man suddenly produced a pistol from behind his back.

"Don't anybody move," he ordered. "This gun is loaded."

The second man stood a couple of paces to his right and pointed his rifle from the waist, levelling it at the British cadets.

Lt Cavendish faced the man. "Who are you? What do you want?" she asked, her voice shrill with anxiety.

The man ignored her. He gestured to the group of British cadets who were standing or sitting a few metres away, their identity obvious because of their different uniforms. "Which one of you is Masters?"

There was a moment of silence. Barbara's shocked mind registered a frozen tableau: Chloe standing on the left, then four or five British cadets standing, and the others sitting up, mouths wide with surprise. The man asked again. He was obviously agitated and angry.

A madman! Barbara thought in alarm, *and with a gun!*

The man gestured angrily with his pistol. "Answer me! Which one is Masters? Step forward or I will shoot this girl," he snarled. He swung the pistol to point it at Barbara.

A wave of cold shock swept over Barbara. *This can't be true,* she thought. *It can't be real!*

There was another tense pause, then Freddy stood up and stepped forward. "I'm Masters. Don't you hurt Barbara. She hasn't done anything to you."

"Shut up and come here!" the man ordered.

Irish, Barbara thought, hearing the man's accent.

She stared at the muzzle of the pistol, which still pointed at her. The black hole of the bore seemed to grow in size and she knew she was terrified.

As Freddy walked towards the man he asked, "Who are you?"

It was Major Grogan who answered that. "Shaemus O'Malley," he hissed.

The man snarled and swivelled his head to look at Major Grogan. "Yes Grogan, you murderous bastard. Now you can pay for what you did!"

Before any of them realised what was coming, or before they could react, Shaemus swung the pistol, aimed it at Major Grogan and fired.

Barbara's mind noted the pistol recoil, the spurt of smoke, the shiny brass cartridge eject into the sunlight.

An automatic, her mind registered, even before the stunning reality of what had just happened struck her with numbing force.

Her eyes widened and she saw Major Grogan reel back, clutching his chest. It all seemed to be in awful slow motion but in fact was over in an instant. Major Grogan fell to the sand.

Shock turned to instant flaming anger. Lt Jeffries cried in rage and Freddy swore and lunged at the man. The man sprang back, swung the pistol to aim at Freddy and fired, even as Barbara screamed 'No!' and began moving forward.

Freddy reeled back. Shaemus aimed again. "This is for my little girl!" he shouted, then fired a second time. This time Freddy went down, the impact of the bullet spinning him round as he did.

"You bastard!" Lt Jeffries yelled as he grappled with Shaemus. Shaemus tried to step back while Lt Jeffries grabbed at the gun. Shaemus shouted, "Let go you fool! Dylan, shoot boy!"

Barbara flicked her eyes at where the other man stood. He shifted the rifle nervously and she sensed hesitation but her attention was drawn instantly back to the life and death struggle going on near her.

Lt Jeffries continued to try to wrestle the pistol from Shaemus. Barbara anxiously wished he hadn't tried to do this as the gun was gripped tightly between the two men's struggling bodies. Then, to Barbara's horror, the pistol went off again. Lt Jeffries grunted and doubled up, then slumped to his knees. Even though he was obviously badly hurt Lt Jeffries tried gamely to twist the gun from Shaemus. Shaemus broke it free from his grasp and stepped back a pace, then raised the pistol to deliberately aim at Lt Jeffries head. To Barbara, now moving forward, it was the most chilling thing she had ever seen. She yelled but was unaware of doing so and only dimly heard others calling out and girls screaming.

Shaemus steadied the pistol and his finger tightened on the trigger. "Now die you British mongrel!" he shouted.

At that moment Chloe struck. She had run forward and now brought her broom stick down on Shaemus's wrist. Even as the gun went off it was struck from his hand. Shaemus yelled in pain and anger and went to pick up the pistol. Barbara did not hesitate. She knew it was all or nothing. There, right in front of her, crouched the man, his fingers scrabbling for the gun. Without even consciously thinking about it Barbara kicked at his head. The blow from her army boot took him hard in the side of the face.

Shaemus was knocked backwards and fell to the sand. Barbara sprang forward and tried to kick him again but he rolled aside and sprang to his feet. "Bloody bitch! You'll pay for that!" he screamed. As he rose Shaemus whipped out a wicked looking knife which he held threateningly in front of him. He also reached up and tore off the balaclava which had been twisted round in the struggle to partially cover his eyes. Barbara noted a florid, round face contorted by rage and topped by grizzled grey hair.

"Back off!" Shaemus yelled. He looked wildly around, seeming to shake his head as he did. The kick had obviously half-stunned him. He snarled in fury, then snapped at the young man near him, "Dylan, shoot damn you!"

Barbara glanced fearfully at the other man, who now swung the rifle to and fro, first to point at Barbara, then at Chloe and then back at the cadets near him, then again towards Barbara. His indecision was obvious. At that moment Chloe moved. She was only two paces from the man and she sprang forward, dropping her broom stick as she did. Her right arm swept the rifle barrel upwards and at the same time she kicked at his groin with her right boot. The rifle went off as the man convulsively pulled the trigger but the bullet flew harmlessly into the air. By then Chloe's boot had slammed into his crutch. He gasped in pain and instantly doubled up.

As he did Chloe reefed the rifle from his fingers with her right hand, to instantly grab it with both hands and reverse the movement, slamming the rifle butt hard back into his face. The man went down in a whimpering heap. Chloe stepped back and swung the rifle around with the butt on her hip. She pointed it at the old man and worked the bolt to eject the spent round. In one flowing movement she inserted a new bullet into the breech.

There was a pause. Chloe, bosom heaving, held the rifle in readiness. Charles stepped up beside her.

"Who are these bastards?" Chloe asked.

"IRA would be my guess," Charles answered. He stopped a few paces from Shaemus and held out his hand. "Drop the knife and surrender mister. We outnumber you rather badly."

Shaemus swore and then turned to look up the slope to his right. His face was working furiously with emotion. "Murty! Shoot man! Cover me!" he yelled.

There was a sharp crack. Barbara's mind registered Chloe spinning around, a spray of whitish liquid splattering away from her as she did.

More of them! Barbara thought in near panic.

She turned her head and looked up, even as her mind registered another sharp whiplash sound. She knew instantly what it was, a bullet. She felt another wave of shock and glimpsed the tiny figure of a man standing right up at the Lookout. From the posture she knew instinctively that he was aiming a rifle at them.

Crack!

Another bullet smacked into the sand. Barbara saw grains spurt up near Chloe, who was stumbling backwards, but still clutching the rifle.

"Back!" Lt Cavendish screamed. "Get back!"

Someone else screamed, "Run!"

Barbara was vaguely aware that all the cadets were now on their feet and that a general stampede was beginning. "Into Snake Gully!" she shouted, stepping back and looking around as she did so.

Shaemus stepped quickly back, still waving the knife in front of him. "Shoot Murty! Kill the bastards! Strike a blow for Ireland!" he screamed.

Once again Barbara heard the vicious crack of the bullet, then the duller thump of the man's rifle going off. She did not know where the bullet went but she was aware that Charles had run to Chloe and was grabbing at her as she staggered around. Fear now almost paralysed Barbara but she realised there were things to do. At that moment another bullet cracked past, the shock wave so close she was sure it was aimed at her. She was conscious of the round striking the sand near her with a hissing, skittering sound.

As she jumped aside she glanced around and saw that the British WO1, Adelaide, was kneeling over the crumpled body of Major Grogan. Adelaide was trying to drag him to safety. As another bullet cracked down Barbara ran, waves of bowel-loosening fear speeding her feet.

She came to where Adelaide knelt and called, "Get up RSM, run!"

"But he's still alive! We can't just leave him," Adelaide yelled.

Barbara paused and looked fearfully up the slope. Leaves now obscured the line of sight.

We might make it, she thought, her whole body tensing in fearful anticipation.

She reached down with her left hand, grabbed at Major Grogan's shirt and began dragging. Without a word Adelaide grabbed his other arm and helped her. There was another shot which came nowhere near Barbara but which speeded her on. As they struggled across the sand Barbara was acutely conscious of the red staining Major Grogan's shirt, and of the nightmarish effort needed to run in soft sand. Her breath came in great gasps and things seemed to be all blurred. Only with an effort could she focus on the open end of Snake Gully. CUO Roberts stood there, urging them on. She then ran out to grab hold.

Within seconds she and CUO Roberts were stumbling into the mouth of the gully. Barbara was aware that they were dragging Major Grogan roughly over exposed tree roots but it did not seem to matter.

We must get under cover! she thought.

There were dozens of cadets crouching there, many huddled up against tree trunks and others blocking the gully. Lt Cavendish was standing in the middle of the gully shouting and nearly hysterical. With a gasp of relief Barbara let go of Major Grogan's shirt. Adelaide at once crouched and felt his pulse. More shouts attracted Barbara's attention and she looked around to see that Chloe and the Honourable Charles were carrying Freddy.

"Oh come on!" she cried, her heart in her mouth with dread.

Chloe was magnificent. She had hoisted Freddy's right arm around her shoulders and was staggering across the sand helped by Charles. In her right hand Chloe still clutched the rifle. At any moment Barbara expected to see them shot down but no bullets came and they staggered into the cover under the trees. With a great cry of relief Chloe handed Freddy over to three British cadets who crowded around to help her. As soon as they had him Charles pointed back out onto the sand.

"We must get Lt Jeffries. He might be still alive."

"No! We must get away from here!" shrieked Lt Cavendish.

"I'm going to get him," Charles replied. He turned and peered up through the leaves, trying to spot the rifleman. "Where is that IRA bastard, the big chap?"

"Shaemus O'Malley? He is over there. He's bolted for it. See, he's climbing the slope," cried a British cadet, a WO2 Barbara remembered as George someone or other.

Barbara got a glimpse of Shaemus as he scrabbled up the steep bank near the abutments of the old highway bridge. A moment later he was out of sight around the curve of the slope. The other man, the one Chloe had kicked in the testicles, was still out on the sand, trying to get up. Near him, on the sand, lay the army radio.

We must get that radio so we can call for help, Barbara thought.

Charles tensed himself to run. As he did the WO2, George, tapped him on the shoulder. "I'll come with you. You grab his arms and I'll get his feet."

Another British cadet joined them. "I'll help with his shoulders."

"Good man Barry, everyone ready?" Charles asked.

"Oh don't do it!" Lt Cavendish cried.

"Hold it!" Chloe called. "I will cover you." She indicated the rifle.

"Can you use that?" Charles asked.

Chloe nodded. Lt Cavendish called in angry fear that she was not to do anything of the sort but Chloe ignored her. Only now did Barbara remember the bullet striking Chloe and she noted that Chloe's trousers were stained with blood on her left buttock.

Charles noted the same thing. He stepped over to her. "Are you up to it? You were hit. Is it bad?"

Chloe glanced down and shook her head. "Hit my water bottle and nicked my bum. It really stings but I'll be OK."

"Let me do the shooting," George offered "This is our war, not yours."

At that Barbara intervened. "No! This is Australia. You won't do anything. I will do any shooting that has to be done. Give me the rifle."

For a moment Barbara thought Chloe was going to argue about it but then she handed her the rifle. "Can I help?" Chloe asked.

"Grab the radio," Barbara said, pointing to where it lay out on the sand. "Now wait till I check this rifle and get into position."

At that moment a British cadet pushed forward and grabbed the rifle "Give that to me! I will sort that murderous bastard out!"

Barbara instinctively tightened her grip on the rifle. The cadet tried to wrench it from her grasp. "No! Let it go!" Barbara cried.

"Give it to me damn you!" the cadet shouted, Cecil, Barbara remembered.

Cecil twisted and pulled to try to break her grip. Barbara was appalled by the look of fanatical intensity in his eyes.

"Let go!" she cried, having to summon all her courage to struggle with the youth. Some instinct warned her not to let him have it

"Give it to me!" Cecil cried. "That bloody terrorist killed my father. I want revenge."

Now the situation became clear to Barbara. She shook her head and hung on grimly, desperate to keep the situation from getting worse. "No! You will not! This is Australia. You won't break our laws. Let go!"

At that moment Adelaide intervened, pushing between them and also gripping the rifle. "Let it go Cecil. She is right. Give her the rifle. That is an order. Cecil! Leave go!"

"No!" Cecil cried, his emotional turmoil clear in his face. "I have waited years for this chance. Now it is my turn." Once again he struggled to break Barbara's grip.

Barbara saw Adelaide shake her head and her mouth tighten. "No. Vengeance is mine saith the Lord. You don't have the right. Help us to bring him to justice, but don't stain your honour, or your hands," Adelaide replied.

For a moment Cecil stood tugging at the rifle, glaring distractedly at Adelaide. Then he abruptly let go and stepped back, sobbing with emotion. Adelaide let go as well and moved to put her arm around his shoulders. "We will get him, don't worry. Now help me look after Major Grogan."

Cecil nodded and moved back to kneel down to where Robbo and Sgt Newell were busy opening Major Grogan's shirt. Adelaide joined them. Barbara glanced at Major Grogan and felt sick.

"Is he alive?"

Robbo nodded. "Yes, but he's losing blood fast. He needs a doctor urgently."

"So does Lt Jeffries, let's get a wriggle on," Charles added.

There was a pause while Barbara dusted the rifle and looked at it. She was no expert but had fired a bolt action rifle several times before. As she held it she was shaken by searing flashbacks to when she and the French Special Forces troops had fought the Dagestani troops at Dotswood the previous year. That had been an intense and bloody little conflict and during it she had several times fired at the enemy in deadly earnest. After the Dags had shot down two Blackhawk helicopters and continued firing on the survivors who were struggling to escape from the burning wrecks Barbara had again fired at them. In her heart Barbara believed she had killed at least one or more of the Dag soldiers and the guilt tormented her from time to time. Now here she was again with a loaded rifle in her hands and people's lives depending on her. She hated the idea of using it but nerved herself.

Some of the others obviously had doubts as well because George asked, "Will you be able to shoot someone if you have to?"

Barbara nodded. "I've done it before," she said grimly. Not only had she shot Dags but she had twice shot men at close range in the leg or arm.

"The devil you have!" George muttered.

"You better believe it," Chloe added in confirmation. Barbara noted the surprised eyes appraising her with interest. She pushed the memories of those other experiences out of her consciousness and gripped the rifle ready.

Time to fret about them later, she told herself.

The rifle felt slippery and heavy in her hands and she hoped she was up to it. Once again Lt Cavendish cried at them not to do anything but Barbara just ignored her. This had to be done.

"We can't just leave Lt Jeffries out there to bleed to death," she said.

"But he might already be dead!" Lt Cavendish cried.

"Might be," Barbara agreed.

"But you could be killed! Oh don't do it!" Lt Cavendish pleaded.

Charles answered that. "We might be, but I'd rather not live with something like that on my conscience thank you. So we are going."

Barbara took a deep breath and moved carefully past the others to the end of the gully. As she did she peered upwards through the tree canopies, her eyes straining for a glimpse of the man. She found it very difficult to find a spot where she could even see the rock face of the cutting below the Lookout but at last she found a place. She stared hard, searching for a glimpse of the man but could not see him. Cradling the rifle into her shoulder she looked through the sights. It took her a moment to get the correct 'eye relief' on the telescopic sight. She then moved the circle of clear vision with its sinister cross hairs slowly from side to side, searching. Still no sign of the man. That worried her and she briefly considered moving, then decided they must act.

I will go out with them, she decided.

"All ready?" she asked.

Chapter 22

ACTION

Barbara noted Charles and George nod and heard Lt Cavendish once again order her not to do it. Ignoring this she cried, "Go!" then sprinted forward.

It was only twenty five metres, perhaps forty paces on the soft sand, but it seemed much further. Barbara ran to the left, towards the slimy pool to get clear of the line the others would be running on, her head tilted up to get the earliest possible glimpse of the man up at the Lookout.

There he is! she thought.

The man was standing, looking down at them, his rifle held across his body. He wore no balaclava, she noted. It was instantly apparent that he had seen them as she saw him move the rifle into his shoulder, even as she skidded to a stop. In icy desperation she raised the rifle, opting for a snap shot to put the man off his aim. With eyes blurred by fear she sighted over the top of the telescopic sights and fired. Even as the weapon thumped back into her shoulder she worked the bolt with desperate speed to eject the spent cartridge case and to feed another round into the breech. Then she swung the rifle up again. Out of the corner of her eye she glimpsed Chloe standing near the man on the sand. She had snatched up the pistol and was aiming it upwards, gripping it with both hands.

Snap! Chloe fired the pistol. Barbara tucked the rifle butt into her shoulder and tried to get an aim picture through the telescopic sight. To her dismay she could not focus and the target area was not even visible in the lens. Desperately she moved it around, trying get the correct eye relief and to find the man. At last she glimpsed him and sighted. Time seemed to slow down and she clearly saw the man up at the Lookout adjust his grip and put his cheek onto the butt of his rifle to look through a telescopic sight, apparently aiming straight at her.

I must shoot first! I must spoil his aim! she thought, her mind numbed by fear and shock.

Bang!

Crack!

The rifle thumped into her shoulder as she pulled the trigger. At almost the same instant the man fired again. Part of Barbara's mind registered relief that the gun had actually gone off while the other part noted that he had not hit her.

"Now move!" she yelled to herself, remembering something an old regular army Warrant Officer instructor had once told her on a cadet camp. She dashed sideways five paces, cocking the rifle as she did. She aimed it again.

She saw the man had moved as well. He appeared to have ducked. Through the telescopic sight Barbara found herself staring straight into the man's eyes. His gaze seemed to lock onto hers, even over the hundred metres up the slope. He aimed and fired again and so did Barbara but this time she could see he was not aiming at her. Knowing that she was not the target helped her steady her nerves. Being shot herself was one thing, but letting down her friends was quite another. She squeezed the second shot much more accurately. This time she had the satisfaction of seeing the bullet strike the rocks of the cutting just below the Lookout and saw the man duck again.

"Barbara!"

It was Chloe. Barbara glanced around and saw that Charles, George and Barry had picked Lt Jeffries up and were stumbling quickly back towards cover. Chloe was standing over the man on the sand, gripping his shirt from behind and pointing her pistol at his head.

"Grab the radio," Chloe yelled.

Barbara glanced up at the Lookout. So did Chloe who shouted up, "You shoot anyone mister and I'll blow this bloke's brains out!"

Barbara glimpsed the man's head. He was being much more cautious now, not standing silhouetted on the lip of the cutting but only exposing part of his head. For a moment she wondered if the man had heard Chloe but no shot came down. As quickly as she could, Barbara ran across and grabbed at the army radio, which lay on its side in the sand. She swung the radio harness over her left shoulder so she could use that arm to scoop up her webbing. Then she ran after the British cadets who were running towards the mouth of the gully. Chloe dragged the man to his feet, showed him the pistol, then placed it against his head and started walking backwards, sheltering behind him. The man was obviously still in considerable pain as he remained bent over and groaned as he moved.

An angry shout from above attracted Barbara's attention and she glimpsed Shaemus up at the end of the old bridge. He was pointing at her and yelling to the man up at the Lookout.

"They are gettin' away Murty! Shoot man! Shoot!"

Barbara saw the man at the Lookout cock his rifle again and raise it. She didn't wait, running with frantic strides back under the trees, the radio falling down to hang on her forearm where it bumped uncomfortably. She was scared, but no longer terrified. Somehow she sensed that the man wouldn't shoot her, or Chloe.

There was no shot, but more angry shouts and threats from Shaemus. "Shoot damn you Murty! Shoot you bloody weakling!"

"I daren't," came Murty's voice, real Irish. "They've got Dylan and I might hit him."

"Ah damn and blast!" Shaemus shouted. "Ye've let them get away! Git down here and give me that bloody gun."

Barbara dashed gasping into the cover of Snake Gully. There was a cheer and she flopped down to sit on the bank, her limbs trembling so much she shivered violently.

"Bloody well done!" Charles cried, clapping her on the back.

Barbara gestured to where George and Barry were ripping open Lt Jeffries' shirt. "Is he alive?"

"Yes he is," George replied, Lord Bramley, Barbara remembered.

Chloe and her prisoner now joined them. She forced him to his knees and snarled, "Sit still or I'll shoot."

The young man did so. Chloe grabbed the top of his balaclava and tore it off. Barbara recognized him at once.

Dylan, the man we met at the Lookout yesterday; Michael's brother. They weren't just local lads driving around. They were watching us.

"Tie his hands behind his back Dunny," Chloe snapped.

Sgt Dunstan took out some nylon cord and began to do this. Barbara sat and recovered her composure, then remembered to check the rifle was on 'safe'. She then glanced at the prisoner again and noted that he looked half stunned and that a livid bruise was appearing across his nose and between his eyes where the rifle butt had struck him.

As she did this there was an angry shout beside her and she saw fear spring into the prisoner's eyes. Next moment he was struck by one of the British cadets, Cecil.

"You murderer! Mongrel! Human filth!" Cecil shouted as he punched at Dylan.

Dylan curled up and tried to protect himself from the rain of blows by putting his arms over his head. Both Charles and George seized Cecil and dragged him back.

"Stop it! Calm down Cecil," George snapped.

"Yes, steady on old boy," Charles added "He is a prisoner so we must treat him properly."

To Barbara's relief Cecil subsided onto the sand and shuddered with nervous tension. Dylan remained cringing on the sand, earning a look of contempt from Chloe.

"What do we do now?" CUO Roberts asked. She was crouched over Major Grogan and was tying a bandage over his blood-stained chest.

CUO Bailey stood up and pointed up Snake Gully. "We get away from here before that man gets down here!" he answered, his voice quavering with fear.

When nobody moved CUO Bailey gestured at the hill and cried, "Come on! We must get away from here before that man arrives with his rifle."

To Barbara he appeared to be on the edge of panic and that made her aware that the whole gully as far as she could see was full of frightened cadets, some crying and others looking fearfully around.

"Stop moving!" she shouted. "Lie down under cover you cadets."

"But the man!" CUO Bailey cried, his voice rising in fear.

"He won't bother us," Barbara spat back. "We've got guns too and he knows it. If he comes down onto the sand he is a bloody fool." She was annoyed with Bailey for acting the way he was. She leaned closer and hissed at him. "Shut up and calm down. You are frightening the younger cadets. Now remember you are a CUO and get control of your platoon."

"But. but.." Bailey gasped, his gaze flicking fearfully out through the end of the gully.

"Shut up and move! Get your platoon together around the next bend there and sit them down," Barbara snapped. She gave him a shove and looked around.

Lt Cavendish was standing nearby in shock but at least some people were trying to regain control. Barbara saw the blonde RSM, Adelaide, pointing and snapping out orders to her own people, sending them into the trees on the right in a group. Sgt Sharon Newell was now crouching with CUO Roberts, giving first aid to Lt Jeffries.

"Robbo, you go and collect your platoon together," Barbara ordered, wishing Lt Cavendish would snap out of it and help. CUO Roberts nodded and stood up to do that. "Keep it as quiet as you can," Barbara added. "Move them all back around the next bend so no-one is visible from out on the riverbed, and put a sentry group up on top of the bank facing the hill on the bank of Deep Creek."

CUO Roberts hurried off, signalling to those of her cadets who were crouched in the gully. Barbara looked around and noted that Chloe was still guarding Dylan, while frequently glancing out onto the sandy riverbed. Charles and his friends were clustered around Freddy.

We need a sentry, she thought.

The senior person standing in view was Sgt Dunstan. "Dunny, take this rifle and sit here as sentry in case those blokes try to sneak up," she said, holding out the rifle.

As Sgt Dunstan moved to take the rifle George stood up and reached out. "Let me. It is our war really."

Barbara had no doubt that George would be much more capable than Sgt Dunstan but she shook her head. "It might be your war but it is our country and I don't want you breaking the law. You will only fire in self-defence, or to save someone else."

She held George's eyes and he nodded grimly. "Yes, OK."

Barbara then handed him the rifle. George quickly checked it, then moved forward carefully to a fire position behind a tree on top of the bank from where he could cover the lower slopes of the hill as well as the mouth of Deep Creek and the open riverbed. Satisfied that the threat from that direction had been temporarily dealt with Barbara looked around, her mind full of things she knew must be done. Problems of deciding on priorities jostled in her thoughts, threatening to fluster and overwhelm her.

First make the place safe, she told herself, squirming fears of the men creeping up on them clouding her mind. For a few seconds she just stood and considered the ground. *The dry riverbed and end of the hill are covered by George and I think Deep Creek is too deep to easily cross between here and the bottom of the hill,* she decided.

But further along Deep Creek curved away from the hill and was dry and easy to cross and there was the low ridge they had walked along to get from it to Snake Gully.

We need to cover the approaches from the west, she thought.

Now, what must we do? she asked herself, deliberately closing her eyes and slowing her breathing for a moment.

The shock was now setting in and she just wanted to scream and run away. It took a conscious effort to keep her emotions under control.

That she was not alone in this was evident from the faces and actions of those around her. Some were obviously in shock and others were plainly terrified. Many stared at the wounded Britons with horror in their eyes. In the gully twenty metres further along she recognised members of her own platoon. They were huddled in a fearful group. Standing with them, providing some control, was Sgt Brady. The sight of him doing that did a lot to increase Barbara's opinion of him.

"Well done Sgt Brady. Just get them together and keep them quiet," Barbara said. He nodded and spoke to the platoon, his words clearly calming a couple.

Even so it was obvious the situation was volatile. Cadets were in tears and whimpering, both girls and boys. Others were calling out to run.

We had better get all this under control quickly, Barbara thought.

She paused to breathe deeply again to stop herself fainting from nausea and nervous reaction. "Calm down!" she called. "Get down and keep quiet."

Then she forced herself to look closely at the wounded. Freddy looked the worst. His shirt had been cut or torn open and there seemed to be blood everywhere. Sharon Newell was trying to bandage him, helped by two British cadets. Sharon was clearly distressed, crying and shaking but still managing to function.

"How is he?" Barbara asked.

One of the British cadets replied. "Not good. He's got a bullet in his chest and another in the shoulder," he said.

Barbara felt her stomach heave as she studied the mangled shoulder. Freddy was writhing and groaning and was obviously in agony.

Barbara then turned to Major Grogan. Adelaide was busy pressing a pad to his chest. Adelaide met her eyes and shook her head. Tears showed.

"I think he is going to die," she whispered.

"What about Lt Jeffries?" Barbara asked.

Three more British cadets were working there. Lt Jeffries was still doubled up and was tensing and flexing, drawing his legs up and then twitching spasmodically. His face was a waxy, greenish tinge and he was sweating heavily. Barbara knew that a wound in the stomach or lower abdomen was very serious.

As she watched one of the British cadets said, "Give him a drink"

Adelaide at once turned and snapped, "Don't! Whatever you do don't give him anything to drink. He has a stomach wound and that will kill him for sure."

"He's going to die anyway if we don't get him to a doctor fast," one of the British cadets replied.

"Doctor! Where are you going to find a doctor around here? We are in the middle of nowhere," sneered another.

No we aren't, Barbara thought, *we are only at Millaroo. We must get a doctor.*

That jerked her thoughts back into action. She pulled out her mobile phone and, with fingers that trembled so much she had trouble controlling them, turned it on. But it showed 'no service'. She tried calling but nothing happened.

Lt Cavendish watched her attempts anxiously. "Any luck?" she asked. Barbara shook her head. "I think the hill is screening any mobile service," she said. She knew it worked further out in the open riverbed but that meant exposing herself to the murderous Murty. Turning to Lt Cavendish she said, "You try yours."

Lt Cavendish did, but with the same result. "Perhaps one of the cadets has a phone," she suggested. All ACS had mobile phones for safety but the army rules stipulated that no cadet was to have a mobile phone at an AAC activity. Barbara only had hers because she was considered one of the adult staff.

"They shouldn't have," Barbara replied. "Lt Cavendish ma'am, can you call the OC on the radio and get him to get the ambulance on his mobile phone?" she said. She knew mobile phones worked at the gravel scrape as she had seen Major Wickham using his.

Lt Cavendish was sitting next to the radio that Barbara had recovered from the riverbed. It took a moment for what Barbara had said to sink in before the OOC reacted. Barbara in fact stood up and began walking towards the radio when Lt Cavendish picked up the handset.

"Hello Hotel, this is Bravo, over."

To Barbara's surprise and relief there was an instant reply, and it was Major Wickham's voice. "Hotel here, send over."

"Oh thank God!" Lt Cavendish cried. As she spoke Barbara saw her hand shake and there was a tremble in her voice. Lt Cavendish went on, "Hotel, this is Bravo, emergency, over."

"Send, over," Major Wickham replied.

"Oh major! Quick! There are men in black hoods shooting at us. They have shot one of the cadets and the two British officers. We need the medics fast!"

There was a pause while Major Wickham apparently had a conversation with someone else. He then asked for details. Lt Cavendish began describing what had happened and ended by saying, "Call the ambulance quickly, and the police."

There was more delay which made Barbara fret with impatience. As she waited she noted Charles helping Chloe to remove her webbing. Chloe's left water bottle was smashed almost in half and her trousers were torn and soaked with blood.

"Is it serious?" Charles asked anxiously.

"Don't think so," Chloe replied "Stings like buggery though."

"How do you know what buggery stings like?" Charles quipped, but he was obviously very concerned.

Chloe poked her tongue at him, then began to undo her trousers. "Oh, I hope it doesn't leave a scar!"

"Why? Nobody will see it, only your beloved," Charles commented.

"Yes they will. I'm a nudist," Chloe replied, looking him in the eyes with a challenging stare.

"By Jove! That must be a wonderful sight to see!" Charles cried. Then he put his arm around Chloe's shoulders and hugged her. "Oh Chloe, you are magnificent!"

Chloe flashed him a smile, then snuggled into his arms for a minute. Barbara watched the by-play with amazement.

Hmm, maybe Lady Matchlock has moved a step closer, she mused. She was torn from this speculation by Lt Cavendish.

"Barbara, something is wrong. Major Wickham just said don't let the men get the wounded, then he was cut off. There is some other man talking."

She held the handset out and Barbara clearly heard a man with an Irish accent say, "Bring all the cadets out to the road, at once, or we will shoot your officers, got that?"

Oh no! Barbara thought. "The terrorists have captured the OC and HQ from the sound of it," she said. She took the handset and replied, outrage sparking her response. "Listen you, we have one of your men prisoner and we will shoot him if you harm any more of our people, you hear me? Over,"

There was a pause, then the Irishman asked, "Who is the prisoner?"

Barbara turned to where Sgt Dunstan stood covering the prisoner. The prisoner was still hunched up and had tears in his eyes and was obviously still in pain from Chloe's kick.

"What's your name?" Barbara asked.

The youth glared at her. "I'm not tellin' you anything."

Barbara held up the handset. "Some old Irish bugger wants to know. He doesn't believe you are a prisoner."

The youth shook his head. His stubbornness exasperated Barbara. "It's Dylan isn't it? You were up at the Lookout yesterday?"

Dylan shrugged, then nodded. Barbara called on the radio, "His name is Dylan, now let our officers go and call the ambulance," she said.

"No chance!" the Irishman said. "Let my boy go or you'll regret it."

Your boy eh? Barbara wondered.

Acting on a hunch, she replied, "No deal. If you hurt anyone else we will shoot him."

"You wouldn't be game," the man answered. "You are bluffing. Now let him go and give yourselves up."

"I might not shoot him," Barbara replied, "but there is one of the British cadets here, a chap by the name of Cecil," She turned to Cecil. "What's your family name Cecil?" Cecil told her and she passed this on. "Cecil Gough-Gore. Apparently your people killed his father in Ireland and he has a personal score to settle. We have already had to restrain him twice, so, if you want your son back unharmed, then do as I say."

There was a muffled grumble from the radio, which then fell silent. Barbara tried calling but was told by another person at the other end to wait.

While they waited Barbara noted that Chloe had now undone her trousers and pulled them down to her knees and had pulled her shirt up to expose her left buttock. Charles was helping her, and obviously liking what he saw. Barbara had the niggling thought that she should order Chloe to have one of the girls do the first aid but Chloe was so obviously encouraging Charles that all she did was shrug.

While Barbara watched, wondering if she should say anything, Chloe used water from her other water bottle to rinse the blood from her wound. The wound appeared to be a crease about ten centimetres long and had already almost stopped bleeding.

"Go easy with that water," Barbara said, realising that she felt very thirsty.

"It's OK," Chloe replied.

"No it's not," Barbara answered. "Most of the cadets left their webbing out on the sand and they will get very thirsty soon."

"There are four water jerries just there at the end of the gully CUO Brassington," Sgt Dunstan called.

Barbara glanced to where the four plastic water jerry cans stood on the sand just out from the end of the gully. "You just keep your eyes on the prisoner," she said to Sgt Dunstan, noting that he, along with most of the others, had their gaze fixed on Chloe's rump.

"Yes ma'am," Sgt Dunstan replied, managing a cheeky grin. He then added, "Cpl Keith, get those water jerries in here."

"Oh poop! I might get bloody shot!" Cpl Keith retorted.

"Crap! That guy won't even see you. Anyway, he's a rotten shot so stop worrying. Just do what you are told," Sgt Dunstan snapped.

Cpl Keith grumbled again but moved to obey. Barbara called to George to cover him, then watched as Charles dabbed Chloe's skin dry. He then took a small bottle of antiseptic from her.

"This might hurt a bit," he commented.

"That's alright," Chloe replied. Charles gently dabbed the antiseptic on and Chloe let out a yowl. "Ow! Aah! Oh shit! That stings," she cried.

"I told you it would," Charles replied, dabbing some more, "And ladies shouldn't swear."

"Swear! I'll give you f... Ouch!... Ow! That will do," Chloe cried.

"Oh golly dash, you mean," Charles commented, but he smiled as he screwed the cap back on the bottle and passed it back to Chloe.

"Do you think it needs a covering?" Chloe asked, hauling up her shirt to look more closely.

"Not sure how we would bandage that," Charles replied, sliding his hand over Chloe's bum, while staring at her thighs.

Barbara intervened, "Chloe! Get dressed. A Band-Aid is all you need."

"I'll put it on," Charles offered.

"You will not," Barbara snapped. "A gentleman would have averted his eyes instead of ogling the poor girl. Sharon, put a Band-Aid on Chloe's bum."

Charles stood up and smiled at Chloe, who smiled back. Charles winked. "I'm only a gentleman sometimes," he added.

"All men are," Chloe retorted with an impish grin.

"Stop it you two!" Lt Cavendish called angrily.

"Yes Miss," Chloe replied. Charles stepped aside as Cpl Keith came staggering along with two water jerry cans. Sharon went over to Chloe.

Barbara turned to Lt Cavendish. "What's going on ma'am?"

"I don't know Barbara. That man hasn't called back."

"They must be up to some trick, sneaking up on us or something," Sgt Dunstan suggested.

"You might be right," Barbara replied.

She felt very anxious and upset, on top of feeling the enormous pressure of responsibility. It was apparent to her that Lt Cavendish was looking to her for leadership. The unfairness of that rankled but Barbara forced herself to think.

We need more information, she decided.

She knelt at the radio. "Hello CSM, this is One One, over."

There was no answer. She tried twice more, then said, "CSM, out to you. One Four, this is One One, over."

"One One, this is One Four, what is going on, over," came CUO Callan's voice.

Barbara opened her mouth to answer when Sgt Dunstan called, "Careful Barbara, the enemy are listening."

"You are right," Barbara said. She then pressed the pressel switch and said, "One Four, this is One One, Charlie, Quebec, Zulu, over."

"Roger, over."

Barbara sighed with relief. CUO Callan had understood the Net Call Sign to switch the radio to the alternate frequency. "Wait, out," she said, then to Cpl Keith, "Keithy, switch this radio to the alternate frequency and do a radio check with One Four."

"Don't know what it is," Cpl Keith replied.

Barbara had to take out her notebook to find it. As she leafed through her notebook she was aware that Lt Jeffries was groaning and twitching in agony. He had gone a queer greyish colour and was sweating profusely.

We must hurry, she thought.

"Ah! Here it is. Forty six twenty three," she read.

Cpl Keith crouched at the radio and began twisting the tuning dials. While he did Sharon stood up and waved her bloodstained hands. "Can we get these people out of here? They need medical help urgently."

"I don't know if we can," Barbara replied. "I don't know how many of these people there are, or where they might be."

"Sneaking up on us through the scrub probably," said Cpl Keith, looking up at the wall of trees and vines on top of the bank.

Barbara's own eyes were drawn to this and she shivered with apprehension. "You just tune that radio Cpl Keith and let the officers worry about tactics," she snapped.

"Yes ma'am, but what are we going to do?" Cpl Keith replied.

Yes! Barbara thought. *What are we going to do?*

Chapter 23

DYLAN

Sgt Dunstan gestured to their prisoner. "What will we do with this bloke then?"

"Find out what he knows first," Barbara replied.

Once again, she looked at the wounded and then shook her head in dismay and looked away. A sense of helpless despair that she found almost overwhelming flooded through her. It brought home to her the truth of something Major Wickham had said.

"If you are in command never do the actual First Aid. Delegate it to someone else and tell them what to do if they don't know. Stay back and try not to become too emotionally involved."

He had pointed out that once you actually touched the flesh of the injured person your emotions were much more powerfully affected, and this could interfere with clear thinking.

"Stay in control, both of yourself and the situation," he had advised.

Even looking at the seeping blood and sweating skin had a ghastly fascination which caused the heart to beat faster and the stomach to churn. With an effort Barbara looked away.

"Hurry up Keithy. What's taking so long?"

"Got him now," Cpl Keith replied, looking both scared and aggrieved simultaneously.

Barbara grabbed the handset. "One Four, this is One One. Bring your platoon back down into the gully but leave a couple of reliable people there as sentries with the radio. Got that? Over."

CUO Callan replied he had. Barbara then went on, "Then run back to here so we can discuss what to do. Collect the other CUOs on the way. Bring the CSM and Colleen with you."

"The CSM and Colleen went with the OC back to the fire at camp, over," CUO Callan replied.

Damn! thought Barbara. "Roger that, do that now, out."

CUO Callan acknowledged. Barbara handed the handset back to Cpl Keith. "Keep a listening watch," she instructed.

Once again she experienced a sharp spasm of annoyance at the fact that Lt Cavendish was just sitting near the casualties, helping with their care.

She is the senior officer. She should be making the decisions, Barbara thought. Then she shrugged and got on with things.

She found herself confronted by a very distressed Sharon, tears running down her chubby cheeks. "Barbara, we need more bandages. I can't stop the bleeding."

"Has anyone got any bandages in their webbing?" Barbara asked. Luckily some cadets wore their basic webbing.

Sharon pointed out onto the sand. "There are a lot in my First Aid Kit."

Barbara looked where Sharon was pointing and felt her hopes drop. The First Aid Kit lay out on the sand 50 paces from the end of the gully.

"We can't get that. It will be too dangerous," she said.

"But... but we need it!" Sharon wailed.

"I'll get it," Chloe said.

Barbara spun to face her. "No you won't. It's not worth the risk."

"Yes it is. I'll walk out with a white flag. Even a terrorist should hesitate to shoot someone carrying a white flag," Chloe said. "Who's got a white handkerchief?" she asked.

Barbara knew she was faced with a terrible quandary. Should she risk someone's life to get a few bandages? "We can rip up shirts to make bandages," she suggested.

To her annoyance one of the British cadets passed Chloe a white handkerchief. Chloe passed it to Charles.

"Tie that to a stick," she ordered.

Charles took the handkerchief and bent to pick up a stick, then straightened up, mouth agape. Chloe had started to unbutton her shirt.

"I say! What are you doing?" he asked.

Chloe shrugged off her shirt, exposing her wonderful womanly shape. To Barbara's relief Chloe wore a bikini top but it was only a tiny thing of two triangles of cloth tied on with thin cords so that most of her breasts were plainly visible. And very prominent! For what seemed like minutes the sight of them held everyone's attention.

"I say!" Charles stammered again, still gaping in admiration. "But why?"

"To let them see I am a female," Chloe explained, indicating her shapeless camouflage trousers. "Surely they won't shoot a woman?"

"You are certainly that!" Charles cried.

"Stop staring and give me the white flag," Chloe said sharply, her nervousness now evident.

"Chloe, don't do it!" Barbara cried.

Charles nodded vigorously. "No, don't go. Let me run out instead," he offered. He continued to stare at Chloe as though bewitched.

Chloe ignored calls from Lt Cavendish and Barbara and just turned and walked out along the gully.

"Cover me George," she ordered.

"By George! I'd rather leave you uncovered," George commented, as he ran his eyes over her.

Barbara saw him lick his lips and realised that all the males were probably having the same reaction.

Bloody Chloe! she thought. *We've got enough problems without her flaunting herself!*

As Chloe walked out onto the open sand Barbara felt her own mouth go dry, but with fear, not lust. Short of physically restraining Chloe she couldn't see what she could have done to stop her.

Chloe walked steadily out from under the tree canopy into the open. At any moment Barbara expected a bullet to strike Chloe down and she felt her heart rise into her gorge so that she had to swallow and slow her breathing.

Instead of a shot there was a shout. Chloe started waving the white flag but kept walking. The voice came again, from just over on top of the old bridge.

"You there! Stop or I will shoot!"

Shaemus, Barbara thought.

"Can you see him George?" she asked. She realised she had run to the end of the gully with Charles to watch.

"No, drat it!" George replied. "He is just around the curve."

Shaemus's voice came again, louder and harsher this time. "Stop I say! Stop or I will shoot!"

"I'm only going to get a First Aid Kit," Chloe yelled back.

She kept walking and was now only ten paces from the First Aid Kit.

"Stop woman! I'm warning you!" Shaemus shouted.

Oh my God! Barbara thought, *he sounds really hostile.*

Chloe did not stop. She walked calmly to the First Aid Kit and bent to pick it up. Shaemus shouted angrily again, "Drop that you Jezabel! Drop it I say, harlot!"

Chloe ignored the threat and turned to walk back, giving a defiant flick of her head and bounce of her breasts as she did.

At that moment Barbara heard another voice shout, "No Uncle Shaemus!" Almost simultaneous with that came the sound of a rifle shot.

Barbara flinched and bit her lip. She saw Chloe tense but keep on walking. The shot had not hit her. Again came the other person's voice, "No Uncle Shaemus! You've done enough damage already! I won't be a party to murder."

"Let go of my rifle boy!" shouted Shaemus.

"No! No more shooting!" the voice cried.

Michael, Barbara decided, *Dylan's little brother, the one Colleen thought was dreamy.*

The sound of a furious argument with words like 'coward' and 'traitor' freely used came to them while Chloe walked quickly back. As she did Barbara was overcome with admiration. She was also struck by Chloe's physical beauty. She had a wonderful woman's body and knew it.

Barbara now took several deep breaths and calmed herself. *I have to take control here. Lt Cavendish isn't going to,* she told herself.

And she knew from bitter experience she could do it. Sharp, searing memories of shooting the pig hunter at Bunyip River two years before and of shooting at the guards of the religious sect nicknamed the Smiley People the previous year came to her. But most vivid and telling was her experience at Dotswood the previous September when she had battled as part of a French patrol against troops from Dagestan. She had been with a mixed group of French marines and French Foreign Legion paratroopers.

2m Regiment etranger de parachutists, my regiment, Barbara thought with mixed emotions.

Even though she was only 18 and a cadet she had seen more action than most regular soldiers experience in a lifetime. It had left her mentally scarred but also with a sharp sense of reality and of what was possible. But it also gave her enormous self-confidence. She knew what she was capable of.

As Chloe reached them Barbara rushed out and hugged her. "Oh Chloe! That was the bravest thing I have ever seen!"

"By Jove yes! Can I have a hug too?" Charles cried.

Chloe squeezed Barbara. "I was scared," she admitted.

Barbara became aware of Chloe's physical presence and of the fact that they were still standing out in the open, the object of many staring eyes. Chloe smiled and gently released her. She passed the First Aid Kit to a tearful Sharon, then stepped over to embrace Charles.

That he was quite overwhelmed by this was obvious. "Oh I say! Oh by Jove! I…" he stammered. "Chloe, that was magnificent."

Chloe released herself and took his hand and led him back into the gully. Once there she began to tremble and Charles held her again, this time with loving adoration in his eyes. Only after a minute did Chloe shake her head and ease herself free again. She then stood there, her delightful female form displayed for all to see.

She is beautiful! thought Barbara, although without jealousy.

Her own breasts were similar and had frequently attracted unwelcome attention to her. For that reason she was careful not to display them. Not so Chloe, who now stood in the middle of the admiring group and appeared to thrive on their attention.

Lt Cavendish was not impressed. "Chloe! Cover yourself up girl! Have some shame."

Chloe was passed her shirt by one of the British cadets and pulled it slowly on. With apparent reluctance she did the buttons up, her eyes on Charles's face as she did. He stared at her with open admiration, licking his lips and clenching and unclenching his hands all the while.

Poor Charles! Barbara thought. *The future Lady Matchlock has used her secret weapons!*

"Stop staring you boys!" Lt Cavendish called. "Now come and help us with this First Aid."

For a moment more Barbara stood to calm her own emotions and racing thoughts. Sheer relief made her tremble for a while. Then she took several deep breaths and walked over to where Dylan sat on the side of the gully, covered by Sgt Dunstan. The situation worried her because she did not want Dylan shot at all, much less by accident, yet she wanted him to believe that he would be shot if he tried to escape. She stared hard at him for a moment, framing her questions in her mind.

"You are Dylan aren't you?"

Dylan nodded. He looked surly and tired.

"How many of you are there?"

"Not saying. Let me go and it might be easier for you," Dylan replied.

Barbara gave a wry smile. "You are the one in trouble. You are an accessory to murder or attempted murder, so start thinking about how you can help yourself in court."

Dylan sneered but made no answer. Barbara was sure the dart had struck home. She said, "There are four of you here: you and your brother Michael, the old bastard who shot these people."

"Shaemus O'Malley," interjected Adelaide, who was cradling Major Grogan's head in her arms. The major was unconscious and his face looked a dreadful grey colour.

"Yes, Shaemus O'Malley, and the man up at the Lookout, Murty someone-or-other," Barbara said. "And there must be at least one other back at the gravel scrape: your dad. What's his name?"

Dylan shook his head and made no reply. Barbara gritted her teeth. Movement along the gully attracted her attention and she noted CUO Roberts, CUO Bailey and CUO Callan making their way past the cowering cadets. She gestured for them to sit nearby and faced Dylan again.

"OK buster, tell us what is going on. Why did you people watch us all yesterday, and why did Shaemus O'Malley come down here this morning and shoot these people?"

For a moment Barbara thought Dylan would not answer, but then he glanced at the group of wounded and said, "Revenge."

"Revenge? For what?"

"For my little sister," Dylan replied.

"Your little sister? I don't get it. Explain," Barbara demanded.

"My little sister Bridie. She was killed by the British army in an ambush in Ulster. It was a long time ago, when I was about two."

"Go on."

Dylan looked at the British cadets, who had grouped close to listen. He licked his lips and said, "It was in Northern Ireland. Apparently my ma was driving in the country with the baby in the back when they were ambushed by a British patrol. The baby was killed in the firing. That was why Uncle Shaemus shot that officer, that bloke's dad."

Dylan nodded at a stony-faced Cecil, then went on. "Later Shaemus and dad went hunting Major Grogan because they heard he was the man who organised it, along with Colonel Masters, the CO of the regiment that carried out the ambush. Uncle Shaemus managed to put a bullet into Grogan but didn't kill him. The family then fled Ireland and came to Australia."

"That's not bloody true!" Cecil cried angrily. "It was no ambush in the country. It was at a roadblock at the edge of the Crumlin Estate. My dad's platoon had been deployed there to stop the two communities from rioting while some Protestant leader made a speech. There was a bomb explosion at St Andrew's Church, a few blocks away, so the platoon began to stop and search every vehicle. Major Grogan had just arrived at the roadblock when a car driven by a woman drove along from the direction of the church and was stopped. When Major Grogan looked in he saw Shaemus O'Malley, who was a wanted terrorist."

"Freedom fighter," Dylan snapped angrily.

"Bloody murderer!" Cecil shouted back.

"That will do! Tell us the rest of your version Cecil," Barbara said.

"It's not my version! It's the bloody truth!" Cecil cried angrily. He glared at Dylan, then went on, "As soon as Major Grogan recognised O'Malley O'Malley shot him. Then he shot my dad who was standing next to him. As the car drove away the troops opened fire. They didn't know there was a baby in the car. They didn't mean to kill it."

"Not it, my sister Bridie," Dylan said.

"Yes, a baby girl. I know the troops were upset. Sergeant Carthew told me about it," Cecil said bitterly.

"They were upset!" Dylan sneered. "What about my mum!"

"What was the baby doing in the car?" Barbara asked.

"Don't know," Dylan replied, "Mum had been shopping I think."

"So what's this story about driving in the country?" Charles asked.

"That's what I was told," Dylan replied.

"Well it wasn't. It was in the middle of the bloody town," Cecil said. "I know. I've been there to look at the place."

"They probably lied to cover up their mistakes," Dylan suggested.

"Lied! You bastards are the bloody liars!" Cecil cried. For a moment Barbara feared he would attack Dylan.

To forestall she said, "So, was Shaemus O'Malley in the car or not?"

"Mum never mentioned him," Dylan replied.

"Then I don't get it. When did he shoot Cecil's dad, and why would he be the one to go looking for vengeance?" Charles asked.

Dylan shrugged and did not answer but he looked worried. Barbara took up the theme. "Yes, why? Why did he come down here and just shoot these people? And what did he mean by shouting 'This is for my little girl!' when he shot them?"

Dylan shook his head and looked even more unhappy. "Don't know," he muttered.

Barbara stared at him. "You people came here to shoot the British cadets didn't you?"

"I didn't know there would be anyone hurt," Dylan muttered. "I thought they were just going to do something to make the Poms look silly, or take hostages or something."

"Or something! Well, it's all gone wrong now!" Barbara sneered. "You don't sound like an Irishman. Are you involved just because your dad and your uncle want to settle old scores?"

Dylan nodded. "We were all brought up in Australia but were taught to be Irish."

"And being Irish includes being a bloody murdering terrorist does it!" Cecil sneered.

"No it doesn't!" Dylan yelled.

"Well, they tell me that the bomb in the church killed fifteen people, all women and kids. Not the Protestant leader. He hadn't even arrived when it went off. Fifteen women and little kids, and you are bleating about you baby sister! You bloody hypocrite! You make me sick!"

The two glared hate at each other. Barbara stepped between them. "That's enough! Raking over old feuds won't help. We have to get these people to a doctor before they die."

"What are we going to do?" CUO Callan asked.

"Sgt Dunstan, you and Cpl Keith take the prisoner further along the gully, then tie his legs as well as his hands, then go and act as sentry at the other end. Cpl Keith, you guard the prisoner and make sure he doesn't get free. Sgt Dunstan, you take the gun, but only shoot in self-defence."

"Yes ma'am. Come on you, up you get!"

While Dylan was moved along the gully Barbara quickly described to CUO Callan what had happened.

Callan listened and then asked, "So you reckon there are more of these IRA characters back at the gravel scrape?"

Barbara nodded. CUO Bailey waved his arms. "Then we are trapped!"

"No we aren't," CUO Callan said. "This is a big area, and we know it intimately. If they have only a few people they will be hard pressed to watch it all. We should be able to sneak out and reach a phone."

"That's what I thought," Barbara agreed. "But who is to go, and where to?" Again she experienced regret that her mobile phone had no service.

"We could trade that guy," CUO Bailey suggested. "They might let us go then."

"Might!" CUO Callan sneered. "They're the ones with the guns."

"What about the British cadets? We can't let the IRA get them," Barbara replied. She was disgusted at Bailey's suggestion and curled her lip with disdain.

"Or the wounded," Chloe added. "That would just be murder."

"But they might kill us!" Bailey cried. Barbara noted he was very pale and sweating. Scared shitless was the way CUO Callan described it later.

Chloe snorted her contempt. "Crap! We've got two guns. They'll be very wary of coming near us," she replied.

"They might be creeping up on us right now," Bailey said.

"You might be right, but that is easy to deal with," Barbara said. She pointed to the thick undergrowth. "They won't be able to creep through that without making a fair bit of noise, so each platoon is to place a sentry group of three up on each bank. If they hear anyone they are to send a runner and we will move the cadets away and send one of the guns to that place."

"What will you do then?" Bailey asked.

"Warn them, then shoot if I have to," Barbara replied. "Now, let's think about going for help. Which is the closest place with a phone?"

"Byrne Valley?" Chloe suggested. "It is only three or four kilometres."

"Landers Creek homestead is about the same distance and you wouldn't have to cross the river," CUO Callan added.

Chloe shook her head. "I wasn't going to. I was just going to call across the water like McArtney did last night," she replied.

"You could take McArtney as a guide," CUO Callan grinned.

"Stop your joking and get a move on!" Lt Cavendish cried. "These people need medical help urgently."

"What about to the north, the pump station?" CUO Callan added.

"Is there anyone there?" Barbara asked.

"Not sure. There are farms that way, and we could flag down a car," CUO Callan replied.

"So who goes, and which place do they go to?" CUO Bailey asked.

"We should go to all those places, just in case one group gets caught," Barbara replied. She had been thinking very hard about who should go and it left her with some cruel decisions to make. The obvious people to go, in terms of physical fitness, navigational ability and fieldcraft, were the CUOs and sergeants. Equally, she could see compelling reasons why they were needed to control the situation here. There was one thing she was sure of and she voiced it now. "The British cadets stay here."

"But we are fit and we know where some of these places are," Charles objected.

"No. You stay together as a group and defend yourselves if you have to. We go for help," Barbara insisted.

"Who goes?" Bailey asked.

"I will go to Landers Creek," Barbara said. "I will take Sgt Dunstan and a corporal. Along the way I will try to use my phone. Mike, you go to the pump station. Go up over the hill near the power line. There is a gully there you might be able to creep up."

CUO Callan nodded. "I know the one. Who comes with me? Chloe?"

"No. I am going to Byrne Valley homestead," Chloe replied.

"Who stays with 4 Platoon?" Barbara asked.

"Who'd want to!" Robbo quipped.

"Hey! Be nice!" CUO Callan retorted. "I will take Cpl Unsworth and Cadet Torrens. Maree can mind the rest of them."

Lt Cavendish had been listening anxiously. "What do I do?" she asked.

"We must have an officer here with the cadets ma'am, so you stay here in charge," Barbara answered. "But give your mobile phone to CUO Callan and he can use it when he gets up on top of the hill."

Chloe stood up. "I am going now. I should be able to make it in half an hour if I hurry."

Barbara wasn't happy with this. She said, "Who is going with you?"

"I was going to go on my own," Chloe replied.

"That's not a good idea," Barbara said.

"I know that, but I can move faster then," Chloe said.

"No. You take Jane and Cpl McPherson," Barbara replied.

Chloe looked around. "Where is Jane?" she asked.

CUO Callan answered. "She is just up on the flat ridge where the track leaves this gully. She was left there by the OC and has a radio. Cpl de Beer is with her," he said.

"Yes, alright. I will pick her up on the way past. Barbara.. I mean ma'am, who will you take instead?" Chloe asked.

"Cpl Ridgeway," Barbara replied. "Now, how do you plan to get there Chloe?"

"I was just going to walk out across the riverbed," Chloe replied.

"Chloe! Have some sense! You would get shot," Lt Cavendish cried.

Chloe shook her head. "I don't think so Miss. I reckon they wouldn't shoot a girl, anyway, they are rotten shots."

"No! You won't take such risks," Charles said firmly. "They use bombs to kill women and children so you will be in great danger. I will come with you."

"No," Barbara said. "All you Poms stay here."

"Poms indeed! Beastly colonials!" Charles replied, but Barbara could tell that he was trying to hide intense anxiety behind a flippant attitude.

"Let's get going," Chloe said. "It's been half an hour already since these blokes got shot."

"But which way are you going?" Barbara asked.

"I'll try to get further upstream through this stuff, then cross the open sand well away from here," Chloe said.

Adelaide looked up. "Follow the fence at the top end of this gully. It leads through the rubber vine to an old road which goes to the riverbank somewhere near Landers Creek."

Chloe pulled out her map and got Adelaide to show her. Adelaide pointed and said, "That is the area I spent half yesterday swanning around."

"OK, get your sentries organised and then meet at the place where our sentry post is up the gully," Barbara said.

As they stood to move Charles stepped over and took hold of Chloe. "You take care please. I want to see more of you."

Chloe's face dimpled into a mischievous smile. "How much more?"

"Lots more, all of you in fact," Charles replied.

"Don't be naughty!" Chloe chided, but she gave him a wicked grin. "Besides, you saw plenty this morning." With that she put her hand around his neck and drew his face to hers. Very tenderly she gave him a good kiss, then hugged him briefly. "I'll be alright. You stay safe here," she said. Then she hurried off.

Barbara sighed and shook her head then turned to Lt Cavendish. "We will be as quick as we can Miss. You take control Robbo."

CUO Roberts looked anxious but nodded. Barbara picked up her webbing and swung it on. As she did it up the radio crackled. Lt Cavendish answered it. She listened, then raised a fearful face to Barbara.

"That was Jane. There are armed men in balaclavas coming towards the sentry post where the track leaves Snake Gully!" she gasped.

Chapter 24

POETIC JUSTICE

Barbara felt her stomach tighten up and her heart began to pound. *More terrorists! And they are moving to cut off our route out!*

She bit her lip and nodded acknowledgment to Lt Cavendish's message. "We will stop them Miss. You keep control at this end."

With that she hurried along the gully. As she passed Adelaide, who still held Major Grogan, she forced herself to give a reassuring smile. Major Grogan looked terrible. His shirt had been almost torn off and was stained with dirt and blood. Blood-soaked bandages swathed his chest and his eyes were closed.

He looks in a bad way, she thought unhappily, *we must hurry and get help.*

As she stumbled and clambered over the exposed tree roots and logs Barbara kept looking at the cadets of her platoon who were sitting, lying or crouching in huddled groups on either side. Sgt Brady gave her a nod and she managed a 'Well done,' in return. She ignored the cadet's questions about what was going on but tried to give them a smile.

These kids look ready to bolt, she thought. That made her wonder whether it was wise for her and CUO Callan to try to go for help. *Maybe I'd better stay here?* she considered.

As she hurried along she was tormented by stories she had read about leaders of armies who fled the battlefield when they realized the battle was lost, leaving their troops to face their fate.

That isn't what I am doing but it might look like that to them, she thought unhappily.

Cpl Ridgeway was sitting with his section. "Come with me," Barbara said as she passed.

Cpl Ridgeway stood up and followed her without any debate, which raised her opinion of him even further. She noted he even had his webbing, another plus.

Just around the first bend, under the big spreading tree, were Cpl Keith and Dylan. Dylan looked very sulky and uncomfortable. Nearby were the cadets of 2 Platoon. Sgt Heidi Hope and Cpl Andrew Wickham stood among them and they both looked relatively calm. The sight of Heidi doing such a good job caused a warm glow in Barbara.

Good old Heidi! She is worth her weight in gold!

Barbara thought that Heidi was one of the nicest persons she had ever met and now she also thought she was one of the bravest. Heidi gave her a smile and said, "Good luck."

"Thanks," Barbara managed to croak in reply, but she was so tense and anxious she found even that difficult. She gave Cpl Wickham a nod as she passed, pleased that he was proving himself to be worthy of his dad.

Twenty metres on, at the next bend to the left, Barbara came on CUO Bailey. He was organising his sentries but his tone of voice gave away the fact that he was scared. His cadet's faces reflected this.

Bloody weakling! Barbara thought angrily.

She glared at several cadets who were blocking the gully. "Get out of the way!" she snapped, then forced her way past, oblivious to their resentful looks.

She hurried past 3 Platoon and on along the gully. There were no cadets here and she suddenly felt very lonely and exposed, even though Cpl Ridgeway was following close behind and she knew that CUO Callan and Chloe's group were somewhere just ahead. The dark, spooky atmosphere of Snake Gully now really gripped her. Added to the knowledge that armed enemy were heading their way it filled her with an almost paralysing dread. To help combat this she forced herself to walk fast without running. Even so she became breathless and broke into a sweat.

Two bends further on Barbara met CUO Callan coming back the other way, followed by Cpl Unsworth and one of his big male cadets.

"Where are you going Mike?" she asked.

"Back to that little side gully where 3 Platoon are. We cut a track up it a couple of years ago, right across to Deep Creek near the bend at the base of the hill. It will be overgrown now but it will be safer than trying to get up across the top of that flat open ridge," he explained.

"Good idea," Barbara agreed. "Good luck."

"Same to you," CUO Callan replied.

He clambered over some exposed roots near her and went quickly on.

Barbara was now fretting with anxiety about how close the enemy might be and she hurried on along the gully. Crawling under or clambering over the big logs slowed her down and made her fret and sweat but she was determined and pushed herself.

A minute later she reached the section of the gully which had long grass on both sides. She pushed through this with barely a thought for possible snakes. After scrambling under the logs and pushing overhanging grass aside she reached the point where the track went up out of the gully. The remainder of 4 Platoon were grouped there. Cpl Maree de Beer was in charge.

"What's going on ma'am?" Maree asked. "CUO Callan said something about terrorists."

"That's right. Irish. They have shot three of the Poms. I am told there are more of them coming from this direction."

Maree nodded. "I saw them. They were over near the power line when I spotted them. We came back here at once."

"Where is the sentry post?" Barbara asked.

Maree pointed up the track. "Just up there ma'am."

"Has Chloe left yet?"

"They just went off along the gully," Maree answered, pointing to the left into the tangle further up the gully. "She had Ben and Jane with her."

Barbara stared at the gully upstream and noted that it looked to be an impenetrable tangle. As it hadn't been cleared, she wondered if it was possible to get along it easily.

Must be possible if Chloe has gone that way. Anyway, worry about that in a minute, she told herself.

"Wait here Cpl Ridgeway," she instructed. She pushed past some of the cadets and scrambled up the steep bank.

Twenty paces on, in among the last of the rubber vines, she found Sgt Dunstan and a male cadet from 4 Platoon crouched under cover. They were peering through the foliage up towards the flat top of the low ridge. As Barbara moved up they heard her and glanced fearfully in her direction, then turned back to their front. Sgt Dunstan had the pistol and was fidgeting nervously with it.

"They are just along the ridge there CUO Brassington," he said, pointing through the bushes.

Barbara went into a crouch behind a bush and looked. For a moment she had trouble focusing her eyes. Then her heart squeezed tight with fear as she noted three armed men in dark green jackets and black balaclavas. They were about a hundred metres away and walking slowly towards her. The first two were solidly built and the last one was a tall, thin man with faded jeans. He carried a hunting rifle. The leading one had an ugly looking black sub-machine gun. The sight of that SMG sent a shiver of pure terror through Barbara and she had to breathe deeply and clench her hands tightly to stop them shaking.

The three men continued walking slowly along, scanning both the creek lines and also the ground.

They are looking for our tracks, Barbara decided, seeing the lead terrorist stop and attract his companion's attention, then point down, then on along the ridge.

For a moment the three men looked carefully around. The man with the SMG stared straight at Barbara and she went rigid with fright. Memories of that dreadful day when the Dag soldier had walked down to the lagoon in Keelbottom Creek at Dotswood the previous year gripped her with paralysing force.

Then sharper memories, of that other man with a sub-machine gun, Berzinski, caused her to shiver and break into a sweat. Berzinski had pursued her obsessively the following year and it had all been a living nightmare. Now here was another evil man with a sub-machine gun. Barbara forced herself to stay still, though every instinct now was to flee.

He hasn't seen me! she thought, relief flooding through her.

She raised her hand to wipe drops of sweat from her forehead, then discovered her hand was covered with sand and leaves which had stuck to her perspiration. She wiped her hand on her uniform and gestured to the other two cadets.

"Get back down into the gully. Take the radio with you. Tell the platoon to move back to the next bend, in under the trees, and to do it quietly." she whispered.

Sgt Dunstan nodded. Barbara saw him swallow and noted he was breathing very rapidly and sweating profusely. She kept watching the three men as the two cadets edged backwards. The army radio was the problem. Sgt Dunstan had it on his back but that made it awkward for him to crawl and he dropped the handset, which dragged in the dirt.

"Hurry up!" she hissed.

The first of the men was almost at the top of the low spur which led down to where they were. She began crawling back as well, her eyes flicking towards the men and around behind to check her route.

Luckily the ground dropped away fairly quickly and she was able to slither back over the crest unseen. As soon as she was in dead ground Barbara rose and scrambled down the slope behind the other two. She was aware they were leaving a trail that an idiot could follow but saw no alternative. The track had been trampled clear by all the cadets passing along it anyway.

The cadets of 4 Platoon were watching with alarmed faces. Sgt Dunstan reached the bottom and began waving them back along the gully. Some cadets immediately rose and began running.

"Walk! Go quietly!" Barbara hissed. She was about to tell them not to panic, then gave a rueful smile and shook her head.

That won't help, she thought. *They will really get the wind up then.*

The cadets hurried back along the gully in a hasty scramble. Barbara glanced to her right up the gully and for an instant wondered if she should try to get away that way, to try to reach 'Landers Creek'.

Chloe's group pushed through there, she thought, noting a few crushed vines and clumps of grass.

But she decided there was no time to do that safely as it would be a noisy process and the men would almost certainly hear it. So she shook her head and hurried after the others, all the while casting anxious glances over her shoulder, fearing to glimpse the first of the men appearing on top of the bank.

I have to stay and try to control this or it will all turn into a disaster. Now is when these cadets need an officer, she told herself. She knew she could not desert the company at such a critical juncture.

About 50 paces back along the gully she found Sgt Dunstan and Cpl de Beer crouching at a bend. Just beyond them was the start of the tree covered section of the gully. Some of the platoon had also stopped there and were looking fearfully back but the others were still running back along the gully. For a moment Barbara considered how to stop them, then shrugged.

They won't go far They will stop when they reach 3 Platoon, she reasoned.

Then another thought came to her. *Blast them! They might spread rumours and alarm when they reach 3 Platoon. Bailey might lose it.*

She gestured to Sgt Dunstan. "Give me that pistol. You use the radio. Call One One and warn them some of 4 Platoon are coming. Tell them we have things under control."

Sgt Dunstan made a face as he passed her the pistol. "Have we?" he asked, his voice laden with sarcasm.

As Barbara took the pistol a new emotion swept through her like a fierce alcoholic drink.

"Yes we have!" she replied.

Her jaw set firmly and she checked the pistol to see that it was ready to use. *I am sick of horrible bloody men terrorising me!* she thought angrily. *If they want trouble they can have it!*

Fired by anger, and a hard sense of duty, Barbara crouched and whispered instructions to Cpl de Beer. "Take your people back to the next bend but keep them together. I want one of your big male cadets who can walk a long way and fast to join us."

Maree nodded. "Kettle will be the man," she replied. She hurried back, moving her people quickly but quietly.

"What do we do?" Sgt Dunstan whispered. He had finished radioing the warning.

"We stop these men," Barbara replied grimly.

"How?"

"Warn them we will shoot," Barbara answered.

"What if they call your bluff?"

"I'm not bluffing!" Barbara hissed between clenched teeth. Memories of the bleeding British cadets mingled with older memories of other fearful events to cause a deep, boiling rage.

She looked carefully around. There was a bend in the gully only ten paces ahead. At that point the sides were over a metre high: steep, eroded soil. Tall grass grew on both sides and overhung the gully so that the lower part was clear but not the top. Both banks were steep and covered with rubber vine.

No-one can rush us through that, she decided.

Now all she could do was crouch against the side and wait. An oppressive silence settled. Barbara realised she was sweating heavily, drops of perspiration dripping off her nose and fingers. The pistol was slippery in her grasp and she had to use her other hand to hold it while she wiped the sweat on her trousers. The sun was almost directly overhead and she realised the air in the gully was still and stifling. Insects buzzed. The loudest sound she could hear was her own heart. She had to swallow and wished she could go to the toilet and have a drink.

Minutes crawled by. With every passing second Barbara became more and more tense. Where were the men? Had they missed the track?

Are they creeping up and about to suddenly spring out and shoot? she thought. Her anger warred with fear. She was shaking and knew it.

Suddenly a man spoke. Barbara tensed and raised the pistol, holding it with her right hand and using her left to steady it. The barrel, she noted, seemed to be shivering. The man was just around the bend.

More voices, too soft for her to hear what they were saying. A bee buzzed noisily. Grass rustled, only a faint breeze. A twig snapped.

They are creeping along the gully, she decided.

Now she wanted to scream with fear as the tension became all but unbearable. Behind her she could hear Sgt Dunstan breathing, short, rasping breaths. His webbing creaked as he fidgeted.

"One Four, this is One One, over," called the radio.

"Oh shit!" hissed Sgt Dunstan. He grabbed at the radio, trying to get it off his back so he could to turn the volume down. In doing so the handset clacked against the case, making more noise. Barbara heard one of the men hiss and knew he had heard. *Damn!* she thought.

For a second she lowered the pistol. She was now shaking too badly to shoot straight and her vision had gone blurry.

The radio came to life again: Lt Cavendish, "One Four, what is going on? Over."

By then Sgt Dunstan had the radio off and he savagely twisted the volume switch, swearing under his breath as he did.

A man's voice suddenly called out from just around the bend. "You there! You cadets, come out with your hands up!"

Another Irishman, Barbara decided, hearing the man's accent.

She went to speak in reply but nothing came. She had to swallow and lick her lips before she could speak clearly. "No! Go away! Leave us alone."

"Don't be stupid girlie. We've got guns and we mean business. Give up and no more of you will get hurt," the man called.

"We've got guns too," Barbara replied. "If you come any further we will shoot."

"Ah crap!" the man replied. "Have some sense kid. I've got a sub-machine gun here. I'll make mincemeat out of ya. Now throw the gun out and come out with your hands up."

"No."

By this time Barbara was shaking so much she feared she would let the pistol slip from her sweaty hands, but she did not dare take the time to wipe the sweat off. But she was determined.

They are not going to kill any of those British cadets if I can help it, she told herself. *They are our guests and these filthy mongrels have no right to bring their ignorant bloody bigotry here.*

That thought rekindled a surge of anger and she quickly wiped her face with her left hand, then steadied the pistol again.

Even as she did she heard the grass rustle up to her left. She moved to aim the pistol that way. As she did she saw movement in the gully. The legs of a man came into view; dark trousers with big black boots. A dark green army jacket and the sub-machine gun gripped by hands encased in black leather gloves. The man's chest and head were hidden by the overhanging grass.

"Go back or I will shoot!" Barbara shrieked, her voice cracking under the strain.

Even as she said it she saw the sub-machine gun come up. Before her disbelieving eyes it began to jerk and little puffs of smoke spurted from its muzzle. Shiny brass cartridge cases flickered in the sunlight. Instinctive terror sent Barbara flat against the side of the gully but even so she was showered with dirt and pieces of grass. Bullets cracked past and thudded into the sand and clay bank. Her body almost lost control as she understood what was happening.

It was only a short burst but it almost stunned her into submission. But enough of her mind kept working to tell her that the man had been shooting blind. It also told her he was utterly ruthless.

He is a killer, she thought and that stiffened her resolve.

Then the man snarled, "Stand up with your hands up or next time I kill you!"

Barbara crouched lower and again raised the pistol. There was a delay of several seconds before the man added, "I'm warning you. I mean business." Then the man stepped forward, holding the SMG ready to fire with his right hand while sweeping the long grass aside with his left.

"Oh God!" Barbara cried, pulling the trigger in desperation.

Bang!

The pistol sounded very loud in the gully. She noted smoke in a grey haze but her vision went blurred without that. She gasped a deep breath and gripped the gun, her senses assailed by a terrible scream. Before her shocked eyes the man crumpled forward.

Barbara saw the sub-machine gun go down into the dirt, but was still sufficiently in control of herself to note it was still in the man's grip. She saw glittering, hate filled eyes glaring at her from the black hood. The man screamed again, a frightful shriek of agony. Then he gasped and tried to raise the gun.

Without thinking about it Barbara sprang forward and stamped her boot down on the gun, flattening it into the dirt. The man screamed again.

From further along the gully a voice yelled: "Kevin, are ye alright?" Terrified of being shot Barbara looked that way and raised her pistol. Another black hood bobbed into view at the bend. Barbara aimed the pistol. She saw the newcomer's eyes widen. Then he was gone.

Fear now motivated Barbara. She pointed the pistol at the injured man's head. "Let the gun go or I will kill you!" she rasped.

The man's eyes filled with a mixture of agony and fear. "Don't shoot!" he gasped. Then he let go and rolled backwards, grabbing at his leg as he did. Only then did Barbara realise she had hit the man in the leg. She saw blood flowing through the man's fingers as he gripped his knee and the sight nearly caused her to faint.

"Oh my God!" she whispered.

Sgt Dunstan called from behind her, his voice frantic with warning. "Watch up on the bank to your right Barbara!"

Only then did the sound of someone pushing through the grass register in her shocked brain. She could not see anyone but jerked the gun up, aimed to one side of the sound and pulled the trigger.

Bang!

"Back off!" she shouted. There was a muffled curse and the sound of someone scrambling back through the grass.

"Now go away!" she added.

She had trouble making herself heard over the wounded man, who was screaming in agony. At each gasp his screams went up a note until it was spine-chilling shriek. The sound was so elemental that it shook Barbara's composure completely. She stepped back and trembled with shock.

"Oh my God! What have I done?" she gasped.

"Shot the bastard in the knee," Sgt Dunstan answered. He was stunned too and was staring at the man's agonised writhing with fascination.

The knee! thought Barbara in horror.

She had heard that it was an excruciatingly painful injury and, worse still, that it led to the victim being permanently maimed.

The man continued to scream. In between he pleaded for help. "Oh help me! Stop the pain! Oh it hurts! Oh help me. Get a doctor."

That helped calm Barbara. "That's rich! You bloody hypocrite! You wouldn't let us get a doctor for the people you shot!" she snapped.

Her fear now blossomed into white hot anger and she steadied herself. There, at her feet, was the sub-machine gun. She scooped this up and looked at it, then passed it back to Sgt Dunstan.

"Take this Dunny and be careful. Don't shoot me in the bloody back."

Sgt Dunstan took the SMG, checked it, dusted dirt off it, then moved into a kneeling fire position over against the other side of the gully. "Move back ma'am. I will cover the gully better with this."

"Don't kill anyone," Barbara cautioned.

"I will if I have to, specially to save you," he replied

Oh heavens! Barbara thought, *another admirer!* Then she put her hands to her ears as the wounded man shrieked again.

There was movement beside her. In near panic Barbara swung round, only to find it was Maree. Maree put up her hands as Barbara pointed the gun at her.

"Steady ma'am! Do you need a hand?"

Barbara tensed, then let out a huge sigh of relief. Suddenly she seemed drained. All she could do for a minute was lower the pistol and slump in a trembling heap. Maree at once hugged her and gave her soothing pats.

"There, there! You are alright. You were great," she said.

After a minute Barbara stopped shaking. The piercing screams of the injured man, and the equally horrifying sight of the blood dripping from his trousers and hands into the sand made her realise she had to act.

"Have you got a bandage?" she asked.

Maree nodded and indicated her webbing.

Barbara pointed to the bleeding knee. "Are you up to trying to put a bandage on his leg?" she asked. She knew there was no way she could touch him. Guilt was now causing anger and revulsion.

"I can do it," Maree assured her.

"Watch out he doesn't try to grab you," Barbara cautioned.

"I'll make the bastard really scream if he tries," replied Maree grimly.

She stood up, took off her webbing and extracted the bandage from it and then moved forward. As she went to pass Sgt Dunstan, he shook his head and stepped out.

"I will cover you," he said, moving forward and quickly stepping over the wounded man who was now curled in a ball.

Sgt Dunstan went 10 paces further along the gully to the next bend. Barbara moved up on the other side and held the pistol so the man could see it. By the time Maree had slit his trousers open with her pocket knife it was obvious to Barbara the man would give no trouble. He was shaking and jibbering and his eyes were rolling up into his head. Every few seconds he let out either a low moan or a sharp scream.

Unwillingly Barbara looked at the injury she had caused as Maree peeled the cloth away. At the ghastly sight of splintered white bone and gristle amidst the pink and red tissue her stomach heaved. Appalled and disgusted at what she had done she bent over and vomited. The retching left her shivering and sweating. It reminded her of that ghastly night when she had shot the gun out of the Smiley's hands to save the slaves in the jungle near Kuranda.

As Maree began bandaging the man's knee he screamed even louder. The screams grew in pitch again, sending shudders of horror through Barbara. She flinched at each one and bit her knuckles. She was even more disgusted with herself when she realised she was sick at heart at what she had done, but also very relieved.

At least the enemy won't come along here now, she thought. Or would they? Would the fate of their friend stir them into some sort of act of vengeance?

That got her thinking. *What do we do now?* she wondered.

It was obviously even more important to get the ambulance. She glanced behind her and noted a frightened face peering around the next bend at her.

The others must be worried sick wondering what is going on, she thought.

With that she moved back to the radio, still keeping her eyes on the top of the grass. As quickly as she could she turned the radio volume back up, then picked up the handset and called Lt Cavendish. To Barbara's relief she answered straight away.

"Barbara! What's happening? What is that screaming?"

"I shot one of the terrorists ma'am," Barbara replied. "We have him prisoner and are putting a bandage on. We have stopped them at this end, over."

"Oh my God! What are you going to do now?" Lt Cavendish asked.

Yes, Barbara thought, *That is a good question. What am I going to do now?*

Chapter 25

COLLEEN

As she hurried towards the gate of the gravel scrape with Michael, Colleen picked up the unit's large First Aid Kit from the CAP. She slung this over her shoulder and then picked up one of the stretchers.

"I'll take that," Michael offered. He looked very upset and glanced several times back at where his father and Kevin were still speaking to Major Wickham and the others. Even now Colleen half expected the men to order them to come back but she got the impression that the old man, Patrick, was surprised as much as annoyed by the news of the shootings.

Maybe that wasn't part of their plan? she wondered.

That got her thinking about what the terrorist's plan might be. She asked Michael this as the pair hurried along the gravel road towards the highway.

"Michael, what were you going to do to the British cadets?"

"Don't know," Michael replied gruffly. "Dad didn't tell me. Dylan and I were just sent to find you and watch what you did."

"Watch us! How long have you been watching us?" Colleen asked. She was dismayed at the thought that she and the others had been spied on.

"Only yesterday and last night," Michael replied.

"Last night! How did you watch us last night?" Colleen asked.

"Dylan and I crept up and watched you at your campfire," Michael replied.

"How close were you?" Colleen asked. She frowned and tried to remember all that taken place.

"Close enough to recognise you and to hear you talking. You were very good in your acts," Michael replied.

"How did you know it was me?" Colleen asked.

"Because you are so pretty," Michael answered. "I thought you were the most beautiful girl I had ever seen when I saw you at the Lookout yesterday. That's why I came over and asked you your name. I really wanted to get to know you."

Colleen was amazed and was not sure if she was upset or flattered. However they had reached the gate and further private conversation was prevented because the other brother, Liam, was waiting there. He had his balaclava rolled up and was standing at the junction with the main road.

"Where are you off to little brother?" he asked.

"Someone's been shot," Michael replied. "We are taking the First Aid Kit."

"Shot! Shit! Who? Where?" Liam was obviously surprised. He straightened up and looked around.

"Down at the riverbed," Michael answered. To Colleen's relief he did not stop walking and Liam did not tell them to.

However Liam did call and ask, "Who's the girl? Why is she going?"

"She's a medic," Michael replied.

At that moment a car came racing around the hill from the direction of the Lookout. Both the men looked anxious and put their rifles behind them. Colleen stared hard at the car, hoping it was someone she could ask for help. She tensed, ready to jump out and wave the car down. But she was cruelly disappointed.

"It's Rory," Liam said, relaxing. He held up his hand to signal the car to stop.

Michael pointed. "Take him in to dad. He will explain what to do," he said, continuing to walk.

He went straight across the main road as the car slowed and turned in. Colleen followed him, her heart beating very fast in case the newcomer tried to stop them. She noted a dark haired, middle-aged man give them a curious look before he stopped the car and leaned out to listen to Liam. By then Colleen and Michael were across the road. To her relief Liam climbed into the passenger seat of the car and it accelerated in along the dirt road towards the gravel scrape.

"Whew!" Michael said. "I was worried they might stop us."

"So was I," Colleen replied.

She was puffing and perspiring now as Michael was walking very fast. Inside she felt so upset and nauseous she just wanted to throw up. A ghastly feeling of apprehension seemed to squeeze her chest and stomach. They reached the light railway and turned left along it.

"This is the quickest way isn't it?" Michael asked.

"I think so," Colleen replied.

"We need to move fast in case dad changes his mind and sends those two to bring us back," Michael added.

Colleen grunted a reply and concentrated on trying to keep up. She was dreading what lay ahead, never having had to treat a really serious injury before. The thought of what a gunshot wound might look like, and how to deal with it, kept her mind busy as the pair strode along, their boots crunching loudly on the gravel ballast.

Michael suddenly stopped and held his hand to his ear. "Did you hear that?"

Colleen did and her stomach turned over with dread. "Gunshots," she whispered.

The sound was unmistakeable. The echoes of the gunfire seemed to wrap her in a blanket of horror. Then more echoes came bouncing back from the hillside and from across the river.

"Gunshots alright," Michael said. He bit his lip and looked very anxious. The two stood and listened for a few seconds. Michael shook his head and frowned. "I hope that doesn't mean more people have been shot."

Colleen bit her lip, then started walking fast. "Come on, let's move!"

To Colleen's relief the gunfire stopped. But not knowing what had happened added greatly to her nervous tension. Three minutes later the pair reached the point where the railway ran off the high embankment over a small gully which led down from the hill, to where it was bench cut into the hillside. The sound of a car came from behind them and both glanced back. However it was a civilian vehicle coming from the south. Seeing it again gave Colleen the idea of trying to flag it down to ask for help.

She asked, "Your dad will have telephoned for the ambulance, won't he?"

"Don't know," Michael replied. He looked and sounded anxious and also eyed the car. Seeing Colleen watching it he added, "Don't try to stop it please. Wait till we know what the situation actually is."

"But it might be urgent," Colleen said, meeting his gaze.

Michael held her eyes for a few seconds, then looked away, plainly embarrassed and upset. "I know, but I can't get dad or Uncle Shaemus into trouble," he said.

Michael then put the butt of the rifle on the ground and leaned the barrel against his body before using both hands to heft the stretcher from one shoulder to the other. He then picked the gun up, his actions betraying his anxiety.

Colleen was appalled at the unsafe weapon handling. "Don't do that!" she snapped.

"Do what?" Dylan replied anxiously.

"Lean the muzzle of a loaded gun against yourself," Colleen said. "If it had gone off you would have.. have shot yourself."

As she said this, she pictured the bullet tearing up through his stomach and into his chest and then out through his back. The image caused her to shudder and again she worried about how to treat a gunshot wound.

"Huh!" Michael grunted, hefting the rifle nervously. Obvious resentment at his actions showed on his face and he turned and kept walking.

I've hurt his male pride, Colleen thought. She shrugged. *So what? Why should I care?* But she knew she did.

By then the car had driven past, the driver not even glancing at them. Colleen felt she had no real option but to go on.

Maybe Michael is right. We must find out what has actually happened, she decided.

The pair hurried on along the railway. As they approached the cutting Colleen kept glancing down into the riverbed at the end of Deep Creek. Trees obscured most of the view but she did see a litter of webbing and many footprints out on the open sand near the big pool at the end of Deep Creek. To add to her anxiety she noted that there was no sign of anyone.

Michael stopped and pointed down. "That's where we are going isn't it?"

"Yes, but it's easier to get down further along," Colleen replied. "We have to get around that big pool down there."

She was now feeling very anxious and her heart was beating rapidly. They walked on through the cutting. At the far end they stopped beside the barbed wire fence. Michael placed the stretcher over, leaning the end on the top strand. He then reversed his rifle and poked it through butt first between the top stand and second strand, leaving it resting with the muzzle on the second strand.

Once again his unsafe weapon handling dismayed her. Colleen shook her head. "You should never do that," she commented.

"Why not?" Michael asked as he crouched to crawl under the bottom strand.

"You should never point the barrel of a gun at yourself. The trigger might catch on one of the barbs and it could go off."

"Huh!" Michael grunted, clearly not impressed. "The safety catch is on," he replied.

Oh dear, Colleen thought, remembering some advice of her mother's about how much males hated to be criticised about anything technical. Then she was exasperated with herself.

Why do I care if I hurt his feelings? He's only a terrorist.

Then, as Michael crawled under the fence, another thought came to her. There, right next to her hand, was the rifle.

I could grab that and stick him up, she thought.

But even as the idea crossed her mind, she shook her head. In her heart she knew she would never be able to shoot anyone, not even to save herself.

And certainly not him!

Instead Colleen took off her webbing and passed it to Michael when he stood up. He then held out his hand for the First Aid Kit.

Their eyes met. "Thanks," she muttered, quite confused about how she now felt about him. She handed him the First Aid Kit and then lay down on her back to go under the fence in the way she had been taught, feet first and face up so she could hold the bottom strand of barbed wire away from herself. A couple of quick wriggles and a roll and she was under safely.

As she stood up Michael handed her webbing to her and she swung it on, not bothering to do up the belt. Then she held out her hand for the First Aid kit. He handed it back to her and she slung it over her shoulder. He then hefted the stretcher onto his shoulder and picked up his rifle. Both sweating and anxious they made their way down through the long grass on the rocky slope to the overgrown old highway.

Michael pointed to the grass on the slope on their right. "Dylan and I watched you from there last night."

"Me? Or the cadets?" Colleen asked.

"Both. I saw you in the light of the lantern. What was all the fuss? Was some kid lost?"

"Yeah, Lance Corporal McArtney, the silly bugger. He got separated from his platoon and walked to the only light he could see, which was all the way along the river there at that cattle station." She pointed to where the sun was glinting on the roofs of 'Byrne Valley' homestead.

"Yeah, it took you a while," Michael agreed. "We got sick of waiting. Oh... good! Here's Uncle Shaemus."

Colleen looked and saw two men in the green jackets and black balaclavas standing on top of the steep slope at the point where the old highway reached the remains of the washed away bridge. At the sight of them Colleen's heart leapt into her mouth and her stomach turned over. These were the men who had done the shooting.

Will they let me do any First Aid? she wondered.

That got her looking around, puzzled. *Where are the cadets?*

It took all of her willpower to walk towards the two men, who now stood watching them. Colleen was very scared and knew it. She stayed behind Michael and began to pray. Both the men had their balaclavas rolled up and she did not like the look on either face. At least only one of them had a gun, the second man, a tall, lanky fellow who had a hunting rifle with a telescopic sight.

Michael held up his hand. "What's going on Uncle Shaemus?" he asked. "Dad wants to know."

"Oh he does, does he? Who's this?" Shaemus gestured towards Colleen, who felt a spasm of icy fear grip her stomach.

"She's a medic," Michael replied. "She brought the First Aid Kit. We heard someone had been shot."

"They have been, but they don't need no First Aid," Shaemus replied harshly.

"Are they dead?" Michael asked, plainly horrified.

"I bloody hope so, God rot their heathen souls!" Shaemus cried.

To Colleen the curse was a terrifying thing and she automatically crossed herself. The action drew the eyes of both men and Shaemus nodded.

"At least you are one of the True Faith girlie. Now, you can go back. We don't need you. Take her away Michael."

Colleen stubbornly stood her ground. "If there are injured people I need to go to them."

"They are only bloody British. Protestant scum!" Shaemus cried, his eyes blazing.

"I don't care what religion they are. It is my Christian duty to help," Colleen replied stiffly. She was shaking with fright and her face felt like a wooden mask.

This man is off his head, she thought, watching the flickering light in Shaemus's eyes.

"No you won't!" Shaemus snarled.

At that moment the second man touched Shaemus on the sleeve and pointed down into the riverbed. "Hey boss, here comes someone."

Colleen looked and saw at a glance that it was Chloe. She was almost naked from the waist up. Even at a hundred metres her breasts were very obvious.

"It's a bloody girl!" the second man cried in disbelief.

"She's the bitch that kicked Dylan! Give me that gun Murty," Shaemus ordered.

He snatched the rifle from a surprised Murty's grasp. Colleen watched in dismay and tensed, ready to try to stop him if he went to shoot. She was also embarrassed at Chloe's display. It was something she did not approve of, although she found it hard to dislike Chloe as a person.

Shaemus raised the rifle butt to his shoulder. Colleen took a step forward and put up her hand, her heart in her mouth. Murty put out his arm and stopped her. "You stay back girl."

Michael now intervened. "She's got a white flag Uncle Shaemus," he said.

"I can see that! So what? It's probably just a trick," Shaemus replied.

"At least see what she wants," Michael added, anxiety clear in his voice.

"Bloody shameless hussy! Walking around like that!" Shaemus muttered, adjusting the rifle more comfortably into his shoulder. He then shouted, "Stop, or I will shoot!"

To Colleen's dismay Chloe continued walking, although she looked up at them.

Shaemus muttered under his breath, then shouted again, "You there! Stop or I will shoot!"

At that Chloe began waving her 'white flag', a handkerchief tied to a stick, but she kept on walking across the sand below them.

"Stop I say!" Shaemus shouted, plainly enraged by her refusal to obey.

Chloe kept walking but called back, "I'm only going to get a First Aid Kit."

By now Colleen was sick with apprehension and her heart was fluttering with anxiety. Her eyes flicked to where Chloe had pointed and she saw one of the small First Aid Kits lying on the sand.

"Oh Chloe! Please stop!" she muttered. Unconsciously she began to pray.

Shaemus shouted again, "Stop woman! I'm warning you!"

By then Chloe had reached the First Aid Kit. She stopped, bent over and very deliberately picked it up. As she leaned forward Murty muttered, "Strewth! She's a good looker!"

"Bloody disobedient slut!" Shaemus snarled. He then shouted at Chloe, "Drop that you Jezebel! Drop it I say, harlot!"

To Colleen's anguish Chloe ignored him, turned with a provocative flounce, then started walking back.

At that Shaemus lowered his cheek onto the butt and sighted at her. Colleen started forward but was grabbed by Murty. Even as she screamed a warning so did Michael.

"No Uncle Shaemus!" he shouted. As he did he sprang across and knocked the rifle away.

Bang!

Colleen screamed, then gasped with relief. The bullet had missed. Chloe kept on walking across the bare sand. Shaemus swore and struggled with Michael, who had grabbed the barrel of the rifle.

"What are ye on about ye ignorant little shit!" Shaemus snarled. His eyes blazed with anger.

Michael clung on grimly. "No Uncle Shaemus, you've done enough damage already. I won't be a party to murder."

"Let go my rifle boy!" Shaemus shouted, struggling to wrench it from Michael's grip.

"No! Let her go!" Michael cried.

He was white faced and obviously scared but equally, very determined. Colleen bit her lip in anxiety, half fearing that the enraged Shaemus would shoot him when he got the rifle free.

"You bloody little coward! Let my rifle go!" Shaemus screamed. Colleen was appalled to see that he was almost frothing at the mouth with fury.

This guy is right off his rocker! she thought in dismay.

Michael shook his head. "Calm down Uncle Shaemus! You have no right to shoot innocent people," he said.

"They are not innocent! They are the enemy! This is a war!" Shaemus cried.

The two glared at each other and continued to struggle over the rifle. To get a better grip Michael dropped his own rifle and used both hands.

"It is not a war! This is Australia, not Ireland. She is just a girl. And she is an Australian, not British!" Michael retorted, gesturing with his head in the direction of Chloe, who was now vanishing back in under the trees at the mouth of Snake Gully.

"A bloody harlot!" Shaemus grated.

"So what? Jesus went around with harlots," Michael snapped back.

"Don't be blasphemous boy!" exploded Uncle Shaemus.

"I'm not being!" Michael cried. "There are people who say that Mary Magdalene was a prostitute. And even if that girl is, you don't have the right to hurt her."

"She should be bloody whipped! Flaunting herself like that!" Shaemus said. By now both men were panting with exertion but Colleen could tell the rage was beginning to abate.

"Jesus preached forgiveness," Michael quoted. "Vengeance is mine saith the Lord; isn't that what the good book says?"

"I didn't know you were a Bible-thumper!" Shaemus snorted, but he now seemed to deflate.

"You and dad sent me to a good Catholic school," Michael replied. He now let go of the rifle and stepped back. Chloe had vanished from sight. "So, what happened Uncle Shaemus? Who got shot and why?"

"I shot three of those bloody British," Shaemus replied with guilty defiance.

"Who? Why?" Michael asked.

He stood with chest heaving but looked his uncle unflinchingly in the eye. Colleen experienced a spurt of involuntary admiration which set her heart fluttering.

Shaemus muttered to himself, then said, "For bloody revenge, to get even with those bastards who killed your sister."

"So what happened?" Michael asked.

"I just walked down and shot them," Shaemus replied. For a moment he hung his head, then he looked up, eyes blazing. "I have waited so long! Years I waited, plotting, hoping; then suddenly there they were, all in one bunch. I... I just... just lost control. I went down and shot them."

"Shot who?"

"That bastard Major Grogan, and the son of that mongrel Masters."

"That is two, you said three," Michael said.

"Yes, a stupid bloody British officer, a lieutenant. He grabbed my pistol and wouldn't let go. He got shot in the struggle," Shaemus admitted.

Michael glanced around. "Where is your pistol? Where is Dylan?"

"The mongrels captured Dylan. That blonde strumpet kicked him in the cods and took him prisoner," Shaemus answered.

"And your pistol?" demanded Michael.

"They got that too. That blonde bitch of a girl hit my wrist with a stick and I dropped it. Then another bitch with ginger hair kicked me in the face during the fight and I couldn't get it back," Shaemus said, indicating a huge bruise on his cheek.

Good old Barbara! Colleen thought. She then spoke up, "Are all three dead?"

Shaemus shook his head. "Obviously not, if they want a First Aid Kit."

"Where were they shot?" Colleen asked.

Shaemus indicated where he had shot each one. Colleen was appalled. The chest and stomach wounds sounded deadly. "I'd better get down there and help then. Michael, you phone for an ambulance."

"No you don't!" Shaemus replied.

"Are you going to shoot me too?" Colleen asked, her emotions focusing into anger.

"I won't let you," Shaemus replied. "I want them to die."

Michael now intervened. "No Uncle Shaemus. You might have a grudge against this Major Grogan, he is the Intelligence Officer isn't he? But you have no right to kill a boy because of something his father did."

"Doesn't it say somewhere in the Bible about mankind suffering for the sins of the fathers?" Uncle Shaemus retorted.

"Yes it does," Michael agreed, "but I don't think that is what it means. You just want an excuse to ease your guilty conscience."

"I do not!" flared Shaemus angrily.

Colleen now spoke again. She was angry too, and feeling increasingly upset and desperate. If the wounds were as described, then time was very important.

"And what about the lieutenant? What did he do wrong? He was probably just trying to save the lives of the kids in his care."

"He is a member of the bloody British Army!" Shaemus spat, "and they are my hereditary enemy."

"That is just ignorant bigotry!" Colleen cried. "You can't justify killing someone just because of their nationality! That makes you just like the Nazis in World War Two!"

For a moment Colleen feared she had gone too far; that Shaemus would strike her. Michael obviously thought so too as he stepped over and intervened.

Shaemus shook his fist in her face. "How dare you speak to me like that girlie!" he whispered hoarsely, but it was obvious to Colleen that her words had gone home.

"Anyway," she went on, "I am going down to help. Shoot me if you want to."

With that she pushed past Shaemus. He made no move to stop her, just muttered under his breath. Colleen then found her route blocked by a sheer drop of ten metres, with a pool of slimy deep water at the bottom. Feeling slightly foolish she turned left and walked along the top of the bank till she came to an easier grassy slope. She then slid down this as quickly as she dared, not wanting to be stopped.

At the bottom she realised she had left the stretcher at the top but there was no way she was going to climb back up to get it. She set off across the sand towards the end of Snake Gully. As she walked she found herself reeling with dizziness. She realised that she was so tense and was breathing so rapidly that spots were dancing before her eyes.

I must calm down or I will faint, she told herself.

But it was hard to do, knowing there was a madman with a gun just above her. At every step she tensed, flinching in anticipation of the bullet tearing through her flesh. She was sweating and gasping for breath but forced herself to walk.

As she approached the mouth of Snake Gully she saw faces peering out at her. Only as she reached the end of the gully did she see the British cadet with the rifle kneeling under cover behind a tree up on the bank. That gave her a nasty shock.

So did the sight of the wounded lying in a row in the bottom of the gully. She noted that the place seemed to be abuzz with activity. Out of the faces one focused into that of Lt Cavendish.

The lieutenant ran forward and cried, "Oh Colleen! Thank God you've come."

"How are they Miss? What's going on?"

"They need proper medical treatment urgently. The English major looks like he might die at any moment and the other two are in a bad way as well," Lt Cavendish said. She was trembling and had tears running down her cheeks. Colleen looked past her into the grief-stricken face of Adelaide, who clutched Major Grogan's head to her bosom. She was also weeping.

"Where are the others Miss? Where is Barbara? Where is Chloe?"

"Oh Chloe! She is mad that girl. She is so lucky she didn't get shot," Lt Cavendish said.

Colleen noted that Lt Cavendish was shaking and having trouble speaking clearly. "I know. I was up there with those men when she came out for the First Aid kit," she replied.

"With the IRA?" asked Charles, stepping forward.

"I brought the First Aid Kit. I'm not one of them," she replied.

"We need it," one of the British cadets called. Colleen looked at the blood-soaked and bandaged figure next to the man. It took her a moment to recognise Freddy.

"How is he?" she asked, moving over to him. Now that she had a real task she found her emotions calm.

"Bad. He needs a doctor fast or he will die from loss of blood or shock," the British cadet replied.

Lt Cavendish crouched beside her. "Has the OC rung for an ambulance?"

"Don't think so Miss," Colleen replied. She began examining the dressings on Freddy's wounds. "The terrorists wouldn't let him. They have him and Lt Forster, Lt Peters and Lt Barker prisoner."

For a minute Colleen worked steadily. As she did she described what had happened at the gravel scrape. The wounds were still oozing blood and she steeled herself to remove one of the dressings. As she did, helped by two others who held Freddy up, she was appalled to see dark red blood actually flow from the bullet wound in a steady stream.

In the lungs, she decided.

With an effort she forced herself to touch Freddy, to place a pad on the wound and to bind it up firmly, all the while keeping her face and voice calm.

For something to distract them she asked, "Where are the others Miss? Where did Chloe go?"

"She and some of the others have gone to try to get help," Lt Cavendish replied.

"Good. I just hope they don't run into any of these men," Colleen said.

"Oh yes! We just had a radio message saying that some armed men were heading for the top end of Snake Gully, that 4 Platoon was moving back to join us," Lt Cavendish replied.

"Ask them on the radio what is going on," suggested Sharon, who had been holding the wounded lieutenant beside them.

"Good idea," Lt Cavendish agreed. She moved to the radio and called. She got no answer so tried again. "They aren't answering," she said

In the distance a shivering, snapping vibration sounded and Colleen felt her heart turn over with dread. "Sub Machine gun!" she gasped. They all looked and went tense with fear. Then there was a distinct 'thump!'. A moment later a terrible, high-pitched scream of agony reached them. The sound made them all jerk around to look. Colleen's whole body broke out in 'goose bumps' and she felt her heart lurch.

"Someone's badly hurt," Charles observed. He stood white faced and with clenched fists.

"Shot from the sound of it," said another British cadet.

"There's another shot," added another.

"I'd better get along there," Colleen said. "There isn't much more I can do here."

She stood up and felt her skin prickle as the awful screams came again. *Oh my God!* she thought. *Who has been shot?*

Fearing that it was one of her friends she snatched up her First Aid Kit and hurried along the bed of Snake Gully past the lines of frightened cadets.

Chapter 26

CONFLICT

As Michael watched Colleen walk across the sand of the riverbed towards the mouth of Snake Gully he was torn by conflicting emotions. Part of him was struck by admiration for Colleen, tempered by the realisation that she obviously despised Uncle Shaemus and his friends, and by extension, himself. Even more he was appalled by the murderous situation that had developed and that he now found himself in. The feeling that he was being carried along by forces outside his control gave him a peculiar feeling of helplessness, mixed with strong resentment. He was also being ripped apart by the conflict of loyalties the situation had exposed.

He was shocked by the image of Uncle Shaemus that had emerged. All his life he had thought of Uncle Shaemus as a cheerful, carefree man, full of jokes and warmth, always with a kind word and a present for a little boy. Now he stood before Michael like a monster unmasked, angry, irrational, deadly.

As Colleen vanished from view Michael turned to the man next to him. "I'm Michael O'Malley. Who are you?"

The man glanced at Shaemus, then said, "Call me what you like."

"Are you IRA too?" Michael asked, nettled by the reply.

"We don't talk about things like that boyo, and if you know what is good for you, you won't either," the man replied.

Murty, his name is Murty, Michael remembered.

Being called a boy rankled even more. He said, "Well, what are we going to do now?"

"Get Dylan back first," Shaemus answered, "Then finish the job."

The implication of that sent a chill through Michael but he resisted the impulse to argue that it was wrong. Instead he turned to Shaemus. "Have you told dad what has happened here?"

"Not yet, haven't had a chance," Shaemus replied.

"Does he know that those cadets have captured Dylan, and that they now have guns?" Michael asked.

Shaemus scowled and looked uncomfortable. "No, not yet. What happened back at that gravel scrape after we left?"

Michael recounted how the cadet officers and cadets had been taken prisoner after they had extinguished the fire. As he talked he was agitated by awful feelings of guilt and apprehension. At last he said, "Have you called the ambulance Uncle Shaemus?"

"No. I don't have a mobile phone," Shaemus replied, "and I wouldn't anyway. I want the bastards to die."

"How are you going to warn dad then?"

"One of us will have to walk back and tell him, unless you have a phone Murty?" Shaemus replied.

Murty shook his head. "Not me... Hey! Look!"

Murty pointed along the riverbed southwards. About a kilometre away two figures in Australian Army camouflage had appeared on the edge of the belt of rubber vines and slid down the steep bank to the sandy bed. As the Irish watched a third cadet joined them.

Shaemus swore. "The bastards are gettin' away!"

As Michael watched the three cadets began walking off across the sand towards the sandy island.

"Only three," Murty commented. "Probably going to get help."

"There's a cattle station homestead across the river over there," Michael said, pointing towards where 'Byrne Valley' was hidden by the trees on the sandy island.

"We've got to stop them! Quick Murty, after them! Here!" Shaemus snapped. He passed Murty his rifle. Murty at once set off at a run along the top of the bank and down the steep, grassy slope.

Shaemus then turned to Michael. "Give me that rifle."

Before Michael had time to think about it, or to resist, Uncle Shaemus had snatched the rifle from his grasp. Michael was suddenly filled with a terrible apprehension.

"Uncle Shaemus, please don't use it! Stop this before it gets worse," he begged.

"It's too late for any of that boy. We must finish what we started, or it is all for nothing," Shaemus replied.

"It is all for nothing anyway," Michael retorted. "It is just pointless bloody murder."

"It is not! Freedom is always worth fighting for!" Shaemus snapped.

In Michael's mind all the images of Ireland that had been drilled into him as a boy warred with his ideas of freedom, and of life in Australia. To him it just didn't make sense.

"This is insane," he said. "I am free, and killing innocent people isn't going to help free Northern Ireland."

"Yes it is! We have to wipe those Protestant scum off the face of the earth, drive them into the sea. They have no right to be in Ireland, they are just bloody immigrant Scots," Shaemus cried.

"They've been there for three hundred years haven't they?" Michael replied, annoyed by the sheer irrationality of his uncle's argument.

"Doesn't matter. They have no right to be there. They are invaders and should go," Shaemus said.

His face was flushed with passion and he ground his teeth in a way that disturbed Michael intensely. He had been trying to watch the three cadets as they trekked away across the soft sand. Murty, he noted, had now appeared on the flood overflow channel and was running across towards the end of the island near the river. In his heart he hoped the cadets would make it to 'Byrne Valley' in time. But the thought made him feel sick inside, not wanting to be a traitor to his own family.

In reply to Uncle Shaemus's argument Michael said, "I'm sure the Aborigines feel the same way about us."

"What do ye mean?" Shaemus demanded.

"Well, we are just invaders here. By your logic we should give Australia back to them and leave," Michael said.

"That's not the same," Shaemus denied. "What about the Aussies who were born here?"

Michael could see that his anger was growing but he didn't care. The thing obviously had to be seen through to the bitter end. He said, "What about the Orangemen born in Ireland? Don't they have as much right to live there?"

"No! They are evil! The Devil's spawn!" Shaemus exploded. "What are ye boy? A bloody traitor?"

That really stung but Michael stuck to his guns. "No. But you are a bloody hypocrite, and a bigot."

"How dare you, you bloody brat!" Shaemus shouted.

At that moment the sharp, flat sounds of what could only be a shots came to them from away off across the belt of thick scrub. The burst of

Sub Machine gun fire was followed by the dull 'snap!' of two more single shots. A moment later the shrill sound of a scream sounded faintly.

"Someone's been shot!" Michael cried. He turned and looked accusingly at Shaemus, "That might be dad, or Liam. I'm going to find out. Let these people go Uncle Shaemus."

"Don't call me uncle, you bloody turncoat! You are no kin to me!" Shaemus snarled angrily. He hefted the rifle and Michael experienced a spasm of fear, lest Shaemus try to stop him going.

To end the confrontation Michael spun on his heel and hurried away up the slope towards the railway. At any second he expected Shaemus to order him to stop, or even to shoot at him but he forced himself to keep walking, his whole body tingling and sweating. An awful feeling of dread now filled him as he heard the scream of agony faintly again. Someone was obviously very badly hurt.

Oh God! I hope it isn't dad, or Liam, he thought.

Sweating with exertion and anxiety Michael scrambled under the barbed wire fence beside the railway and set off back along it. He ran through the cutting and on along the strait. After two minutes he was opposite the point where Deep Creek turned away but had to slow to a fast walk as he was winded. He wiped sweat from his eyes and strode along, panting and feeling so sick in the stomach that he wanted to throw up.

From time to time he heard more screams and each time it caused him to flinch and feel ill. He bit his lip and hurried on, his mind trying to grapple with the situation and the possible consequences. All of a sudden his future looked very bleak.

The police will be involved soon and we will probably all go to jail, he thought bitterly.

All his dreams of the next few years became bitter regrets. The regret on top of his conscious mind was the thought that Colleen would have nothing to do with him.

What decent girl would want anything to do with a jailbird and terrorist? he told himself.

Suddenly Michael stopped in shock. Movement in the deep gully between the railway and main road had attracted his attention. People in Australian Army camouflage uniforms were crawling up a gully. They had seen him, but too late. They then made the mistake of moving to try to get under cover, instead of just freezing. But what to do? Michael stood staring down at where the cadets had gone to ground in long grass.

They must be trying to crawl under the road through that culvert, he decided, seeing the ends of a small concrete pipe at the base of the embankment that carried the main road over the gully.

The gully went on diagonally up the side of the hill, dwindling as it went until it ended near the saddle where the power line went across.

That is where they were trying to go, Michael deduced. *One group to Byrne Valley to try to get help and another one to the north. That must be their plan.*

But what to do? In his heart Michael really just wanted to let them go, to call the ambulance as quickly as possible.

But that means the police as well, he thought unhappily.

That raised the issue of loyalty: loyalty to the concept of a Free Ireland; and, more importantly, loyalty to his family. For a minute or so Michael stood and wrestled with his conscience, being torn apart by the conflict. The cadets remained cowering in the grass, obviously hoping that, as he hadn't called out, that he had not seen them.

Michael's dilemma was made worse by him hearing the distant screams again. "I must do something!" he muttered. But go on, or try to capture the cadets?

His dilemma was suddenly resolved in an unexpected fashion. A man called out to him from along the railway to his left. Michael jumped as though stung, then stared in shocked amazement. A hundred paces away, and hurrying towards him, was a man in black trousers, green jacket and black balaclava. The man had an automatic shotgun.

"Are you Michael?" the man called out.

"Yes," Michael called back.

Oh bloody hell! he thought. *What do I do? Do I tell the man or not?*

Even as he thought this the man called, "What are you lookin' at?"

Feeling like a real weakling, and a traitor, at least to his idea of himself as a decent person, Michael pointed. "Some cadets, trying to sneak out of the area."

The man swore and broke into a trot. When he arrived he pointed his gun down and nodded. "Yeah, I see 'em. Haven't you got a gun?"

"I had one. I gave it to Uncle Shaemus," Michael replied.

"Where is he?" the man asked.

"On top of the riverbank just through that cutting," Michael replied, pointing back along the railway line.

"Oh yeah. What's goin' on? Jesus! What's that?" the man gasped as another shrill scream of agony came from the rubber vine area behind them.

"Someone's been shot I think. I was going to find out when I saw these kids," Michael replied.

"Yeah, Rory said someone had been shot. I'll find out." The man pulled a mobile phone out of his pocket and hit the redial button. While he waited he shouted down into the gully, "You cadets come out with your hands up and come up here, and be bloody quick about it!"

Michael had no desire to have to look the cadets in the eyes, knowing that it was him who had betrayed them.

"I'll get over there," he said. "You bring the cadets with you."

The man nodded, distracted by the phone which showed it did not have service at the same moment as the first cadets came out of the long grass, hands high and faces taut with fear.

"Get up here you kids! Damn! Bloody phone doesn't work! Never mind, Pat gave me this little cadet radio."

The man pulled out a small hand-held CB radio and spoke into it. "Trevor here Pat. What's the screamin'?"

Michael turned and studied how to reach the area where the screaming was coming from. Across the open flat to where Deep Creek curved again he decided. He started walking quickly along, looking for the easiest way down off the steep embankment. To his relief the man, Trevor, kept talking on the radio while keeping his eyes and gun on the cadets, two of whom were still scrambling up the steep slope.

In his haste to get away from the situation, and to reach the noise, Michael pushed down through the long grass beside the track heedless of possible snakes, or of the rocks and logs in the grass. He was barely aware of barking his shins, or of stumbling on hidden rocks. While crawling under the fence he snagged his shirt on the barbs, tearing it and scratching his skin. He barely noticed that, but pain made him aware of the prickles he had picked up in his hands and knees.

As he hurried across the bare open flat beside Deep Creek he picked and scratched to try to get the burrs out. They were, he noted, two different types: normal 'Bindis', and tiny, two pronged ones which really stuck in and were hard to remove. The mixture of physical and emotional distress had him sobbing by then and he reached the belt of rubber vines and lantana on the bank of the creek with tears streaming down his cheeks.

Michael paused for a moment to recover his breath and to find an easy way through the tangle. A cattle pad or animal track led down into the creek bed and he went down this, then followed it up through the thick belt of rubber vines on the other side. He went as quickly as he could and was soon gasping for breath.

Ahead of him the country opened out to scattered trees and sparse grass on a wide, flat ridge. As Michael reached the crest he stopped and looked both ways. Which way? This was answered by another scream. It came from over to his left and was abruptly cut off.

Moaning and a man's voice sobbing, "No! No! Take it easy! Ah! It hurts!" came clearly to him.

Michael went along the ridge and saw movement down among the rubber vines to his right: two men with green jackets.

Dad, and Liam, Michael noted.

As he walked down a dusty foot track towards them, they heard him and looked around, guns at the ready.

"Oh, it's you boy," Patrick said. "What are you doin' here?"

"Uncle Shaemus sent me to find out who was screaming," Michael lied, despising himself as he did.

"Kevin's been shot, smashed his knee," Patrick replied.

The notion of a smashed knee cap made Michael wince at the imagined pain. The thought also crossed his mind that 'knee-capping', the deliberate smashing of a person's knee cap, was a punishment for traitors and informers that he had heard was widely used by the terror groups on both sides in Northern Ireland. It was, along with the murders of people shot down in their own homes in front of their families, and the bombs which mutilated innocent women and children, one of the things that most revolted Michael about the so-called battle for freedom. He was secretly ashamed of the blot on the good name of the Irish, a blot that he sensed would linger for hundreds of years.

His father reinforced the feelings by unwittingly adding, "It's ironic really. Kevin knee-capped plenty of Orangemen and traitors in his time."

To that Michael said nothing, but he did consider that maybe there was a God, and that sometimes justice might be done. To avoid another dispute he asked, "Where is he?"

"The cadets have him prisoner just down the gully," Patrick answered.

Michael eyed the narrow gully and tangle of long grass and weeds and shuddered. "Who did it?" he asked.

"Bloody ginger-haired bitch of a girl cadet," Liam answered. "Shot him with a pistol."

"Shaemus's," Michael said with a spurt of malicious pleasure in doing so. "She took it off him when the cadets captured Dylan."

"When they what?" cried Patrick.

"They captured Dylan. Apparently Shaemus and he went down to the cadets and Shaemus shot three of the British Army people. The cadets attacked them and took their guns and took Dylan prisoner."

"Yeah, they said that on the radio, but I didn't believe 'em," Patrick replied. "Bloody hell! That means they've now got three guns."

Liam swore. "One at each end of this gully then," he added, eyeing the tangle of thick country. "Bugger! We won't get at 'em easy in there."

"They'll be trying to sneak out too," Patrick added gloomily. He suddenly looked very old and tired.

"They are. Murty went off to try to catch some that are trying to get across the river and Trevor has another group back there at the railway line," Michael explained.

Patrick held up a small CB radio. "I know about the bunch Trevor has. I told him to take them back to the gravel scrape and hand 'em over to Rory," he said. "How did you know about them?"

"I saw them and showed Trevor where they were hiding," Michael replied.

"Good boy!" Patrick said.

The praise gave Michael very mixed feelings. At that moment Kevin moaned again and Michael asked his father, "What are you doing here?"

"Trying to negotiate with the cadets down in the gully," Patrick replied.

"What are we going to do?" Michael asked. "We can't stay here. Whatever plan you and Uncle Shaemus had has obviously all gone wrong. Have you called the ambulance yet?"

"Don't you tell me what to do son. I'm not ready to give up yet. We can really make news out of this," Patrick replied.

"But we must get the people who have been shot to a doctor or they might die!" Michael cried.

"Kevin yes, but not the others. I don't care if they die. That's why I came here, to get my revenge," Patrick answered.

"But you told me that no-body would get hurt," Michael said. He felt very mixed up and hurt.

Dad lied to us! he thought in sick dismay.

He was even more shocked by the burning hatred and lust for revenge that both his father and Uncle Shaemus exhibited.

His father grunted and did not answer that. Instead he asked, "Who did Shaemus shoot?"

Michael had to struggle to remember the names. "Two British officers, a major and a lieutenant, and a cadet named Masters."

"Masters eh! Good, that is vengeance. His troops killed my daughter, now we have killed his son!" Patrick exulted.

Watching his father's face at that moment caused Michael a wave of revulsion. He shook his head in dismay. Liam saw this and sneered.

"What's wrong you little sook? Can't you take it?"

Michael shook his head. Before he could frame an answer his father asked, "Was the major's name Grogan?"

Michael nodded. He was feeling so sick he felt faint.

"Good!" Patrick cried. "Got the bastard! He was the cause of many a good man being caught, the rotten mongrel!"

At that moment a girl's voice called out to them from down in the gully. "Hey! You up there! What are you going to do about this man? He's losing a lot of blood and needs a doctor urgently."

"Bring him up and we will look after him," Patrick called back.

"No way! We don't trust you. You come and get him, but only after you let all our people you have captured go," the girl answered.

"Bloody bitch!" Patrick muttered. "No!" he shouted back. "We want Dylan back as well."

"Bring Major Wickham here first," the girl demanded.

For the next five minutes the argument went on. Neither side would give way. Michael stood there feeling increasingly distressed. He realised he was dizzy from exhaustion and heat as much as the revolting situation. Every moan and whimper from Kevin set his flesh on edge.

How can I end this? he wondered.

Another girl then called out from down in the gully. "Don't shoot. I am coming up."

Colleen! Michael thought.

His heart leapt, then fell again. He watched anxiously as she came into view. She looked very strained and he noted with dismay that her hands and clothes were now stained with what could only be blood. She had to struggle to make her way up the steep slope of loose sand on the bank of the gully.

When she reached the top Colleen stopped a couple of paces from them. For a moment she stood there, panting for breath. She pushed a strand of hair back up under her hat and gave them all a hard look. "That man down there has a badly smashed knee. We can't stop the bleeding. He needs urgent medical attention. We are not going to use him as a hostage. I have persuaded the others to let you have him."

There was a pause while Colleen looked directly at Michael, her eyes like stone. "We also want you to telephone for the ambulance to come and get the three badly wounded British cadets."

"Damn the bloody British!" Patrick snarled.

"We have to do something," Colleen replied. "They might all be dead soon. Do you want that on your conscience?"

Dead! Michael thought in horror and dismay. *Then it really will be murder!*

"Do it dad!" he cried. "This has all gone wrong!"

"No," Patrick replied. "You can keep Kevin, if that is the deal."

"It isn't a deal," Colleen replied with a sigh. "We want you to take him now, quickly, and get him to a doctor. I don't want his death on my conscience. We will negotiate over your son Dylan, but not over the wounded. Now come and get him."

Patrick thought about this for a minute, then said, "How do I know we can trust you lot?"

"I will stay here as a hostage," Colleen replied, "And some of our cadets will help carry him up here."

Patrick grunted and nodded. "Liam, you watch her. Michael, come with me."

"You sure you trust 'em dad?" Liam asked. He moved over and pointed his gun at Colleen, who stood to one side of the track and ignored him. Michael stared at her anxiously but she avoided his eyes. Feelings of bitterness and regret added to Michael's distress. With a heavy heart he followed his father down into the gully.

Snake Gully was a horrible place, all long grass, closed in and hot, and the smell of blood and shit hung in the air. Kevin had soiled himself. Flies buzzed and the whole place was claustrophobic to Michael. The cadets stood or crouched near where Kevin lay on a stretcher made from saplings and ropes. Michael noted that one cadet was pointing a sub-machine gun at him but he felt no fear. It was all too far gone for that to matter.

A female cadet officer, a long-legged young woman with red hair, holding a pistol in her hand and looking very military in her camouflage uniform and webbing, gave the orders.

"You two IRA go at the front," she ordered. "You others, hands on! That is both hands you pair. We don't want anyone to slip. Prepare to lift! Lift up!"

Michael experienced a surge of resentment at being labelled as IRA and he felt the urge to deny it but moved to obey the girl's commands. They set off back along the gully. It was hard going as the gully was too narrow and they had to push through the grass on either side. Within ten paces Michael found he was gasping and struggling to hold the weight. He had never carried a stretcher and was astounded at how heavy and awkward it was.

The cadets were obviously finding it hard going as well as he could hear them puffing and grunting with effort. At the point where the track left the gully the red-head ordered halt and told them to lower the stretcher. She then moved a second group of cadets up to take over the back end and to help lift it up the hill.

At her word of command they lifted the stretcher and struggled up the slope. The red-head gave more instructions so that the people at the front held the stretcher down near their knees and those at the back held it up above their heads to keep it level. It was all very awkward. It took the combined efforts of about a dozen of them to get it up the 10 metres of slope. As they reached the area where the slope levelled out Michael noted that cadets were letting go and hurrying back down into the gully but he ignored that. As they came up to where Liam and Colleen waited Colleen came over and took hold of the stretcher near him.

They struggled on for another 50 paces, right out past the last rubber vines. "That will do," the red-head said. "You people can take over from here. Prepare to lower, lower!"

The stretcher was lowered and they all stood back to recover their strength and breath, except Colleen, who knelt to check Kevin's pulse and dressings. Michael noted that both Kevin's legs were splinted together and that he had now passed out. Colleen did a quick check, then said, "I think he's going into shock. I'll stay with him Barbara. You go back. I'll speak to Major Wickham for you."

The red-head, Barbara, nodded and gestured to the cadets with her. They turned and hurried back down into the rubber vines and out of sight. For a moment Michael thought Liam was going to try to stop them. However he just watched with a suspicious and angry look on his face. Then he said, "How the hell are we going to carry this great lump all the way back to the road?"

"There are four of us," Colleen replied. "We will do it in short stages."

"I don't want to leave this end of the track unguarded," Liam replied. "The cadets might escape then."

"Not with three badly injured people they won't!" Colleen retorted, "Now stop talking and hands on."

"No," Liam replied. "They might send a small group to try to get help. Dad, go back down into the gully and keep them bottled up. And call Rory and tell him to send that Trevor here to help us."

Patrick nodded and took out his mobile phone. But it had no service either so he called on the small radio he had obviously taken off the cadets. He contacted Rory and told him to send Trevor.

Colleen then interrupted him. "While you are at it tell him to bring the prisoners from the gravel scrape. They can help carry the stretcher and you can negotiate with Major Wickham."

For a moment Michael thought Patrick was going to snap back at her but instead he nodded and said, "Rory, both of you come, and bring all the prisoners with you. They can help carry the stretcher."

Patrick ended the call, then said to Liam, "When you get there tell Trevor to drive Kevin to Doctor O'Farrell. He'll know what I mean. You come back here and bring that cadet major with you."

"Yes dad. Now you get down into that gully. OK you pair, I will carry the back. You take the front. Let's go," Liam ordered.

Michael bent to grip the end of the stretcher, very aware of Colleen beside him. Several times he glanced at her, his mouth feeling the sour taste of failure. Once she met his eyes but there was no friendliness there and she looked quickly away.

Bloody hell! Michael thought. *What a stupid mess!*

The next half hour was a real strain. Rory and Trevor met them near the powerlines with their prisoners. These were a dozen cadets and four cadet officers under guard. To Michael's relief they also had a proper army stretcher. As soon as the groups met Colleen started explaining things to the cadet major, and demanded they call the ambulance at once.

"Shut up girl!" Liam snarled. "Don't start telling us what to do. We are the ones with the guns. Trevor, you are to drive Kevin here to Doctor O'Farrell. Do you know where?"

"Yep. No problems," Trevor replied. "Do I come back?"

"Yes, as quickly as you can," Liam replied. "Rory, you take this mob back to the gravel scrape and tie the adults up again. And don't let them use a phone, or let them talk you into using one. We will be back in the gully there."

"What are you going to do?" Rory asked. He looked very worried.

"Going to get Dylan back. Major, you come with us," Liam ordered.

Liam then pointed with his rifle and the major moved in front of him. Michael stood uncertainly, unsure which way to go. He wanted badly to go with Colleen. Liam ended this.

"Michael, come with us," he ordered.

Not knowing what else to do Michael turned and followed Liam and the major. As he walked he glanced back wistfully several times and just once saw Colleen looking in his direction. She immediately looked the other way and began giving directions to move Kevin to the proper stretcher.

Five minutes later Michael, Liam and Major Wickham were back at Snake Gully. They made their way cautiously down the slope into the gully. Patrick was waiting at the bottom, gun at the ready and facing along the gully towards the bend where the cadets were hidden.

Patrick pointed along the gully. "OK major, tell them to let my boy go and I will then let you and all those others join them."

"No. We would still be prisoners," Major Wickham replied. "You call the ambulance first, then I will negotiate."

Patrick shook his head. "The Australians can go, the British stay."

Major Wickham also shook his head. "Never! They are our guests. I will not leave them."

"You aren't in a position to argue major," Patrick snapped.

"Let me talk to them," Major Wickham temporised

"OK."

Major Wickham called out, "Hello! Hello cadets! Major Wickham here. Speak to me."

A voice answered from just around the bend, a girl's voice. "Yes sir. Here we are. Is it alright?"

"No Robbo. I am a prisoner. Is Lt Cavendish there?"

"She's at the other end sir. I can call her on the radio," the girl replied.

"Do that please," Major Wickham called.

As she did Liam said, "That isn't the same girl who was here earlier, the red-head. Her name is Barbara."

"So?" Major Wickham replied. "I've got two female officers and two female Cadet Under-Officers."

"Maybe," Liam replied, but he sounded suspicious. "Where is the red-head?"

"How should I know?" Major Wickham replied.

"She was in charge here. She helped carry the stretcher up the hill," Liam said.

He looked around, then walked a few paces back along the gully and looked on along the gully past where the track went up the bank.

Michael saw at once what Liam was looking at: boot prints in the dust. They lead on along the gully, and beyond that he saw white sap leaking from a cut rubber vine. Liam walked quickly along the gully and held the cut end of the vine to study it.

"This has been cut recently," he said. It was now obvious to Michael that someone had cut the vines to make a path up the otherwise overgrown gully. Liam suddenly turned and swore. "Bugger! That bitch has escaped! I'll bet she took off while we were still talking up there." He nodded towards the slope.

"Where would she have gone?" Patrick asked.

"To get help of course!" Liam cried. He turned to Michael. "You know the area. Where do you think she is heading for? Where is the nearest telephone?"

Michael had experienced a surge of emotion he thought might be joy at the idea that Barbara had got away. That would mean an end to the nightmare, but now he was dragged back into helping prolong it. He pointed to Major Wickham. "These cadet officers have mobile phones I think."

Liam shook his head. "No. We took them off them. Where else?"

Michael knew at once, but hesitated to say. Then under Liam's intense stare he said, "One group was trying to cross the river to the station homestead there, but Murty went to cut them off, and we caught another group trying to go north over the hills, so I reckon she has gone south, to the station homestead over there." He pointed towards 'Landers Creek.'

"Do you know where it is?" Liam asked, urgency clear in his manner and voice.

"Yes. It is called 'Landers Creek'. It is back along the main road about three or four kilometres and a couple in along a side road."

"Right! Dad, you stay here and guard this lot. Major, you come with us. Come on Michael, we must get there before her or we are done!"

Chapter 27

TO 'LANDERS CREEK'

B arbara crouched in the bottom of Snake Gully and stared in horror at Kevin while Maree tried to staunch the flow of blood. As Maree worked she obviously caused extreme pain as Kevin screamed, moaned and writhed. Each time he did Barbara flinched and felt like throwing up. She also felt very distressed and guilty at having caused such agony and damage.

She tried to divert her thoughts from this by thinking about what should be done next. At the top of her mind was getting help. A quick check revealed that her mobile phone still had no service.

How can I get past these mongrels to get to a phone or to high ground? she wondered. In her mind she ran over possible routes. She placed the pistol down and took out her map.

Movement in the gully behind her caused her to look around. She saw Colleen hurrying along the gully and at once felt a surge of relief.

Colleen! Good. Now we can care for the wounded better.

Colleen nodded to her but concentrated on the casualty. She at once knelt and checked the man's pulse and temperature, then began discussing with Maree what she had done and what they should do next. She nodded approval at Maree's bandage.

"That's as good as we can manage," she said. "Now, let's splint the two legs together to limit the movement. Barbara, can you organise a group to make a stretcher?"

Barbara nodded. She turned to Cpl Ridgeway. "Run back and get CUO Roberts and ask her to come here."

Cpl Ridgeway nodded and hurried off. Barbara next instructed Sgt Dunstan to give his machete to Cadet Kettle. As the CQMS Sgt Dunstan was the only person who usually had a machete.

"Cadet Kettle, start cutting two suitable saplings, plus stretcher poles. Make them at least five centimetres in diameter," she ordered.

Cadet Kettle hurried back along the gully. He looked almost green with nausea and Barbara wondered if she looked the same because that was how she felt. She rinsed her mouth, had a drink, then picked up the pistol again and knelt under cover while she considered the next move.

"How did you get here Colleen?" she asked.

While Colleen worked she described what had happened back at the gravel scrape, and how she had walked long the railway with Michael.

"Michael eh? I'll bet you don't think much of him now," Barbara replied.

"He's alright," Colleen said. "He had the guts to stop that Shaemus shooting Chloe. I think he has gotten involved because his family is."

"Do you think we could get Major Wickham's mobile phone?"

Colleen shook her head. "No. Not easily." Colleen described the situation as far as she knew. She then said, "This bloke is losing a lot of blood Barbara. We can't stop it properly. I think he should be moved to a hospital as quickly as possible."

That led to Barbara's attempt to negotiate with the men. She was very determined about this and would not consider handing over their prisoner as part of the deal. As she said this Colleen moved over beside her.

"Barbara, stop the haggling. This man will die if he doesn't get medical help quickly. Do you want that on your conscience?"

Barbara shook her head and felt even sicker. "No," she muttered.

"Nor do I," Colleen said. "We are not going to use the injured as bargaining chips. We just hand this bloke over," she insisted. "We can negotiate about prisoners later."

"What about the three wounded Poms?" Barbara asked.

She noted that Cpl Ridgeway had arrived back with CUO Roberts. Two of the British cadets, Charles and Cecil, were with them.

Colleen shook her head. "Two of them have really serious wounds. They will probably die in the next hour or so if they don't get proper medical treatment."

Barbara gulped and felt awful. "So what can we do?"

"Get this bloke out of here so it isn't another one," Colleen said.

"What about the three wounded Pommies? We can't let the terrorists get them," Barbara said. She saw Charles and Cecil nod in agreement.

"No, we have to keep them here and try to get these men to see sense," Colleen replied.

"They won't. We must get to a phone," Barbara said.

"That could take hours," Colleen said.

Barbara shook her head. "Not if Chloe or Mike have made it out."

"We can't plan on maybes," Colleen pointed out. "I am going to go and negotiate with these men."

"That's an awful risk. What if they hold you hostage again?"

Colleen shrugged. "I'm a prisoner here anyway. I have to go."

"What about the three wounded back there?" Barbara asked.

"We've done all we can. Sharon will just have to manage," Colleen replied. "So I'm going."

Barbara nodded. She could not see any moral alternative. "Yes, OK. Just wait a moment while we organise what we are going to do."

At that moment Cpl Ridgeway pointed and said, "Don't move suddenly CUO Brassington ma'am. There is a snake right next to you."

Barbara went cold with fright and slowly swivelled her head and eyes to look. Only half a metre from her a snake was moving in the grass on the slope level with her head.

That's all we need! she thought in horror, *Someone bitten by a snake and no way to get them to a doctor!*

"It's two snakes!" Robbo cried in amazement.

"What are they doing? Are they having a fight?" Colleen asked.

By then Barbara had edged away. She focused her eyes and saw that it was indeed two snakes, intertwined and writhing around.

"No, they aren't fighting. They are having a f… er, you know," Sgt Dunstan called.

"Dunny! There's no need to be crude!" Robbo chided.

Barbara noted Colleen blush and that made her like her even more. *She is a really nice person,* she thought.

She had now identified the two snakes as being yellow-bellied blacks, each about a metre long. Her rational mind told her she would be unlikely to die from the bite from one but that did not help the panic which was building. She moved further away, until she was several metres back. She found herself pressed between the two British cadets who were staring at the snakes with horrified fascination.

Now that she was safe Barbara stared at them as well. *I've never seen snakes having sex,* she thought.

"I wonder which one is the male?" Maree commented.

"They might both be male. They might be gay," Sgt Dunstan added.

"Don't be crude Dunny," Colleen said.

"Yeah, sorry. But how do they do it?" Sgt Dunstan persisted.

"That's enough!" Barbara snapped, although she had been wondering exactly the same thing. "Never mind them. Let's get organised."

To her own amazement she had a plan. She quickly gave orders and the group got ready. While they were doing this Cadet Kettle arrived back with the improvised stretcher and three more male cadets from 4 Platoon. He carried the stretcher past Barbara.

Sgt Dunstan pointed and said, "Cadet Kettle, there are two snakes there."

"Shit!" Kettle cried. He sprang aside, then stared back at them. "What are they doing? Are they hurt?"

"Never mind the bloody snakes!" Barbara snapped. "Get ready."

She gave final instructions. As she did she noted that Charles and Cecil were both casting frequent fascinated glances at the snakes, which still slithered and writhed around each other. To Barbara's relief the two snakes parted and slid off up the bank and vanished.

"OK, all ready? You two British cadets go back around the bend out of sight. OK Colleen, off you go," she said.

Colleen called out to the terrorists and then went along the gully out of sight. Barbara tensed for the sound of a shot but was relieved to only hear voices. A couple of minutes later the older man, Patrick, and his son Michael came along the gully. It was a very tense moment which Barbara overcame by pretending she wasn't scared and by giving quick orders.

Once Kevin was on the improvised stretcher they picked it up and carried it along the gully. Barbara walked behind it with a second group of cadets. When they reached the point where the track went up the bank she ordered a halt and changed the carrying party over. As the group began struggling up the bank Barbara met Cpl Ridgeway's eye and he nodded and stepped aside to take out his secateurs.

Barbara went up the bank with the stretcher. As they reached the more level ground she tapped several cadets on the shoulder and they hurried back down into the gully. They now reached the most critical moment of Barbara's plan. She feared the terrorists might order them to hand the stretcher over while the bed of the gully was still visible, but to her relief they did not. They were too absorbed with the problem of getting the stretcher up the slope.

As soon as Barbara was sure none of the terrorists could see down into the gully Barbara turned and gave Cpl Ridgeway a nod. Ridgeway and Kettle at once ran along the gully past the point where the track went up and began cutting a way through the rubber vines which blocked the gully to the south.

The next moment of crisis came after the stretcher was lowered out in the open. Barbara feared that the terrorists might try to hold them prisoner, or might walk back immediately to the gully. To forestall this she had Sgt Dunstan covering her with the SMG from the bushes at the top of the slope. But he was not needed and she at once set off back with the two remaining cadets.

As she passed where Sgt Dunstan crouched under cover she said quietly, "OK Dunny, get going." He at once rose and followed her, the SMG still ready to fire.

As they reached the top of the bank she glanced over her shoulder. Now was the critical minute!

To her intense relief the terrorists were still standing talking to Colleen. Heart in mouth Barbara slid the last few metres to the bottom then handed the pistol to one of the cadets and said quietly, "Give it to CUO Roberts. Now go! Hurry!" Sgt Dunstan moved back past her, the SMG still aimed up the slope.

Satisfied she had done all she could Barbara gave a thumbs-up to CUO Roberts, who was watching from the next bend, then turned and hurried along the bottom of the gully to her right. As she did she had to consciously resist the urge to run, being very aware that the sound of army boots thudding carried a long way.

She had fewer qualms about leaving the group now, sure that the terrorists would be very wary of trying to sneak in through the rubber vines.

They can see what I did to Kevin, she thought grimly. *That will make them think twice.*

Twenty paces up the gully she came to the first point where rubber vines had overgrown and choked the bed. Dripping white sap indicated newly cut rubber vine. "How the hell did Chloe and her patrol get through here without cutting the vines?" she murmured.

Cpl Ridgeway answered that. "They weren't wearing webbing," he explained.

"Knowing Chloe it's a wonder she was wearing anything," Cadet Kettle commented.

"Sssh! Whisper," Barbara hissed, acutely conscious that the terrorist were only about 50 paces up to her right. "And no more talk like that thank you!" she added.

Barbara pushed though the tangle of vines and at once saw the sense in Chloe's decision as her own webbing was almost immediately snagged. Careful not to make all the vegetation shake and thereby attract attention she eased back and quietly snipped some more vines and then slowly pushed forward. As she did she snagged her webbing a couple of times in her haste.

She came out in another short stretch of ten metres which was like an overgrown trench with a thick tangle of rubber vine and bushes on both sides. Anxious to be away from the area she hurried along it. At the end of that section she glanced back and was relieved to note that she could no longer see the area where the track came down into the gully.

Thirty paces on she had to push through another tunnel in the rubber vines for twenty or so metres and found Cpl Ridgeway and Cadet Kettle waiting on the other side.

Cpl Ridgeway pointed and said, "There is a junction. Which way do we go?"

Barbara had to pull out her map. She knew it was about 4 kilometres in a straight line to the 'Landers Creek' homestead but was also aware that the direct route might not be the best. Earlier she had noted that a creek led off in the direction they wanted to go and she now decided this was the one. It led to some of the culverts which 3 Platoon had been guarding the previous day.

We should be able to get under the railway and road unseen that way, she thought.

"That way, to the right," she said, indicating the branch she wanted.

"The rubber vines have been cut going to the left though," Cpl Ridgeway said.

"Chloe's patrol will have done that," Barbara replied. "Come on, let's move."

Cpl Ridgeway began snipping away the dozens of tendrils which blocked their path. Barbara watched for a minute then said, "Don't waste time on perfection, just enough for us to crawl through."

"What if there are wild pigs?" Cadet Kettle asked, looking anxious.

"Too bad! We climb a tree. Now get a move on!" Barbara answered.

The gully was narrow and deep and blocked for a length of about twenty metres. As they inched along Barbara noted from time to time that she was able to get glimpses up to the open flat ridge on their right. She kept a careful eye on this area in case the men appeared, but most of her attention was taken up with guarding the rear.

It was slow going, and very hot. Barbara drank the remainder of one water bottle and began to fret. It made her glad her team had their webbing and worried that Chloe's group, without water bottles, might suffer heat illness.

They can drink the river in an emergency I suppose, she consoled herself. The responsibility now weighed heavily on her and she shuddered from the stress and harrowing memories. *This is much too slow!* she thought. But a check of her mobile phone showed that it still did not have service so she urged them to hurry.

It took nearly ten minutes to make their way around two bends and forward 50 paces. To Barbara's intense relief they then came out in open country in a small vale a few metres deep and about fifty wide. The dry creek bed was sand and a metre wide and wriggled across the grassy flat at the bottom of the depression. Open timber provided some shade and clumps of rubber vine helped provide cover but Barbara was acutely aware that if one of the terrorists appeared on the crest of the gentle ridge on the right or rear then he could not help but see them.

We are depending on being in 'dead ground', she told herself. *But we must take the risk. Speed is important.*

She now took over the lead, striding quickly along the bed of the creek. In it they could quickly duck down out of sight if they spotted the enemy first. As Barbara walked rapidly along the creek bed her eyes scanned from side to side and particularly along the grassy top of the embankment along which the railway ran. No one was visible so she continued moving as fast as she dared.

The culverts came into view. They were smaller than the ones she had defended and were half full of sand. Without pausing she walked bent double straight into one that appeared to have been used the day before. Within ten paces she had to stop as it became so dark she could not make out where she was putting her boots.

Cpl Ridgeway walked into her, then Cadet Kettle bumped into him. "Ow! What's wrong?" Cpl Ridgeway asked.

"I can't see. Wait a moment till our eyes adjust to the dark," Barbara answered.

"Yeah," Cadet Kettle agreed. "You wouldn't want to stand on a big snake. They'd like to live in a place like this."

Thanks! Barbara thought in annoyance as fear caused her heart rate to shoot up.

"Shut up about snakes," she snapped. "This isn't Snake Gully. That was the other one."

In fact it wasn't snakes which bothered them, but bats. Half way through the tunnel they had to proceed on hands and knees as the sand had filled up so much of the culvert. At that point Cpl Ridgeway let out a shriek of terror. Barbara felt her own heart leap and flutter, only to realise that the black things swishing around her head were bats.

"Sssh! Shut up! They are only bats," she said.

"They might bite!" Cpl Ridgeway cried, ducking flat.

"Yeah, some bats carry deadly diseases," Cadet Kettle added.

"They aren't bloody vampire bats! Come on!" Barbara snapped.

She rose and hurried on, tensing herself and gritting her teeth. The others followed with much muttering and gasps of fright as bats swooped and fluttered around them. Barbara saw that the bats were in fact only about 15 centimetres across the wingspan but even so she found she was anxious.

They reached the far end with a rush and it took will power on Barbara's part not to run out into the open, despite the other two bumping into her and pushing from behind.

"Stop shoving!" she ordered. "Let me check there are no enemy up on the road."

Twenty metres ahead was the embankment with the main road on it. Culverts ran under that as well, but they were larger. The embankment was covered with long grass but Barbara could not see any enemy against the skyline. Beyond the next culverts she could see that the creek bed was full of trees and bushes.

At her signal they hurried across the open ground between the two embankments and into the next tunnel opposite. There were no bats in there but at the far end they encountered another unexpected nuisance.

Wasps had built their nests hanging down from the roof and the disturbed insects began to attack them.

A wasp bit Barbara on her neck and she let out a yelp of pain before she realised what it was. The others were likewise stung and cried out in alarm and pain. Flailing at the insects they ran out the far end until brought to a halt by a barbed wire fence across the creek bed. They paused here and looked to ensure the wasps had not pursued them.

What a hopeless mob of noddies we are at fieldcraft! Barbara thought ruefully.

At that moment a vehicle drove past northwards. Barbara just glimpsed the roof of a brown truck. That set her thinking, but she had already made her mind up when Cpl Ridgeway voiced the same thoughts.

"Why don't we flag down a car?" he suggested.

It was very tempting but Barbara shook her head. Cadet Kettle answered for her. "With our bloody luck the first car to come along would be the bloody crooks!"

"That's right. Come on, it is only about two kilometres, twenty minutes if we hurry," Barbara said. She noted it was now getting on for 1100 and that it was very hot.

She led the way on Southwest along the creek bed, still scouting carefully but also glancing frequently back towards the main road. They had only gone another hundred paces when an unusual vibration caused Barbara to stop. She crouched behind a bush and looked around

"What's that?" she asked.

"A train," Cpl Ridgeway replied, "Coming from the north."

"The crooks wouldn't be on that," Cadet Kettle added.

"No, and those trains all have radios," Barbara said. "Come on!"

She turned and went running back along the creek bed. Much of it was small rocks the size of oranges and it was difficult to run on. She ignored several sharp twists and pushed herself to run. The fence held her up for a few seconds as her webbing snagged on the barbs of the bottom strand but she tore herself free and scrambled to her feet, then dashed into the culvert, completely forgetting the wasps until another one stung her.

All the while she could hear the train getting closer and by the time she was half way through the culvert under the main road she knew she had lost the race as she heard the engine go past. By the time she dashed out the far end the locomotive was fifty metres past her. Still she did not give up. She dashed up the steep, grassy slope, cutting her hands on sharp grass as she did.

The train crew might see me! she thought hopefully, even though the glimpse she had of the driver had shown him sitting in the cab looking bored and staring ahead.

Barbara's next idea was to try to climb onto the train and travel with it but as she neared the top she saw that was a hopeless idea as well. The embankment was so narrow at the top that the wire bins overhung the sides and there was no clear, flat track to run along to match their speed.

All she could do was stand in gasping frustration until the last wagon went past. That was the yellow brake van but by then the train had picked up speed on the long straight and she knew she had no chance of catching up. As the train clacked off southwards she stood and gasped for breath and felt like drooping with defeat.

Then she remembered she was now up on the skyline. She quickly looked around and slid back down the steep bank. Cpl Ridgeway and Cadet Kettle were waiting at the bottom, slapping at wasp stings and muttering. They did not look happy. Barbara said nothing, just led them back under the main road, using a different culvert this time. This resulted in them having to push through spider webs instead.

They crawled under the fence again, then paused for another drink. Cadet Kettle swilled the remaining water in his water bottle around and drained it. "I'm out of water now," he said.

Damn! Barbara thought. *Another worry.*

"Let's move," she answered, resuming the walk.

They set off along the creek bed for the second time. The creek was a few metres wide here, lined with trees but with low banks which sloped gently up for hundreds of metres through open savannah woodland. Having no practical alternative Barbara led them at a fast walk. She was now getting very hot and upset, and was acutely aware that time was passing. The idea that another person might die just because she did not walk fast enough distressed her deeply.

After a couple of hundred paces they passed under the power line in its clearing. Barbara was cautious here, frequently glancing back to her right rear in case the enemy were on the main road near the pylon she could clearly see and which was marked on her map.

That's the pylon 3 Platoon were guarding yesterday, she thought. In the distance beyond it she could clearly see where the power line went up over the Big Hill. *Oh, I hope CUO Callan has made it over that,* she thought.

There was no sign of any of the men so they hurried quickly across the clearing and passed safely into more open savannah woodland, lots of tall, straight trees with thin trunks, a mixture of smooth barked eucalypts and iron barks. Several small creeks coming in from the right gave Barbara a few navigational worries but she opted each time to go left and to keep aiming south.

As they trudged south the creek became smaller and smaller until it was just a rill in a gentle dip and they had no option but to walk in the open savannah across the flat land. As they did Barbara kept glancing to her left, hoping that they were not observed by any of the IRA who might be on the main road. A check of the map showed her that their route was diverging from the main road but was almost parallel to the power line. From time to time she glimpsed one of the big steel pylons through the trees. Seeing them reassured her that her navigation was accurate.

For the next fifteen minutes they went almost due south until they came to a field of sugar cane. That was so unexpected that Barbara paused and studied her map. The sugar cane was not marked and she could only shake her head and assume it had been planted after the map was made. Then she remembered to try her mobile phone and to her delight she noted one tiny bar of service.

With her heart beating with both hope and over-exertion she tapped 000 and waited. The phone rang for a moment but then dropped out. Biting her lip with frustration Barbara tried again. But again it dropped out.

"Not connecting," she muttered. "Come on, it can't be far now."

Barbara now led the way along to the right, following the vehicle track beside an irrigation pipe along the side of the field. As they walked, she kept looking to her left every couple of paces. The field was full of ripe, uncut sugar cane ready for harvest and was so tall they could not see over it. Ahead of them were the foothills of Mt Dalrymple.

At least the navigation is easy, she thought.

She could clearly see the peak of Mt Dalrymple all of the time and way off to her right rear she could even see the hill above the gravel scrape. It now looked a long way away and she felt hopeful they did not have far to go. Her immediate concern became heat exhaustion as both she and Cpl Ridgeway drank the last of their water and she noted the sweating and red faces of the other two.

It's when they go pale and stop sweating I really have to start worrying, she reminded herself.

Another five minutes of walking brought them to the end of the standing cane. Ahead on their left was another huge open field that had obviously been recently harvested. But what made Barbara's hopes suddenly surge was the sight of two farm houses and some sheds at the other side of the field. She wasn't sure if that was the homestead of 'Landers Creek' Station or not but she said, "They will do. There might be a phone there, or people who can take us to one."

So she turned left and began striding towards the farm houses as fast as she could go, her eyes searching anxiously for signs of people. It took five minutes to walk the length of the field and they came to a bitumen road. The houses lay beyond it. For a few moments Barbara paused to look around before leaving the relative cover of the standing cane. Seeing no sign of anyone she led the other two forward into the open, crossing the bitumen while she aimed for the left hand house.

It was an old low-set house of simple plan. At the open front door Barbara paused to listen and look around. At the bottom of the short flight of three steps she said. "Cpl Ridgeway, go and look in that other house over there. See if there is anyone around. Cadet Kettle, take our water bottles and find a tap to fill them up. I will go inside."

Barbara pulled out her two water bottles and passed them to Cadet Kettle, then walked up the stairs and knocked on the doorpost.

"Come in!" called a man's voice.

Before she thought about it Barbara had stepped into the cool interior of a lounge room, only to stop in stunned surprise. Standing to one side, pointing a gun at her, was a grinning Liam.

"G'day Ginger. You took a while to get here," he said.

Chapter 28

CRISIS

When Liam and Michael reached the entrance to the gravel scrape Michael was so winded he could hardly speak. Liam shouted at him to keep up. "Come on you little slug! You are just unfit. We've got to get to that homestead before that red-headed bitch."

Michael gritted his teeth and forced himself to run on. When they reached the area where the cadets had their bivouac he saw that nine cadets and four adult officers were seated in a group under a tree near the Command Post tent. Guarding them was a worried looking Rory.

Liam shouted to him, "Rory, come with me. Michael, come and get this gun and take over as guard."

Liam led the way to where their ute was now parked under a tree. He reached in behind the seat and extracted the bolt action .22" rifle from there. After rummaging in the glove box for a moment he pulled out a packet of bullets and thrust them into Michael's hand.

"It's only a single shot so keep well away from them. Don't let any of them stand up or walk around. If they do then shoot one to show the rest you mean business," Liam instructed.

The instructions appalled Michael but he said nothing. He took the rifle and loaded it as he walked back to where Rory had been standing. By then Liam and Rory had climbed into the ute and the engine had been started.

"Get one of those little radios there and switch it to Channel Twenty Eight. That way we can talk to you or you can talk to dad. We'll be back as quick as we can," Liam shouted as he accelerated the ute out along the gravel track.

Michael was left standing alone, scared and confused. He licked his lips and then ran his eyes over the prisoners, noting first that the three male officers were both tied hand and foot and looked very hostile. Then his eyes met Colleen's. He had known she was there but had not wanted to face her. Now he knew he had to, or he would despise himself for the rest of his life.

Colleen glared at him from where she was seated among the other cadets. "What is going on Michael?" she asked.

"Did you get that bloke away to the doctor alright?" Michael replied, not wanting to get drawn into an argument or discussion.

"Yes. Where are those two going in such a hurry?" Colleen persisted.

"To the homestead at 'Landers Creek'," Michael replied reluctantly. He found he could not ignore Colleen and did not want to.

"Are they going to call the ambulance?" Colleen asked hopefully.

"No. They are going there to catch some cadets to stop them using the phone," Michael replied unhappily.

"What cadets?" Colleen asked.

"Not sure. Liam thinks it is the girl with red hair who shot Kevin."

Michael was then annoyed to see the cadets all grin to each other and heard them mutter 'Barbara'. "Shut up!" he snapped. "No talking."

"Why not?" Colleen queried.

"Because I said so," Michael replied. He was feeling very stressed and wished fervently he wasn't there.

"What will you do if we do talk?" Colleen asked in a sarcastic and challenging tone, "Shoot us?"

Michael couldn't answer that. He met her eyes momentarily and then looked away. To his horror she then stood up. "Sit down please Colleen," he pleaded.

"I won't try anything," Colleen answered. She walked over and stood facing him from several paces away. A tense silence settled on the watching cadets and one of the officers, the older, solid one, called, "Colleen, don't take any risks please."

"It's alright sir," Colleen replied to the officer.

Then she faced Michael and he had to look her in the eyes. It made him sweat and his stomach tightened up even more.

God she's beautiful, he thought, *I wish I hadn't mucked this up.*

"You can end this madness now," she said. "There should be a phone over there in Lt Barker's vehicle, or Major Wickham's might still be here somewhere. Use it to call the ambulance."

Michael experienced the most acute pang of anguish he had ever known. "I can't do that Colleen. I can't betray my own family."

"It seems they have betrayed you," Colleen sneered, her eyes blazing. "If you are a man you will get that phone and call the ambulance now."

"I can't!" Michael cried.

In his distress he gripped the rifle across his front and twisted it in hands slippery with sweat. Colleen stared at him with a look of contempt on her face which cut even deeper. It was movement among the other cadets which diverted Michael. He noticed a big lad move into a crouching position.

In near desperation he stepped back and levelled the rifle at the boy. "Sit down! Don't try anything! Don't make me shoot."

Colleen stood her ground. She glanced around and said quietly, "Sit down CSM. There's no need for heroics. Michael knows what is the right thing."

Michael did but the conflict of loyalties tore him apart. "I can't!" he cried again.

"If you don't then you become as much a murderer as if you had aimed the gun and pulled the trigger," Colleen said coldly. "You know that there are three people dying down in Snake Gully. I know what condition they are in because I went and carried out the First Aid. They will all die if they don't get medical help quickly."

Michael nodded. He was panting and sweating and hating himself. "They might be dead already," he muttered.

"Oh you bloody weakling! Why can't you be strong like you were when you stopped your uncle shooting Chloe? That must have taken a lot of guts. So show me you do have some," Colleen snapped.

Michael could only shake his head because his throat had choked up in silent misery. Colleen kept up her attack. "If one of those people dies it will be on your conscience for the rest of your life. Can you live with that? I couldn't."

That made Michael even more distressed as he knew in his heart he was a facing a dreadful choice.

Whichever way I decide I am going to bitterly regret it, he thought miserably. *If I let them use the phone Dad and my brothers will cut me off for ever.*

What Uncle Shaemus and his men might do in revenge did not bear thinking about, although he suspected that knee-capping might be the least of it. Fear gripped Michael in a bowel-watering grip.

One of the younger male officers now called, "Who are these people? What is it all about?"

"Be quiet!" Michael cried.

"No," Colleen said. "I want to know too. What is this madness all about?"

Michael wiped sweat from his face, then wiped each hand in turn before proceeding to explain the family story of the tragedy in Northern Ireland. Colleen listened in silence, shaking her head in amazement. "So this is all a mad act of vengeance by your father and brothers for the shooting of a baby sixteen years ago!"

Michael nodded. Colleen went on, "This little sister, Bridie, did you know her? Do you remember her?"

"No, I was only a baby myself, one or two years old," Michael replied.

"And that is why your father and uncle left Ireland, to escape the law?"

Michael hesitated, then shook his head. "No. I think they were wanted for other things, for fighting against the Orangemen and British." Now he felt sick about what those 'other things' might have been.

"These other men, Kevin and Rory and so on, are they some of this Irish Republican Army?" Colleen asked

"I don't know. They didn't say, but I think they must be. They obviously know Dad and Uncle Shaemus and take orders from them," Michael replied.

Colleen shook her head and looked disgusted. "Well, I think the whole situation is insane, and revolting," she said. "You can try to justify it to yourself anyway you like but I think it is just immoral. What is more I won't be a party to it. I am going to use the phone."

Panic leapt into Michael's heart. "Oh Colleen! Please don't."

"You can shoot me too if you like but I don't want to live with myself knowing I let others die if I could have stopped it."

Colleen turned and started walking towards the parked vehicles. Michael stood in miserable defeat, knowing there was no way he could stop her. At that moment, a vehicle came roaring in along the gravel road. Michael spun around to look and felt his heart sink even more. It was the ute and it was being driven by Liam.

"Colleen! Please sit down," Michael cried in anguish

To his relief Colleen stopped, gave him a withering look and then went over to the others and sat down. To Michael's further distress he saw that she had burst into tears. To his added consternation he saw that there were people in the back of the ute, three cadets and Rory. One of the cadets was the girl with bright copper-coloured hair.

She didn't make it! he thought.

Inwardly he groaned. He had been trying to salve his conscience by hoping that she would have called the ambulance and he would not have to betray his kin. Now he saw that he was presented with a stark choice.

As the prisoners were ordered out of the ute Liam gloated to him. "We got the bitch! Now she can pay for what she did to Kevin."

"What do you mean pay?" Michael croaked.

Liam gave him a wicked grin, then leered at Barbara, who now stood defiantly beside the ute, her hands tied behind her back. "I can think of a few things," Liam hinted.

Barbara just gave him a look of cold disdain, then walked over to where the other cadets sat. To one of them she said, "So they caught you too Mike?"

The cadet nodded. "Got us trying to get under the main road at the bottom of the hill."

Hearing that added to Michael's guilt and he fervently hoped the boy named Mike would not mention that it was he who had spotted them.

If I'd pretended not to see them they would have reached a phone by now, he thought miserably.

"Never mind Mike. It was a good try. Anyway, Chloe might have made it," Barbara replied. She then sat down. The cadets with her did likewise. They began answering questions from the others. Liam snapped angrily at them, "Shut up you lot!"

Michael could not endure the pressure any more. He moved over near Liam and said, "This is wrong Liam. We must let these people go."

"Crap little brother! We have too much to lose. You are just a soft weakling. Now shut up and watch the prisoners," Liam replied. He turned to Rory. "Take the ute and drive to the Lookout. You'll find another cadet officer tied up in the back of a Land Rover. Make sure he hasn't wriggled free, then take the radio there down to Shaemus. That way we will be able to talk to each other at least. Oh, and give him this pistol."

He passed a pistol to Rory, who said, "This radio, what frequency is it on?"

"Same as the one under that tent there I suppose. Is that so mister lieutenant?" He addressed the solid officer who shut his mouth in a stubborn line.

"Don't be stupid mister officer. I will hurt one of these girls if you don't tell me." He walked over and swept his eyes over the group.

Oh please don't pick Colleen! Michael thought in panic.

To his intense relief Liam pointed to a sulky looking blonde. "You, you are one of the smokers from down at the dunny aren't you?"

The girl gave Liam a scared but venomous glare, then nodded. The cadet officers looked at her and shook their heads sadly. Liam went on, "What's you name sweetie?"

"Micki," the girl replied.

Liam laughed. "You look more like Minnie to me! And you look a bit of a goer. Now sweetie, you go and show Rory how to make sure these radios work."

Micki blanched and glanced at the officers in panic. Liam guessed her fear. "No, all you have to do is show him how to use that radio there under the tent. You don't have to go off into the bush with him. But if you don't get the radio working then I'll take you there right now."

At that Rory laughed aloud. "That might not frighten her Liam me boyo. We caught her down in the bush gettin' up to mischief remember."

Liam laughed too. Michael just felt sick. He noted Micki give a sickly smile and blush but she then walked over to the CP tent and proceeded to nervously explain to Rory how to set the frequency. While this was going on Michael stood in near despair, wondering how to resolve the apparently insoluble. As he did, he became aware that Colleen was staring at him, her face a mask of contempt. That really hurt.

But it was his own contempt for himself that was hurting the most.

I am a weakling and a coward, he told himself.

To avoid those hard eyes he moved to the tent and picked up a water bottle. Only as he began to drink did he realise just how dehydrated he was. He almost drained the bottle, then had to turn back to face the group.

Rory stood up with a radio and leered at Micki as she also stood up. "OK love, I got that. You sure you don't want to come for a walk with me? I've even got cigarettes."

Micki gave him a terrified look, then scuttled back to sit with the others. Rory gave a great belly laugh, then said to Liam. "What are you going to do?"

"Take this whole bunch down to that Snake Gully to where dad is. That way we will have them all in one place at least. At the moment we are scattered all over the place and out of communication, so you get moving with that radio. I will carry this one."

"Yeah but what are we gunna do?" Rory persisted.

"Get Dylan back and get out of here I reckon," Liam replied.

"We could shoot a few more of the bloody British before we go," Rory said. That stunned Michael even more.

"You wouldn't!" he gasped.

Rory gave him a pitying look. "I've shot a few of the bastards already boyo. Why do you think I'm on the bloody run, eh?"

Hearing that chilled Michael to the heart. But what followed depressed him even more. Liam indicated where the cadet officer's mobile phones were and also a bag containing mobile phones belonging to cadets.

"Take them with you Rory," he said.

Rory collected the phones and tossed them into the cab of the ute. Then he climbed in, slammed the door, started the engine and drove the vehicle back out along the dirt track. That left Michael feeling even more torn. Seeing Colleen give him an 'I-told-you-so' look did not help.

Oh God! What can I do? he asked himself in anguish.

Liam now began giving orders to the cadets and their officers. "You lot, on your feet! Stand in a line on the road. You, untie the officer's feet. You bloody officers don't try anything stupid or I will shoot one of these kids."

Michael was even more appalled. He had always thought Liam was a happy-go-lucky type. Now another person seemed to be speaking. As the cadets formed up in a line on the road Michael moved to the rear, his mind and emotions in turmoil.

Colleen walked over and stood near him. "Well? What are you going to do?" she asked.

"What can I do?" Michael whispered bitterly. "I might not shoot but my brother will."

To Michael's infinite distress Colleen gave a shrug and turned her head away. Liam came walking along the line counting them.

"Just making sure how many there are. We don't want to lose any on the way," he explained. "You go at the back little brother."

Michael swallowed and forced himself to speak. "Liam, this is all wrong. We must call the ambulance."

Liam sneered. "Getting soft are you? Bothers your tender little conscience does it? Or has she been getting at you?" He gestured to Colleen who stood next to him.

Michael shook his head but Liam sneered. "Be your own man you weakling. Now let's get moving."

"Liam! It isn't right," Michael cried. "We must get the people who have been shot to a doctor."

"People! They aren't people! They are bloody British shit!" Liam replied.

At that Colleen exploded. "You disgusting creature! You are just an ignorant bigot. You haven't even met these people."

Liam spun to face her and raised a hand. "Shut up bitch! Mind your mouth or I'll belt you."

To Michael's dismay Colleen gave Liam a look of contempt and said, "You make me ashamed to be Irish."

Fury blazed in Liam's eyes and he stepped forward to strike her. This time Michael acted. He stepped between Liam and Colleen and shook his head. Liam gave him another sneer but lowered his hand.

"Tell your girlfriend to keep her mouth shut or I will shut it for her," he threatened.

Liam then spun on his heel and walked over to the tent. He had a drink, then picked up the radio and pulled it on, getting tangled in the harness and dangling handset as he did. At last he had it on and he started walking. "Start moving!" he ordered.

The line began moving. Michael felt his heart sink into his boots. Despair and defeat welled up in its place.

As they walked along Colleen fell back beside him. "Well, I hope you are satisfied," she said, then closed her mouth in a grim line.

Barbara, who was walking just in front of Colleen, spoke over her shoulder "Let's hope Chloe made it."

At that Michael remembered the three cadets crossing the open sand of the riverbed. It struck him in the chest like a blow. For a few steps he was unable to speak. Then he shook his head.

"I don't think she did. Her group was seen trying to cross the bed of the river and Uncle Shaemus sent Murty to catch them."

"So nobody knows!" Colleen muttered. She gave Michael another hard look, then said, "I am going to get help."

"Oh don't. Liam will shoot," Michael replied.

"Then you go," Colleen answered.

Michael nodded. By then they had reached the gate and the head of the line was at the main road. Liam paused there to check for traffic. Michael found himself walking forward. Colleen followed.

"What is it little brother?" Liam asked as he reached him.

"I am going to call the ambulance," Michael heard himself say.

"What, and get us all in the shit? Where's your loyalty you weakling. Stop being selfish," Liam retorted.

"I think this whole thing is wrong. I also think I have been lied to and used, and I won't be a party to murder. So I am going," Michael replied.

He was trembling with fear and he had the impression he was seeing things in a tube with fuzzy edges.

Liam turned to face him. "So you are a traitor as well as a coward!"

"I'm not a traitor. I was brought up to be a good Christian, and I am going to be true to my faith, and to myself. And I'm not a coward either. You can shoot me if you want, because that's what you'll have to do to stop me."

With that Michael turned and started walking back towards the gravel scrape.

Chapter 29

DECISION

"Michael!" Liam shouted.

Michael forced himself to keep walking. He was aware that Colleen was walking beside him but he did not look at her. All he could see was the dusty road curving ahead, and a long, bleak future.

"Michael! Come back here!" Liam yelled. "Come back or else!"

Somehow Michael made himself keep walking, moving as though in a dream. He was now so swamped by surging emotions that he felt numb.

Bang!

The smack of a bullet throwing up a plume of sand and stones just in front of him made him flinch, but he managed to keep control of his bowels and to keep walking. He was already sweating but now began to tremble. As he forced himself to keep putting one foot in front of another, he realised he was now so depressed he didn't care if he was killed.

That would be a quick end to it all, he thought. But then another, far worse thought came to him. *He might shoot Colleen.*

"Colleen, go back," he managed to croak.

She made no answer but Liam added to his fear. "Stop Michael, or I will shoot the girl."

At that Michael stopped and spun round, raising his rifle to his shoulder as he did. "If you do," he shouted, "then you really will have to kill me, because I will bloody well shoot you!"

"Mike! I'm your brother. Be fair!" Liam replied. He also had his rifle in his shoulder but was not aiming it directly at him.

"So? You are my brother. Why can't you be fair to me? What about mum? Where does she fit into this?" Michael retorted.

"Don't let us down Mike! Don't betray us," Liam cried.

It was the closest to pleading Michael had ever heard from his big brother and it wrung his heart.

Michael shook his head. "Your cause is unjust. It is wrong. It has nothing to do with freeing Ireland. It is just ignorant bloody revenge. The right thing to do now is to try to fix up the mess."

"But we could go to jail," Liam replied.

"Aw, so what! We deserve to. We have deliberately come here to kill these people. Besides, it would be better than having to go on the run and then have to live a lie for the rest of our lives," Michael answered.

Liam now lost his temper. "You gutless little shit! What about dad and me? What about Dylan?"

"The best thing you can do is take these cadets and trade them for Dylan, then get the hell out of here before the cops arrive," Michael said. "You should have time. It will take the cops a while to get here."

Michael saw Liam glance at the line of cadets beside him and noted that his face was a mask of anger and anguish. He sensed that the moment of decision had arrived.

I must take the initiative here, he thought. *If we just stand here arguing it could all turn into a stalemate, or a shoot-out.*

Having decided that he turned and resumed walking, expecting at any second to be struck down by a bullet. He was dimly aware that Colleen was striding along beside him.

From behind him Liam shouted, "Michael you gutless little bastard, come back!"

Michael kept walking but sensed that he had won. Liam screamed after him, "Coward! Weakling! Traitor!" but no shot came.

By then Michael and Colleen were 50 metres from him and through the open gate. When he heard Liam shout, "Don't you try anything, you ginger-headed bitch! I might not shoot my brother but I will bloody well shoot you," he knew they had managed it. He glanced back and saw Liam urging the line of cadets to start marching. The bend in the track then hid them from view.

To his relief Colleen said nothing. She just kept walking beside him. He realised he was crying, the tears streaming down his cheeks and blurring his vision. He felt so upset it was as though his heart would burst.

The pair made their way to the CP. Colleen was careful not to look at him, for which Michael was grateful. It allowed him to regain some self-control and to wipe his eyes.

"They are not here," Colleen said, turning over some gear.

Michael realised she meant the officer's mobile phones. "Rory took them," he said.

"There might be one he didn't get," Colleen replied.

He followed her over to the 4WD. Colleen looked inside and rummaged around. "None here either," she muttered.

She then walked over to the blue station wagon and searched it.

"We had better hurry," Michael managed to croak. "When Liam tells dad then he or Uncle Shaemus will come after us." Suddenly Michael was terrified of Uncle Shaemus. "Or one of those gunmen. They will shoot us for sure," he added.

Colleen faced him. "There are no phones here. Your people must have taken them all. We will have to walk to a phone."

"We could flag down a car," Michael suggested, hearing one passing out on the main road.

"Not here. We could get caught by those men at the Lookout," Colleen replied.

"We could go the other way, and if there isn't a car we could go to that cattle station," Michael suggested.

Colleen shook her head. "No. Barbara tried going there and got caught. Liam knows it. Besides, we need to be where we can meet the police and explain the situation. They will come from the north, from Ayr."

"Which way do we go?" Michael asked.

Colleen pointed at the hill. "Over that. Come on."

"Do you know the way?" Michael asked as he and Colleen began walking towards the bottom of the hill.

"I spent half of yesterday up on it," Colleen replied. "Besides, I have my map, not that I need it. I know the lie of the land."

Michael followed Colleen up the slope beside an old barbed wire fence which bordered the gravel pit. On the lower slopes of the hill above the gravel pit Colleen stepped through a gap in the fence and set off diagonally up the hill, aiming for the saddle where the power line crossed. She went as fast as she could and Michael soon found he was panting. After a bit they came to an old bench cut with an overgrown and washed out road on it. This clearly led to the saddle, so they turned right to follow it. But after a hundred more paces Michael came to a gasping standstill. They were about half way up.

Colleen stopped and looked back at him. "Your brother is right. You are unfit," she said.

Michael could only nod and suck in air. His heart was hammering furiously in his chest and he felt dizzy. To steady himself he looked out over the tree tops to the flat area inside the curve of the railway, hoping to see Liam and the cadets. They were nowhere to be seen.

As soon as he had recovered some breath Michael nodded and resumed plodding on upward. Colleen led the way again. Within a couple of minutes they had reached the crest under the power line. Michael was surprised. "This hill isn't as high as it looks," he gasped.

"No, it only looks big," Colleen agreed, but she didn't stop.

She went straight on over the crest and began picking her way down the rough vehicle track that went down the steep slope on the north side. Michael saw that ahead of them was a semi-circular valley about half a kilometre wide. On the left was an even higher extension of the ridge they were on. Ahead were two conical hills, one large and one small, marking the far side of the small valley. They were about 500 metres away. The large conical hill was almost directly in front of them and the power line ran in a clearing across to a saddle on its left, between it and the steep, stony ridge which marked the head of the valley. Down to the right, just visible through a scattering of spindly eucalypts, was the main road. It went over a low rise to the right of the large conical hill, between it and the small conical hill.

"We could angle over to the main road there," he suggested.

"OK," Colleen agreed. She at once changed direction and began tramping through knee high grass. Michael followed, surprised at how confidently Colleen moved cross-country.

As they walked down the rough slope Michael battled with black thoughts and bitter regrets. He suspected he had broken with his own family irretrievably and it was heart rending. Just as distressing was the thought that he would now go to jail and that would forever exclude him from many jobs.

And decent girls like Colleen won't want anything to do with criminals like me, he thought. His whole future now looked very grim and bleak.

For several minutes they made their way down towards the road, picking their way over the rocks and ant hills which were mostly hidden in the long grass.

As they reached the flatter ground near the bottom of the slope Colleen suddenly pointed to her right.

"There's a car," she called.

They were now only a couple of hundred metres from the main road. Michael looked and saw a vehicle which had come around the hill from the right. Then he felt his heart stop, then pound. It was their ute. Even as he watched the ute stopped and a man got out, Shaemus.

"Get down! It is Uncle Shaemus," Michael cried.

It was instantly obvious they had been seen as Shaemus leaned on the roof of the ute and aimed a rifle. Michael and Colleen lay flat but the area they were in was short grass studded with scattered trees with thin trunks and offered little cover.

Crack! Thump!

The bullet snapped past very close, striking a small tree just past them. Michael felt a wave of icy terror sweep over him and he flattened himself into the grass. Shaemus obviously meant to kill them.

"We can't stay here," he gasped, raising his head slightly to look around. Twenty metres ahead was a small creek line. "When I say run, bolt for that creek," he added.

Crack!

That shot was so close Michael felt the shock wave and it caused him to prickle with goose bumps and another wave of terror.

"Go!"

They scrambled to their feet and darted forward.

Bang! Crack!

The bullet plucked at Michael's shirt, creasing his back as it did. A sharp pain made him wonder if he had been hit but his legs were still working so he kept running. He saw the creek getting closer in a blur. Then he was diving into it, rolling down a small grassy slope and coming to a stop in the narrow bed. To his intense relief Colleen slithered to a stop beside him. He glanced around. It wasn't much cover, only a few metres wide and about two deep, but it was just enough.

Cautiously he raised his head behind a tree. His worst fears were confirmed, Uncle Shaemus was walking around the front of the ute, obviously intending to hunt them down. Michael looked behind him. The creek wriggled its way up the valley to end as a steep re-entrant in the side of the high rocky hill at the western end. In all other directions the ground sloped gently upwards, covered with short grass of varying heights.

Colleen had looked as well. "We will have to run for it," she said. "We will never be able to crawl away without being seen. He will be able to walk faster than we can crawl."

Michael nodded and felt sick. "I'm sorry Colleen. It is my fault you are in danger. You start crawling up the gully and I will wait here and stop Uncle Shaemus." He held up the .22.

"You can't shoot your own uncle!" Colleen gasped in horror.

"To save you I will," he replied. "Anyway, when I shoot he might back off. If that doesn't work then I will get up and run and decoy him away. When he starts shooting at me you make a run for it."

"Can't you fire some more shots?" Colleen asked.

Michael nodded. "I can try," he replied.

But before he went to fire he felt the pocket where he had placed the packet of bullets. It was empty.

Did I put it in another pocket? he wondered, his stomach lurching with a sickening jolt as the potentially deadly seriousness of the situation struck him.

But he could not find the packet of ammunition. "I... I've lost the bullets!" he croaked, his eyes watering with tears of defeat and misery as he met Colleen's.

The horrifying knowledge that his only option now was to shoot to kill sent him gasping for breath as anxiety gripped his chest.

Miserably he shook his head as he again patted his pockets.

Oh, you careless fool! he berated himself.

He quickly looked over the lip of the gully to see if the packet of bullets was lying nearby. But the desperate hope that it might be somewhere close was quickly dashed, first by nothing being visible in the grass he had run through and then by another shot from Uncle Shaemus which struck the ground just near his face, hurling grit into his eyes and sending a wash of fear though him.

With his heart pounding with terror and with emotions surging through him that set him sweating and trembling Michael ducked back down. Shaking his head he looked at Colleen and was again struck by her beauty and character. The sight stiffened his resolve and he met her eyes again.

"This is only a single shot and I've dropped the packet of bullets somewhere. So you will have to run if I don't kill him."

"Can't you just wound him; shoot him in the leg or something?" Colleen asked, plainly aghast at his plan.

Michael shook his head. He knew Uncle Shaemus better now. "No. This is only a twenty two. A hit will probably only wound him and that is not likely to stop him. If I don't kill him he will just keep moving and shooting. He will really be out for blood then. We don't have a choice. Now get going!"

"Oh Michael!" Colleen cried, her face softening with concern. "You mustn't. He will kill you."

"He will kill us both otherwise. Please Colleen, I love you. Don't argue. Do this for me." he pleaded.

Again Colleen's eyes softened, then tears filled them. She moved over and put her arm around his neck and kissed his cheek, her gratitude and admiration obvious.

"Thanks," she whispered, then kissed him again.

"Go!" Michael whispered, his voice all choked up with emotion. She bit her lip, turned with a sob, and began crawling away.

Michael again raised his head and was appalled to see that Shaemus was now walking into the bush, rifle at the ready and eyes searching.

"God forgive me," Michael prayed, "and keep Colleen safe."

He tensed, ready to shoot. It was the worst moment of his entire life and his whole being revolted at the idea. He nestled the rifle butt into his shoulder and sighted it through the grass.

When he is at that tree, Michael decided, selecting a tree about twenty paces away.

A glance behind showed that Colleen was gone from sight up the bed of the gully. That was something, but Michael knew that, if he missed, it would be a desperate thing for Colleen to try to outrun Shaemus.

He's got a telescopic sight on that rifle, he thought unhappily, remembering times his uncle had tracked a racing kangaroo, then knocked it down at three or four hundred metres.

"It will have to be a head shot," Michael muttered, sick to the very pit of his stomach at the thought.

He moved the foresight till it settled on his uncle's head. By then Michael was shaking with emotion but was very determined.

Colleen must be given the chance to live, no matter what it costs me, he told himself grimly. He began to pray for forgiveness.

Suddenly Uncle Shameus stopped and faced back towards the main road. To Michael's astonishment Shaemus brought his rifle up and fired it at a car that had come into view over the low rise. The reason was instantly clear. It was a police car. The bullet must have hit it because the car skidded violently to a stop. Shameus fired again as it stopped in a cloud of dust in the long grass of the ditch on the other side of the road.

The police! We are saved! Michael thought.

To his relief he saw men in pale blue shirts tumble out of the open doors into the long grass. Shaemus began running back towards the ute, firing from time to time.

From the ditch a policeman began shouting at Shaemus to stop and to drop his gun. Shaemus ignored the commands and kept running, firing and shouting obscenities. The police called again for him to stop but he ignored that as well. Only then did one of the police fire. To Michael's relief the shot missed and Shaemus reached the ute and went to ground. From there he began firing back at the police.

For a couple of minutes Michael could only lie and shake with emotion, his whole being flooded with relief at not having had to shoot. Then he remembered Colleen.

I'd better find her and get her out of here, he decided.

He turned and began scrambling up the gully after Colleen. Behind him he heard a police loud hailer boom out, calling on Shaemus to surrender. The loud hailer was coming from the crest of the low rise but Michael could not see anyone for the trees and the swell of the ground at the base of the large conical hill. Satisfied he was hidden from the police he stood up and began running, eyes searching feverishly for Colleen.

Suddenly she was in front of him. "Here I am Michael," she called. She jumped up and began running with him. Michael aimed for the saddle where the power line went over the crest to the west of the large conical hill. It was easy running, the grass being fairly short and with few logs and no rocks. Fear kept them going till they were well up the slope and winded.

They came to a gasping halt in a small dip near the crest. Michael stopped and looked back, his heart pounding and breath coming in hot gasps. He could no longer see the ute through the tree canopies.

"Safe!" he gasped. "We made it!"

Both flopped down and lay panting till their heart rate slowed and their breathing eased. Michael then got to his knees and looked over the lip to ensure they were really not being followed. A shot and faint shouts back in the direction of the ute indicated that Shaemus was busy with the police. Michael stood up and held out his hands to help Colleen up.

"We'd better keep going," he said.

She took his hands and got to her feet, then stood holding his hands and looking into his eyes.

"That was a very brave thing you did," she said.

"I would do anything for you," Michael replied. "I think you are the most wonderful girl I have ever met."

At that Colleen stepped forward and put her arms around his neck. Her eyes filled with tears and she kissed him gently on the cheek. Michael was overcome by a surge of emotion. He let the rifle slip to the ground and hugged her to him, then kissed her on the lips. She responded, holding him tightly and kissing with a fire Michael had never experienced.

After a minute they parted. Michael continued to hold her. His eyes explored hers. Then bitterness at what might have been welled up. He let her go and stepped back. "I'm sorry. I love you but I have no right to involve you in my life."

"Why not?" Colleen asked.

"Because I am a murderer. Because I am going to go to jail. Because I have no future to offer you," he said.

They were both silent for a minute while Colleen considered this. "You really are a good man," she said at last.

"You are the sort of girl I want to marry," Michael said. "But I have made a real mess of everything."

"You haven't," Colleen replied. "You just found yourself dragged into something by your family. Anyway, I don't want to get married for a few years yet. I want to do my Nursing Degree at university, then work for two or three years. I plan to start having my babies when I am about twenty three or four."

"That's nice to think about," Michael replied, trying to hide his misery by being light-hearted.

"What is?" Colleen asked.

"Helping you make babies."

Colleen snorted and blushed, but then she smiled. "You men! That's all you can think about."

"When we are with a girl as lovely as you it's hard to think of anything else," Michael replied. But then his self-control failed and his eyes filled with tears. What a wonderful dream! What a hopeless situation! "I can't ever ask you. It wouldn't be fair. You would not want to be married to a criminal. Besides, it wouldn't be fair to the kids."

"I might," Colleen replied. She stepped forward and kissed him again, then gently wiped his tears. "But that's not a promise," she whispered. She then stepped back. "We can see how things are when you come out of jail. You can look me up if you want. But I have to add I won't be waiting for you. If I meet someone else I fall in love with then that will be that."

"That's fair," Michael replied, his heart leaping with hope. "I can't ask you to wait for me."

"You might not even go to jail," Colleen said.

She bent down and picked up the rifle. For a moment Michael wondered if he had just made a real fool of himself, that she had tricked him and was going to arrest him. But she did not look at him but instead skilfully and carefully ejected the bullet and slipped it into her pocket. Then she closed the bolt and snicked on the safety catch.

"Always handle rifles safely," she lectured him, indicating the safety catch. She then handed the rifle back to him. "Now come on, let's find the police."

Smiling she turned and started walking up the hill. Michael went with her, his heart much lighter.

Chapter 30

BELOW THE LOOKOUT

When Michael and Colleen crossed the saddle all Michael initially saw was bush stretching away into the distance, and the midday heat haze shimmering along the power line clearing. Then, as they picked their way through long grass down the vehicle track under the power line he saw an irrigation canal full of water. The canal started near the base of the slope and extended off away from him and around the bottom of the hills to the left.

It wasn't until they came further around the hill that the main road came back into view, then the buildings of the pump station. For the first hundred metres the pair aimed for them, hoping there might be a phone there. Then they saw the vehicles stopped on the road over to their right, just back from the crest of the low rise.

"Over there," Michael said, indicating where a police car and two ordinary cars were stopped beside the road.

Three police were visible, one walking back along the road to stop traffic and to urge the people from the cars to go back.

As Michael and Colleen walked across the open, grassy lower slopes on the north side of the conical hill they saw two vans with TV logos on their sides come racing along from the north. The vans were waved down by the policeman on the road and pulled up at the rear of the line of vehicles. TV crews spilled out with cameras and other equipment. One man climbed onto the roof of his van and began erecting a satellite transmission dish.

"We are going to be in the 6 o'clock news," Colleen observed. "Major Wickham always said that if we caused that he wouldn't be happy."

"It will be world news," Michael added gloomily. He had no desire to be the centre of such attention and infamy.

The pair were 50 paces from the road by then. Colleen said, "You'd better be careful with that gun Michael. You don't want to be shot by mistake."

"Yes, you are right," Michael agreed.

He raised his hands into the air, the rifle held horizontally at the point of balance in his left hand. It was only then that he noticed one of the TV newsmen pointing to them. The look on the policeman's face when he turned to follow the newsman's pointing finger almost made Michael laugh out loud it looked so comical.

He heard the policeman say, "Shit! Where did they come from?"

The policeman whipped out his pistol and dived behind a car. This precipitated a mad scramble by the watching civilians and TV people as they also took cover. Channel 9 and Channel 10, Michael noted.

"Put the gun down and come over here," shouted the policeman. He then yelled to his boss, who was standing up at the crest, loud hailer in hand. "Hey Sarge! We got some back here."

Michael placed the rifle in the grass and continued walking. Colleen stayed with him. "It will be alright. I will tell them what you did."

"Thanks," Michael answered.

He felt tired now, rather than scared, but knew he could not relax just yet. The situation was a long way from being resolved. The pair had to roll under another barbed wire fence in long grass and then both he and Colleen lay down on the mowed verge. Two policemen, one the sergeant, came running back down the road, guns at the ready. As the two policemen began searching them a helicopter arrived overhead and began circling: TV news, Channel 7, Michael observed.

Having been searched Michael was told to get up. Colleen stood beside him and dusted the grass off herself. The newsmen came out of cover to get pictures.

"Who are you? Are you one of the cadets?" the sergeant asked.

"My name is Michael O'Malley and I came with the IRA men," Michael replied.

Colleen stepped forward. "He's not a terrorist. He has been helping me to escape," she added. "He saved my life. He is a real hero."

The sergeant looked doubtful. He studied her camouflage uniform.

"Oh yeah? And who are you? Are you a cadet?" he asked.

Colleen nodded and gave her name and explained the situation. The sergeant obviously did not know whether to have Michael handcuffed or not. Finally he decided he would. Michael made no protest. He was now reconciled to the humiliations to come.

"Sit him in the car," the sergeant said to the constable beside him.

"Wait!" Michael said. "I can still help you. I know all the gang. Most of them are from my family. I can help you talk to them."

"How many are there? Are there any more round the back of that hill?" the sergeant asked.

"Not that we saw," Michael replied. "There are only six of them here, plus the two that left earlier."

He gave their names and details, then began describing how Kevin had been shot and then taken to a doctor known to the gang.

Colleen then asked, "How did you know to come? Who told you we were in trouble?"

The sergeant grinned. "We got a phone call from one of your girls, Chloe someone or other," he said. "She rang up from the homestead at 'Byrne Valley'. Apparently she had swum the Burdekin to reach them and the landowner told us she had almost no clothes on."

"That would be Chloe!" Colleen replied. She did not know quite how to react, partly pleased, partly annoyed.

The policemen all smiled and that did annoy Colleen. She stood in silence, wondering how she felt about a lot of things, how she felt about Michael in particular. Michael was asked what weapons and communications the gun men had. He proceeded to give a highly detailed description of each man and how he was armed.

While he was doing this another helicopter arrived, a blue and white POLAIR. It landed at the turn-off to the pump station and three more police got out, one a senior officer and the other two dressed in dark blue with helmets, bullet proof vests and automatic rifles with telescopic sights. The sight of them made Michael feel sick with dread. The helicopter then lifted off and flew southwards following the river.

The senior officer arrived and introduced himself as an Inspector. He asked what was going on and the situation had to be explained to him. The sergeant, Michael and Colleen did this. While they were talking more and more vehicles kept arriving, keeping the constable busy controlling the growing crowd. A road block was set up and only the media people were allowed to stay near them.

Two coaches arrived. Colleen gestured to them. "Here are the army coaches to take us home. They might have a bit of a wait."

"Yes, I'd better inform the army. Hello, what's going on there?" the Inspector said, looking back to the end of the line of cars.

Michael glanced that way and saw a large woman trying to push past the policeman. "Mum! That's my mum! Let her past," he cried.

The Inspector called out and Mrs O'Malley was allowed past. She hurried up to where they stood. She went to embrace Michael but was stopped by another policeman. "Oh Michael!" she wailed, "What have you done? What's going on?"

"Who are you please?" asked the Inspector.

"Mrs Eileen O'Malley," she replied. "Oh please tell me what has happened! Oh, I just knew it was something bad."

Michael was astonished to see his mother. *She has come all the way from Mount Isa to try to find us,* he thought.

"How did you know where to come Mum?" he asked.

"I just knew something was up when your father got all these phone calls from his old cronies and from Shaemus on Saturday morning. I overheard him say something about the newspaper. Your father then told me he had to go to Townsville urgently on business but was vague about why. He left within the hour. I didn't have a paper, so had to go and get one," Mrs O'Malley explained.

She bit her lip and was silent for a moment then said, "The moment I saw the photo of the British cadets with Major Grogan I just knew. But then it took me quite a time to get organised. I had to wait till this morning for the next flight, then had to hire a car in Townsville, and then find out where you were. I'm obviously too late aren't I? What has happened?"

Michael told his mother what had taken place. As he talked he was torn by the looks of anguish that kept crossing her face. When he told her that Major Grogan and two others had been shot she cried aloud and began to weep.

"Oh Shaemus! You stupid bloody man! What a thing to do after all these years!" she cried.

"So there are three badly wounded people in there?" the Inspector asked.

Colleen answered that. She took out her map and showed him the layout. He looked very thoughtful and then took a radio and began talking to the helicopter, then to a higher HQ somewhere else. Michael stood in the sun and slowly wilted in the heat. He felt exhausted and had to ask for a drink. Colleen gave him one.

There was a sudden flurry of shots. Michael flinched as several cracked overhead. At least one ricocheted off a rock up on the hillside with a fearful whine, making them all crouch for cover.

"What's going on?" the Inspector yelled to the police in black.

One of them pointed along the railway. "That one's crossed the road and is now in the long grass beside the railway sir. I think he's moving back towards the end of the hill," he called.

"Right, follow up, but don't take any chances," the Inspector ordered.

Mrs O'Malley looked fearfully along the road. "Who? Who are they shooting at?" she cried.

Michael answered. "Uncle Shaemus. He was trying to catch us."

"Oh my God! Please let me talk to him. I might be able to get him to surrender," Mrs O'Malley said.

The Inspector nodded. "Right, come with us then," he agreed.

He then turned to give orders to three more police who had just arrived. They went running off through the long grass to the railway and then across behind the small conical hill to the riverbank. Two more police went into the bush on the right to the base of the big conical hill.

By then the police in black had vanished forward over the crest. The sergeant reported that a road block was now in position at the Landers Creek Bridge and that all traffic had been stopped. He had no sooner said this than the blare of a locomotive's horn sounded and a diesel loco appeared around the bend of the hill. The sergeant looked foolish.

"Bloody hell! A train! I forgot about the railway," he said.

The Inspector glared at him and the sergeant hurried to radio further instructions. The train went rattling past northwards, the driver and his offsider staring at them curiously.

The two helicopters continued to circle. The police helicopter was radioing a stream of information to the Inspector but Michael could only hear snippets of the messages. He gained the impression that it was reporting two men with guns on the railway below the Lookout.

After another ten minutes the Inspector said, "Right, our people are at the next bend and up on the hill. We will go forward to the bend. Get in those cars."

Michael, his mother and Colleen were placed in one of the police cars and driven forward. The TV crews came driving and running forward after them but all the other people were held back behind the low rise. As the cars reached the bend where the road began to climb towards the end of the hill they suddenly pulled over, in response to crackling warnings over the radio. Michael heard the thump of rifle shots, the sound muffled by the end of the hill.

The Inspector got out of the car in front of them and came back to them. "We had better walk from here. The two men are shooting at our people from just around the bend."

Colleen bit her lip. "Can you rescue Captain Hamilton please sir? He is tied up in the army Land Rover parked at the Lookout," she asked.

"Where is that? Describe it to me," the Inspector demanded.

Colleen did so. As Michael climbed awkwardly out of the car the Inspector gave more instructions over the radio. Then, as they started walking forward he said, "One of the men has surrendered. He is walking this way along the railway line."

"That will be Rory," Michael said. He just knew it wouldn't be Shaemus.

He was right. A few minutes later a handcuffed Rory was led out of the long grass beside the railway by two armed policemen. As he went past he gave Michael a very malevolent look but said nothing.

The Inspector ordered Rory to be placed under guard in the car they had just left. He questioned Rory for a couple of minutes but obviously got no satisfaction because he re-joined them looking annoyed. They then continued walking slowly forward, the newsmen being held back by a grumpy senior constable.

When they reached the point where the road began to climb away from the railway, Colleen pointed to the gravel road leading up to Cornford Lookout, and said, "If you go up to the Lookout you will have trouble getting down to the river or railway. There is a very deep cutting with steep sides. If you want to get down to the river you must get onto the railway here."

"The Lookout is just up there?" the Inspector asked.

"Yes sir."

The Inspector spoke on the radio while staring up the hill. He then spoke to two police wearing bullet proof vests over their blue shirts. They nodded and edged forward along the side of the road, their automatic rifles at the ready. The group then made their way through the fence to the railway. Colleen wriggled under quickly as she had been taught, feet first and on her back, and stood up. Michael had to lie down and wriggle under, then roll onto his back, getting a few scratches in the process. Colleen helped him to his feet, earning a curious glance from his mother.

That part of the railway was a shallow cutting which led to a bench-cut section just before it curved into the deep cutting. From where they were, they could not see the riverbed. Michael could see the two men in black crawling up the end of the cutting onto the knoll between it and the riverbed. The sight chilled him. The men looked so calm and efficient that he feared for his uncle and family.

"We can safely move a bit further along I think," the Inspector said.

There were still two police with them and one led the way, cautiously peeking over the grass every few steps. The other brought up the rear. Michael walked slowly along and experienced real difficulty keeping his balance. He had not realised how much he needed his hands and arms for balance. Colleen noted him stagger several times so she helped by walking beside him and holding his arm.

The Inspector listened to his radio, then pointed up the steep side of the cut on their right. "The captain is alright. They have rescued him and set him free," he said.

"Oh thank heavens for that!" Colleen said.

The group had now reached the point where they could see down onto the grassy area of the old highway and beyond to the riverbed and island. One of the policemen waved them down.

"No further please sir, the two men are just down there."

He pointed further along the slope to the right. Michael could not see anyone but was puzzled. Two men? Who was the other: Liam or Murty?

At that moment there were shots and Michael saw the two men in black spring up and throw themselves over the crest to lie flat on top, facing back to their right rear towards the cutting. There were more shots and shouting and then the shooting stopped.

"Some of them in the cutting," Colleen said.

Michael had dropped to his knees and crouched against the low bank Colleen pressed herself against him. He was more concerned about his mother, who was standing waving her arms and crying out to stop it.

"Mum! Get down!" Michael shouted.

To his relief she moved to bend down with a lot of puffing and wheezing. There was more shouting and the Inspector called loudly to the two men in black, "Hold your fire! Don't shoot! We will negotiate."

Negotiate? Michael thought. *That means hostages.*

He had already deduced that the people coming through the cutting almost certainly had to be either his father or his brothers.

That question was answered a few seconds later when a group of people came shuffling through the cutting in a huddle. They were over against the outside cliff and were looking up. As he saw who it was Michael's heart sank. It was his father and brothers, three of the male cadet officers and the ginger haired female cadet under officer. The only cheering thing about the scene was that Dylan was with them.

They must have swapped him for those other cadets, Michael decided.

He saw that Liam and his father were both crouched behind the male cadet officers and had their guns pointed at the officer's backs. At that moment they saw the group on the railway and came to a standstill.

"Get out of the way," Liam shouted. "Let us go or we will kill some of these hostages."

At that Mrs O'Malley stood up and strode forward, ignoring the attempts by the crouching police to restrain her.

"Oh no you won't!" she roared. "No son of mine is going to turn into a murderer! Now let those people go at once!"

Despite the deadly potential of the situation Michael had to smile at the reaction of his father and brothers. They goggled, then looked sheepish.

Mrs O'Malley placed her hands on her hips. "Let them go I said! And put those stupid guns down before someone gets hurt," she commanded.

"Mum! But... but... but Mum!" Liam began.

Patrick also tried to argue. "Stay out of the way you silly woman. We are going to get out of here."

At that she exploded. "Don't you silly woman me you stupid man Patrick O'Malley! I don't know why I married you. You've got concrete between the ears instead of brains. Is this how you want your sons to end their lives? Now stop being silly and put that gun down."

"No! We are going to get out of here," Patrick shouted back. He looked and sounded quite desperate. He turned to the Inspector. "Get your men away from here or I will shoot a hostage."

At that Michael cried out in protest. "Oh dad! Don't do it! This is all wrong. Give it up."

Patrick glared at him. "You, you bloody traitor! Shut your gob!"

The accusation burned, but Michael persisted. "I will not be quiet! You promised me that no-one would get hurt. You lied to me!"

At that Patrick swore and shook his head. He then looked at Michael and answered, "I'm sorry. That wasn't part of my plan. I don't know why Shaemus had to go and shoot those people."

"For revenge of course!" Mrs O'Malley cried. She was visibly distressed. "Oh Patrick! Please surrender before anyone else gets hurt."

Patrick wasn't mollified. If anything his anger appeared to increase. "Bugger Shaemus! It was none of his business. He may have had some reason for wanting to kill Grogan, but those other two were mine."

"Ours," Liam added. He also looked very determined and had his gun pressed against the base of the solid lieutenant's skull.

"Oh no!" Mrs O'Malley cried. "None of you has any right to take such revenge. Now please give up."

"She was our sister mum," Liam shouted.

Michael saw his mother shake her head and whimper. "You don't know the whole story," she said. Tears were now pouring down her face.

"Yes we do!" Liam shouted. "Those bloody Poms shot our little sister for no reason."

At that Mrs O'Malley cried out in anguish and shook her head vigorously. "No. They didn't know the baby was in the car."

"But they still had no reason to ambush you," Liam persisted.

"They didn't!" Mrs O'Malley cried. She was now wracked by sobs and could hardly speak. Michael was moved to hug her but was restrained by the policeman and his handcuffs.

"So what happened?" Liam demanded.

There was silence for a moment. Michael tensed, sensing that this was a critical moment in his life. His father ended it. He had a peculiar look on his face. "Yes Eileen, what really happened?"

Still Mrs O'Malley did not reply. Instead she stood sobbing. It was Dylan who spoke next.

"Those British cadets have a different story, Dad."

Liam reacted to that. "Them! You wouldn't believe them! They would just lie to cover their crimes!"

Dylan shook his head and looked doubtful. "There was one of them there who said that Shaemus shot his father at a road block. He thought he was the one who should have revenge."

"He may have," Liam snarled, "But that would be against Uncle Shaemus for some other thing."

Dylan shook his head and briefly met Michael's eyes. He looked very unsure and unhappy. "No. It was when Bridie was shot. They said that the car was being used as a getaway vehicle after some bomb attack. They claim it was stopped at a roadblock. That major who Shaemus shot, Grogan, apparently looked into the car and recognized Shaemus. They say that Shaemus had a gun and that he shot Major Grogan and then the lieutenant next him, that British cadet's father. That was when the soldiers opened fire, as the car drove away."

"Lies!" Liam cried.

But it was Patrick who spoke next. He looked suddenly old and drawn. "Tell me Eileen, was that what happened? Was Shaemus in the car with you?"

Michael felt his heart being squeezed by emotion as he realized that there was real tension between his mother and father. After a moment his mother nodded. She stood sobbing and put her arms up, then dropped them to her side.

"Tell me what really happened then," Patrick demanded.

"Only if you promise to surrender and let these people go unharmed. I've got enough blood on my conscience as it is," Mrs O'Malley replied.

There was a more tense silence, before Liam cried, "Don't do it dad! We can get Uncle Shaemus and get away."

"Be quiet boy!" Patrick replied. "I'm not sure I want to, if what I suspect is true." He faced Mrs O'Malley and said, "Well woman, what really happened? Was Shaemus in the car?"

Mrs O'Malley nodded. "Yes," she whispered. Then she said, "Promise me you will give up."

"Yes, now tell me the truth," Patrick cried.

He looked very distressed and Michael knew that some long-standing issue between his parents was involved.

Chapter 31

MOMENT OF TRUTH

After a moment Mrs O'Malley sighed, then said, "Shaemus wanted to get a bomb through the checkpoints to try to kill that Reverend Paxton. And he needed a getaway car. So he asked me to help. I took Bridie for a drive, then met Shaemus. We talked, then I got the baby basket out and Shaemus placed the bomb under the bedclothes. I put baby Bridie in on top and tucked her in. We reasoned that the British soldiers or police wouldn't search under a baby."

Michael was aghast. So obviously was his father for Patrick cried out in horrified anger, "You tell me you that you risked our baby by putting her in the same basket as a bomb! How could you do it woman? You had no right to risk my daughter without asking me."

"She wasn't your daughter," Mrs O'Malley whispered.

"Eh? Not my daughter! What are you saying woman?" Patrick cried.

"She was Shaemus's daughter," Mrs O'Malley replied.

For a moment there was stunned silence. Michael stared at his parents in shock, hoping that what he was hearing wasn't true, yet knowing deep down that it must be.

His father found his voice after a minute. "You are telling me that Bridie was not my little girl? I don't believe you."

To Michael's surprise it was Dylan who spoke up. He stared accusingly at their mother. "That would explain something that has really been troubling me. When Shaemus shot one of those British cadets he shouted, 'This is for my little girl!' I didn't know what he meant. It didn't make sense. Now it does."

A look of great anguish crossed Patrick's face as he assimilated this. Then he faced Mrs O'Malley.

"So my suspicions were right. You and Shaemus were having an affair?"

"Yes we were!" Mrs O'Malley cried defiantly. "You were so busy with your bloody politics and work you never had any time for me! I was just a bloody convenience, someone to do the cooking and washing! You didn't love me then, and you don't love me now. Shaemus did love me and he gave me what I needed; a bit of care and attention."

"But you stayed with me," Patrick replied, shaking his head in pain.

"Only because of the children and my marriage vows," Mrs O'Malley replied.

"These are my sons?" Patrick asked in a hoarse whisper, indicating the boys beside him.

"Yes!" Mrs O'Malley snapped, much to Michael's relief.

He was now feeling very distressed himself, as well as ashamed that all this was being said in front of strangers. But it was also now clear to him why Uncle Shaemus had acted the way he did.

He must have been nursing that grudge all these years and just snapped when he saw all those British officers and cadets together, he thought.

Mrs O'Malley shrugged. "I'm sorry. It was a long time ago, and it's been over just as long, but that is the truth. So that is how Shaemus and baby Bridie both came to be in the car with me. Shaemus left his gun in my car and was able to pass through being searched at the check points with no difficulty. I went a different way with Bridie and no-body even bothered me. We were right, who suspects a mother with a live baby?"

She went on, "We met at the church and I gave him the bomb, then walked back to the car with Bridie. Shaemus planted the bomb, then walked back to meet me."

At that stage Mrs O'Malley faltered and burst into tears. She sobbed for a while, then wiped her eyes and went on.

"But something went wrong. The bomb went off early. Instead of killing the Protestant leaders it killed those poor women and children who were there for church! Oh God! You have no idea how I have suffered over that! I have even thought it was God's punishment that I should lose my little baby in payment for such a dreadful crime!"

Once again there was shocked silence. The images of the horrible story gripped them all. Mrs O'Malley went on, "We drove off but ran into the roadblock. It would have been no problem if that major hadn't been there, but he recognised Shaemus. So Shaemus shot him, then he shot the officer standing next to him. He shot the lieutenant because he had a gun. I didn't even know Shaemus had taken the gun out till he fired it."

"The bloody fool!" Patrick cried. Then he bit his lip and swore before glaring at Mrs O'Malley. "So I've been believing a lie all these years! You deceitful creature! I should shoot you!"

Michael felt his blood go cold as his father turned his gun to point it at his mother. "Dad! No!" he cried, but was ignored.

Mrs O'Malley nodded. "Yes, I deserve it. It is time I paid for my sins. The wages of sin is death it says in the Good Book."

But Patrick shook his head sadly and lowered his head. "No. You are the boys' mother. They might need you." He now lowered the gun and stood, shoulders bowed in defeat.

Michael sighed with relief but was still all choked up with conflicting emotions. His mother now strode over to Patrick and put out her hand. He scowled but handed his gun to her. She tossed it into the drain on the other side of the railway. She then turned to Liam.

"And you, Liam!"

Liam sighed and stood up, dropping the gun. "Yes Mum!" he muttered, plainly disgusted with the turn of events.

Mrs O'Malley then proceeded to get stuck into Patrick. "Oh you silly man! What were you thinking about! Wanting revenge after all these years! And sneaking away after telling me fibs about urgent business in Townsville! Why, I wouldn't have minded so much if you'd been sneaking off to meet some fancy woman! And as for dragging my little boys into this to help you with your dirty work! You should be ashamed of yourself! I should box your ears. I will give you a good talking to about this later. Now turn around the lot of you and let the police handcuff you, you stupid boys!"

To Michael's relief they did as they were told. The two constables ran forward to search and handcuff and the Inspector moved up with them. As they worked one of the policemen in black moved into a kneeling position so he could see down into the cutting better.

Crack!

A shot rang out and the policeman in black was knocked flat. Only the strong arm of his partner prevented him from plummeting head first into the cutting.

The bullet had been fired from behind and below the policeman, from somewhere on the top of the riverbank. The police up at the Lookout responded at once with a fusillade of shots. Michael and Colleen huddled together and he wished he could put his arm around her. All the people in the cutting threw themselves flat. Michael saw the police in black both wriggle around and begin firing down the slope, using short, savage bursts from their ugly looking automatic weapons. The policeman had obviously been saved by his bullet proof jacket.

"Got him!" cried a voice.

There were more shots while Michael nearly vomited with apprehension. Got who? Uncle Shaemus? He hoped not.

"Cease fire!" shouted a voice down to the left somewhere. After several attempts the command was obeyed.

"Where's he gone?" called another unseen policeman.

"He went over the bank. He's dropped his rifle," called a voice from up at the Lookout.

Michael craned to look but could see no-one. The police helicopter came circling around again and there was the constant chatter of radios.

The Inspector shouted, "I want him alive. Fire only in self-defence or to save someone else."

"Sir, the chopper reports there are three people down on the riverbank. Two are men with green jackets and the other appears to be a girl. She is being held hostage. One of the men is hurt and the other is bandaging his arm. Both have weapons. The injured man has a pistol which he is aiming at the girl. The other man has a rifle."

Has Shaemus been hit, Michael wondered. *But who is the girl?*

*****

Colleen crouched beside the fence and tried to calm down. Listening to the O'Malley's had distressed her and her overwrought emotions now manifested themselves in a severe bout of trembling.

As she calmed herself, she watched the Inspector came back along the railway to where she and Michael crouched. The Inspector called loudly, "All you people are to stay here while we find out what is going on."

But Colleen was gripped by anxiety. "What about the British cadets who have been shot? We must get a doctor to them," she called back.

"Don't worry, we've got the ambulances just back there and a helicopter is on stand-by," the Inspector replied. "As soon as we have dealt with these fellows they can move in."

Colleen shook her head. "That is not good enough. They were shot at about nine O'clock and it is now nearly one. That is four hours. We must get them out."

"It is too risky while those men are down in the riverbed," the Inspector replied.

"No it isn't!" Colleen flared. "If these three men are here then there are none of them at the other end of Snake Gully. We can get in that way. I can show you the way."

At that Major Wickham spoke up. "You are right Colleen, but you won't go. Lt Barker can show them the way."

The Inspector needed convincing but Major Wickham became very angry. "It will be safe. Listen, we've been doing bivouacs here for years. We know every track and gully. Now organise the medics and let's get them in there. If need be we can carry the casualties out the other way."

At this the Inspector relented and used his radio to start organising things. He called two policemen down from the hill above the Lookout to go with the rescue team and then spoke to the ambulance on his mobile phone.

Major Wickham turned to the officers. "Ash, you take the stretcher party and cut across Deep Creek to Snake Gully as soon as you can get down off the railway. Duncan, you lead the vehicle around to the gate to this paddock and show them the way in. They should be able to drive almost to where the track down into Snake Gully starts. Barbara, you stay with me and for a start check on young Colleen here. Now get moving!"

They moved. Lt Barker went hurrying off along the railway with two police while Lt Forster hurried back along the railway towards the cars. As he passed Colleen he gave her a smile.

"Well done," he said.

Colleen tried to smile in response but was too anxious about who the men had as a hostage. Barbara joined them, looking a bit worn. "Who have they got as a hostage Barbara?" Colleen asked.

"I don't know. Did you call the ambulance?"

"No. They were here by the time we got over the hill," Colleen replied. She then shuddered at the memory of those terrifying minutes when she and Michael were being shot at by Shaemus.

Major Wickham moved over and crouched beside her, giving Michael a glare as he did. "Who called them then?" he asked.

"Chloe," Colleen replied. "Apparently she swam the river to the 'Byrne Valley' homestead and rang from there."

"Swam the river!" Major Wickham cried, plainly aghast at the risk she had taken. "The silly girl! She's lucky she didn't get taken by a crocodile."

Colleen could not bring herself to mention that Chloe had probably performed this feat apparently nude. She did not want to get her into more trouble. Instead she said: "I heard she swam some mangrove river full of crocodiles on some island out in the Pacific to rescue some president."

Major Wickham harrumphed and Barbara nodded and said: "Yes, she did. I was there. She saved me and a couple of others as well."

Then she gave a wry grin and said, "I'll bet she took a few clothes off again."

The Inspector answered that. "Yes, I'm told she arrived there nearly as naked as Eve. All she had on was a very skimpy bikini."

"Bloody Chloe!" Major Wickham cried in exasperation. "But thank God she made it."

Colleen could only add 'amen' to that. She was starting to relax and to wilt in the heat. What distressed her most was the look on Michael's face as he watched his father and brothers being seated against the side of the cutting. His mother stayed talking to the others and looked very upset. A policeman stood guard over the group.

"Back off you buggers!" snapped Major Wickham.

Colleen glanced to see who he was speaking to and saw a group of TV cameramen. She turned her back on them and wished it was all over. The helicopters kept clattering and buzzing overhead, adding to her annoyance.

The group remained seated in the cutting for another ten minutes while one of the policemen tried to persuade the gunmen to surrender. Colleen began to sag with weariness and kept licking her lips. She was very thirsty but did not want to leave till it was all over.

The relative silence was shattered by a shot down on the riverbank to the left.

Oh no! she thought. *Someone has been shot.*

She stood up and joined the others in peering over the lip of the cutting, almost jostled off her feet by the TV people. Michael struggled up beside her, his face deathly pale.

"Christ, I hate this!" he muttered. "What a bloody mess!"

They stood and waited, but there was just that one shot. Then voices began calling, even further to the left. The Inspector listened to his radio and said, "We have got another one. He has surrendered."

"Who is he?" Michael asked.

"Murty O'Reilly," the Inspector replied.

"Ask him who the hostage is please," Major Wickham asked.

He had been using the Inspector's mobile phone to contact the army and their school principal and looked very distressed.

The Inspector sent the query by radio. The answer came back in a few seconds. "Chloe," he said.

At that Barbara cried out with dismay. "Oh no! How did those mongrels catch her? She reached safety."

Colleen joined her, anxiety making her very agitated. "Oh do something please. You must save her."

"We are trying," the Inspector replied, "but Shaemus O'Malley is threatening to shoot her if anyone comes near them."

Mrs O'Malley had been listening. She came over. "Let me try please Inspector. He might listen to me."

Colleen bit her lip in anxiety and wondered what she could do. As she did she heard a cry and spun round to look.

"There she is!"

Half way across the bare open sand between the bottom of the hill and the tree-covered 'island' were Chloe and Shaemus. Even at two hundred metres Colleen could clearly see that Chloe was almost nude. The bikini that she wore was just two tiny triangles of cloth at the top and a single small triangle at the bottom. It was secured by thin cords. Her buttocks appeared bare, with just a thin cord at the back. Shaemus was standing gripping her by the hair and using her as a shield. He was edging backwards across the sand away from them, crouching behind her so that no sniper could risk shooting. He had a pistol pressed into the small of her back.

"Oh my God!" Mrs O'Malley cried.

She began to scramble through the fence. In the process she snagged her dress and scratched her legs but she ignored this. She also ignored calls from Michael to stay under cover and shook off the hand of the Inspector.

The Inspector was not so easily put off. He grabbed her again and dragged her back.

"Let her go, you filthy bloody copper!" Patrick shouted, getting to his feet.

"Shut up dad! Mum, stay here please!" Michael cried.

"Don't you tell me to shut up, boy," Patrick yelled. "You bloody traitor!"

"Be quiet!" Mrs O'Malley screamed. "Don't you call your son names like that Patrick."

"He's not my son anymore!" Patrick shouted, his face livid.

Colleen glanced at Michael and saw him blanch. A look of utter desolation flickered across his eyes.

Oh poor Michael! He was damned if he did and damned if he didn't, she thought. But in her heart she was sure he had made the right decision.

Mrs O'Malley flared into anger also. "If that is the selfish way you think then I am not your wife anymore either!"

She was very distressed now but gave up her attempt to get through the fence. She stared down her angry husband and snapped at him to shut up. To Colleen's relief he did.

Colleen helped Michael up. A policeman gripped Michael and held him but did not stop him standing to watch. By then everyone else was lining the edge of the cutting and watching as well. The newsmen had their cameras going and were busy transmitting live broadcasts. Patrick, Liam and Dylan were allowed by their guard to join the group watching.

Colleen bit her knuckle in anxiety as she watched. The Inspector kept hold of Mrs O'Malley and tried to calm her. Major Wickham stood beside them, clenching and unclenching his hands in frustrated anxiety. Movement over to the right caused Colleen's heart to skip with icy dread. It was the two policemen in black moving down to get a better fire position.

"Shaemus!" Mrs O'Malley shouted. "Shaemus, it's me, Eileen."

Shaemus heard her and Colleen saw his head turn in her direction.

Mrs O'Malley yelled again, "Shaemus, let the girl go please."

"No! She is my passport out of here," Shaemus shouted back.

"She hasn't done anything to you. Let her go," Mrs O'Malley called.

"Yes she has, the slut! She captured Dylan, then she went across the river and called the bloody cops," Shaemus yelled angrily back.

"She doesn't deserve being shot! That isn't right," Mrs O'Malley cried.

"She does! She's just a disgusting whore! Look at her! Running around like a harlot!" Shaemus screamed.

Barbara shook her head and muttered, "He's got a problem with women that one."

Mrs O'Malley shook her head. Sadly she said, "No, the woman he loves is married to someone else." She then turned back to Shaemus. "Shaemus, it's too late for that now. It's over. You've got your bloody revenge, now please, for my sake, let the girl go and give yourself up."

"It isn't over!" Shaemus screamed. "Ireland still isn't united and isn't free."

"He's off his bloody rocker," a constable commented.

Shaemus continued to edge backwards. The watchers stood transfixed at the potential tragedy of it. Mrs O'Malley tried again but Shaemus ignored her.

"You had your chance Eileen," he shouted back. He then growled at Chloe. "Stop squirming and walk faster, you slut!"

They did not hear what Chloe said back to him but it sparked an explosion. Shaemus let go of her hair and struck at her head with his left hand. "Don't you call me a murdering coward who hides behind women you foul mouthed trollop!" he screamed.

"I wish she hadn't done that," Michael muttered in anguish. "I think he's going to shoot."

"He will regret that he let her go," Barbara added. "He doesn't realise that his prisoner is Chloe the Warrior Princess."

Shaemus whacked the side of Chloe's head a second time with his hand. She tried to protect herself and was hit a third time. And this time she moved. Moving so fast it was hard to tell what actually happened she spun and grabbed the hand with the gun with her left hand and used her right foot to kick back and up to hit Shaemus in the testicles. He gasped in agony and began to double up. In a blur of rapid motion Chloe swung round, gripping his right wrist with both hands and twisting his arm as she did. Next moment Shaemus went flying through the air. Shaemus landed on his face on the sand. In a flash Chloe pounced. Still gripping his arm, which was now hard up behind him she knelt on him. Then she twisted his right arm harder up behind his back.

"Let go the gun or I will break your arm!" she warned.

Shaemus screamed a flood of obscenities and tried to heave her off.

"Don't swear in the presence of ladies, you bad-mannered oaf!" Chloe snapped. "Now stop struggling or you will get hurt."

In response Shaemus shouted more obscenities. "You aren't a lady, you slut!"

He then gave a convulsive heave and tried to throw Chloe off. A moment later he gave a piercing scream and Colleen saw that Chloe had twisted his arm even more.

"Oh my God! She has broken his arm!" Mrs O'Malley cried.

"Well, she did warn him," Major Wickham said.

Chloe now grabbed at Shaemus's little finger with her right hand. "Let go of the gun or I will break your finger," she warned. There was another scream of agony from Shaemus and they saw the gun drop onto the sand.

"He's a slow learner that one," the Inspector commented.

Chloe reached over and picked the gun up, then tossed it further away. She then tightened her grip.

"Come on!" Barbara cried. "She's got him! Help her!" She dropped and rolled under the fence.

"Stop here!" shouted the Inspector but Barbara ignored him.

"Come on!" Major Wickham shouted.

He also rolled under the fence and began racing down the slope, followed by the others.

Chapter 32

CHLOE'S CLOTHES

Barbara ignored further shouts from the Inspector to come back. She ran down the grassy slope as fast as she dared, dimly aware that others were running behind her. Ahead on her left she saw the two policemen in black dashing forward. They vanished over the edge of the steep bank as Barbara reached the flat area where the old highway ran along to the washed away bridge.

At this point, Barbara lost sight of Chloe and Shaemus because of the ground. Anxiety spurred her to run even faster and she reached the top of the steep bank at full tilt and nearly fell as she went over it. Even so, she did not slow down. By some nimble footwork she avoided a fall and continued on down the slope, half running, half slithering and jumping.

To her relief she saw that Chloe was still kneeling astride Shaemus, whose arm remained twisted firmly up behind his back, despite groans and pleas for her to let go. By then the two policemen were half way down the bank. Off to the right, running across the open sand from the mouth of Snake Gully, Barbara saw four figures in dark British Army camouflage running towards Chloe. One had a rifle and she recognized him as the WO2 named George. The others were Charles, Cecil and Adelaide.

Near the bottom Barbara stumbled. She fell and rolled the last three metres to the bottom, ending on her back on the sand. In an instant she scrambled to her feet, ignoring the bumps and dust. As she ran on across the sand, she saw that the two policemen had reached Chloe and Shaemus.

"Thank God! She is safe!" Barbara gasped.

The soft sand slowed her and the effort winded her but Barbara did not stop running till she reached them. The four British cadets arrived at the same moment. It was an astonishing sight. Chloe, almost totally naked and apparently quite oblivious to it, still knelt astride Shaemus,. Barbara could not help taking in the sight of Chloe's long, tanned legs, her wide hips and lovely, mischievous smile.

One of the police ran over beside Chloe, slinging his sub machine gun as he did. "OK girlie, you can get off him now," he ordered.

The other policeman aimed his ugly black automatic rifle at Shaemus's head. His companion moved behind Chloe while taking out his handcuffs. As he bent to place the cuffs on Shaemus's other wrist, the policeman had a good, close-range look at Chloe's bum, which was covered only by a single thin cord. The sight of that caused Barbara to shake her head with annoyance and to blush with embarrassment.

Bloody men! she thought. *And bloody Chloe!*

Chloe stepped to one side and the second policeman moved in to hold Shaemus. Shaemus screamed in pain as the policeman tried to put the handcuffs on.

"He's got a dislocated arm," Chloe said. She then faced Charles, who was staring at her in open-mouthed amazement. "In a minute," she said, fending off his attempt to put his arms around her. She turned, saw the puffing Inspector and called to him. "You'd better call down one of those helicopters straight away and get those wounded people to hospital."

The red-faced and panting Inspector stared at her with an incredulous look on his face, then nodded. He put his pistol away, snatched up his radio and began talking on it. As he did Major Wickham and half a dozen TV news people came racing over to join them.

Chloe ignored them and turned to the British cadets. "Get those casualties out on the sand, quickly!" she ordered. She stood there, upright and proud. To Barbara she seemed to be the very essence of femaleness, all curves and lithe grace, but with more than a hint of the tigress.

"I'll do it," George replied. He ran his eyes over Chloe and shook his head in disbelief, then turned and went running back across the sand, shouting as he did. Adelaide turned and went with him. Barbara looked towards Snake Gully and saw people appearing: Robbo, Lt Cavendish, Lt Barker, Lt Forster some ambulancemen, and a mixed group of Australian and British cadets carrying a stretcher.

Major Wickham gasped as he reached them. He was flushed and winded from his run. "Chloe, well done, now get your clothes on."

"Yes sir," Chloe replied. "Get the injured to the doctor first."

"That is being done," Major Wickham replied, pointing to where a helicopter was already coming in to land 100 metres further upstream. More police were running that way and two more uniformed police joined the group around Shaemus, who was now groaning and cursing.

"You bitch!" Shaemus shouted at Chloe. "You've broken my arm."

"You assaulted me, you brute," Chloe snapped back, "and you pointed a gun at me. I didn't like that. And you called me crude names. You are lucky I didn't break your neck!"

Cecil stepped forward and spat. "You deserve it you murderous bastard!" He stood in front of Shaemus and glared his hatred. For a second Barbara feared he might try to take some sort of revenge and glanced around to check who had the rifle. To her relief she saw that George still had it.

Shaemus was rolled over and one of the ambulance men was called over to give him First Aid. The Inspector pointed to him. "Keep this one here out of the way. He can go on another helicopter. Use the one that is landing now to get the wounded to hospital," he instructed.

At that Shaemus swore and then groaned but was ignored. The group moved away, leaving two constables and the paramedic with him.

Barbara watched the helicopter settle on the riverbed, its rotor wash blasting out a swirl of grit and fine sand that caused them all to squint and shield their eyes. As the disturbance subsided her attention was then drawn back to Chloe and those around her.

Charles still stood admiring Chloe, his face showing open admiration. "Chloe, you are magnificent!" he cried.

At that Chloe smiled and stepped over and put her arms around his neck. "And you are very brave," she said. She pressed herself against him and he hugged her, his face radiant with pleasure.

By then Robbo and Lt Cavendish had joined them. Lt Barker and Lt Forster came running across to join them. Barbara indicated where groups of cadets, paramedics and police were hurrying another casualty on a stretcher towards the helicopter, which had now slowed its engine so that the rotors were not blowing out so much sand. The second stretcher was loaded aboard.

Where is the third casualty? Barbara wondered.

A glance towards the mouth of Snake Gully answered her question. Moving towards the helicopter was another group of British cadets. They were carrying a stretcher on which lay another casualty. Walking beside it was an obviously very distressed Adelaide. She was holding the casualties hand, tears streaming down her face.

Major Grogan, Barbara thought sadly. *Poor Adelaide. She obviously cares deeply for him.*

"Are they still alive?" Barbara asked.

"Yes, but only just," Robbo replied. "Another half hour and they would be dead I reckon."

"Yes, help arrived just in time," Lt Cavendish added. "Who got through to the police?"

"Chloe," Barbara replied. "I got caught at 'Landers Creek' by that Liam mongrel."

Lt Cavendish turned to Chloe. "Well done Chloe, now please get dressed."

Chloe eased herself away from Charles. "Aw Miss! Do I have to?"

"Yes, you are almost naked in that outfit," Lt Cavendish snapped.

Chloe shrugged and glanced down at her bikini. "It's more than I would wear on a beach in Sydney," she commented.

"We aren't in Sydney, so please cover up!" Lt Cavendish snapped.

Chloe nodded and sighed but then thrust her breasts out, all sexy voluptuousness. Barbara could only shake her head and marvel.

She is certainly all woman, and very beautiful!

She remembered being naked on a couple of her own adventures and suddenly found she could forgive Chloe for her nudity anytime.

Not so Robbo. "Chloe!" she cried. "All these men are looking at you."

Chloe glanced around and gave a wicked grin. "I know. That doesn't bother me. I do that for a job."

Lt Barker laughed and gestured to the half dozen news cameramen, "You are on live TV."

Barbara had forgotten them. She now saw that three TV cameras were focused at close range on the scene. All the male cameramen were staring open mouthed.

"Chloe, get dressed! You will get hundreds of disgusting offers from all over the world otherwise," she cried, moving to stand in front of one of the cameras.

At that Charles stepped forward and took Chloe's hand. "By Jove! I will make you an offer right now!" he said, his face alight with wonder.

"I was hoping for an honourable one from you," Chloe replied, taking his other hand and looking him in the eyes.

"Oh yes! Please marry me Chloe," Charles replied.

Chloe smiled. "That would be nice, but I'm a bit young yet. I'm only sixteen you know. Maybe in another four or five years when I have finished school and lived a bit more."

"Five years!" Charles replied in dismay. He ran his eyes up and down Chloe's almost nude form. "I don't even want to wait five minutes!"

At that Chloe laughed and threw herself into his arms. "I didn't say we couldn't have a bit of fun in the meantime," she said.

"Oh I say! I say!" Charles stammered, rendered speechless by the situation.

Lt Cavendish was scandalized. "Chloe! Stop that sort of behaviour and get dressed."

Major Wickham shook his head. "Chloe, you are too young. Now please put your clothes on before the police arrest you too."

Chloe released Charles and stood facing Major Wickham. "I like being naked sir. It feels natural and it feels nice." She glanced at the policemen who were standing staring at her.

Bloody men! Barbara thought.

It was obvious from their faces that the thought of arresting Chloe for her nudity was the last thing on the policemen's minds.

She snapped at them, "All you men might look the other way! And you people could stop taking pictures!"

To Barbara's annoyance the TV people kept on filming and the police only looked away half-heartedly. Charles moved to unbutton his shirt.

"Have this," he said.

"No thanks. I will just take it off again," Chloe replied. "If you don't like me being a nudist then you'd better fall out of love with me otherwise you will only get hurt."

Oh Chloe! Barbara thought, knowing she was being hypocritical, *Don't say that or you will never be Lady Matchlock!*

But she realised Chloe was right. Whoever married her would have to love her and accept her as she was, not be the jealous type.

Conversation was then drowned out as the helicopter lifted off. As it flew overhead, the wash from its rotors again showering them with dust and grains of fine sand, Barbara heaved a sigh of relief.

Thank God! she thought. *They are on their way to hospital at last.*

When it had gone Major Wickham turned to Chloe. "Chloe, where are your clothes?" he asked.

Chloe pointed upstream. "Back there, where I swam the river, sir."

Barbara was now resigned to the fact that Chloe was going to stand there for all to see and quite unabashed unless somebody actually forced her to cover herself.

She is truly beautiful though, she conceded.

Chloe pointed upstream. "I crossed the sand with Jane and Ben McPherson up there near the bend," she explained. "We reached the bank opposite the 'Byrne Valley' homestead and called out but no-one answered. So I decided to swim. I couldn't see any crocodiles and I reckoned it was a fair risk in the circumstances."

"You are damned lucky!" Major Wickham cried in exasperation. "I thought my orders were no swimming?"

"Yes sir, but there was no other way," Chloe replied. "Anyway, I had just stripped off behind a big rock when we saw one of the terrorists come out of the trees at the far end of the island. He was nearly a kilometre away but had a rifle so I told Jane and Ben to run off to the south to decoy him away. They did. He saw them and yelled out but they got away. He then ran after them."

"Ben and Jane! Where are they now?" Major Wickham asked.

"Safe I think sir," Chloe replied. "I told them to head for the farms the other side of Landers Creek."

"So how did you get caught?" Barbara asked.

"Well, I hid till the man had gone into the trees further up the river, then I swam across. That was no fun, as there were lots of rocks, and nor was going up the bank because there were a lot of Bindis."

"A lot of what?" Charles asked.

"Bindis," Chloe said. "Prickles. Anyway, I went to the homestead and found three young men at the stock yards." At that she giggled. "You should have seen their faces! They positively goggled," she said, and hugged her breasts, squeezing them up to form a real cleavage. That got all the males present goggling too and Barbara had to shake her head.

Chloe went on, "They forgot about their horses and took me to the house where a nice lady wrapped me in a towel and phoned the police. I explained the situation and then had a lovely cool drink. After that I swam back across the river."

"But why?" Robbo asked in amazement.

"Because I thought I might be able to help. I was worried about Jane and Ben too," Chloe said. "The people at the homestead didn't want me to go, but I went anyway. The boys came down to the riverbank with rifles. They wouldn't swim across with me but said they'd shoot any crocs."

"They just wanted to see you without any clothes on again," Lt Barker suggested.

Chloe laughed at that. She then went on, "Well, I swam back and went to find my clothes. Instead this man popped out from behind some rocks and stuck me up."

"You are lucky that's all he did!" Cecil cried.

Chloe just shrugged. Barbara had heard many stories about Chloe and sex so suspected the idea of rape did not worry her too much.

Chloe went on, "He was very hot and angry because Jane and Ben had given him the slip but he had obviously noted there were three of us and he had come back searching for me. I suppose he followed our footprints and found my clothes. He brought me back here at gunpoint and we had just arrived when the helicopters and police showed up. The rest you know."

"And he didn't even let you get dressed?" Robbo commented.

"No. I suppose he liked what he could see," Chloe commented, wriggling her hips.

"Disgusting beast!" Lt Cavendish said. She obviously did not approve of Chloe's nudity at all and frowned her disapproval.

"That would have been Murty, the man we shot at," Barbara said.

"Yes, it was," Chloe agreed. She then turned to one of the TV reporters. "Is that really a live broadcast?"

The reporter, a young man, blushed and nodded. "Yes it is. There's a satellite dish up at the Lookout there. Half the world can see you now."

Chloe smiled and waved to the camera. "Hello Mum!" she called.

"Chloe! That's enough!" Lt Cavendish said. "Go and get dressed."

Barbara agreed. She looked around and saw a long line of cadets walking towards them from the mouth of Snake Gully. "Yes Chloe, here come the cadets."

Chloe shrugged. "Most of them have seen me like this before."

Major Wickham shook his head. "Maybe, but some of them might be offended or embarrassed, and I know a few of the girls are jealous. Besides, I don't want the unit, or the army cadets getting the wrong reputation."

"We will get a flood of boys wanting to join now," Lt Barker added.

"That will do Ashley!" Major Wickham said. "Now go and get dressed Chloe before I ask the police to arrest you."

At that the Inspector, who had been busy talking on his radio and mobile phone, in between giving orders, looked at Chloe, shook his head in disbelief and nodded.

"Your missing cadets are safe Major," he added. "They are at a farm five kilometres south of here. Now go and cover yourself girlie before I have to act."

Chloe pouted but nodded. "OK. Come on Charles."

She took Charles' hand and turned to go.

"Where are you going?" Major Wickham asked.

"To get my clothes sir," Chloe replied. "We won't be too long."

Major Wickham shook his head. "That is not suitable. Besides, you don't have to go. Someone can lend you something and we can collect your gear some other time."

"No sir. I know where my clothes are. It will be a while before we leave won't it? The police will have to look around and ask questions and so on won't they?" Chloe replied.

Major Wickham had to agree. "Yes but you can't go with a boy while you are dressed like that. Go with a couple of girls please."

"I'll go with you," Robbo offered.

"OK. Thanks ma'am, come on," Chloe said. "See you later Charles."

With that, she reached up and gave him a kiss on the cheek, then turned and walked off, her lovely back profile presented to the cameras. As Chloe walked away, it seemed to Barbara that she was deliberately wiggling her hips and buttocks, but she had to concede they were unkind thoughts.

Chloe always walks with a wiggle, she told herself. In spite of everything she now really liked and admired Chloe.

"She has done a great job," she commented.

"By Jove yes!" Charles agreed. "She has saved at least three lives."

"She can go round naked as much as she likes as far as I am concerned," Barbara said. "She has earned it."

"Yes... well," Major Wickham said, shaking his head.

The Inspector stared hard at the departing Chloe and then turned to Major Wickham. "Is she the same Chloe that saved the day when that bikie gang caused you problems at Mingela a couple of years ago?" he asked.

Major Wickham nodded. "Yes, and she has saved the day again," he commented.[5]

"She deserves a medal," the Inspector added.

"She already has one, a Bravery Medal," Major Wickham replied, turning to stare at Chloe and then again shaking his head.

By then the company was filing past up the grassy slope towards the railway, many of the cadets staring after Chloe and Robbo as they walked off across the sand.

Major Wickham looked around. "We'd better get the troops organized," he said.

As they turned to follow the cadets Lt Barker pointed to the TV cameras, which had at last shifted focus from Chloe to the cadets. "We will be on the six O'clock news tonight sir."

"Yes, blast it!" Major Wickham replied with a scowl. "And I will spend hours answering questions from the army and writing reports. And I thought it would be a nice ordinary bivouac!"

Barbara followed Sgt Brady up the slope, smiling back at her grinning cadets, even though she felt anything but happy. In the distance she glimpsed Chloe and Robbo, now two tiny figures trudging up the dry riverbed. Even at that distance there was no doubt Chloe was female.

At the railway the cadets crawled underneath the fence and headed left along the line towards their bivouac area. As Barbara stood up she noted that Colleen was standing beside Michael. The police were moving the terrorists off the other way. Colleen was crying but also smiling.

"I love you," Michael said to Colleen.

"And I will think off you often," Colleen said. "I think you did the right thing and that you are very brave."

"Can I write to you if I go to prison?" Michael asked.

"Yes," Colleen answered. "And I will come and visit you. I think you are a good man and worth it." She then leaned over and kissed him gently on lips before turning and walking along the railway after Barbara, her eyes streaming with tears. Behind her Michael's face lit up with hope and he was smiling as the police led him away.

Oh, I hope so! Barbara thought, her own eyes misting with emotion.

---

5   Read *Mischief at Mingela* by C.R. Cummings

SEQUEL

And did Chloe get discharged for her behaviour? Well, no. Not only had she been a public hero and saved the day but even Lt Cavendish had to admit there were mitigating circumstances. This time Chloe had not been completely nude.

"Although she may as well have been!" the OOC had snapped viciously.

And both Barbara's and Chloe's courage and leadership had to be rewarded. Barbara was nominated for a Bravery Medal for her actions in rescuing Major Grogan and Lt Jeffries. This was granted. As Chloe was already the recipient of the Bravery Medal Major Wickham and the police inspector nominated her for the next level up, the Star of Courage. But this was not granted. Instead she was awarded a bar to her Bravery Medal. Barbara and Chloe went to Government House in Canberra the following January to be awarded their medals by the Governor General.

And Chloe's obviously outstanding leadership also had to be recognized so in December Chloe was selected to attend the Cadet Under-Officers Course. But that is another story. Chloe's career is not over yet.

Enjoy more C.R. Cummings stories

The Air Cadets

The Navy Cadets

The Army Cadets

www.ingramcontent.com/pod-product-compliance
Lightning Source LLC
Chambersburg PA
CBHW030919260626
47169CB00002B/317